THE HEROIC FACADE

FORSAKEN DESTINY TRILOGY
BOOK ONE

ANGELA FUNK

To my mother
To my grandmother
To everyone who believed

THE HEROIC FACADE

LEGEND
Port City
Town
Village
Castle
Broadcastia
Wall
Deserted Village
CELESTI
TAHNU
LAENTE
BUVION
RALYITZ
EBBERSOL
TAVANO
SILVASA
KULTAL
XIVIS
DEVOSI
ELVOS
INORE
WEXEL
MYLYAI
Unclaimed Land
JEATAR
REINTA
EDNA
ABBERSTEIN
HELMINCH
Outer
Inner
NEW GUAYI
UBAS
FELDEN
KELTERNAM
PELVA
NYEAT
ILLAI
GIAN
YELBAH
MIDRAL

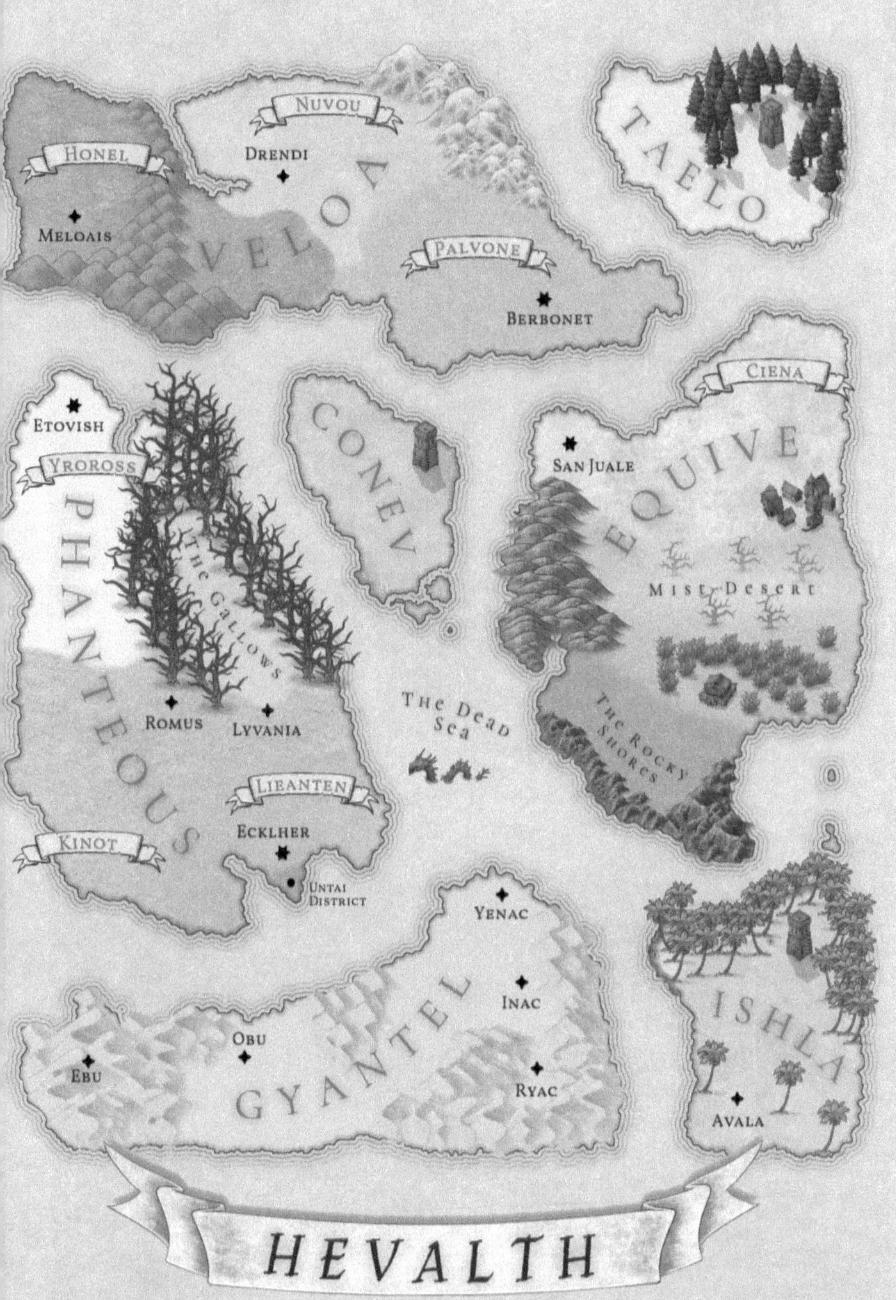

HONEL
MELOAIS
NUVOU
DRENDI
VELOA
PALVONE
BERBONET
TAELO
ETOVISH
YROROSS
CONEV
CIENA
SAN JUALE
EQUIVE
MIST DESERT
PHANTEOUS
The Gallows
ROMUS
LYVANIA
The Dead Sea
The Rocky Shores
LIEANTEN
ECKLHER
UNTAI DISTRICT
KINOT
YENAC
INAC
RYAC
GYANTEL
OBU
EBU
ISHLA
AVALA
HEVALTH

PART ONE

AND SO THE JOURNEY BEGINS

CHAPTER 1

LEO

- 34 HOURS BEFORE -

LIFE WAS UNRAVELING before his very eyes. Fields wrapped around the horizon; fields of grass and flowers and navy-spotted cows. Mornings always began with a long line of cattle stretching around the barn as they waited to be milked, but today the milking station stood vacant. The sun shined brightly between the clouds and the breeze was fair, the type of weather cattle laid in for hours on end, the type of weather that pushed milking to sundown.

Although navy-spotted cows were considered to be low-maintenance—especially compared to the widely utilized and sought-after violet-spotted—they would be milked when they wanted to be, and no amount of wrangling would convince them otherwise. Their laziness was just his luck; it was the one morning he'd rather work than have time to himself.

Dutiless, Leo stood on a hill, the tallest hill of all the hills that scattered their land, and tried his best not to think. It was here he could see everything. His family's farm stood a few yards away, the barn a worn shade of deep orange. The wood was chipped in several places and protruded at awkward angles.

Their cream-colored house sat beside it, a tiny little thing that could barely hold three people, much less their family of four, and a small shed of the same color stood behind it.

Leo took a deep breath; he'd never smelled something both sweet and sour before nitren, a flower native to Edna. His family harvested them in the warm months and sold them to the Corporation of Pharmaceuticals for a price he was never told. His parents kept funds tight to their chests, but based on the slim meals they could afford, he knew they made next to nothing. "Enough," as his mother so eloquently put it. "We make enough."

When had that become a lie?

He closed his eyes and cocked back his head. A swell of sadness pooled in his gut as he took a final, intoxicating breath. The nitrens overwhelming fragrance sent him to tears. He would miss this, the silence he had to himself. But, at the same time, he was ready to go. He'd been listening to his own thoughts for too long.

Leo took off down the hill, the anticipation of what was to come drawing him into a full sprint. His feet crashed to the ground with knee-shattering force, but adrenaline outweighed the pain. His thoughts temporarily ceased as he became enthralled by the sound of his heart thumping in his ears. He'd give anything to never think again.

He reduced his pace to a brisk walk as he neared the shed. The thick double doors were wide open, exposing his father's workspace. And there the aging man stood, his back hunched over the table inside, tufts of gray overtaking his once dusty brown hair. Unlike Leo's ear-length, messy brown curls, his father's was cut just above the scalp and so thin that Leo could see the wrinkles overtaking the back of his neck.

His father swung a thick hatchet overhead and split a piece of wood in two; the pieces clattered to the concrete floor as he got to work on the next log. Words rose to Leo's mouth, but he watched without a sound. If he spoke now, he'd be met with a last-minute scolding, common to the one he'd gotten the night before, and every other night since he told his parents of his plans to leave. Leo suspected his father wouldn't be upset by the lack of a last goodbye.

Leo checked his watch and gulped down his anxieties. There was time, but it would never be enough. He jogged past the shed and ungraciously clamored through the back door of their house. The kitchen was scrunched in the far-right corner, visible from where he entered, and his mother was in her usual position, leaning against the counter.

She hummed to herself, sawing a dull knife through a pink apple, the sweetest of apples. Her dark blonde hair was tied back in a tight ponytail and her green, knee-length dress was hidden beneath her apron. Her eyes were drawn to her work, pushing thinly cut slices to the side with her dainty fingers, no doubt to be used in the creation of cinnamon apple pie.

It would be the fifth pie this week. He had a sneaking suspicion she was attempting to bribe him. After all, his father was getting older, and they needed a strong hand around the farm. Keeping the cattle in check was proving to be the hardest task for the man's aging knees, and bending for flowers was no better for his back. And Leo's sister, well, she was a lost cause. She was two years younger and utterly uninvested in life there. Leo scoured his memory for the last time he'd seen Noelle, landing on what must have been an entire month ago.

"That looks good," he said as he leaned against the kitchen doorframe. The heat from the oven made the room notably warmer than the rest of the house and added to his already mild discomfort.

His mother jumped, releasing a soft "oh!" as she set the knife down and touched her chest. He braced himself for a reprimanding, but she offered a pleasant smile and kind eyes instead. If they avoided the subject altogether, he told himself, it'll all be fine.

"They're just apples," she remarked, furrowing her brows in confusion.

"Yeah, but apples mean a pie is on the way, right?" His stomach clenched at the prospect of another incessant pie, but he smiled back.

She nodded and turned her attention back to cutting. She was unusually chipper, her voice airy as she said, "Cinnamon apple."

"Ah." Leo crossed the kitchen and sat at the tall dining table; it stood in the left corner with a long, open window beside it. The sticky room made him nauseous; his stomach tied in turmoil, and his neck was starting to perspire. He reached for the latch of the window, desperate to free himself.

"Don't," she said, her eyes never leaving the cutting board. "I like the heat."

No, he thought, you like to sweat. He kept quiet and leaned back, rubbing at his temples in a bold and fruitless attempt to scare away a budding headache. There wasn't much time until the bus arrived.

They lived miles away from civilization and they hadn't the money, nor need, for a car. To his relief, the buses were generally safe and easy to acquire using the mailing system. All he had to do was send his address to the Bureau a few months before his desired departure with the date of his choice, and they mailed back a departure time.

He checked his watch again. Three minutes had passed. Twenty left. He clasped his clammy hands together and twiddled his thumbs on the tabletop. "I'll be gone before you finish."

His mother turned to him with pleading eyes, whatever

happiness she'd held now gone, and his gaze quickly bounced away as he squirmed in his seat. Why'd he say that? He'd take pie over this.

"You don't have to be," she said. "We can pay things off another way."

"It'll be alright. I can take care of myself."

"You know you don't know that."

"There are no other options, ma, we all know it. Give me one right now and I'll stay." His raised voice made him cringe, and he clamped his mouth shut. She stared back, hurt written across her face. This wasn't how he thought things would go, how he thought he would act. She shook her head and turned back to the apples.

He understood her frustration, he did, and he certainly understood her longing to keep him there. Of course, he was utterly terrified to leave; his sleepless night attested to that. The prospect of adventure was exciting, but the idea of socializing with strangers was excruciating. He scarcely talked with others outside his family, and when he did, it was the same doctor he'd had since birth.

Leo sighed. "I'm sorry for raising my voice, ma, I am, but we're backed into a corner here. There ain't no other way out. They'll take it all except us and we'll have nowhere t'go."

"I trust you'll make the right decisions, but I don't think you can handle it, not alone, and there's no way your father and I are goin'. I can't go back out there. We can't. And you? You're not depraved, son, and that's a good thing. I love you for that. But the people who take that exam? They are. You'll have your back turned and they'll kill you. Please. I don't want to lose you. Not over a stupid debt."

He took to looking at her, absorbing the silence that followed and wishing he could blink the next twenty minutes away. She was fragile; her skin was beginning to sag and wither, though there was a faint beauty behind her baggy eyes and thinning brows. He glanced at her scar-covered wrists, a product of her past. Leo never queried her about her upbringing, and she divulged but one detail after drinking a little too much wine some years ago.

"I grew up in Yroross," she'd said, her broken farmvillian accent morphing into one of fluent Latarian. Of the two universal languages, they taught Leo only one. Edna natives had their own dialect, a mix of both, and it was rare to speak Latarian formally. But that night, her voice came out as a smooth, tumbling wave. *"Ech a'slav ta mar eitholet."* The streets ran with blood.

She'd seen more horrors than Leo could ever come to imagine, and her apprehension was further proof of how over his head he truly was. His mother and father were survivors. And he was... what? A poor, sheltered farmer's boy, like any other in Edna? Boring. One of many. Average. And certainly not equipped to fight.

"You won't," he finally said, pulling together what little positivity he had left. "I won't. I promise you. No killing and no dying."

She stared at him for an uncomfortably long time. Her eyes were wide and glassy, his words unleashing the unspoken and throttling what little hope she still had.

Leo gulped and extended his hand with a warm smile. "Here, let's shake on it. Those are the two rules and I'll follow 'em."

She stared a moment longer before waving him away. "I don't want your hand. I want you to stay."

"Even if we end up homeless? What about the cows, ma? They'll be sold, you ever think about that? No one spoils 'em like you 'n pa. They'll go mad." She smiled softly, easing his fear of disappointing her. How could he disappoint her when she had no faith in him to begin with? "Have some faith in me, alright? I'll do whatever it takes to help our family."

"That's why I'm so worried." She went back to cutting. Leo watched while playing out fantasies of the upcoming exam in his head. He pictured himself standing tall and triumphant with a bulky award held up in both hands, a shit-eating grin plastered on his face. Leo would come home with the money, and his parents would cry and celebrate. He tapped his fingers on the counter.

If he came home.

When it was nearly time to go, he grabbed his backpack filled with sparse essentials, gave his mother a tight squeeze, and left through the front door. He sat on the swinging bench, invoking a screech of protest from the rusty chains with every kick of his legs.

The bus arrived fifteen minutes late. It chugged down their dirt road, trailing dust behind the wheels as it shrieked to a halt in front of their estate. The door flung open, exposing a large woman in a solid blue uniform behind the wheel. Leo dashed down the porch steps and waved, his other hand clenching the strap of his bag. He could hardly breathe, nervousness crushing his lungs and squeezing sense from his brain.

He stopped and peered up at the driver, unsure of what to do next. Her gaze was indolent, each eye blinking sluggishly in succession with the other. He gulped. This was it. It was his last chance to turn around.

"Well?" the driver asked, her gruff voice bringing him back to reality. She stuffed a piece of chew into her mouth and watched him with increasing perplexity.

Leo snapped into action, grasping the handrail as he skipped up the steps inside. There were fifteen rows, two chairs on each side of the aisle, and it was packed with people. Most passengers didn't look to be citizens of Edna, their clothes too bright and... fashionable, he supposed.

He scanned for a vacant seat and locked onto his preferred destination beside a window. He made it halfway down the aisle when the driver cleared her throat and hoarsely called back, "Hey! You need to confirm where you're going!"

Leo jumped and twirled around, his freckled face becoming bright red. He scratched the back of his head. "S-sorry! Midral!"

The driver appeared pleased with his answer and closed the door with a grunt. "It's a fourteen-hour drive. We'll be making six stops along the way." She winked in the rearview mirror. "Feel free to come up here and keep me company."

The engine roared to life, and he stumbled forward as they drove away. Leo wasn't sure how to respond, so he caught his footing and scrambled to the chair he wanted, hopping awkwardly over the man who took up the aisle seat. He was old, fifty or so, and looked at Leo with disdain. Eventually, the man fixed his attention elsewhere and Leo was left with thirteen hours and fifty minutes of road to look forward to. Of sitting. Of waiting.

He'd left a full day and a half before the exam started; a suggestion made by his mother. There was a pre-exam, she warned, a task to find the location of the International Exam itself. Clues in the form of advertisements would be scattered throughout twenty select cities, but she told him of merely one —Midral. A Tier 3 city. A safe city. And, evidently, the closest one to Edna.

Not much else was known about the exam aside from the prizes, which were bolstered everywhere, along with the tagline 'eighteen or older to apply.' Take the exam on either January or July 1st and, if successful, win a bucket load of money, a list of magical items, more money, and the title of an Expedition

Overseer. EOs often went down as legends for the new land, foods, and fortunes they discovered.

Leo's hand gravitated toward the strap of his bag, and he rubbed at it gently with his thumb. Each swipe soothed his racing heart, as did the growing disinterest of his seatmate. Leo didn't want trouble, and he didn't want small talk. So far, he had to say, this was going perfectly.

The two straps of his backpack only left his shoulders when he needed something, the bulky contents jutting into his spine and creating a rather unpleasant experience. He knew his back would pay later, but thieves could be anywhere, be anyone. Leo eyed up the man beside him suspiciously, but now he was snoring, his head lolled to the side. Not everyone was out to get him.

Leo spent the rest of the trip doodling in a leather-bound notebook he brought; a present from his sister a year prior. He attempted to draw a city skyline, buildings piled atop each other with a rising moon and shining stars. With each line, he began questioning how he'd be able to afford anything in an upscale city. He was strapped for cash with the 60 quill he'd saved over the years. Would people buy his drawings if he couldn't afford a lodge? Would he have to sleep on the street? Leo hadn't begun to wonder what he'd do if he failed the exam. Bus fare was cheap, but not without a Q to his name.

Day turned to sunfall turned to night, and eventually, his vision became too impaired to finish the face he was working on. He put his drawings away and watched the trees and buildings whizz by until the bus slowed to a stop. He leaned closer to the window, nose pressed against the glass as he peered outside in awe, the bus station staring back. It was wide and lofty and made entirely of gray stone. The front entrance was between two thick pillars, each engraved with swirls and waves.

The building was labeled 'Midral Sector' in gold embroidered letters.

The driver pulled around the building and into a long parking lot full of similarly stylized busses, all aligned parallel to each other. There were far fewer people than he expected. Next to none, in fact.

Leo became trapped in the flow of bodies swarming into the station. He weaseled his way out and stopped by a line of vacant chairs. Leo took some deep breaths and let his surroundings sink in. He was there. He made it. But what was he supposed to do now? His mother hadn't prepared him for that.

The station was scarce. He noticed bolts on all the bus lot doors and guards walking about with guns in their holsters. Everything was made of gray concrete, even the ticket stands, which were now protected by thick metal bars extending from the floor to the ceiling. The security was tight tonight.

He checked the time. Midnight. He cocked an eyebrow, his eyelids becoming heavy at the prospect of a cushy bed and proper rest. His stomach growled, but he ignored his feverish hunger and followed two short and stocky women into the streets of Midral. The buildings were ragged and broken, windows smashed in, and walls covered with brown overgrowth.

His mother had told him stories of Midral, how it was lively and bright. There were apartments that reached the skies and vibrant signs that speckled the streets. But all he saw now were broken down, deserted buildings and sidewalks lined with chipped, flickering lights that abruptly stopped at the end of the block. Beyond was darkness, shadows dancing atop each other. Leo shivered and quickened his pace in the opposite direction.

Beside the station was a brightly lit and somewhat busy

restaurant, labeled via a neon sign of noodles splashing out of a bowl. The display was wildly fascinating; the sign was warm and welcoming, but the structure of the building was rotting, wood peeling in black shavings to the thin walkway below. The next building over proved to be the most promising. It was taller than the others, the front covered in a slew of curtain-drawn windows. 'Fantisimo' was written above the entrance, each letter aglow in red and orange.

He hesitantly walked through the double doors, hoping it would be an affordable lodging site. Upon a quick glance around the packed and well-guarded lobby, he had no expectations, the decor a hodgepodge of luxury and filth. Pairs of fine, red velvet couches decorated the four corners of the room, a marble fireplace between them. The floor was tattered and stained, and the light fixtures were turning a rusty shade of gold.

Leo waited in line for a room, using the extra time to size up his potential opponents. Some wore exuberant and long, modest dresses and tuxes, donning heavy powdered makeup and fancy top hats. Others were dressed casually, closer to that of himself. He had chosen comfort over style—a red checkered flannel, blue jeans, and sneakers—determining that was best for combat and running situations.

The line moved at a sluggish pace, and a moment of panic unraveled within him—panic that convinced him the lodge would be full before he reached the front desk. His frets persisted with every sideways glance at his adversaries. Leo had developed a great deal of muscle from growing up on the farm, but he didn't have the training regimens others clearly had.

He stepped up to the receptionist nervously. She was kind-faced and duty-driven. Bangs dangled over her pointed eyebrows; black hair chopped to her shoulders. Her blue eyes were dark and uninterested, but she smiled and gave a rehearsed greeting. He almost gasped at the price of a single bedroom. 30 quill for one night.

He contemplated arguing down the price but deduced that he was too tired for such a grueling endeavor. Thoughts were becoming entangled within each other, ideas lost in fragments. Leo nodded with a stroke of his chin and reluctantly handed over his Q. Already, half his life savings were gone.

She placed her hand face down on the desk and slid the room key across the counter. Leo's attention gravitated toward her coffin-shaped nails, each painted black with a segment of a white, scaled snake down the center. The triangular head of the snake stared back at Leo from her thumb, tongue-less.

Then, before he could think to react, a forked tongue sprouted from the tip of its head, only to disappear seconds later. The movement was so sudden that Leo gasped and took a startled step back, his frantic gaze bouncing from her haunting blue eyes to her nails. The tongue was no longer there.

Was his mind playing tricks on him?

The corners of her lips curled into a smirk, her eyes aglow with newfound amusement as she lifted her hand. He swiped the key off the counter, afraid the snake might strike if he lingered for too long. "Do you know how to get to the, uh, city part of Midral?"

Her smirk gradually grew. "First time here?"

Inside, he was screaming. There was no way to know who was listening, who was jotting down his appearance and responses for a later note. For all he knew, she could be testing him. He straightened his back, trying to play the part of someone built on courage.

Leo opened his mouth, but she interjected with a raised finger. "I already know the answer," she said. "You'll have to take a taxi into the city."

He almost lost his composure, his shoulders seconds from

sagging. What held him together, however, was his want, his *need*, to look in control. "How much would that happen to cost?"

The receptionist put a finger to her chin and looked up in feigned contemplation. His eyes never left her thumb. "Well, the inner city is what, eight miles away? That'd be, say, 25, 30Q? Depending on the traffic and drop-off spot, of course."

He couldn't very well walk eight miles and make it in time for the advertisements to start. It was crucial to have all twelve hours before the exam to adequately prepare and find the location. His stomach growled then, badgering him for something that wouldn't come.

"Thanks," he said meekly before walking away.

"Wait," she shouted after him. The ample chatter within the lobby simmered to a dull whisper as eyes and ears were drawn to him.

He turned around tentatively to see a revived smile and delighted gaze.

"Did I forget something?" he asked.

"No, but... I think you should know you don't look the sort to pass."

"Excuse me?"

"If I were you, I'd go back to wherever I came from. No offense or anything. The exam isn't for average people."

The room hushed. If he wasn't afraid of thugs killing him before, he certainly was now. Her words rang in his head. It was one thing to *be* average, but to be *told* he was average was unsurprisingly offensive. Did she call out everyone who didn't fit whatever boxes she needed checked?

If he didn't act fast, he'd become an easy target.

Leo offered her a sly smile of his own, and what he perceived to be cunning eyes. He sauntered over to her, threw his hand out for a shake, and said, "You wanna bet on it?"

Her lips parted in disbelief. He couldn't tell if she was about to laugh or tell him off. Despite her baffled reaction, he kept his sense of bravado. All he could do was hope it was persuasive enough for their audience.

"What's your name?" she asked, a brow raised. Her skepticism sent a wave of self-doubt through him. There were no clues as to how he should act, no one around to whisper the appropriate thing to say or do in his ear.

"Leo. Leo Montero. And you?"

The receptionist pointed to the name tag above her breast. *Marcella.* He blushed at the roll of her eyes, embarrassed for overlooking something so obvious. It was a messy mistake.

She took his hand and gave it a firm shake. "A bet wasn't what I expected, but I'll take it. If you fail the exam, you owe me 20Q."

"Deal," he said, knowing he'd be broke after the taxi ride the very next day. But, he reminded himself, he'd be a millionaire after the exam. "And if I pass," he added, "I'll give you 50Q."

Marcella chortled. "Good luck."

"Don't need it, but thanks," he said with a cocky smile, his eyes never breaking from hers. He set off for the elevator, ready to be rid of the attention Marcella generated, and hoped the rest of his evening would be quiet and uneventful.

As he pressed his floor number and the elevator door slid closed, a hand intercepted. The door reopened to reveal a tall, tan man who appeared a few years older than Leo. Leo looked him over; his suit and dress shoes were pitch black, and he had hair of the same color that stretched to his ears. His belt pinched at his waist, accentuating the slight pudge of his stomach.

"Can I help you?" Leo asked.

The man smiled and ran a hand through his side bangs. "I

thought you'd never ask. I'm Eli. I happened to overhear your conversation back there. You're looking for the exam location?"

"And if I am?"

Eli raised his hands in defense and entered the elevator with a lackadaisical shrug. Leo took an instinctive step to the side, creating substantial room between them within the limited space. "Well, it so happens that I am, too. What if we, say, teamed up?"

"Why?"

"You made an impression on me. That and I'm not very confident in my detective skills. Besides, what's the harm of having a little help? And," Eli added, "we can split the taxi fare."

"How do I know you aren't going to use my expertise to slide by?"

"How do I know you won't do the same?"

Leo was careful not to show his shaken thoughts, keeping his expression blank. In truth, he desperately wanted to say no. His gut told him to trust no one. But the temptation of affording food later outweighed caution.

He grumbled inwardly but nodded with the faux confidence Eli was so attracted to. "Alright. But if you try to sabotage me, I'll get my revenge."

Eli shook his head, dispelling some of the distrust Leo held, and his shoulders relaxed the tiniest of amounts. "Don't worry. I need to pass, too. There'd be no point in sabotaging you if it meant sabotaging myself."

The look in his hazel eyes told Leo everything. Eli was determined, as was he, to find something at the end of this exam. Not only the prizes and title but something else much more tantalizing.

The elevator halted and dinged at the second floor, one

below his. Leo was dumbfounded by the chime; he hadn't noticed Eli press any of the buttons.

"Tomorrow," Eli said as he stepped off. "5:30 in the morning. We'll meet in the lobby and eat before we go. There's a café a few blocks from here that I saw open. Sound good?"

Leo responded with a nod. The elevator door slid closed with Eli's proud face smiling back at him. The idea of working with someone else was inviting at first glance, but people were unpredictable, unsafe. He'd have to remain cautious.

He took a deep breath and rubbed at his backpack strap subconsciously while staring at his metallic reflection. His eyes were wide and terrified, and he began to wonder if he'd been able to feign confidence as well as he'd first thought. Oh well. It was too late to change anything now.

Tomorrow.

Tomorrow, it began.

CHAPTER 2
OTHELIA
- 34 HOURS BEFORE -

THE **PRINCESS WASN'T** fond of doing her daily chores, especially when they required her to awaken at the crack of dawn. By now the sun was pouring over the edges of the staggering mountains that lined the island. The air was sticky and hot, sweat peeking from her pores as she wandered down the streets of Avala, the largest town on Ishla.

Small, wooden shacks stood on either side of the cobblestone street; a marketplace packed with townspeople. Occasionally, a bell would chime, and a horse-drawn carriage would emerge from the crowd. Locals moved in unison, ebbing out of the way and flowing back once the carriage pulled past.

Normally, Princess Othelia would begin her day by cleaning the stables and feeding their six horses. The King believed all his children should participate in work equally around the castle. It would build character, he explained, and help them gain discipline. For the most part, she didn't mind it. The stables were calm and quiet, though she could've done without shoveling horse dung every morning.

Today was different. Today, she drifted down the red-bricked road wearing a stable boy's uniform that she'd stolen the morning before. She'd stuffed it underneath clean clothes in her wardrobe, knowing no one would go looking for it there. Her father wasn't going to be too happy about that, but there was something she needed to do, and she was going to do it.

Her blonde hair was wrapped in a bun that rested atop her head, stuffed in a billed cap. Billed caps were rare in Ishla, as they were typically seen as informal. But staff—stable boys and such—gave caution to the wind and walked around proudly in white caps. Their rebellion against normalcy worked in her favor, as did the bagginess of the uniform she'd grabbed. Her hair and boobs were hidden well, and she looked rather boyish without her usual splash of makeup on. This plan would work, it *did* work, and she found herself in town, alone, for the third time in her twenty-two years.

Her personal guard, Alexander, was probably searching for her already. Honestly, Othelia wouldn't be surprised if he'd already found her and merely lurked in the shadows, watching. She could hear his chiding words now, ringing so clearly in her head. "You're a strange one, Princess. Your insolence is incomparable to anyone I've ever met."

Alexander had spoken those words after giving her a beating some years ago, as per order from the King himself. Her parents had important guests over for dinner, and she'd chosen to arrive with scrapes and bruises running up her arms and legs. To top it off, she showed up twenty minutes late, hair in shambles and dress splattered in drying blood. "I beat up the stable boy," Othelia had said with a boastful point of her thumb. "Broke his nose."

She gulped at the memory, her chest tightening at the thought of the beatings to come if Alex noticed she was gone.

When he noticed. No, no, *if*. She had to give herself the benefit of the doubt.

Othelia pushed her grievances aside and continued forth. This was a necessary trip, she told herself. There was no need to be afraid. If she found what she was looking for, a few punches wouldn't matter. Not in the long run.

There was something special in town, a force tugging at the corners of her mind and body—as if a string was wrapped around her finger and someone was pulling her forward from the other side. She'd felt this pull twice before but was never able to reach the source. It wasn't a feeling that should be ignored, whatever it was and whatever it would bring. This time, she would get what she wanted.

The streets were bustling as usual, but Othelia slithered through the crowd somewhat quickly. Most of the Ishla citizens had dark brown skin and hair, though there were a handful with Othelia's dusty blonde hair and russet tan.

She walked with her head held high and a stagger in her step, reaching the sealine with ease. The marina stretched nearly a mile along the coast with long docks that extended into the water. A myriad of standard sailing ships bobbed in the choppy waves. The docks were somewhat filthy, though not offensively so, covered in dark green moss and white splotches of seagull dung. A few fishermen littered the edges in groups, smoking cigarettes and tossing back bottles of whiskey. She passed them with her eyes glued to the horizon.

The invisible pull led her to the second to last boat. It was a dinky little thing with a deck big enough for three people. The dark red paint was worn and cracked, revealing slivers of cream wood underneath. She scanned the vessel with dismay. Nothing worthwhile would be on this floating hunk of garbage. She kicked the side of the boat in frustration.

After all this time, it was all in her head.

But that answer wasn't good enough. She wasn't crazy. There had to be something there. If not on the boat, then in the water below. Othelia glanced around, hoping no one found her suspicious after the scene she made. She didn't notice any eyes on her, so she took that as a sign to keep going. She moved with haste, her steps blending in with the dry wind as she walked on the balls of her feet.

Othelia jumped over the taffrail and landed on the deck. The ship rocked in the uneven ripples her added weight created but made no discernible sound. She nodded to herself and wiped the sweat from her brow. Before she continued, she checked her surroundings a second time. No one seemed to care about the stable boy in a white cap, and Alex was nowhere in sight. Good. Her gut, this attraction, was real. It had to be.

The upper deck was empty of items aside from open sails, a flyer pinned to the mast, and a net. A quick inspection led her to realize there was no lower deck, either. She put her hands on her hips and huffed, looking around for any loose boards or cabinets. There was nothing, her vision either failing or leading her to the end of her quest.

Othelia walked up to the flyer and ripped it off the wood, splinters scattering onto the deck. Thick, bold Latarian words read, 'Interested in a lifetime of money and fame? Test your knowledge with the one and only International Exam! Join the EO now! Summer testing begins with the pre-exam July 1st.' She raised a brow. She'd never heard of the EO before. Intrigued, she folded the flyer in half and shoved it in her pocket. At least she found something worth noting.

She turned to leave when, miraculously, a risen board caught her eye. The edge protruded a minute amount, but it was enough to send a rush of adrenaline through her. A rare sense of excitement produced a smile on her face as she crouched down and picked at the corner eagerly. It was stuck well, her long nails proving useless.

Othelia cracked her neck and closed her eyes, her hands trembling and heart pounding. She pictured jolts of silver rushing through her arms and pooling at the tips of her fingers. Power rushed to her aid, producing a burst of raw strength that allowed her to yank the board off completely. Few people could access this type of power, a power they called 'maoho' on the island. *Murder.* But the Royal family could. They were special. She was special.

Her blue eyes glistened at the sight of a small black bag with a purple string tied tightly around the top. She couldn't help herself and undid the bag's binding. It crinkled open, revealing three wilted flower heads. They looked to be eliases, a flower with long red petals slowly turning brown. Yet, the bottom half of the flowers remained a vibrant red, and the cut stem was a healthy, light green. She marveled at their beauty before her thoughts came to a crashing halt.

"These are completely useless!" she exclaimed in Ishlish. She kicked the wooden paneling and curled her fingers into fists, crumpling the flowers inside.

"Are they?" a voice sounded from behind, their Latarian broken, and accent lilted. Othelia froze. Whoops. What was she to do now? She ignored him and inspected the flowers. Though two of the petals had fallen off from her grip, they were otherwise bright and lively. She cursed at her carelessness and faced her foe.

The man was a towering height, complete with a beer belly and a thick, dark brown beard. A brown satchel was wrapped across his body, a long tunic underneath. His slightly baggy pants were stuffed in oversized mountain boots, which were considerably disheveled, and, perhaps most notably, a small carving knife was clutched in his right hand.

Othelia straightened her back and asked in fluent, smooth Latarian, "Why's that?"

The man cocked his head before throwing it back with a hearty laugh. "You think I'd tell you, boy? You're a thief with a keen eye, but those won't be any good to you. Put the bag down and leave and I'll let you keep them eyes."

She raised a brow, remaining arrogant in stature. His maoho tugged at her in strong spurts, a menacing pull toward unforeseen darkness. What business did he have on the island?

Othelia placed the half-dead flowers back in their bag and stuffed them in her pocket. She let out an annoyed sigh and crossed her arms. "You have the audacity to threaten me but not the guts to tell me why?"

Her eyes flickered to his weapon as his grip tightened around it. At that moment, he hopped onto the boat with an immense force that sent them rocking. Seawater splashed onto the deck as her world tilted and her footing was lost. She flailed her arms around helplessly in an attempt to stay upright.

The man lunged forward, aiming for her lower abdomen. Othelia regained balance and dodged to the right, evading his knife by mere inches, and grabbed his weapon-wielding wrist. She knew her raw strength wouldn't be enough against him— he was too big—so she pictured the same silver, electrical jolts rushing to her other hand.

She punched him in the gut, and his body flew backward, his feet sliding against the floor until he slammed into the mast. As he crumpled to the ground, the base layer shattered into a pile of wood chips. The mast swayed and billowed a horrendous, defeated moan; the sails held it up a moment longer, a momentary lapse in gravity. And then it slowly came crashing down, destroying half the ship in the process and landing in the water with an eye-drawing splash.

The man held his stomach and groaned, his chin resting on

his chest. Some of his bones were undoubtedly broken, but that was hardly any of her concern. There was a more pressing matter at hand; water was pooling onto the deck. The boat was very much sinking, and she somehow felt bad, terrible even, to think about leaving him to drown. She was stealing his goods. The least she could do was save him.

Othelia dragged him up and over and off the ship with exhausting effort, her arms aching as she plopped his unconscious body onto the dock. She could've used her ability for further strength, but people were gathering now, people who could judge and deduce who she really was.

She gasped from her exerted energy and kept her head down, avoiding eye contact with the congregating bystanders. There was nothing she wanted more than to leave, but she had one last thing to do. She got on her knees and put her ear up to the man's parted lips. His breathing was shallow but there. She'd accidentally destroyed his ship *and* underestimated her power, but at least she hadn't killed anybody.

Othelia left the port with swift steps. It was easy to lose the gaping onlookers when she reached the main road, and the walk home was serene once she left town. Though there were tall trees on either side of the street, the forest wasn't dense this far inland; each palm tree was evenly spaced from the other. It was impossible to find cover, so she boldly walked to and fro Avala without any. She was amazed by the lack of carriages that passed.

The stone wall of the palace was within her eyeline now, the four golden conical roofs gleaning in the hot sunlight. She had twenty-five minutes until she reached the gateway, where the two guards waited for their payouts. She didn't have access to her family's money, so she bribed them with her lips. Two kisses before and two after. A crude part of the plan, but one that worked. No one could resist adhering to the princess's requests.

A few beautifully quaint minutes had passed when a rustling erupted from behind. The sound was soft, the culprit concealing their presence immediately after presenting it. Othelia spun around and jumped back at the sight of Alexander. His fist was reared and ready to strike. She reacted within seconds, blocking his attack with her forearms.

His strength sent her sliding backward. She dug her heels into the dirt to slow her momentum, puffs of dust swirling around her feet. Her body skid to a stop and they stared at each other, her chest heaving and eyes wide with wild fear of what would come next.

Alexander's lips were drawn in a tight line, his heavily bagged eyes squinting in concentration. He looked as he always did, dressed in a tux and sharp, black shoes. His short black hair was slicked back, and his hands were hidden with thick gloves. The kind he wore when he was about to fight and didn't want to rough up his knuckles. And, she realized with budding dismay, his shoes were smudged. She took a deep breath and tried to prepare. He'd been following her for a long time, maybe the whole time.

She tentatively opened her mouth. What she said now would make or break his reaction. "Ale—"

He disappeared, cutting her off with the brief silence that came before his attack. The trees swayed in the breeze. She listened, her body tense and fists ready.

She didn't hear him, no, but she heard the change in the wind, felt the way it got warmer behind her as he reappeared. Othelia whirled around and raised a hand to block him. She missed, and a fist slammed into her stomach. The air was thrust out of her lungs. She wheezed as another connected with her side. She fell to her knees, involuntary tears streaming down her cheeks as she released stifled sobs.

Every breath she took sent a stabbing pain through her chest. He crouched beside her and watched as she gasped for breath, her body paralyzed. His expression remained hard and unreadable while he eyed up her bruises and tears, no doubt criticizing how easily she'd been beaten. A royal guard had two purposes: protect the royal family and train them. Othelia had disobeyed the rules, giving Alex the authority to train her how he wished.

And he wasn't finished yet.

Alexander pulled off her cap and grabbed a handful of her hair. She tried to wriggle away, but his grip only became tighter. He dragged her down the road with harsh and unbearably painful pulls, ripping hairs from their roots. Her screams bounced off the trees, but no one was around to hear. Alex stopped walking and tossed her to the ground.

She stared at the dirt and sniffled. "I—"

He cut her off with a kick to her stomach. She curled into a ball, defenseless as every muscle in her body throbbed in agony. Her hair was a knotted mess of blood, her scalp rubbed raw. It'd been a long time since she'd gotten a beating, and she'd had the useless faith that Alexander would go easy on her this time around. She thought they'd been getting along recently.

Any movement Othelia made sent a thousand needles stabbing her organs at once. A groan escaped her lips, and she stopped trying. The fight was over.

Alexander pulled her up gruffly and stored her under his arm, using his tight grip around her ribs as further punishment. She released another scream but couldn't find it in herself to retaliate further. Her mouth was dry and her eyes puffy, but her face remained undamaged. No one could know of what the King allowed.

"What were you thinking?" he asked in a low whisper. Drool fell from her mouth as she tried to respond, but her lips sputtered, and she wheezed again. Her lungs and bruises burned.

Alex shook his head and carried her back to the palace without another word. She could already feel the swell of bruises growing underneath her garments. A familiar pang of defeat and failure coursed through her, but she quickly found a way to rationalize the pain she had to endure. An unfortunate price to pay, but the mission was still a success. And, as a bonus, she wouldn't have to kiss those guards again.

Usually, after a beating, Alex would drop her off in her bedroom and bring her an ice pack. A nurse would come to bandage her up later. When she saw the familiar painting outside her room's double doors, Othelia became excited. Finally, she would be free of his wretched grip.

But then he passed the painting and the double doors and hauled her down the hall. Right to the throne room, where he tossed her in front of her father. She landed on her hands and knees, biting back a yelp from the sudden shot of agony coursing through her.

King Sandoval sat atop his yellow-embroidered wooden throne and stared down at her with a fiery unlike anything she'd ever seen. Alexander bowed before stepping off the strip of golden carpet that stretched down the center of the marble floor. Pillars stood parallel on either side of the carpet; an S was carved in the middle of each.

Othelia took her time to stand—knowing each second added to his rage—and wiped off her clothes.

"Tell me, Othelia, does our family's name mean nothing to you?" His voice was demanding but not booming, a hint of fatigue resting somewhere underneath his disdain. "Does the legacy we've built and the reputation we've upheld hold any regard to you whatsoever?"

Othelia stared at him, unable to respond. Despite his old age, he was big and burly, thick with intimidating muscle, and his narrow gaze reduced her to a piece of filth. His absurdly long beard sat over his yellow sash and black tunic, lush with light blond strands interspersed with sparse gray.

She hadn't told anyone of the connection she'd felt toward the flowers. Even worse, she didn't know of their importance. There were few things more embarrassing than looking her father in the eyes and admitting she had no idea what she was doing. Reluctantly, she pulled out the bag; she couldn't bring herself to lie or tell him half-truths. He was an honest man, albeit harsh with his words and actions. Ultimately, he wanted what was best for his children. Or perhaps he just wanted them to be the best.

She opened the bag and looked down at the contents, mortified for being drawn to something that looked so minuscule, and sighed.

"I was brought to these. I'm not sure why, but..." her voice trailed off. She didn't want to sound as crazy as she felt. "Late last night, I felt this sort of, I don't know, tingling in my body. Every time I closed my eyes, I could see a path leading to something, but I couldn't see where or for what."

"And you decided to follow this feeling by yourself?"

She shrugged, keeping her eyes on the flowers. She wanted to say something snappy, something along the lines of 'you wouldn't have let me go anyway,' but instead, she met his gaze and said, "Evidently."

He leaned back. "You realize any number of things could've gone wrong, correct? You could've been seen by someone, raised speculation, or worse, been tricked. What if this 'path' was planted by an enemy? What then?"

"I—"

"You would've been handing yourself over on a silver platter." He gestured toward her disguise in disgust, then rubbed at the bridge of his nose. He shook his head, eyes diverting from her to the wall as if she were a mess he could no longer bear to see.

"I don't think—"

"No. You don't. Now bring them closer."

Othelia curled her fists and clenched her jaw, using every ounce of control to stop herself from arguing, and climbed the six steps to his throne. The pained lines along her father's face were beginning to fade as she came closer. Was the way she struggled to stand and walk enough for him to feel satisfied? Or did he actually feel an ounce of pity for his daughter and what he allowed the royal guards to do?

The sudden change in his reaction made her second guess his intentions, and she debated turning around and running out of the room. No, she denied herself, that wouldn't be possible in her current state. There were guards at his side, at the door, and lining the gold carpet sporadically. She had no choice.

She stopped in front of him and held out the bag. It was rare to get this close to the King, even for his children. Often, she'd go weeks, if not months, without seeing him. It should've been an honor to stand before him, but she couldn't wait to leave.

Her father leaned forward and inspected the flower heads, stroking his chin and nodding when he came to a satisfying conclusion. He settled back on his throne and gave Othelia a familiar, contemptuous look that further confirmed his antipathy toward her. It was her own fault, she knew. She actively went against his wishes. He had no reason to trust her, to love her. He didn't even know her, not really.

"These," he began, "are called *talithes,* which roughly translates to 'of the lost' in Ishlish."

Othelia released her breath, thankful for his kindness, and gawked at her treasure with wide eyes and newfound curiosity. Flowers of the Lost. She wanted to know everything. Where they came from, where they were going, why that man was hiding them so well. "What do they do?"

He shook his head. "They don't do anything, my dear. They're a collector's item, an auction prize. It's been said they cure sadness, but that's merely a folk tale. They're pretty little flowers with enough mag trapped in them to not completely wilt away. You've disobeyed me for nothing. Tell me, how does that feel?"

Othelia shook her head, momentarily surprised by his lack of interest, and then smiled. She tied the bag up, put it back in her pocket, and made her way down the stairs. She didn't bother with asking about the flyer she found—she knew what his answer would be.

Othelia stopped when she reached the double doors and turned to him for the last time. "You know that's not true, Father. I thought you had more integrity than to lie like that."

CHAPTER 3

LEO

- 15 HOURS BEFORE -

HIS NERVES WOKE him every hour until he finally gave up and got up. When he pulled open the rickety shades of the lodge window, the moon was up, too. Whatever time it was, he didn't care. His stomach was in knots and his head was overheating. He pried open the window and leaned out, the cool air soothing his nausea. At least he wasn't hungry anymore.

He looked up at the night sky and traced constellations with his finger. His mother had once prayed to the stars, claiming the little specks were watching over humanity and judging their actions. If the good outweighed the bad, you'd be sent to live among them and carry out their will. But somewhere along the way, she lost that faith, and Leo could never seem to find it, either.

It was too early for such thoughts. He rubbed away the crust from his eyes and peered at his watch. Three in the morning. He sighed and laid back in bed, staring at the ceiling as time slowly passed, his anxieties growing into a dreadful pool of unanswered questions. How had the receptionist moved her nail polish? Was Eli trustworthy? There was only one way to find out, and he hated it. He was stuck in a corner.

Leo got ready to take a shower and turned the knob. He frowned, the showerhead waterless, and looked around for an explanation. A coin slot was beside the knob, a sign that read "5Q per minute" underneath. He wasn't about to spend 5Q on a quick wash. So next was drawing, because what else was he to do, and the sketch was good. Great, even. For a second, his nerves were calmed. And then he focused on the thrum in his ears with each beat of his heart and he was back to square one.

When it finally hit 5:15, he made his final preparations. He'd changed from a red to bright blue flannel and tossed yesterday's clothes into his backpack. Atop them, he placed his identification card, a water bottle, and a switchblade. His notebook and pencils were shoved in there, too. Everything was accounted for. He brushed his teeth and was off, his jaw clenched as he imagined the day ahead. He could get all the clues wrong. Eli could choose not to show up, or he could be a trickster. Or a murderer. In fact, most of the scenarios Leo concocted ended with his death.

A rush of relief washed over him as he made his way into the lobby; Leo spotted Eli almost immediately. He was sitting on one of the red-velvet couches, looking down at a rectangular device in his hand. His unmistakable side bangs dangled over his eyes. Leo raised a brow at the phone—equating it to wealth —and his skepticism of Eli grew. He couldn't find it in himself to trust people who had money, especially since Eli suggested splitting the taxi fare instead of covering it.

Leo whistled and waved for Eli's attention, who stood and smiled once he realized the whistle was directed at him.

"Glad to see you're awake," Eli said, nodding for Leo to follow. They stepped outside, the sky still dark. The streets were jammed with headlights and impatient honking. Most of the citizens surrounding them were a mix of buff ruffians and those wearing rags and carrying garbage bags. The homeless, he guessed. Their dead-set eyes and shambling legs made him shudder. An ominous look into his future if he failed the exam.

People crowded the outer edge of the sidewalks, arms flailing as they shouted for a taxi into the inner city. Another symphony of honks filled the taut air as Eli and Leo swerved through the sea of stalemated cars. Just yesterday, this place was an empty wasteland. Now it was impossible to walk around without getting shoved. One thing was for sure: there wouldn't be an easy way to hitch a ride.

Leo kept his eyes on Eli's back, weaving through the city and down two blocks before he remembered where they were going. A café. His stomach involuntarily rumbled, a song of lustful, mouthwatering hope. They rounded the corner and there, in all its delicious glory, was one of the few places that remained open.

The café in question was bigger than he expected, the exterior a light blue. A bright yellow sign above the door read 'Deluxe Baked Goods and Café' in large Latarian letters, translated into what he presumed to be Baltarish underneath.

Eli propped the door open, and the heavy scent of freshly baked bread wafted into Leo's nose, overwhelming his senses. His mouth watered as he thought of home and the bread his mother would make. He envisioned the dough rising inch by inch, gradually turning golden brown around the edges.

Inside, the bakery had booths along the walls and tall tables sprinkled throughout the center. They were all occupied, conversations bouncing off the walls in a constant ramble. A bar area sat in the back, labeled 'sixteen and older,' with bottles lining the wall behind the counter. Light bulbs were strung above the counter with wires, and a bartender with a thick mustache was wiping away residue left by previous guests.

Leo held his head high as he followed Eli to the barstools. Leo was freshly eighteen but looked far younger, and the other two seated at the bar were easily in their late fifties. Eli called over the bartender and the mustached man reached out a hand for their identification cards. Paranoia sunk in yet again. What if he thought it was fake and kicked them out?

The bartender nodded and handed the cards back. "Drinks?"

"Make that three shots of taq, please," Eli said. "And bread. Loads and loads of bread. There's a discount here, I heard?"

"Half off."

"Two baskets, then. I'll pay." He offered Leo a smile. "Anything to drink?"

Leo shook his head and crinkled his brows skeptically. Eli was ordering taq? At this hour? Leo's father was a big fan of taq but drank rarely. His eyes always gleamed when he spoke of drinking, a spark that had otherwise died the day he stopped partaking in it regularly. Leo didn't like that look, and although Eli didn't have it, there was something unsettling about a man ordering liqueur this early in the day.

"Uh... grab me some water as well," Eli added. "Fetch a glass for him, too."

While the bartender prepared their order, Leo leaned his elbows on the countertop and gave his new partner an accusatory stare. "Do you start every morning like this?"

Eli waved him off. "Only when I need that extra boost. Helps me think. What about you? You look exhausted. You sure you don't want to order anything else?"

"We don't have time to drink."

The bartender dropped off Eli's shots, and he gulped them down like water. When he was done, Eli shivered from their presumably bitter taste and looked to Leo with a wide grin.

"We don't have time to eat, either. Not with this flow of traffic. We probably should've gotten up earlier."

"I've been up since 3," Leo grumbled along with his stomach.

"Early riser? I hate waking up before 11, hence the help." Eli raised his hand for the bartender to come back. Leo grabbed his arm and pulled it down with forceful ease.

Eli shot him a glare. "What? I've only had three so far."

"Wh—only? No, no, I'm not working with someone who relies on liqueur." Saying yes to this man was a mistake. He could see that now. "I'm not hauling you around if you're dead weight."

"I don't *rely* on it. I like it. There's a difference."

"If you use it every day, you rely on it." Leo shook his head. "You're going to have a hard time during the exam, you know."

To his delight, the bartender placed a basket of baked wheat and whole bread rolls in front of them, the butter on a separate dish, sculpted into a flower. Leo watched the steam rise in hungered anticipation. With this, he hoped the conversation would end, mostly because he knew chastising someone could push them away. Practically speaking, there was a slim chance Leo could find the exam location alone. But after that, he and Eli could go their separate ways.

"Relax a little. My actions are my own and I'll deal with them as such," Eli said, picking up a roll and breaking it in half. To Leo's surprise, Eli didn't come across as disheartened or annoyed. In fact, he didn't appear to care about Leo's warnings at all.

Leo dropped the topic and took to spreading a thick layer of creamy butter on his bread before taking a ravenous bite. Eli didn't talk or look at him for the rest of the meal, and Leo was left wondering what he'd gotten himself into.

CHAPTER 4

ISABELLE

- 13 HOURS BEFORE -

THE EVENING ENDED like any other. She was perched in front of a fire that crackled and sparked against the moonlit village. A skinned deer rotated on a spike over the flames, its searing flesh bringing tears to her eyes. While she enjoyed the hunt, she despised the notion that humans were allowed to kill and eat creatures made from the hands of Gahi.

Reinta was lively at night; residents sat outside their huts with their own handmade fires and spoke jovially with family and friends. Copious chatter filled the mountainside as stars sparkled in the night sky, illuminating a barren, grassy land. There were but fifty villagers scattered about the area, their lives bound by the constraints of the vast, empty land surrounding them. No one dared speak to her family.

Her father sat across from her, watching with intent eyes as though he knew her later intentions. They sat in silence; her father watched her as she watched the deer slowly become meat to be consumed. After her family had been torn apart, bit by bit, her father had slowly lost any words to be had with his daughter. At first, it had been disconcerting that he was progressively growing quieter until their time together was void of any conversation. But as the months grew on, she became accustomed to the silence, and it had become almost peaceful. Almost.

After their dinner—she'd allowed it to roast too long, creating a burnt aftertaste—her father retreated into their hut with a grunt that signaled 'goodnight.' She tossed a bucket of water onto the fire and watched as the flames turned to ash. Her plan replayed in her mind. An effortless plan, she thought. Once she reached the fences.

Isabelle used to never make note of how fast her father drifted to sleep—there was no need—but she'd been keeping track of him the last few weeks. Sneaking beside him as he slept was rather easy, though nerve-wracking. She surmised he fell into a deep sleep within minutes, his snores loud enough to raise complaints from the villagers over the years. Her ability to rest throughout childhood was certainly troublesome with the ruckus that came from his mouth at night.

But tonight was no night for sleep.

Isabelle made sure the fire was out, stood with a stretch and a yawn, and headed inside to prepare. She moved to her side of the hut and slid the cloth shades closed before quickly stripping off her traditional garbs—a short-sleeved, long blue dress that stretched to her ankles.

She reached underneath her mattress and produced a black hooded shirt and tight pants of the same color. A leather sheath clipped around her waist, a dagger resting within. Although Reinta did not have mirrors, it was apparent her new attire stuck out against the rest, but the only way to escape home was by blending into the night. Finally, she prepared a pack of all the berries and water they owned. Her father would probably never forgive her, but that would matter not. Sometimes, she didn't know if she would ever forgive him.

She stepped out of the hut and was immediately faced with the priestess, Yalien. "Where are you going?"

Isabelle stammered, nervousness written along her sputtering lips. "To fetch some water. My father is thirsty."

His snores rumbled through the door of their hut, and she winced. She hadn't expected to be caught so soon, or at all. Isabelle wasn't sure what she expected Yalien to say or do, and she didn't want to wait around any longer to find out. She began to slowly walk toward the road that separated the other huts.

"What are you wearing?"

Isabelle gulped. "It is as Gahi preaches, my priestess. 'Those who wear black signify a deeper understanding of the less fortunate.' I must be going now."

She turned and quickened her pace down the dirt path, praying her nonsensical explanation was enough to postpone Yalien's inevitable actions. The fences were 500 meters away, just far enough for the horses to be undisturbed by the fires and people. She could reach it in a matter of minutes if she just—

"Protectors!" Yalien yelled. Isabelle glanced over her shoulder to see Yalien pointing in her direction as those who remained outside turned to watch. "We have a disturbance!"

Isabelle took to running, listening for the heavy steps of the Protectors that followed. She glanced over her shoulder to find them advancing quickly, their torches ablaze. What good was wearing black if they could light up the world around her? She cursed her ill-timed exit, expecting the worst as she reached the fences. They were short and easy to maneuver over, but the flames approaching were beginning to frighten the horses. Their fearful whinnies echoed through the night, and she knew if she didn't act fast, she would be caught. And trampled.

She didn't have time to grab one of the saddles hanging along the fences or pick a horse accustomed to long journeys. No, she had to pick at random—whichever was closest and easiest to cut loose from their ropes. As she approached the nearest, it stood on its hind legs with a cry, towering over her small frame like a ravenous beast.

Isabelle gasped and ducked, veering off her path and to one of the smallest steeds. The footfalls of the Protectors were nearing. She was afraid to turn around, to see how close they now were. Any false movement would be a squandering of what little time she had left. She had to persist; she had to go.

She whispered to the horse, "Come light a new path with me."

Then she used the rope tied loosely around his neck to lead him to the nearest fence. She climbed on top of the wooden barrier to mount the horse but found herself being pulled backward instead.

"I got her," a man yelled, wrapping his arms around her waist with a tight squeeze. She reacted without thinking, swinging her head back into the man's nose. His grip loosened, and she used her arms to push him off her. She whirled around and punched his face, pain immediately shooting up her arm. Isabelle stood, stunned. She'd never punched anyone, nor did she have any desire to. But the mission she set forth on was one that could not be delayed. Adrenaline was the only power she had now.

Isabelle jumped back on the fence, watching as more torches drew closer. The horse stood attentively, her words keeping him calm. For reasons unknown, she had an affinity for horses. They trusted her; they listened. Isabelle climbed atop him and kicked him in the sides.

"Now! Now!" she yelled. The horse whinnied and veered away from the fence she'd just climbed, pulling her to the right.

She hunched low as she held onto his mane; her body bounced roughly against his. She closed her eyes, feeling the wind rush through her hair. Butterflies filled her stomach as the horse jumped over the fence and ran. She didn't open her eyes until she was sure the Protectors weren't following; once someone was gone, they had no jurisdiction to follow.

A long night was ahead, but she'd made it. For the first time in her life, she was in the unknown. People rarely left the village, and if they did, they weren't allowed back. Not without extensive punishment. But that didn't matter. She wouldn't be coming back.

Tears streamed down her face as she rode. She'd miss her father, the people, and the Priestess. Regardless of the whispers throughout the village about her family, she loved every single person. Reinta was home. And now, she'd left her father with no one and nothing, a fate she wouldn't wish on anyone. But she had something to do, and she'd stop at nothing to do it. Even if it meant never seeing her father again.

THE TRIP LASTED three and a half days across the continent of Ubas. Her small village was far off in the mountains, and she neither ran into civilization nor found another mode of transportation. Thankfully, her father had primed her for lack of communication, and the journey was peaceful.

With her unexpected quick departure from Reinta, she had grabbed one of the short-distance horses that belonged to the Gatherers. She remembered riding this particular steed by the silver entangled in his brown mane. Aogra, a horse she used to ride with her late mother whilst finding nearby berries and fruits to eat. One of her mother's favorite horses. Upon this revelation, she expected a bout of sadness to overwhelm her, but it did not come. Such was to be expected after the wretched things her mother had said to her brother, Micah. Things Isabelle didn't dare repeat in her thoughts or prayers.

Isabelle wagered that Aogra hadn't ventured farther than six hours. Her luck, it seemed, did not exist. And now, she was facing the consequences of a trip any longer, namely because Aogra began to refuse things.

First, it was his treats. Isabelle would offer an apple after a huge feat, and Aogra happily chomped them down. It wasn't until the end of the second day—after trekking through a shallow river—that Aogra stopped accepting them. He stared blankly ahead with his mouth clamped shut, a look of annoyance etched in his empty, black eyes.

Then he moved on to his second refusal: walking. He stopped when he pleased, which happened to be far too often and for far too long. Like now, for instance. Aogra neighed as his hooves clanked to a stop on the concrete roadway.

This particular stretch of road was unlike any other, held up by concrete pillars and curving until it reached the top of the wall separating the inner and outer city. The wall abruptly ended at the bay on both sides, where large military ships sat with their cannons pointed toward the outer city.

The very top of the wall had a heavily guarded checkpoint with five armed men in protective vests. Three worked on a line of cars, unloading them and patting down the passengers, and the other two monitored a line of horse travelers.

When it was her turn to step up, Aogra kept his hooves planted a few feet away from the checkpoint and sufficiently held up the rest of the line. She kicked her legs lightly at his sides. He wouldn't budge. The two guards appeared unamused. Rather angry, really. She smiled half-heartedly and let out an awkward huff of air meant to be a chuckle.

Her Latarian accent was no good, she knew, but she

pushed the words out with stammering fervor, "Sorry! Sorry! Give... me a second...?"

She kicked Aogra harder, praying to Gahi that he would move. Her face grew hot in both frustration and embarrassment. Isabelle had never been disobeyed quite like this before, and certainly not in front of so many people.

Isabelle jumped off and planted her hands on her hips, bending to get a good look in Aogra's eyes.

"What's the hold-up!" someone yelled from behind. Her body became tense, the notion of confrontation overwhelming.

She took a deep breath and did the only thing she could think of—talked to her horse. She spoke in Urkinian, her native language. "You chose the worst time to be doing this. We're so close, Aog. So close. Come with me." She put her forehead to his and closed her eyes. "Dub askla, rypkhod'te." Please, come.

But he stayed. Tricky little thing. So much for her ability to persuade horses. If only she'd been able to stick to her plan and bring Raldolph instead, but this was no time to think of what could've been.

One of the guards—a man of average height with short, stubbled hair—stepped forward while eyeing up her oversized friend. His brows were furrowed, but he spoke with kindness. "You need to move him, miss."

She winced, his Latarian fluid and hard to understand. Urkinian was specific to villages beyond the vast mountain realms, deep within the western underbelly of Ubas, and they had no need to learn the universal languages. Her brother had been the one to teach her about them. "There are two, but Latarian is the one used the most most often. Two mosts; that's how favored it is."

Isabelle had laughed then, a young sixteen-year-old

entranced with her older brother's intelligence. He'd been the lone adventurer, daring enough to stray from home and come back. "Why's it more favored? Shouldn't they be treated equally if they're both universal?"

Micah had shrugged, twirling a sharp knife through his fingers with little effort. It looked as though he were morphing the steel into a line of liquid. "There are many unknowns. For instance, what did I do when I was away from home?"

His sharp green eyes were cunning and bold. She wished she had his strength, his ability to get others to do what he wanted. Better yet, she wished he'd waited for her, so they could've taken the exam together. Won together. But it was too late for all that.

"Miss? You need to move the horse, or we'll have to escort you off the highway."

"I'm trying," she snapped in Urkinian. The guard reached for the gun at his side, and she threw her hands up, her heart dropping. Yelling was no way to get what she wanted, and it was no way to speak to someone with a gun.

She took a deep breath and thought hard about her Latarian literacy. She knew words and phrases, but stringing them into sentences was a task she admittedly struggled with. How to make him understand...

"The time to move, um, sirs... sires?"

"Sir."

"Right. Sorry, sir. Now is not the time."

The guard tsked and pulled the gun from his holster. Isabelle gasped and raised her hands again as a sign of resignation. "Please, no!"

The guard pointed the gun at the ground and fired twice at Aogra's feet. Isabelle sprang to the side with a startled squeak. Aogra neighed furiously and held his front legs high in the air. The guard shot a third and final time, sending Aogra galloping back the way they came, his tail swinging in choppy successions. The other horses in line were notably disgruntled, the ones nearest fighting with their riders to turn away.

Isabelle kept her distance from the man, the gun still in his hand. She clenched her fists and glared at him. "My horse!"

"You can chase after it if you want," the man said with a scoff as he put the gun away and reached out his hand. "Identification card."

Herein lay her third problem: she did not have an identification card. Why should she? Her village forbade going anywhere that required one. Why hadn't Micah warned her of this? Though, she supposed the last time they spoke was two years ago. Perhaps these were new requirements. Or perhaps he'd forgotten to mention it, never expecting his sister to take the exam herself.

She shook her head and confidently stated, "I am from Reinta."

The man tossed back his head and released a single, sharp laugh. "Isn't that one of those tiny little villages across the Row?" She nodded, and he laughed again. "Long way from home, are ya? Very well, you ain't no harm. You can pass. Just stay on the far-right side of the road. That's the side for walkers."

She gave a curt bow. "I offer my gratitude."

Isabelle did as she was told and made her way down the road, which was similarly designed to the other side, descending back to the ground at a curve. Horses and cars alike passed on by, not a single one stopping to offer help. It was the crest of dawn when she passed that first checkpoint, and she arrived at the second two hours later. There, she was laughed at by grown men again, this time both because she came on foot and without an ID. Again, they waved her through.

Midral was as Micah described: rambunctious and

crowded, but also bright and diverse. No one looked exactly like the other. Large balloons drifted overhead, and animated screens switched between models and soundless animations. The streets smelled of fried dough and cooked meat. Her mouth watered. All she'd brought were assorted berries, of which she'd devoured after her second day of travel.

She had to stop marveling at this new world and get back to the task at hand. The city was overwhelming, unlike anything she'd ever experienced, and if she wasn't careful, she'd be stuck staring for hours. But where to start? Isabelle knew to search for advertisements that could be deemed fake—Micah had told her that much. But as she looked around, she realized she had a fourth problem: she couldn't tell what was real and what was not. Although there were hundreds of advertisements, they all came packaged with their own snappy one-liners and striking short names.

As time ticked away, she became increasingly aware of how little she knew about the exam or how the city worked. Instead of giving into dread, however, she scuttled through the hordes of people taking up the sidewalks and attempted to rework her initial plan.

She found an open bench and sat down, inspecting the hodgepodge of individuals that passed. The eye-catching crowd would be overwhelming for most, but Isabelle was able to focus on the smallest of details, a trick taught to her by her father while they hunted boar. "If you know what you're looking for," he'd say, "and you can focus on its every move, you've already won."

Isabelle listened to his words and scanned the crowd for anything distinct. There had to be a way to weed out those looking for the exam from the locals. She tried to watch people's gazes, see which advertisements grabbed their attention. When that failed, she inspected the clothes they wore and the languages they spoke. No two people pointed her in the same direction.

And then she noticed someone holding a clump of papers. And then another. And then she saw an image on a faraway screen that corresponded with one of the papers. She counted the sheets in each person's hands as best she could; about a third had a total of four, the highest amount she'd seen.

She smiled to herself, relieved, and looked for a viable target. Who seemed gullible? Who seemed arrogant and brash? Who appeared approachable *and* had all four papers?

Her eyes stopped on a tall, beautiful man with long, golden brown hair tied back in a ponytail. He passed the four pages around his crew of two. The crew in question were twins, their heights and enormous muscles identical. The sole difference between them was a jagged scar on the left brother's nose, spanning from cheek to cheek horizontally.

She focused on the handsome one, his swagger palpable and unlike anything she'd ever seen. It was time to cut that confidence down.

Before making her move, Isabelle looked for street names and addresses, choosing whichever ones she could read. She walked a block down and crossed the street, careful to blend in with the pace of her peers. When the three men were in sight, the twins were standing beside each other, her target to the far left of them. She prayed to Gahi for forgiveness for what she was about to do.

As she passed, Isabelle feigned a stumble and bumped into her target. She would have to channel her brother's cunning ways to a perfect degree if she wanted to pull this off.

"Hey, watch i—" he began, cutting himself short when she turned around.

Her eyes were wide and apologetic. "I am so sorry! I'm

so..." she trailed off, "I am new to... how do you say, area! Do you know why it is so busy here?"

The scarred twin scoffed. "How could you possibly be unaware of what's going on?"

"I move here two day ago from Reinta. They don't teach... a lot. I live," she said, pointing to a random building with wide windows. "505 Shellbrook Lane."

Isabelle didn't like to lie, largely due to her fear of looming damnation. Gahi would understand in time and through prayer, she was sure of it. Despite this trepidation, her mind and nerves were clear. She felt content in her ability to tell a lie, and even more so in her ability to run away if needed. She just had to maintain her composure and hope she picked the right people for the job.

The men exchanged glances. The scarless brother shook his head. "I'm not buying it."

The target raised his hand to silence his partner. "I've heard of those people before and, based on her rather poor Latarian and... unique accent, I'd say her story checks out. She wouldn't know anything about the exam. They don't learn like we do."

The three men continued to size her up. The twins appeared unimpressed.

"I-I swear," she said, placing a hand over her chest, "I was, uh, inte-interestated?"

"Interested," the target corrected with an amused smile.

"Yes, interested, yes! Interested in." She gestured at the enormous crowd, then at him. "And I think maybe you could help? You all look so... so nice."

"Aw," the target said, his golden-brown eyes glistening with unsettling hunger. "How about now, Marcious? Do you believe her now?"

Marcious, the scarless twin, squinted at her, but she refused to break character. She was so close. Finally, he said, "Sure, Abe. I do if you do."

Abe nodded. "Oh, yeah. I do. People on the other side of the river don't concern themselves with matters like ours. I'd be surprised if she even knew what we were saying."

The scarred twin rubbed his chin. "I think I remember learning about Reinta. How they don't got an education and do nothin' but hunt all day."

She restrained a wince. First, the roadway guards had laughed at her, and now this. This city was filled with vile creatures, and it took all her strength to not punch the twin directly in his already crooked nose. Gahi would understand that action without prayer.

"They're made extra fine, though," said Marcious, skimming her body greedily. Isabelle held in her rage with a confused furrow of her brows.

"What are these?" She pointed at their papers. She could make out one image—waves. It looked similar; no, it was certainly the same ad she'd seen on a passing blimp. Something about a boat. "Many have?"

Abe produced a pompous smirk as he looked down at her, golden-brown eyes narrow and glistening. She had to hand it to him; he wore that look well. "These are for the pre-exam."

"Pre... exam? I'm not familiar..."

"Wow, they really don't teach these people anything," the scarred twin said. His brother laughed, but Abe kept his eyes on Isabelle. One wrong look and he would know she understood. She debated fighting them for the papers, but she hated fighting, too, and lashing out wouldn't solve anything. It wouldn't change their opinions of her or her village.

"Oh, uh, can I see?" she asked sheepishly, pushing back a strand of dark brown hair that had fallen out of her tight ponytail.

They conferred amongst themselves before reaching a consensus. Abe handed his paper to her, the twins following suit with theirs. She looked over the ads in stunned amusement. They'd really fallen for it, and now she had all four in her hands. The paper was yellowed and flimsy; the ink was faded but legible. She was lucky. No, not lucky. This was the work of Gahi.

She looked up at the men, smiled, and said in Urkinian, "Ya'lyke." Give thanks.

And then she ran.

CHAPTER 5

LEO

- 10 HOURS BEFORE -

THE INNER CITY of Midral was immensely close to the outer, yet it breathed on a different level. Tall buildings lined the sky with boisterous colors bouncing off screens. Swarms of people took up every nook and cranny, boisterous chatter drifting into their taxi as a group crossed the street. Blimps and hot air balloons floated aimlessly in the graying sky, advertisements flashing against the clouds.

Eli and Leo were dropped off south of the marina at a pink sign labeled 'Taxidrop.' The driver took their money and shooed them out with a displeased flick of the wrist. He swore incoherently as Leo shut the door.

"He's mad even though we paid him?" Leo asked.

"No tip," Eli said. "I think he might've expected one. I always forget about that type of stuff; it's not common where I'm from. Guessing it's the same for you?"

"We don't have a taxi service." His answer was lost with the flock of bodies that tugged them along. If the outer city was packed, the inner city was overflowing.

Leo managed to sneak out of the crowd, pulling Eli with

him by the cuff of his suit. The bench they stood in front of was decorated in red and orange swirls reminiscent of the wind. It was sandwiched between two buildings with yellow-striped umbrellas hanging above the doors. Leo observed the sky until he found one of the flashing blimps. The screen switched between two images.

The first was written in bold, capital letters: 'Hails, the newest horror series!' It faded after ten seconds, a new ad in its place. Leo widened his eyes. This could be it. This could be a clue.

The second had pixelated blue waves flowing on half the screen, white fizz crashing into a scrolling bar of text that read, 'It's now or never! Get your boating license, 50% off! Avoid getting pulled over by the sailor patrol!'

Leo was ill-prepared. Neither of the advertisements pointed to anything of note. Perhaps he was wrong, and his optimism clouded his judgment. Maybe they were average, boring ads, and maybe every ad he gravitated toward was average because that's what he was. Maybe, maybe, maybe. His mother was right; he was in over his head. He shouldn't have come.

He'd been so absorbed in his thoughts that he hadn't noticed Eli watching him. Unbeknownst to Leo, his shoulders had begun to sag, and an indent had formed between his brows.

"Don't count yourself out yet," Eli said, grabbing Leo's shoulder lightly. "We have to think things through."

"That sounds funny coming from a drunk guy."

"Hey, I want help with the exam, not my rigorous drinking habits. You're very judgmental, you know."

"Practical."

"Not when you're wrong. I'm not drunk. Now, let's focus on the task at hand, shall we? We have two clues right up there." He pointed to the blimp. "I'll tell you how I know in a second. Now, what about the people walking by? Notice anything about them?"

Leo shook his head and Eli added with a sly smile, "Look harder."

He wasn't sure what he was looking for, but Leo felt his shorter height left him at a disadvantage. He climbed atop the bench and took in the view of jumbled faces and movements. A group of ladies wearing revealing outfits and fuzzy boas around their necks passed by, followed by men carrying computers under their arms, and a group of flannels and overalls behind them.

Physique ranged from fat to chiseled abdomens to bulging arms to anything in between. He wished there was a way to know everyone's past, everyone's desires and interests. Aside from clashing cultures, there was nothing out of the ordinary. Except—

Leo cracked a smile and pointed to the computer-wielding men, a small set of papers clenched in each of their hands. "Most of them are carrying a collection of papers."

He watched as a couple walked by, their heads hunched over a copy, two other pages hidden beneath them. He couldn't hear what the pair was saying, nor could he see what the papers said. But he noticed that some had two, others four.

"Good. You figured it out. I knew I made a good decision picking you, even if you are judgmental. Yes, pages are scattered throughout the city, usually at random shops or street vendors. It's first come, first serve, though, so we might not have any luck."

"I have principles. That doesn't make me judgmental."

"Sure, it does."

"Anyway, how do you—"

"I did my research. This type of information is pretty accessible on the net."

Leo flushed. His mother's words flashed through his mind. "There ain't nothin' on there you need to be seein'." But apparently, there was plenty. What else was she wrong, or lying, about?

"I didn't grow up with the net, either." Leo regretted his forwardness. Such honesty! To a complete and utter stranger, no less. Any sign of weakness was bad, and yet he laid it out on a platter for this man. "But I know of computers, of course."

His fears grew as Eli responded with, "Hmm."

He'd have to prove himself, and fast. Leo took off his backpack and sat down, taking out his notebook and preparing a pencil. He could feel Eli watch as he got to work; his silence was racking every nerve in Leo's brain. He wasn't a less valuable partner because he didn't have the net. No. He could do this. He had to shake his anxiety and push forward.

"So, four is the highest, would you agree?" Leo asked, sketching the advertisements from the blimp on two separate sheets of paper. He rewrote the text word-for-word.

"I would. Say, that's a good wave."

"Thanks. We have these two, so let's try to find the remaining two and I can draw them. Saves us the time of looking for the papers ourselves, and it'd be harder to solve them without physical copies."

"Wow," Eli inched closer, his shoulder touching Leo's. "If there's an art phase, you'll pass with flying colors."

"Is there an art phase?"

"Not that I know of, but the phases are different for every exam. I don't see how art would pertain to joining the EO, though, so don't get your hopes up. How'd you do that, write them word for word?"

Leo smiled but kept his gaze down, hand moving, lines forming. "Words and images just sort of stick after I see them. I have to think it's important enough to remember, though."

When his work was done, Eli snatched the notebook and inspected the details.

"Now, this," Eli said with chagrin, "this is what I'm talking about. From what I could gather about the pre-exam, each advertisement will point to the country and city of the exam and nothing else. It's the easiest part if you know your geography."

"How does a discounted boating license correlate with our destination? How do we know it means anything?"

Eli pointed to the drawing of the waves and boat, his finger underlining the phrase '50% off boating license.' "I can see why you'd ask that if you don't know—"

"That's the point of a question."

"—But you don't get discounts on a boating license. It goes against the Accordance of Licenses. The number is probably what's important here. Ask me how I know."

"How do you know?" Leo asked impatiently. They didn't have time for this.

"I'm glad you asked! My father owns a famous cruise line. I know everything about the rules of boating, inside and out. A license is something to be earned, not bought." He turned his attention back to the notebook. "I also doubt Hails is a real horror game. It's a strange name."

"That's your reason?"

"What could a game named Hails possibly be about? It's fake."

"Huh," Leo said, more confused than ever. "Who comes up with this stuff?"

"Hails," Eli muttered, ignoring Leo altogether. Eli continued to look the drawing over until something seemed to click. He snatched Leo's pencil and wrote what looked to be gibberish beside the video game title. It took Leo a little too long to fully understand what Eli was doing. His eyebrows shot up when he finally figured it out.

Hials. Hilas. Hilsa. Ialsh. Ilsha. Ishal.

Eli sucked in a deep breath, his hand shaking. "I-I can't believe it. I know what it is." He wrote the final combination. Ishla.

Leo scratched his head. "Ishla? That island off the shores of eastern Gyantel?"

Eli nodded, something wild sparkling in his eyes. "Good, you know your geography, too! Very good."

His transparent passion was enough to ignite Leo's belief in their mission. His ambition was quickly derailed as he realized Ishla was far—too far to reach in ten hours. The continents of Gyantel and Phanteous were sandwiched between Ubas and Ishla, making it a two—or more—month journey.

"I've come across some illegal forums on the E-net that suggested unscrambling words," Eli explained. "Of course, the post could've been a bad lead and I could be completely wrong here."

Leo didn't know what the E-net was compared to the regular net, nor what illegal forums could entail. Instead of asking about either, he stroked his chin. "Do you think you're right?"

Eli's grin widened to an impossible length. "Undoubtedly."

"Then we'll look for things related to Ishla. Do you think the boating ad implies we need to get there by boat?"

"No, probably not. That's far too... self-explanatory, you know? Especially if you know Ishla doesn't have any aircraft ports, which I happen to."

Leo crossed his arms. "If you know all this already, why ask me to help you? You said you'd be bad at this."

"'Knowing some things doesn't mean you know everything,'" Eli said in a mocking tone. "An old adage from my pops' time. Never thought I'd have to use it on someone else."

"You're avoiding my question."

"I'm actually not; I told you back at the lodge. Do we really need to go over this again? I'm not fond of your continual, and might I add, unwarranted, implications."

For whatever reason, Leo couldn't shake his suspicions of Eli, but he'd have to put them on hold for now. It wasn't probable that Eli was lying about his guess. What would the benefit be for him?

"Why do you need to pass the exam?" Leo asked.

"Is this really necessary?"

"Yes. I can't trust you until I know for certain that you actually plan on taking it."

Eli grimaced, and the silence between them began to linger. Leo stared at him until he finally broke. "Fine. I want to become a politician. There are other tests for that and being part of the Expedition Overseers isn't required, but it looks better on a resume. Shows you can make snap decisions. The EO-MC-T is pretty cool, too. I also enjoy the idea of swimming in boatloads of money, pun intended."

"EO-MC-T?"

Eli raised a curious brow but didn't provide an answer. "What about you? You must be taking the exam for the money if you've never heard of EO-MC-Ts. What do you need it for? To buy yourself a computer?"

"I have a debt to pay off."

"Ah, classic." Eli interlocked his fingers behind his head and leaned back. "I believe you. Can you believe me, so we can get going?"

Leo scrutinized every inch of Eli's face, analyzing every line and movement. Nothing indicated he was lying, though that didn't mean much. People were unpredictable. Leo stood and stretched with a deep inhale. "We should start looking for the other two."

He stuffed his sketchbook and pencil back into his pack while Eli stood. Leo took a gulp of water from his bottle, the plastic crinkling beneath his grip as he guzzled down the lukewarm liquid. "Are there any typical signs of a fake ad?"

"Not really. They're usually scattered around the city in different forms. I've heard paintings have been used before. Some ads can be in plain sight, like on a blimp, or they can be hidden quite well."

Leo rolled his shoulders and took two firm steps onto the sidewalk when a girl bumped into his shoulder. He stumbled forward with a gasp. Eli caught his arm before he hit the ground and pulled him upright.

The girl skidded to a stop and faced them. Her brown ponytail twirled as she turned, revealing warm yet stern emerald-green eyes. Her skin was dark brown, a sight unseen in Edna, and her outfit was peculiar yet riveting—a tight black bodysuit with a hood and flat-bottomed boots.

"Sorry," she panted, but her focus was placed on something behind him.

"Give those back," someone shouted. Leo whirled around and spotted a rather attractive young man running toward them, trailed by two broad and muscular henchmen.

Leo looked back at the girl and noticed the papers in her hand. Her frantic gaze swapped from him to the approaching men. His pulse quickened, his vision developing spots from loose nerves. He gave her a close-lipped smile and the sole solution he could think of.

"Don't be," he said. "Just run."

They took off, dodging and weaving around the city streets until Eli suggested ducking into a coffee shop. Leo checked behind them as they entered to make sure the girl was still there. She was, though she lingered at the door before turning to him with a nod. "All clear."

A success. For now. But there was still plenty more to do.

They chose a booth to sit in—one of the last available spots. The air smelt of bitter beans and toasted cinnamon, and their table was still messy from the last occupants. The girl didn't have money, nor did she ask them to order her anything. She watched Leo and Eli intensely, the papers clenched in her hands and hidden underneath the table.

Eli ordered them water as the waitress cleaned off the table and apologized profusely.

"It's okay, miss," he said. "We'd just like those waters when you have the time, please, unless either of you would like anything else?"

The girl shook her head.

"Yeah, I'll have a coffee," Leo tried. "I've never had one before." If Eli was offering to pay, Leo would buy.

"Bitter or sweet? Ice or hot?" the waitress asked.

"Sweet? Hot?"

"Are you sure about that? That's not usually—"

Eli laughed and shook his head. "You heard the man, miss, one sweet 'n hot coffee, too."

The waitress scurried off and Leo was left with an order that was starting to sound like a mistake. There were more pressing matters at hand, however, like the girl sitting across from them with all the answers. She certainly derailed Leo's 'use' to the team.

She continued to stare at them, keeping the clues out of sight. Leo cleared his throat.

"Leo," he said with a small smile. "And this is Eli."

He could hear the rustling of the papers being set on the seat beside her as she narrowed her eyes. "Isabelle."

"Nice to meet you," Leo said. "I couldn't help but notice

those." He gestured toward the papers he couldn't see. "We could help you solve them if you'd like. We already have an idea of where the exam will be."

Isabelle didn't answer, instead examining both of them extensively. Though Leo wasn't fond of adding another partner to their group, he couldn't deny how much they needed those papers. It could take all afternoon to find the right ads on the street.

Leo leaned back and nodded. "I understand. You don't trust us. I wouldn't, either, so don't worry. All I can say is that I'm telling you the truth, that Eli and I want to help you find the exam. We have no intention of deceiving you. We all need this for one reason or another."

She looked over the pages one last time before nodding to herself and placing them on the table. "I need help, too. My Latarian is not... the best. If you could read them to me, please?"

Leo nodded excitedly and started looking through the papers. He held two of them up and explained what they'd gleaned from them, about Ishla and their theory about the importance of the 50 in 50%. Then he read the remaining two in a hushed whisper.

One was a sentence long, placed in the center of an otherwise blank page. "'It's easy two find the right way to follow the red-bricked road.'"

Eli snatched it from Leo's hand and fished in his backpack for a pencil. He hastily circled the word 'two' while the waitress brought their water and Leo's coffee. The water was in tall, pastel green glasses, whereas his coffee was in a small glass with a handle. He eyed it up suspiciously, heeding the words of the waitress. The steam rising from the top further persuaded him to stay away.

The last page had a small, yellow-feathered bird trapped in

a cage. A speech bubble wrapped around the words, "'Banished, I am. Wings clipped at the ends of the earth, for I am nothing without my horizon.'"

Isabelle's eyes widened, and she recited the last line without looking. "'And the horizon is nothing without me.'"

"How do you know that?" Leo asked with astonishment. He'd never read such poetry before, but its somber sadness resonated in him for reasons he didn't quite understand.

"My father. He loves this one."

"What could it mean, though?" Eli asked. "'Earth?' What's that supposed to be?"

Leo shook his head with a sigh. "That, I know, at least. It's from an old fable. 'Earth' was another name for Hevalth in the story, a cautionary tale of greed and wasting resources. As for its significance, I can't say..."

"Banishment," Isabelle said suddenly. "Without a clear sight of what your future holds."

Leo snapped his fingers. "Or it's literal. There are mountains surrounding Ishla, right? You can't see the horizon from certain positions."

Isabelle shook her head and circled the bird. "It means he's stuck. On land. Can't get off."

"So, what we need to find is on land?" Eli confirmed, and she nodded.

"Both those theories are good, but what about the boat?" Leo added. "What if it meant we needed to find a boat?"

"Maybe... the marina in Avala is the only way onto the island, though, so that'd be a bit... obvious."

"But we're sure... sure it's on this Ishla?" Isabelle asked. Both Leo and Eli agreed, and she continued, "Perhaps we should just... go?"

Leo didn't like this, the uncertainty surrounding Ishla and what would be there when they arrived. They spoke a whole new language, and their customs were unknown. He rubbed at his backpack strap and stared down at the caged bird.

"She's right," Eli said. "We should get going. Ishla's pretty far from here. A few hours, at least. And there's also the issue of which side of the island the marina's on."

"Since when does it take a few hours to cross the sea? And how are we going to get there?" Leo added.

"There are many secrets in this world," Eli remarked. "Many, I do not know. But I know more than you. Don't worry; we'll get there. Ask me how I know."

Leo glared at him. Eli's jokes were getting old with every word he spoke.

"Oh, don't look at me like that. Drink your sweet n' hot; it should be less hot now."

"How?" Isabelle asked.

Eli smiled. "Well, I'm glad you asked. My father bought me a boat for my 18th, and I just so happened to arrive in it today. Figured it'd be a good thing to have. And, there's a way to cross the sea faster than you may think. You'll see what I mean soon enough."

Leo could feel his confidence rise again, and he took a deep breath to calm his nerves. At the very least, they had a rough estimate of where they were going and how to get there. He'd made the right decision about trusting Eli, he reminded himself, and Isabelle. As long as Eli's cryptic answer didn't lead to their downfall, they would be fine. As long as he kept making the right decisions, he would be fine. Now he just had to trust himself.

"What about the 50%, the 'two,' and the bird? What's the purpose of—" Leo began, but Eli cut him off.

"We'll keep that information with us, and we'll keep the printouts, too. If we encounter something that may be reminiscent of a clue, we'll deal with it then."

Leo agreed reluctantly. They began packing up to go, moving as one in silence. A unit ready to set out for their next destination. He'd never seen a boat before, nor had he seen or sailed the ocean. What was it like, to feel the salty breeze blowing through his hair, to see the waves dance? Being surrounded by water and sea creatures was an enchanting yet harrowing dream, one that was soon to play out.

As they stood, Isabelle bowed. "I offer my gratitude."

The boys stopped and stared at her for a moment too long. Then, with a radiant smile, Leo said, "No need for all that. We needed your help as much as you needed ours."

CHAPTER 6

OTHELIA

- 9 HOURS BEFORE -

AFTER MEETING WITH her father, and partaking in an 18-hour resting period, she searched high and low for anything that could explain the mag flowers. She even ventured to their robust library, a place she stepped foot in only when absolutely necessary. Which, evidently, was never.

The circular room was piled high with book-stuffed shelves separated by long, curtainless windows. Because of her rather bruised abdomen, she had her servants climb the rolling ladders and look for any books on magical items or royal powers. All they could find were empty spots where the books had once been, dust in their place.

She became shameless about her questioning, asking guards and her siblings alike. Her mother had been the helpful one, at least regarding information, but there was no point thinking about what could be.

Most of the servants looked at her in worried confusion, wondering why someone would care about a bag of half-dead flowers. She understood their confusion; she couldn't explain the attraction she felt toward them herself. Either way, they were certainly cool, and she hoped they weren't as useless as her father claimed.

She'd accused him of lying, but truth be told, she didn't know if he was or not. The empty bookshelves could've been indicative of many things, but she had to believe her father was hiding them, along with the true purpose of the flowers. Even if that meant facing her fear that he wasn't as honest as she once thought.

Her efforts were fruitless, and she stopped looking, heading off to the kitchen to appease her hunger. She wasn't about to find anything worthwhile in this desolate place.

Now, the talithes were in her room, safely tucked in their pouch. She'd been extra careful when hiding them, stuffing them in a shawl pocket at the very bottom of her wardrobe. She knew someone would try to steal them. Whatever their value, it was enough to make that man attack her. And there was a possibility that others were drawn to the flowers, too.

Othelia could still feel that initial pull no matter where she went, even as she stood in the kitchen making stove-toasted bread.

"Are you sure you don't want me to make it for you, Princess?" Philip, the morning cook, asked. He was the youngest at twenty and by far the cutest of the palace staff, though he was the type to think otherwise.

She turned and pointed her spatula at him, her yellow dress twirling delicately around her ankles. Her long and wavy hair was down today, dangling freely against her back. "Surely I can put a knife to bread on my own."

"Of course, Princess. I didn't mean to offend."

Othelia cocked her head. "The only thing that offends me is that you call me princess. I think we're past that. Don't you?"

He took a step closer and leaned in, his thick lips inches

from hers as he whispered, "I don't think that's appropriate to talk about here. But I'll be happy to discuss these matters later tonight."

"Hm, and what kind of discussion will it be?" she asked, transferring her toast to a plate. She kept her back turned to him as she spread homemade jam along the slices. His eyes bored into her, undoubtedly full of lust. Othelia smiled to herself; the power she had over him was quite titillating, as was the sex they'd recently been indulging in.

"I'll see you tonight, but I can't engage in any unspeakable acts for the week," she added, her bruises a secret to everyone except her father and Alexander, and her lovers were no exception.

"Doing the peasants' work again, are we?" her brother's unmistakably deep and condescending voice cut in. She slapped the two pieces of bread together and glared at him. His hair was a dash lighter than hers, his blue eyes a dash darker.

"Looks like it. Next thing you know, I'll be the help."

"Your childish humor never ceases to be just that. I heard you met with Father the other day. What'd you do this time?"

Philip interjected with a bow. "I'll be off now, Your Highnesses. Princess, do tell me how you like the jam. I made it myself yesterday morning."

"Will do. Take care."

Samuel scoffed as Philip turned to leave and peered down at Othelia from his advantageous height. He, too, wore royal garments—a standard black tunic decorated with gold chains and lace, his pants solid black. There was a long sword sheathed at his side, a turquoise emerald in the center of the diamond embroidered handle. Despite his relentless efforts to show it off, she'd never seen him use it.

She stuffed the gooey sandwich into her mouth, maintaining her glare. Usually, he returned a similar scowl, but today he was nothing short of giddy. His eyes were particularly delighted, a look he got after conversing with the King. She could see their father's features vaguely in his, a prophecy set in stone. But behind his cocky judgment, she could see a fit of ferocious jealousy clawing at the back of his mind.

"That's between me, Father, and the audience of guards that were with us. Sorry, little brother, but you're staying out of this one," she said, allowing his jealousy to fester. He never did like being reminded that he was two years younger and second in line.

Her jeers were working too; he looked like he may burst, his fingers curling in on themselves. But to her disappointment, he relaxed with a sigh. "It's no matter. I was simply curious. Once I prove myself to Father, nothing you do will be of any concern."

She watched him carefully, noticing the way his lips curled and his dimples formed. Although they were prone to getting under each other's skin, he'd never made such a bold claim before.

"What does that mean?"

"Oh? You haven't heard? Father is sending me on a mission. There's been talk that the eldest princess isn't suited for the crown."

"Excuse me? What kind of mission could he possibly be sending you on?"

"Sorry, sister." He patted her on the shoulder. "Looks like you're staying out of this one."

Othelia stuffed the rest of her sandwich into her mouth with a frustrated huff. "So, what? Did you find me just to gloat?"

"Actually, I was hoping someone would make me lunch, but you've chased all the help away. Unless you'd like to make me something?"

"Sorry. Guess you'll have to do the peasants' work."

She brushed past him and sped down the corridor with soft steps. She enjoyed being the mouse in their castle, scurrying around without the distraction of guards or Alexander on her tail.

Sweat sprouted on her forehead. Were her brother's words true? Had she made one too many mistakes? None of them had been sent on a mission before. Not that she knew of. The thought alone sparked more fear, enough for her pace to quicken. *Am I the failure?*

She reached the hallway to her bedroom and paused at the sight of two guards, their voices bouncing off the walls between laughs. Othelia ducked behind the corner before they could spot her and listened. Any of the guards could know of her brother's assignment, and any of them could know of her possible... reassignment.

Based on the even level of their voices, they were standing still, maintaining their assigned positions for the day. Othelia glanced around the corner and looked the men over. They were in their late thirties and unrecognizable. Othelia wasn't one to remember the names of their guards, instead referring to them by rough estimates of their heights. These two looked to be six-foot-one and five-foot-eight, both wearing their brown hair chopped short. There were a lot of six-one men in the castle.

Their conversation was frivolous, detailing the gambling session the guards had the night before. She reached for the flyer hidden underneath her dress, stuffed in the top of her tight stockings. If there was any time to ask, it was now. The chance of Alexander or her family telling her the truth was far slimmer than some unexpecting guards.

Othelia readied herself and strode around the corner, pretending to pass them. The guards straightened up immediately as they noticed her, their airy banter lost in silence.

She stopped mid-step and turned to them with a warm smile. "Oh! I was just looking for someone!"

The men bowed dutifully, a hand placed over their hearts. "Princess, your highest honor," they said in unison. When they looked at her, their brown eyes shone with excitement.

Five-eight was the first to speak. "Princess Othelia. How are you today, your beauty?"

"I am having quite a fine day, thank you. And yourself?"

His eyes widened ever so slightly, and he hesitated to answer; it was rare for a Sandoval to speak to the guards with anything other than orders. "I fare well, Your Highness. What are you in need of?"

"Ah, yes! Well, I was searching for my dresses in the cleaning room, and, well, I found this." She pulled out the flyer and unfolded it. "Have you heard of this exam before?"

The guards exchanged glances. How much did they know that she'd never been told? A flutter of anger and spite coursed through her. *How* did they know?

She wanted to pry deeper—ask if they'd heard of her brother taking the exam as well, but she knew it was too risky. There was a chance they didn't know, and she didn't want them to think less of her or spread rumors.

"Y-yes, Your Highness," said six-one, "to join the EO."

"Which is?"

He paused. Longer this time. She kept her smile, determined not to show how nervous she was. They knew something she didn't. It replayed in her mind until her blood was boiling.

"The Expedition Overseers. They're known to be quite the heroes. From what I've heard, the exam happens twice a year and lasts for a few days. It always takes place somewhere new. We think it's here this year."

She raised a brow. "What makes you say that?"

"W-Well," five-eight stammered, "my girlfriend works down at Waxandle. She said there were large foreign ships there. Didn't get close enough to see who was entering or exiting them, but they were there, can't miss them. And a lot of travelers, too."

"Do you know when the exam starts?"

"No, Your Highness," said six-one. "I'm guessing it's sometime today."

"How'd you hear about it?"

He shrugged and avoided her gaze. "People talk. Traders and travelers, mostly."

"I don't really know anything, either," five-eight chimed in.

She bowed. There was nothing else to gain here. She was beginning to think the entire palace was completely useless. "I give you my greatest thanks. Keep up your diligent work."

Othelia took to leaving but stopped and turned around after her first two steps. "And I'd be careful with what information you give out. You never know when the walls are listening."

"Y-yes, your beauty," they said as she walked away. Might as well make them squirm a bit.

Othelia crumbled up the flyer and stewed on her new findings. There was no timeframe, nor a concrete explanation for the importance of this exam. Not only was it kept hidden from her, but for her father to send Samuel? A wave of disgust washed over her at the thought. There was absolutely no doubt in her mind; what else could her brother be entrusted to do? He wasn't smart enough for political dealings, and he wasn't skilled enough to be sent on a fighting mission.

An exam was perfect for Samuel, hunched over a testing booklet. Which was exactly why she needed to take it and pass.

She didn't have a bag of any sort, a restriction brought on after her first escape attempt. She'd have to bring the bare minimum. Was anything required? Did she have to sign up ahead of time? These were all problems she thought vaguely about and then promptly discarded. The least she could do was scout the area and see if she qualified.

Othelia tossed on a dark blue skirt with deep inner pockets, ones where she could store the bag of talithes. She'd made the pockets herself in case she ever wanted to escape for good. Alexander, in an act of kindness, had handcrafted a leather protective case for her dagger, which Othelia had sewed to the outside of her skirt.

Alexander. He would prove to be a challenge. Hopefully, if she worked fast enough, she'd be able to sneak out before he noticed.

Othelia caught sight of the gauze wrapped around her arms as she put on her long-sleeved shirt. The bruises on her stomach may have been temporary, but the scars from the various cuttings and whippings she'd received throughout her life were permanent. Her legs were in similar shape and covered —always covered—by a layer of gauze. The scars brought about a wave of embarrassment and shame, though she knew it was silly for her to feel so. Her siblings were given the same treatment.

There were no excuses for what her parents allowed or commanded. Although she loved her mother, the Queen was as cruel as her husband. Their beliefs on discipline were tired and old and did not work. Not on Othelia. There were no excuses for Alexander, either. He'd been her Royal Guard for years. They'd been friends once, long ago, before she went rogue. But now, he wanted nothing to do with her. And that was fine. She could hate him, too. She already should've.

Annoyed both at herself and the situation at hand, she closed her dresser drawers, swept the floor, and made her bed.

The final preparations to make it look as though she were never there.

"Ahem."

She spun around. Alexander was blocking the doorway, leaning against the frame with his arms crossed over his chest. She should've known.

He looked her over with a bemused look, the bags beneath his eyes heavy. "Planning on leaving again?"

It made sense that she'd be under stricter supervision. For a short while, she was allowed to spend most of her time alone or with Alexander far behind her trail. But whenever a red flag was raised, her father sent him over to keep a closer watch.

"You know, I was just thinking about you," she said, sitting on the edge of her bed.

Alex clasped his fingers behind his back with a sly smile. "I'm glad to hear that. Would you care to answer my question?"

"I care not."

He sighed. "That's fine. I've been ordered to keep you in your room today, anyway."

"That's curious."

"Is it? You ran off yesterday. Did you think you'd be free of supervision?"

Othelia examined the beige walls she'd been surrounded by her whole life. She didn't like how he looked at her, with the smile of someone who enjoyed her pain and discomfort. It was sickening.

"I did run off yesterday. So, Alexander, why haven't you been keeping an eye on me until now? Why am I suddenly ordered to stay in my room?"

He responded with his usual cold and hard stare. His silence was all she needed. "Hiding something, are we? You can tell me. It'll be just between us."

Silence.

"Come on, Al," she pleaded. "Who am I going to tell? Would it happen to have anything to do with the exam?"

His eyebrow twitched. A fraction of a second worth of movement, but it was enough.

"Father doesn't want me to know about it."

"He wants you to be safe," he blurted, "and the exam doesn't concern you."

An uncontrollable swell of frustration ignited in her, but she clenched her jaw shut. Everyone knew about the exam except her, even the guards. Even the *locals*. Disgusting. She felt like a fool.

"Ah, but it concerns my brother?"

He shook his head. "I wouldn't know anything beyond what the King has told me, which is what I just told you. You're to stay here for the day. I'll be watching your door, and there are two guards watching the window, so please spare us another one of your escape plans."

She shrugged. "Don't worry, I'm trying to learn from my mistakes. That being said, you cannot deny you're curious about all this. It must be of some importance."

"It doesn't matter what I think, and it doesn't look like you've learned anything, either."

She slumped her shoulders and pouted. This was a technique that had only ever worked on Alexander twice before. Once, when she'd wanted to fight an intruder that had tried to break into the castle. The second, when she'd wanted to eavesdrop on a conversation between her parents. She was never sure why he buckled for those requests and not, say, breaking into the stables and riding the horses at night, but she prayed to add this occasion to the list.

"Please, Al, we'll only be gone for a short while, that's it. If you suspect I'll run off, you can say something, and we can turn right back around. I just want to know what's going on."

"That's precisely why the King hasn't told you about it."

"I understand, really, I do. It's hard for you to believe me, especially now. But I need to know what father is sending Samuel to do, and—"

"No, you want to *beat* Samuel. I know you, Othelia, and so does the King. This is for Samuel to pass, not you."

Othelia crossed her arms. "I thought you didn't know what the King had planned for Sam?"

"I—"

"—don't know anything beyond what the King has told you? Because it sounds like he's told you quite a few things. But that's no matter; this exam is for *us* to pass. Come on, we've been stuck on this island for our whole lives, and now there's a chance for us to go. Can you honestly sleep well tonight knowing there's something out there that you don't know?

"Father is hiding things. By the looks of it, books have been missing from our shelves for years. He's lying to us, and you don't want to know why? We deserve to know. You deserve to know." She took a shaky breath and continued, "I overheard the guards out in the hallway. They said it takes a few days. What kind of exam lasts that long? And Father left this morning, didn't he? I heard the thrice tolls."

There were a series of toll variations, each with its own meaning. Once meant it was noon. Twice meant shift change, and thrice meant a Kingship meeting was called. It occurred early in the morning, jolting her awake. An urgent meeting with the six kings. A rarity, indeed.

"He won't know we've left," she added, "and we'll come back after we take the exam."

He stared at her, his emotions a phantom. Sometimes she

could catch glimpses of his old self, the one that longed for adventure and had heaps of hope coursing through his veins. What happened to that spark? It had to be reversible. Her childhood friend was in there, somewhere.

"The people will recognize you," he relented, his queries indicative of interest. "And the other guards will notice us leaving."

Valid concerns, ones she'd have to be quick to resolve. There was also the deeper issue of Philip, who would certainly take notice of her absence when she didn't meet with him later that night. What would he gain from reporting her missing, though? He had yet to tell anyone of their physical encounters, either. Yes, she could trust him. She was sure of it.

Othelia hopped off the bed and opened her wardrobe. Sifting through it, she pulled out a thick, wooly cloak. It was essentially a hooded sac that stretched just below the knee. Yet another item she'd collected in case of a needed disguise. It was also good for harsh winters. At least, that's what she assumed, as Ishla lacked cold weather for her to try it out. "This should work, don't you think?"

She pulled it on and tossed the hood over her head. Alexander's hands were now at his sides, his posture a mess. He was deep in thought, she guessed, and it looked like he was having a hard time coming up with an answer. Finally, he said with a pained sigh, "I think it could work. If we were to convince the guards of something."

"You worry too much. We're leaving together. Father's orders."

"Forgive me for thinking things through," he said, "and they'll be wondering why you're dressed in a cloak... you should take off your makeup, too. Put up your hair. That'll be best for your disguise."

She smirked. "You're taking me to a new training site and

want me to wear this in case we pass any commoners. See, Al, it's easy to come up with these things, and you know they'll believe anything you say."

He rolled his eyes. "Just hurry yourself up before I change my mind."

Othelia raised a brow but didn't question him—it was best not to—and prepared. She couldn't help but smile as she pulled back her hair and looked at herself in the mirror. There was nothing useful at the palace, her poor excuse for a home, and the exam was the perfect place to look for answers. And Alexander was going to help her get one step closer.

Alexander closed her door lightly and appeared behind her, his reflection staring at her with piercing, apologetic blue eyes. "I'm sorry. For the things I've done and do to you. But you must understand I do it because I have to. Because you break the rules and rules need to be enforced. But, for what it's worth, I'm sorry."

It was too late for an apology of any kind—especially his botched attempt at one—but she finished up her hair and turned to him with that same smile.

"You're forgiven," she whispered. "It's time to go."

"Actually," he interjected with a sly smirk, "the exam isn't for another nine hours. So, I guess you're stuck with me until then. Come, let's train. See if you can take the exam with more bruises."

She sucked in a deep breath. It was going to be a long day.

CHAPTER 7

LEO

- 2 HOURS BEFORE -

IT HADN'T BEEN too hard to find the island once they had a proper map. Eli was handy with his ship, cruising idly through the vast sea that separated Ubas from Ishla. Leo wasn't familiar with seacrafts in the slightest, but Eli was happy to fill him in on the details.

"She's a class XYO cruiser, first of her kind. Grandmother invented it, if you can believe that. The sails provide easy maneuvering and transport, and the motor in back helps propel us if need be. She also has a rather special addition, but that's a secret just for the family. I'll give you a hint, though: we'll be there far faster than you think."

The seacraft in question was of medium height; low enough to be boarded with ease, but high enough for the waves to be out of reach. There were two cloth sails dancing in the breeze and enough space on the upper deck for ten people, at least.

It'd been a smooth trip for them, complete with crystal clear blue skies and calm waves. Somewhere along the way, he'd blinked, and his body felt like it was being thrust through a windstorm. But when he opened his eyes, the air was still, and the border of Gyantel was peeking through the horizon. What should've taken two months had taken nearly an hour. He opened his mouth to enquire about whatever secret Eli was hiding, but nausea took hold, and he doubled over.

He found himself face-to-face with the water. It rippled along the side of the boat, creating a white fizz among the deep blue. He couldn't see anything beyond that, and he couldn't help but wonder what lived down there. Most of the world was composed of the sea, and yet they didn't know the first thing about the creatures that lived below. His thoughts were negated by his nausea, and he hurled.

After six hours of sailing, they finally reached Ishla, only to find that the docks were overflowing with boats, not a single docking port available. They sailed alongside the tree-infested island shores until they found a sandy beach that was no bigger than their boat.

As they approached land, Eli and Isabelle dragged the seacraft out of the water. They pulled with a decent amount of effort, beads of sweat forming on their temples as they worked away. Leo watched them briefly, thanked them, and then laid on the deck until they were done. His eyes were clamped shut as every tug through the sand jostled his body.

Leo was filled with superb delight when his feet finally hit the small patch of golden sand that lined the water. His legs wobbled to the tune of the sea.

Eli slapped him on the back with a laugh and he stumbled forward. "I haven't seen anyone react like that before! It's not what I expected from the confident and put-together Leo."

Leo shot him a glare and grumbled back, "Yeah, well, that's what you get for judging me at first glance."

"Not by first glance, but by confidence."

"Same thing," he said before taking a final hurl onto the

sand.

Isabelle came up from behind him and rubbed his back. He stiffened at her touch, but soon found it soothing, his stomach settling. When he was done, he looked up at her, perplexed by her calm nature. She acted like a natural, born to take on the ocean. Leo found himself growing envious, wishing he had the ability to control his vertigo.

"Il layek," Isabelle said, taking in their surroundings. "So beautiful."

Leo followed her lead and looked around. The beach ended abruptly with a cliff to their right and a sea of palm trees to their left, leading to the marina they'd passed along the way.

"Yeah," Eli agreed, peering over Leo's shoulder at the mess he made. "It's rare to see pink vomit. Must've been the sweet in that delicious sweet 'n hot."

"Funny." Leo collected himself, wishing he could brush his teeth and rid himself of his embarrassment. His lack of composure was a clear weakness, and he didn't trust either of them, not really. He wanted to. They were nice so far, but he couldn't shake his unease.

Leo helped them haul the boat toward the tree line and gathered palm leaves to hide it. The job was haphazardly done, splotches of white paint seeping between the leaves. Although there was no sign of civilization in the area, there was no telling when someone would stumble upon the beach as they had.

Eli shrugged. "Eh, it's fine. If all goes well, I can buy another one." He clapped his hands. "Now, Avala is that way," —he pointed through the trees—"Where the marina was. I'd say that's our best bet."

Leo took a deep breath in. "I hope you're right."

Eli smirked. "I'm always right, except when I'm wrong. But this time I'm right."

They walked through the forest of evenly spaced palm

trees. Occasionally, one would be misplaced, adding some variation to the otherwise perfect scene. Leo spotted a tiny reptilian creature—one he recognized from his homeschooling. The ramna was short and no longer than five inches, its scales a light green and blue. Its distinguishing feature was the streak of dark blue along the center of its back. He marveled as they passed, but didn't dare disturb it, and took a deep breath in. They'd stumbled upon a paradise.

His walk morphed into a light jog. It'd only been two days, and yet he already missed the thrill of running. Leo didn't look back for the others; their footfalls were close behind. They kept pace until the marina came into view and the trees tapered out. They reached the outskirts of Avala, standing atop raised land where they could see the small town. There were at least two hundred vessels docked, each of varying size and shape.

Eli was heaving profusely, sweat staining the collar of his suit. His hair stuck to his skin in clumps. Leo, too, was in a similar state. He hadn't anticipated this type of weather, with a sun so heavy and the wind so stagnant that it was hard to breathe. A flannel and jeans were certainly not the best choice. Clearly, a suit wasn't either.

The marketplace was crammed with people and loud chatter. They followed the red-bricked road while holding shoulders to not lose each other. He made note of a few narrow passageways between shops as they passed. Each led into the forest, a peculiar place to lead unless people lived somewhere beyond there.

"Where should we try first?" Eli asked, marveling at the surrounding sights. They all were, and Leo realized they hadn't talked to each other since they'd left the beach.

"The docks," Leo said. "Might as well get that theory out of the way."

They made their way to the marina, where they could spot

three large ships, identical in every way aside from the numbers painted on their sides. Isabelle took the lead, walking two steps faster than the boys. She walked tall, with pride. Even her ponytail swayed with determination.

As they made their way closer, the ships were vastly larger than anything he could've imagined and made the other boats look small in comparison.

"No offense, but I'm not sure you'll last another boat ride," Eli said, tapping Leo lightly on the back.

"I really hope there's a running portion, so I can say the same to you."

"I kept up, didn't I?"

"Barely."

Eli ran his fingers through his mop of wet, stringy hair. "Hey, barely is good enough. At least I didn't puke."

"Fight later," Isabelle said, stopping at the end of the long line leading to the ships. There were at least forty people waiting, if not more. At the very front stood a podium, a short and smiling man regulating who got on. A sense of relief washed over him. They had found it. They were there.

But then he heard Isabelle say, "Too easy, too obvious."

She unzipped his backpack before he could protest and took out the advertisements. She pointed to the poem, to the phrase 'wings clipped at the edges of the earth.' "Can't be here. We are not on the edges of the eart—Hevalth."

Leo looked around while considering her theory. The docks were packed; the line was long. Logically, exam takers from around the world would gravitate towards docking at the only marina. Why would the exam location be conveniently placed there?

He pictured the advertisement that was a sentence long; 'It's easy two find the right way to follow the red-bricked road.' And then he realized, and he walked off without a word.

"Hey, what—" Eli yelled, but he ceased speaking when Leo's pace quickened. Off the docks and back onto the red-bricked road of the marketplace. 'Right' and 'two' jumped out at him, namely because of the passageways he'd seen before. Walking through, they'd been on the left-hand side, but coming this way, they were on the right.

He passed one passageway, then veered into the second. The path stretched into the forest, twisting into shrouded unknowns. He looked back to find a surprised Isabelle and a confused Eli.

"You're right," Leo said with shocked glee. "It's on land. Or, at least, the boarding is. I still think we're looking for a boat."

"We were right there," Eli said. "You saw that line. That man. Those ships were unlike anything I've ever seen. I couldn't place the model or make at all."

"Isabelle already explained. That'd be too obvious. Think about it. Avala is the porting city, right? Where would everyone dock if they thought they needed to find a boat?"

Eli opened his mouth to protest and then clamped it shut. He nodded and opted to follow Leo and Isabelle until they reached a shoreline similar to the one they'd arrived at, with cliffs surrounding one edge and trees along the other. The sandy shore was long and two white ships with golden trim towered against the waterline. There was even another podium, with a man identical to the one from before. Same height, hairstyle, and facial features. The resemblance was uncanny. The numbers were different on each boat.

There was no one in line, but footsteps in the sand were a good indicator that others had come up with the same idea. It gave him a sense of hope and comfort; he was able to solve the clue. Him. He was one step closer.

CHAPTER 8

OTHELIA

- 1 HOUR 30 MINUTES BEFORE -

LEAVING THE CASTLE had been surprisingly easy, needing not an explanation as the guards were too preoccupied with mindless conversation. There were never any threats on the island, and the King was kind to the citizens who lived on it. Since there was never a need for an uprising, days of standing attentive and still for hours had morphed into guards becoming lazy. Othelia couldn't blame them. It was a dutiless duty.

Othelia and Alexander arrived at the Avala docks, squished between people of ethnicities she'd never seen before. Ships of all sizes spanned the marina, sticking out against the more polished and small boats owned by the natives. At the very end of the docks, there were three gigantic boats, each lined with thin windows. They had no distinguishable differences between them aside from the black numbers painted on their sides.

As they got closer, she could see wooden loading ramps leading up to each boat. A short, burly man stood at a podium outside them, a long line of travelers itching to board standing in front of him. She watched as the podium man spoke with the person in front, who then picked a ship and disappeared into the belly of the seacraft.

Alexander lingered behind while Othelia bypassed the line.

"Excuse me," she said softly in Latarian, her words pointed. "Is this the exam location?"

He nodded with a grand smile. "Yes, ma'am! Your last task is to choose the right boat! Once it's your turn, I'll ask which of the three you'd like to board. Once you cross onto a ship, you can't unboard until the pre-exam is over and the right ship sails. If you choose the wrong one, you'll be allowed off and may return home and wait for the next exam to try again."

She peered up at the large ships. They loomed over her with their ominous and perfectly whitewashed paint. She'd never seen a ship of this magnitude, let alone three.

"Thank you," she said, and she sped back to Alexander to relay the news.

His eyebrows shot up at the mention of a pre-exam. "So, we'll have to base this on luck?"

"No. Instinct." She examined those who waited in line. None of them stood out to her. "Let's wait awhile and see which one the others pick."

He scoffed. "I can't wait to see what your instincts tell you."

They stood off to the side and in plain sight, keeping close to a group of Ishla fishers discussing their daily catches. The overwhelming majority of travelers arrived at the exam alone and talked to no one. Occasionally, there were groups of people who looked and spoke the same. What type of exam allowed people to work together? Based on her homeschooling, that would be considered cheating.

Two people weren't allowed to board at the same time; a rule she found useful. The consensus seemed to be the middle and right ship, but there was no way of knowing which was correct, and no one memorable jumped out at her. Her heart thumped in her chest as they continued to watch.

Almost an hour had passed when she felt a tug of mag. Othelia fought the urge to smile and feigned a yawn to keep her true intentions from Alexander. She glanced to the right. There were too many people to discern whom the mag belonged to, but something, or someone, interesting caught her eye. A girl. More specifically, her attire.

She wore black from head to toe, a hood on the back of her shirt. Othelia had never seen that type of material before, but the way it shimmered slightly in the sun delighted her. The thick boots the girl wore were laced over her tight pants, fur peeking out from inside. Othelia was immediately fascinated; there were few things more enticing to her than a fashion statement.

Othelia turned back to Alexander and pointed to the next person in line, an average-looking man. "That's the one."

"Are you sure?" he asked, a hint of disappointment in his voice. "I thought you'd pick someone more interesting."

"The instinct never lies."

They stood in the long line silently. All the while, Othelia glanced over at the girl, who was conferring with two men. Othelia hadn't noticed her companions until then—they were all dressed so differently that she hadn't thought they were together.

Othelia blinked and the flannel companion was heading back into town, followed shortly by the girl and her third partner. Othelia gulped. They were turning away? She looked back at the line and sighed. There were ten more people left. All the while, her ticket to freedom had hurried away.

"You look nervous," Alexander interjected her thoughts.

She smirked. "Of course, I am. You used to grade my exams. I might end up having a hard time."

He let out a sharp laugh and nodded. "That is true. Maybe you should be nervous."

They arrived at the podium and the short man greeted them once more. "Have you made your decision?"

Othelia and Alexander nodded.

"You will choose one at a time. Once you cross over the platform, you cannot leave until the pre-exam is over. May I ask who is the oldest?"

Alexander raised his hand partially. "I am, but I don't see why that matters."

The man chuckled. "We like to keep it fair for groups. Sometimes people fight over who should go first. It's silly, really, but that's the way it's done."

"How long until the ship sails?" Othelia asked.

"Ah." He checked his watch. "There's still a little under an hour left. There are restrooms on all the ships, if need be, as well as food and drinks. Now, sir, please step up and choose your path."

Alexander took a reluctant step forward. He paused to look back at Othelia. His icy blue eyes were uncertain, scared. But she could see it, that boyish wonder. His mouth curved into a smile as he said, "See you soon."

Othelia saluted him and watched him board. When he was out of view, she nodded to the man behind the podium and thanked him. Then she turned and jogged away, down the marina and off the docks, back into the packed streets of Avala.

Her abandonment was inexcusable. She knew by the heaviness of her heart that what she'd done could never be undone, but she wasn't being dragged home once they were through with the exam. With luck, Alexander would try to cover for her, a man determined to save his own skin. If her father were to find out the truth, there was no telling how he would react. She may have just gotten Alexander fired, or worse, killed.

Othelia pulled herself back to reality. There was a time and a place to worry about her father and now was not then or there. If Alexander had come with her, there would be no way to evade the inevitable. He'd fight to take her home and probably succeed. Yes, she had to dispose of him now.

She caught hold of the mag pull and followed it as it grew stronger. She paused in front of a path sandwiched between two stores that she'd never noticed before. The sky was bright, and the path was well lit, yet it brought about a foreboding danger that forced her to take a step back. The mag was strong, stronger than before. Was it the girl, or was it something far more sinister?

It mattered not. Whatever was beyond the forest was nothing she couldn't face. She was trained, and she was ready, despite her shaking hands and beating heart. Othelia edged toward the path, the powerful mag pushing back at her instead of forward, sending a shiver down her spine.

Something in the back of her mind screamed for her to turn around, to make sure Alexander wasn't there, seething with anger and ready to drag her home. But when she glanced over her shoulder, no one was there, and she knew she'd have to live with what she'd done.

CHAPTER 9

LEO

- 30 MINUTES BEFORE -

THEY APPROACHED THE short man, whose long mustache twirled up at the ends. His black hair was perfectly combed to the side, and his smile was bright and wide.

"Are you three together?" the man asked overzealously. His hooded eyes were lit with excitement as if he'd been waiting for them to arrive. Leo responded with a nod, and the man continued, "Delightful! With groups, we like to let them choose in order of age. Which one of you is the oldest?"

Leo, Eli, and Isabelle exchanged glances.

"Oh," Leo said. "I guess we don't really know. I'm 18."

"19," Isabelle said.

Eli pointed to himself in awe. "You mean, I-I'm the oldest?"

"You're first," the podium man said, gesturing for Eli to step up. "The right boat is number 05, and the left boat is number 50."

Eli's oozing poise dissipated; his shoulders slumped as he

thrust his thumb toward his companions. "I—oh, that's okay, really! One of these guys can—"

"Those are the rules, sir. Please come forward and make your choice. Once you cross a platform, you must wait on the ship until the pre-exam is over and the right one sets sail."

"The day I rue being 21 has finally come, I suppose." Eli gave one last hopeful look to Leo and Isabelle. "What do you guys think? It's got to be 50, right?"

Leo nodded, though he had his doubts. As Eli had said throughout the pre-exam, '50' seemed too obvious to be correct. But now was no time for second-guessing. It was simply a gamble. "That's what I would guess. Isabelle, thoughts?"

"Yes. But, um, we should make a rule. Help when we can but can't be expected. Focus on—" She gestured toward herself. Her Latarian was rough, her thick accent hard to decipher.

"That is the exact opposite of teamwork," said Eli.

"Makes sense to me," Leo affirmed, without offering insight as to why he thought so. Truthfully, he was ecstatic. He didn't have to trust them, because they were all there for themselves.

Eli ran his fingers through his hair, pushing the bangs out of his eyes. "I-I guess you're right. Don't be surprised if I make all the right choices."

Just like that, his confidence shone through again. How much of that was fake, Leo wondered. It came across as genuine enough, more so than Leo could say for himself. Doubt pervaded his mind. What if his interpretation of the advertisement was wrong and all three of them failed? There could've easily been a trick involving the 50%—tiny print that said 05 that he just missed. Their failure would be his fault.

Eli didn't hesitate any further and headed toward the left

boat. He ascended the wooden plank up to the deck and disappeared on the other side. Isabelle followed suit, leaving Leo alone with the podium man and his own terrifyingly destructive thoughts. Boat number 50 felt like the obvious choice, which was precisely why his heart fluttered at the prospect of being wrong.

If he'd journeyed there alone, which would he have chosen? No, it didn't matter, because he already knew which one he was going to pick, even if it was wrong. Leo took a step toward the podium, standing directly beside the wooden stage, and asked, "What's your name?"

The man raised his thick eyebrows in surprise. "Magenta Magnum."

Leo reached his hand out to shake. "Leo. Thank you for giving us this opportunity."

Magenta's intrigue permeated from the gaze he gave Leo. "You're a strange fellow, aren't you?"

"How so?"

"You're the first to ask of my name."

Leo responded with a warm smile. "Of course! I'd like to know the names of all the people who contribute to helping my family, whether the help is indirect or not."

Magenta looked Leo up and down, taking in his clothes and physique with an uncomfortably long stare. Magenta opened his mouth to speak when his eyes drifted to something behind Leo. Leo turned to find a tall, thin man with silver hair and a smirk. The man wore a silver suit and dress shoes, a hand tucked in his pocket.

"Good luck, Sir Leo," Magenta said, his smile dropping. "Please choose one, now."

Leo hurried forward, the look of fear on Magenta's face temporarily sending him into a state of unease. What he'd just witnessed, he didn't know, and he didn't want to know. He couldn't turn back, and it terrified him to climb up the ladder onto the boat. No matter how hard he held onto the railing, he couldn't steady himself completely. His apprehension was ludicrous. His family depended on his strength, a strength he should have.

But it was a painful process, one of psychological torture to climb over the shoreline and swing his leg round to the deck. He somehow found it in himself to persist, forcing his trembling body along the solid wooden planks that held the floor together. There was no way to turn back now. He tried to remind himself there never was. If he didn't get the prize money, they would be evicted, their house and farm torn away right before their eyes. The cows would be slaughtered or sold, and his family would be stripped of the clothes on their backs.

Now was not the time to stress of such things. He needed to focus on the present.

At the end of the main deck, there was a large navigational center that required a climb up a ladder to enter. There, he could see the silhouette of someone pacing the glass enclosure like a caged animal. Not another soul stood about, wiped from existence as though they had never boarded. A white sign stuck out against the horizon, a black arrow pointing down a set of stairs. As he got closer, he could vaguely hear voices drifting up from below.

The stairs were polished and had circular, low-beam lights carved into each of their sides. He held onto the railing in fear of slipping, his legs wobbling with every step. By the time he reached the lower floor, his legs had steadied. The sway of the boat was almost entirely unnoticeable, relief flooding him as he looked around for Isabelle and Eli.

The lower floor was a single, long ballroom with flooring made of marble. Chairs were set up in front of a stage raised all but seven feet in the air. Every seat was taken, and there were at least six dozen others standing about. The stage was unattended and empty aside from a microphone standing in the center.

He had just finished assessing his surroundings when Isabelle's body was thrown past him and into an occupied chair. Her back slammed against the rough metal and pushed the chair and its occupant a few inches forward as she dropped to the ground. The man she was flung into stood and turned around. His long, black hair was tied with gold and purple tassel and resting on his shoulder. He stared down at Isabelle with monolid gray eyes and thinly drawn lips, his hand on the sword sheathed at his side.

Isabelle struggled to stand, using the back of his now vacant chair to prop herself up before making eye contact with him.

"May I ask what is going on here?" he asked. Leo wanted to react without thinking, but words eluded him. He took a few steps forward, his stomach clenching. This man was taller, stronger, and clearly more willing and able to fight. And the sword. He thought sword fighters no longer existed, a relic of the past. A man who fought with swords was a man who killed.

Leo opened his mouth but let the silence linger so he could gauge their surroundings. There, in the direction Isabelle had launched from, he spotted twins and their presumed leader scowling at Isabelle with a look of grandeur. They'd made one annoying enemy.

"Some guys have it out for us 'cause we outsmarted them," Leo said, nodding toward the three men. "One of 'em tossed my friend into you."

The man looked between them, put his hands at his sides, and bowed. His buttoned-up jacket was white with black trim along the front and pockets, and a dazzling green emerald rested against his chest, glinting in the overhead lights. Isabelle glanced at Leo with what he perceived to be mild nervousness and confusion. He had no words of comfort or answers to give.

"Hanako H. Byrde." The man looked up and gave Isabelle a soft smile. "Please let them know that if anyone touches me again, I'll cut off their hands."

"Duly noted," Leo said, finding Hanako's oddly specific threat frightening.

"Sorry," Isabelle mumbled, brushing herself off.

"Oh, goodness, no. Never apologize for someone who instigates violence." Hanako sat back down, and a wave of relief washed over Leo. Unfortunately, there were still three more enemies waiting to be dealt with.

Eli must've had the same idea; he started walking up to the trio with clenched fists and furrowed brows. The scarred twin jeered, "Who should deal with him, Abel, you or me?"

The man standing in front of the twins smirked and gestured toward Leo. "You get that one. I want the girl."

"Hey, what about me?" Eli charged forward with a fist reared back. Abel extended his left hand and Eli was tossed back in an instant, an unnatural and invisible beam slamming into his stomach. He let out a grunt and he, too, flew back. Eli's body missed Isabelle by a mere inch, veering to the right and away from the chairs. He slid against the marble floor until he hit the bottom of the stage.

Leo tried to piece together what he saw. He saw nothing. Yet Eli had been pushed. Was it the wind? Could someone control the air? But, no, humans couldn't use mag. Mag was for the dirt and plants and animals. It wasn't for humans. Surely, he had blinked and missed a punch.

Isabelle rushed to Eli's side and helped him up, her eyes wide with bewilderment, and asked, "How? I flew! I fly without being touched!"

Abel approached them with the scarred twin trailing

behind. Both were sneering with bared teeth, like wolves waiting to prey on navy-spotted cows. Leo took a step forward, unsure of what he was going to do, but determined to do something.

Isabelle lightly grabbed his shoulder. Her golden-green gaze sent chills down his back, certainty written clearly in them. "My fault. Please, let me."

"Are you sure?"

"Oh yeah, I'm sure." She ran straight for Abel and, instead of throwing fists, tossed her entire body into the wretched man. A yelp escaped his throat as he flailed to the ground with Isabelle on top of him.

Leo took to action. His legs moved freely along the pristine marble, his mind muddled. He approached the scarred twin and got ready to punch, bracing himself for impact and pain. His opponent pulled out a thin knife and Leo realized with dread that he had forgotten his own weapon. He was going to be stabbed, and his punch would be weak.

He launched his fist, but it didn't budge. He opened his tightly shut eyes and turned to the culprit; a tall, slender woman with a pointed nose and slanted eyes stared back at him. Her black pencil skirt and blazer suggested she was a woman of poise, but her emotionless gaze suggested otherwise. Those faded yellow eyes replaced every single thought with one—run.

He attempted to pull away, but she clung tighter, her sharp nails digging into his flesh. Leo winced at the shooting pain erupting from her grip. "Please be civil before the exam begins, or we'll escort you out."

He gulped and suppressed his fear—pleading with himself to calm down. Think of flowers. Yes, flowers. Beautiful blue peyunas, black speckled and filled with scarlet pollen. The sweet smell of eliases. Dazzling, yellow lilaces. Nitren. Home.

He nodded, his voice level. "I understand. I'm, we're..." He signaled to Isabelle and Eli, purposefully leaving out their three foes. "Sorry for inconveniencing you."

The woman let go, crescent-shaped creases indenting his skin. One was already beginning to bruise, a ring of black and blue forming. He stared at the woman's exquisitely wrapped heels, avoiding her impossibly narrow and glaring eyes. Then, without a word, she walked off and stood along the wall, clasping her hands together and staring blankly ahead as though nothing had happened.

Leo brought his attention back to Eli and Isabelle. A wide, muscular man stood between Eli and the other twin. Eli immediately backed off and explained his intentions, but did not apologize for his actions. Abel's bleeding nose indicated Isabelle had gotten some swings in before being intercepted. Another woman hoisted Isabelle off of Abel and carried her over to Leo.

The scene ended abruptly; the three men backed off and headed to the food and drink tables set up at the other end of the ballroom. Those who broke up the fight dissipated back into the crowd.

"What the stars was that?" Eli hissed as he made his way over.

It was unsettling to know they'd be stuck taking the exam with those men, especially now that Abel revealed... something. Could all three of them fight like that?

"I don't know," said Leo. "But I really, really want to know."

"I hope that man gets food poisoning," Eli said, rubbing at his wrist despite his lack of fighting.

"Wishing ill fate on him will bring that fate to you," Isabelle said, garnering a look of surprise from both Eli and Leo. She seemed to know certain phrases and words better than others, a product of whoever taught her what little she knew.

They remained in the middle of the showroom, standing behind the last row of chairs. Again, he scanned the walls and seats for any people to stay away from, people with bulky muscles and cruel looks. The tone in the air had shifted after their fight; the room had become more hushed as people sneaked glances around the room.

One of particular notice was a man leaning against the wall with arms folded over his chest. His eyes were closed, but he appeared attentive regardless. A long scar ran along his cheek, down to his jaw. Leo's attention bounced to the person standing beside that man, a person wearing a burly wool coat. They were purposefully trying to hide their face, their gender and physique unknown.

They were two of the few that elicited his sense of unease. The vast majority were more average than anything else, a blessing in his mind. He wondered how many of them had tried the exam before, if any of them came for fun. Did such a person exist?

Leo was lost in thought when a boy of the same height approached them. He looked to be Leo's age, his hair short, blond, and shaggy. Thick-rimmed glasses covered his heavily bagged and deep-set green eyes. He stuttered as he said, "H-hi, uh, I was wondering, uh, do you know what that man did?"

"Thank Gahi you saw. I feel crazy," Isabelle said.

"Unless, of course, we're all going crazy together," suggested Eli.

"It looked," the boy stammered again, his voice soft and barely audible. "Well, it looked like mag."

Leo's ears perked up at that, almost fearing he'd heard wrong. But, as far-fetched as it sounded, there were no other explanations for what had occurred. Technology wasn't that advanced.

"What's your name?" Leo asked, noticing the boy carried himself sluggishly, shoulders slouched so that his long-sleeved, maroon crop top was nearly a regular shirt. His stomach hung out partially, revealing only a glimpse of his navel, and his black sweatpants were tightly tied around his waist. Leo had never seen such an attire.

"Galen." He didn't look to be someone who would want to take the exam, his quiet nature the first they'd encountered. He wasn't noticeably armed, either, unlike those scattered about wearing straps full of knives or holsters with guns. "Sorry for bothering you, I—"

Loud feedback screeched from the microphone as someone tapped on it. Leo winced and covered his ears while pulling his attention to the front. The woman with a pointed nose stood on stage. When the feedback died down, she spoke. "Excuse me. Yes, hi, I would like to inform you that the correct ship will leave in approximately thirty seconds."

Leo's heart skipped. He gravitated closer to Eli and Isabelle, taking comfort in their presence. For a second, he was happy he wasn't alone. If he failed, he wouldn't be the only one. They could leave with their sorrows and take Eli's wretched boat anywhere they wanted. Have a laugh. Be homeless together.

Those thirty seconds dragged on, everyone collectively holding their breaths.

And then the engine of the ship roared to life and began drifting to sea. The woman on stage smiled and leaned into the mic. "I'm Exam Leader One, Emmarcia Parigold. Congratulations. You've found the exam."

PART TWO

THE EXAM

PHASE I

CHAPTER 10

OTHELIA

THE SHIP ERUPTED in cheers upon the Exam Leader's announcement. Othelia clapped along solemnly, standing with her back to the wall between two men. The one to the left was unextraordinary, but the one to her right leaned against the wall; his eyes had been closed since she arrived. His fitted black jumpsuit accentuated his muscular body, and the scar across his cheek exemplified his past. A bow and arrows were bound tightly to his back.

Othelia found him the most interesting upon setting foot on the lower level, so she'd nestled into the spot beside him, the stage a few feet away. She hoped to strike up a conversation, but he had yet to awaken.

The announcement was preceded with nothing more, no destination or estimated time of arrival. She was hopelessly confused as to what this exam was and why so many people were taking it. Perhaps if she'd had access to electronics, she would know, but her parents had long since forbidden them. She knew her father had a computer in his office but, no matter her antics, she'd never been able to bust through those locked doors. She should've tried harder.

Othelia stood in the same spot for as long as she could muster until her stomach growled. She soon found herself meandering toward the food tables with her head held low, all the while attempting to sneak glances at everyone she passed. There were easily two hundred people on board—maybe more—crammed together like tiny, packaged fish.

She passed the group she followed, noticing their new member for the first time. Where had he come from? She contemplated introducing herself but kept her head down and cover intact. If they were meant to meet, they would. They were bound to if they all made it to the end of the exam. If.

Her brother was nowhere in sight, but she sensed he was near. She pictured Samuel lashing out once he saw her, swinging around that stupid sword of his. He was to be avoided like the second plague.

And the place reeked of mag. It was pulling from all directions, weighing down on her like a thick blanket. It was nearly suffocating. Wherever they were going, she hoped they got there soon. No matter how large the ship was, she felt trapped.

Othelia reached for a fruit bowl when she saw Samuel from her peripherals. She instantly jerked her head away, her heart skidding to a stop. If he caught even a glimpse of her face, her cover would be blown. It was too early to confront him. With any luck, she wouldn't have to.

"Hiding from someone?" a husky voice emerged from thin air. A man she'd noticed earlier with gray, monolid eyes and a long white jacket stood beside her, filling a bowl with berries.

"My business is my own."

Othelia attempted to shrink away from him with her berry bowl, but he trailed behind. When she thought there were enough bodies between her and Samuel, she stopped and looked around. The man stopped next to her, silently watching her watch the room. She was too absorbed in her prickling adrenaline rush to care.

Samuel was there, all right, standing tall and proud, joking loudly with Abel Casterral. Of all people, *Abel* was there. The Casterrals were part of the Kingship, leaders of Xivis, an island across the sea that was slowly rotting due to air pollution. Their families would have them train together every few years, and she never failed to beat Abel. And yet, there he was, sent by his father as Samuel had been.

Othelia couldn't help the jealousy and frustration coursing through her, knowing Father had given up on her. She cracked her knuckles; her face grew hot with seething rage. When had she started letting emotions get to her?

She had the burning desire to have her mother at her side. The Queen's charm was alluring; people would often reveal whatever she wanted. Father could never plot against her because she was always one informant ahead. She would've gathered all the answers and relayed them to Othelia.

"It appears someone has you riled up. Did something dishonorable occur?"

Othelia turned to the man with a raised brow. She didn't know ass-kicking would be number one on the agenda today, but she didn't oppose it. "I do not know you, sir. Please leave me be."

"Ah, yes. I suppose one should introduce themselves. Hanako H. Byrde."

He extended a gloved hand for her to take. She stared down at his invitation and crossed her arms. "Okay? And?"

A man who followed her about and disregarded rejection was unappealing. She had her fair share of unsavory princes trying to lay with her, and Hanako came across no differently.

"I was wondering if you'd like to work together," he proposed, his gaze welcoming, or at least attempting to be. "I've heard the exam is easier with companions, and I've only brought myself and my sword. You're alone, too, unless I'm mistaken?"

She swirled her finger in the bowl of berries and popped one in her mouth, chewing it with care to prolong her inability to answer. Finally, she swallowed and said, "I don't mean to offend, but I can't work with people I don't trust."

Hanako gave her a sad smile. "What a shame; I'm a very truthful man. You'll be experiencing intense headaches and nausea soon. Remember, I could've helped with that."

"Excuse me?" Baffled, she examined his features and contemplated reaching for her knife. That was a bold threat to make, but his face was still kind and unmenacing, and his hurt appeared genuine. She almost regretted rejecting him, but his hauntingly unusual irises were pools of unnerving clouds.

"May you do your best. I hope for nothing else than to see both of us as champions." Hanako H. Byrde walked away at a leisurely pace, hands clasped behind his back. The white heels of his knee-high boots clanked against the marble flooring as he made his way to the stairs. She watched him disappear beyond the threshold. Had it been a warning and not a threat? No one was capable of foreseeing the future. She'd attracted a loon.

An hour went by of intermittent snacking while she took to thinking about the exam to come and found her optimism resurfacing as she reminded herself of how weak Samuel and Abel were. Looking around, she couldn't spot any others from the Six Royal Families, making it increasingly apparent that her father and Casterral were planning something. And she was unstarly thankful that, out of all the royal children, Abel was the one there. If she saw Helarii Kahale, prince of the island of Yelbah, she'd lose her mind and, undoubtedly, her life.

She had to admit that she was curious about her family's motives. One thing was for sure: she didn't think their plan would pan out. Othelia believed in her brother as he believed in her.

By now, many of the contestants were moving upstairs. As she noticed the thinning crowd, she decided the best course of action was to join them. Her brother and Abel were still on the lower deck, and she'd rather run into Hanako again than either of them.

The outside air had cooled considerably as the sun slowly set over the horizon. She looked over the nearest railing, peering out into the vast blue ocean. Hues of purple and red sitting atop the waves reminded her of paint delicately brushed onto a page. There were no birds this far out, and nothing but their boat disturbed the water. She loved the salty smell of the sea, the calmness of the waves, and the slight teetering of the boat.

She headed to the stern. Her island was no longer visible, replaced by the endless sea. Home was gone, and she was alone.

Something below the deck popped, and the ship rumbled and rocked ferociously. The sudden jolt made her stomach drop, and she automatically grabbed onto the railing with an iron grip. She peered over at the propellers, which now sputtered to a stop as the ship released a low moan. Othelia held her breath and clung desperately as the jagged tilt of the boat sent her shoes sliding against the slick wooden floor.

Those who didn't have the same strength or instinct slid feebly with every sway, screaming until their voices were coarse. She watched them struggle, unable to intervene. She wouldn't have helped even if she could. They didn't matter. A common goal meant common enemies.

The rocking eventually subsided, and Othelia found her footing. The propellers were no longer moving, and large pockets of bubbles burst as they hit the water's surface. Another moan bellowed, and her heart sank with the ship.

A sharp buzz from electronic speakers cut through the air. She couldn't identify where the sound system was, but she could hear the person speaking as if they were shouting directly into her ear. She recognized the voice as the Exam Leader, although Othelia couldn't remember her name.

"335 contestants have successfully found phase one. There are currently six remaining lifeboats on this ship. Each can hold twenty-four people. All lower decks will be full of water in one hour, and the ship will be entirely submerged in two. Those who survive and find us will move on to the next phase. We have already left."

The speaker clicked off, giving way to momentary silence. Othelia was frozen, her mind reeling. She thought the exam would take place in an arena or testing room. Not on a sinking boat with three hundred people.

Othelia came to life, looking around for any sign of the lifeboats. They were probably lined against the large vessel, she thought, and she dashed toward the left side. A group of men were fighting each other, blades and guns drawn as they all clamored for a lifeboat. There were perhaps forty people surrounding her, and more were spilling out of the staircase in a massive hoard pressed shoulder to shoulder. Soon everyone would be on the main deck, and it would be a bloodbath. She'd either have to join the fight or wait until they evened each other out.

A gunshot rang within the cluster in front of her, and a man dropped at her feet. She yelped and ran the other way, but not before catching the body's lifeless gaze. His mouth hung open with a stream of blood drizzling from his lower lip, a pool forming around his head. She'd never seen a dead body before, not even at a funeral. Another gunshot pierced the air, and she ducked while her feet propelled her away. The brawls were no different on the port side, though there were fewer people by about twenty. That would have to do.

She lifted her heavy garment and reached underneath for her dagger. It slid out of the leather pouch with ease. Othelia rubbed her thumb over the handles' engravings as she ran; three infinite gods with hands raised toward the blade. She found no solace in religion, but the artwork was simply riveting and soothed her in moments of high stress.

A man in her peripheral waved his gun, and she jumped to the side as the pop sounded. The bullet landed in the railing beside her, where her thigh would've been. Realizing the error of her ways—there was no time for comfort—Othelia reduced her thoughts and relied on instinct. She released a final breath and sprung to action with a single idea flashing through her mind. Pick a boat and defend.

Many were already in battles of their own, fighting with swords and guns and weapons she'd never dreamed of using. A hatchet user was cornered at the outer wall of the navigation deck, her tight fingers white against her auburn skin. Her opponent, a man in a bright orange robe, thrust a spear at her stomach. The blow never landed.

Othelia diverted from her path and slit his throat. It was over and done with in one swift motion, and she was gone before his body dropped. When she was halfway down the deck, she realized she should've killed the woman too. They were all enemies now. The game had begun.

Her hands were shaking immensely, her heart jittering at an inconsistent beat. She didn't look at the bloodied blade in her hand or focus on what she'd done. Enemies, she reminded herself. They were all enemies. Again and again until the words were painted in bright red in the darkness of her mind. And the more people she eliminated, the better chance she had of winning or passing or whatever happened at the end of all this. The question was, who would be next?

She chose two women fighting with fists a few feet ahead. One was in fairly good condition and the other was done for. Her hair was matted with blood, and dark black bruises were forming along her cheeks. Still, she aimed a final, meek punch at her opponent before being pushed into the water below. The worn woman's hoarse screams were cut short by bubbling water.

Othelia channeled her power into her arms and punched the remaining woman. The woman was caught off guard, giving Othelia enough time to hoist her over the railing and toss her into the sea. She continued her way to the front of the boat.

The few people at the front were all preoccupied with their own battles. She used this to her advantage and looked over the railing. Sure enough, there was a lifeboat dangling high above the water, attached via a rope pulley system and suspended by crane-like arms on either side. The lifeboat was long and wooden and sturdy. Two oars rested vertically over six wooden seats. Would they really be forced to row to their next destination? How far would they have to go? The unknown was maddening.

She focused on the task at hand; others could attack at a moment's notice. The cranes were connected to the deck by large, metallic boxes, of which had cranks that would manually send the boat down. There were two boxes, two cranks, and they required two people to work properly.

She thought of jumping into the lifeboat and cutting the ropes, but the chance of the boat crushing on impact was too high. Perhaps she could run between cranks and slowly but surely send the craft halfway down. Then she could jump into the lifeboat, cut the ropes, and hope her bones didn't break. An all-right plan, if she could execute it in time.

"I can help with that," a voice said from behind her. She jumped in surprise and held her knife between herself and a man. She recognized him as one of the people she'd followed onto the boat. The suit-wearer. The other three were nowhere in sight.

"Where are the people you came with?" Her voice was sharp and demanding. He held his hands up in defense, his eyebrows drawn in worry. She could see no blood on him, nor any muscle or noticeable weapons.

"We've, uh, split up. But, like I said, I can help with that." He gestured toward the ropes. "I come fro—"

He was cut off as Othelia grabbed his sleeve. She pulled him forward and away from a giant man who came up behind him. She let go and rushed forward with a fist. It was about to connect with his nose when an outstretched foot flew between them and slammed directly into the giant man's side. He was thrust a few inches from his spot. Their newest group member, the blond boy, landed on his feet in a crouch. He stared at her as he stood before his attention flickered to the suited man.

"Galen! You came, too!"

"Did you find a lifeboat?" Galen asked as the giant attacked once more. She couldn't help but watch in awe as Galen easily dodged. His effortless victory piqued her interest, the way he slithered around his opponent, trapping them. He moved on to someone new, someone with a hammer.

"Well, it looks like he's got that under control," the suited man said. "I'm Eli, by the way. As I was saying, I come from a family of cruise owners. This stuff is within my expertise."

She hadn't realized how close he was standing to her until she turned around. Othelia hopped back in nervousness, uncomfortable with the weight of his breath on her shoulder.

His hazel eyes were glued to her, and the incessant staring made her skin crawl. "A cruise? What's that?"

"Oh, uh, people pay a lot of money to go on luxury boat rides."

His answer raised her suspicions. "Even when something like this could happen?"

"Ships don't sink often," Eli answered. "And the rich will do anything with the word 'luxury' tacked on. It's in their nature."

She was nearly offended, knowing very well that she was one of the so-called detestable rich. But she didn't think he was right. Her family treated the island well. There was no famine or spreading of disease. The air was crisp, and the food was bountiful. They hardly relished in materialistic things, aside from the famous paintings that lined their hallways. What made him think this way? What types of people had he encountered?

Aside from his heated words, she couldn't gauge any ill intent and he didn't seem to recognize her. Othelia nodded and lowered her weapon. He and Galen very well could've killed their companions and planned to do the same to her, but this process would be far slower without someone's help, and no one else was offering. "All right. You take that one."

They split up, lowering the boat in unison. It was remarkably hard to do, her muscles aching. She had to reserve her power for later—if she used a copious amount within a day, she would become sluggish and worthless.

"Hey!" Eli yelled as fingers wrapped around his collar and yanked him back. The attacker held him up over their head, Eli's feet dangling off the deck. A grunt escaped Eli's lips as he was thrown into the railing, his body connecting with a painful thud. The air looked to escape him, and his body went slack, giving the man time to wrap his arm around Eli's throat in an impenetrable chokehold.

Eli released a series of muffled grunts and groans as he clawed at the man's arm. His efforts were unsuccessful, and his face was turning a deep shade of red. And she was letting it happen. One less competitor, right?

She shook her head and glided her knife into the man's back, pulling it along his spine before taking it out. His grip on Eli's neck tightened as the attacker screamed and writhed. She pulled the knife out and stabbed him again, driving the blade down to the hilt. Her thoughts were empty; her actions were no longer associated with herself. This had to be done, and if she had to turn off her brain to do it, so be it.

One more did the trick, and Eli dropped. He released a series of coughs and gasps as he rubbed his neck. Fury burned in Eli's assailants' eyes as he fell onto his stomach and looked at Othelia. He propped himself up on his elbow and pulled out a knife. He swung the blade haphazardly in front of him, knowing this was his last resort.

Eli came up from behind him and wrapped his tie around the man's neck. Startled, the man reached backward to slash at Eli. Othelia launched at the man and cut his arm. He dropped his weapon and began clawing at the tie around his neck. Othelia did what she had to do and stabbed him in the chest.

Eli released his tie, his skin paling. "Oh, my."

"Back to work," Othelia said, turning back to the lifeboat crank she'd been attending. Eli hesitated before joining her. "We have to hurry."

Eli jumped back into action, and they cranked the lifeboat until it was halfway down. She peered over the boat. "How are we getting down there?"

"These cranes are called a davit. Usually, the crew is responsible for lowering guests. However," he said, pointing to large metal clips that connected the ropes and the boat. "A few years ago, they added those, in case the crew is unable to help. Smart, right?"

She nodded, gulping at how far they'd have to jump. "This is unbelievably dangerous, though."

He shrugged and looped one foot over the railing. He straddled it and gestured for her to do the same. She swung her leg over awkwardly, laying with her nose against the smooth alloy and her arms securely wrapped around it. She was still shaking, nerves taking over.

"It's certainly not a perfect solution, but it's one we can work with," Eli assured. "Don't worry, I've done this jump plenty of times."

Before following through, Eli looked around the deck. She followed his gaze back to the blond boy.

Eli cupped his hands together and yelled, "Galen!"

Galen doled out a final punch to his current opponent and dashed over, a puff of wind daring to ruffle his hair. Ten, fifteen bodies scattered the ground around him. One was rolling around with her nose in hand, blood gushing and throat wailing. None of them looked dead, merely unconscious or in severe pain, and it was all the work of the boy who strolled up to them.

Was he a royal son she didn't know about? Galen had the pale and creamy skin of a northern island native, one with both yearly snow and warm summer months. Or was he just an average person with good self-defense techniques? Or was he something else entirely?

Galen looked at them with confusion until he got a look over the railing, and then he whistled. Blood splattered his face, and his knuckles were a bruised mess, but he stood tall and composed; the demeanor of someone who liked to fight and fought often. He didn't have a weapon, which meant he either used maoho or his strength was raw. In both cases, she simply had to fight him. But not now.

"No one but us. I'm getting the others," he said, his voice soft but stern.

Eli saluted. "We'll see you soon."

And the boy was off, darting back to wherever the others were. She gulped as she studied the drop. Eli was insane. But it was comforting to know he hadn't killed his companions. Unless he was trying to kill her right now. Which was entirely possible, since the fall looked agonizing.

When she dared to look at Eli, his hand was outstretched. He didn't smile, but there was something calming there, written on his face. "Here, grab my hand. It'll be okay."

Othelia certainly didn't want to. That level of trust was far from earned, but there was no way she would push herself off the railing herself. Irrational, maybe, but it was something she simply could not do. But there was nothing worse than relying on others.

She grabbed his hand. He looped his other foot around and rested on top of the railing by the edge of his butt, his legs dangling freely a few feet above the lifeboat. She followed suit, his hand helping her balance as she struggled to sit up. The metal dug into her lower backside; this was one of the most uncomfortable positions she'd ever sat in, and she desperately wanted to get their escape underway.

"Jump on the count of three, alright? At the same time."

Othelia nodded, and on the count of three, they jumped. Nothing could've prepared her for the drop of her stomach and the pause of her heart as they plummeted through the air. An impossible moment passed between feeling alive and wondering if she'd live.

And then her feet connected with the wood and the impossible moment was over, replaced by a very sudden, pulsing pain. She dropped to her knees and gasped. She looked up and laughed involuntarily, temporary shock and elation dictating her thoughts and actions. They had fallen through the air and survived.

"You're crazy," she said between each giggle. Her heart wouldn't stop racing. She was breathless and in pain, but very much alive.

"That hook," Eli said, unfazed and unharmed. A man born to jump off boats. He ignored her look of awe and pointed to the hook closest to her. "We have to do it together, or else it won't work."

She slowly scooted over to the lifeboat's side and reached for the hook. "My whole body hurts."

"Yes, but once you get used to it, you get to free fall for fun."

She let out a groan in response while grabbing onto the hook. She found its release mechanism and met the calm eyes of Eli. He was already in position. "Count of three, okay? And hold on to the boat with your other hand."

They counted together and unhooked the ropes. Her clamp got stuck, and the boat fell at an angle. She held on with dear life—her legs trailing for a millisecond before the hook gave way. The boat connected with the water and bobbed haplessly.

Her eyes were shut tight, and her fingers burned from her tight grip on the boat's edge. Her eyes snapped open at the sound of a gurgled yell. Eli was gone. She searched the side of the boat for any sign of him and found nothing.

He resurfaced on the other side seconds later, his arms flailing wildly. Othelia thrust herself across the boat and reached down for him. She grabbed his forearm and pulled him into the boat with a firm tug. His body sloshed onto the wood with a thump. He rolled onto his side, water spilling from his lips as he coughed harshly.

Othelia sat beside him, her chest heaving and her eyes heavy as the adrenaline coursing through her faded.

"What"—he released a series of rough coughs—"should we do now?"

Othelia took in their surroundings. There was nothing but water and a bright orange dot on the horizon, bobbing in the same spot. A buoy or another boat. She pointed in that direction. "Think that might be the phase two destination?"

Eli sat up with a wobbling arm and followed her finger. "I'd say that looks like the right way to go. But we need to wait for the others."

She shook her head. "We should get rowing. If we stick around, people will probably try to jump down and hijack the boat."

He considered the scale of the ship. "I don't think anyone could survive that. Not with their legs."

"But someone may not know that and try. If someone tries to get down here or gets thrown overboard, our lifeboat is at risk."

"We're ditching them? That's not what I agreed to."

"You want to pass the exam?"

"Of course, but—"

"Then think for yourself. It's not like you lied. You promised you wouldn't let anyone else on. We aren't, are we? We're leaving instead."

He stared at her, mouth agape. His teeth were a radiant white against the growing darkness of the sinking sun. "I may have initially left them behind, but I can't leave knowing Galen plans on coming back. How about this? If we wait thirty minutes and they don't come, we'll go to the examiners. For now, we'll paddle a suitable distance away and wait until the others wave us down."

"And how are we keeping track of time, exactly?"

"With our instincts, naturally. We'll wait until we feel like it's been thirty minutes." Eli smiled as though he was the funniest man she'd ever met. He moved to the front and picked up an oar.

"It's already felt like an hour sitting here with you," Othelia mumbled before letting out an aggravated sigh. She tossed her hood over her messed hair. "Ten. We wait ten minutes."

She pushed the paddles into the water hesitantly as Eli explained how paddling worked. The black sky reflected off the water, but the ocean waves were calm, and the world was quiet. They found their rhythm after a few errors, disappearing into the growing darkness.

What a wretched situation. She didn't want to deal with other people, let alone four, but Eli's decision wasn't one to be persuaded. Besides, they were an interesting group, but interesting often meant smart, which often meant cunning. She really, really didn't want to deal with people.

If he didn't recognize her, she supposed there was no harm in giving her name. She was stuck with him, after all. It took her a while to find the courage to fill the dead air. When was the last time she'd introduced herself to someone outside the palace?

The words slipped out in Ishlish, a lapse in forethought. "I'm Othelia, by the way."

He offered her a dashing smile, dimples forming on each side of his oval-shaped face. And then her world folded in on itself as he uttered the Ishlish royal greeting with the cadence of a native-born speaker, "Taylek du'la stoilés."

Blessed by the stars.

CHAPTER II

ISABELLE

THE EXPLOSION CAME from two or three levels below. The chair she sat on slid forward until the legs gave out and she was tossed onto the marble floor. She had no time to register the pain coursing through her forearms as momentum pushed her around the ballroom like a useless sack. Her shoulder collided with the wall, and she let out a sharp cry. Somewhere, Leo's voice called out to her, but it was lost in the screams and shakes of the ship.

And then she, along with everything else, rolled the other way as the ship rocked. It went on for what felt like forever, her hands shielding every loose item that flew her way.

When the teetering subsided, she pushed herself onto her back and relished the coolness of the marble, her eyes fixated on the flickering lights above.

A hand waved over her dazed eyes. A voice, Leo's voice, ebbed in and out like a rippling puddle. "Isabelle!"

She sat up and rubbed her arm, wincing at the soft throb that erupted underneath her touch. Leo helped her stand as Eli and Galen rushed to their sides.

"Is everyone okay?" Eli asked. He stretched one of his legs while assessing his calf, the pant leg ripped at the seams. Galen was unharmed and unshaken, and his eyes darted around the room, looking, but looking for what? She wasn't sure what to think of him yet. He exuded harmlessness, but his quiet nature kept her on edge. She couldn't tell if he was shy or hiding something, and she didn't care to find out.

"What's going on? Are we being attacked?" Leo asked, ignoring Eli's previous query.

Isabelle shook her head, embarrassment running through her. They should've known something would happen. The exam began an hour ago. "It's started."

Her ears rang as Emmarcia's voice blasted from invisible speakers. Isabelle's eyes widened. She felt like a fool for not being prepared. They had two hours and six lifeboats. Six chances.

"...those who survive and find us will move on to the next phase. We have already left."

People reacted immediately, stampeding up the stairs in a frantic hurry. Abel and his crew were among the crowd, and she made a mental note of their new comrade—a blond man in exuberant attire. Another person to look out for.

"We should stop the boat from sinking," Leo suggested rather matter-of-factly. She looked at him incredulously, unable to comprehend his absurd proposal. They weren't there for other people; they had no obligation to save anyone. "If we stop the water soon enough, the boat should stay afloat."

"What?" Isabelle asked. She couldn't bring herself to ask anything further, so taken aback by his readiness to try the impossible. It had to be a joke.

"Are you crazy?" Galen hissed. "Even if we stopped the water, how could someone steer the ship back to land with no propellers or sails?"

"I'll have to agree with him on this one," Eli said. "I like you guys, but that's too risky for me. Good luck."

With that, Eli turned and jotted up the stairs and out of sight. The ballroom was now devoid of others, three dead bodies littering the ground.

Galen, to her surprise, stayed. "Why would we do that?"

Leo pleaded with doughy, round eyes. Isabelle was unconvinced; his idea was ludicrous, and they were wasting time. She shook her head and gestured at the world unraveling around them. "Too dangerous."

"The people who don't get onto the lifeboats will die," Leo said. "You heard the examiner. All she told us to do was 'survive.' They're perfectly fine with letting the losers drown."

"So?" They looked at Galen in unison. "They knew the consequences of taking the exam. Death is always one of them."

"That's at least a hundred lives," Leo said, his brows furrowed. "People with families and friends. They don't deserve to die any more than we do."

Galen sucked in a breath, disgruntled. "Okay. I'll find us a lifeboat just in case, and I'll come back to help. Good luck." Sarcasm dripped from his crooked smile, and then he turned to leave. A strange boy, indeed.

Isabelle hadn't known that death was a consequence. Her brother had revealed only that the International Exam was necessary for the line of work he was interested in. If he became an Expedition Overseer, he could apply to become a full-time hitman. Micah didn't offer any insight on what that position entailed, but he'd explicitly told her that he "erased scum from hevalth and got paid for doing it."

But her fellow contestants weren't scum. They were just people. Surely Gahi would turn Their back on Isabelle if she let people needlessly die. Who was she to decide if her goals and dreams were superior to theirs?

"Fine," she said. "Hurry."

Isabelle and Leo ran for the next flight of stairs; the floor was sticky from juice and blood and squished berries. A small girl was huddled in the corner with fingers gripping her hair tightly. She was whimpering, eyes clamped shut as she rocked in her spot and recited an unfamiliar prayer. The lights were flickering and the muffled shouts above filled the air. This was unlike anything she could've expected—a splintering, unknown world. How had Micah left so many details out?

The second floor was dark aside from the setting sun pooling in from circular windows. Her eyes took a second to adjust, and when they did, she saw the floor was dry. There were bare mattresses raised on wooden frames, somehow unbothered by the earlier commotion. At the opposite end was a doorway leading to another staircase.

"The examiner said we have two hours," Leo said. "So my guess is the damage isn't all that bad. We could have a chance at plugging it up."

She didn't ask how he planned to do so; she knew he wouldn't have the answers. He was reacting with a sense of duty, not out of rationality. Isabelle's thoughts and actions were disconnected. She wished she'd never known the failures could die so she could turn back, but she kept going.

The smell of salt hung in the air. She could hear the water sloshing on the floor as they approached the lower doorway. Leo stopped at the top of the descending stairs and turned to her. She avoided his gaze and peered down the steps; the third floor was submerged in water.

Leo started down the stairs without a word. Isabelle gulped. She didn't follow at first, her hope waning. She didn't know how boats worked, or how they could be unsunk. If that was possible, even. But she had to remind herself that abandoning lives was as good as murder, and she did not want to spend an eternity in the Unholy Land. No amount of prayer excused murder.

Was Micah there now, being tortured by a thousand scorching suns, for the killing he'd done?

She shook her head and made her way down the stairs. Pesky intrusive thoughts.

The water went up to their ankles, instantly numbing her feet. It was beyond freezing, and she hopped out in shock. It was nothing like the warm tides of Ishla. Her shoes were now drenched, and she shivered; her teeth chattered as she rubbed her arms. This level had lights lining the edges of the ceiling, and they flickered during their last moments of life. Water splashed against Leo's feet while he waded through the water.

The third level was split into six sections by large metal doors. They were flung open, exposing a hole in the final compartment that looked no wider than a few feet. The excess water was entering at a rapid pace, thoughtlessly dragging them towards death.

Isabelle forced herself back into the water and paused beside Leo. He was frozen in front of the first door, fists clenched. She tried to follow his gaze but couldn't find an explanation for why he stopped. She verbalized her hasty fright. "Have to work fast. It's filling."

But he didn't respond. She rolled her eyes as she passed him and journeyed to the last door. The water was rising faster than she'd thought; it was already up to her knees. When she reached the sixth compartment, she noticed a second hole letting in water. Her heart was pounding, but she remained calm. She'd agreed to this, and now she had to pull through.

Isabelle pushed on the thick door. Rushing seawater fought back, a formidable opponent against her tired arms. She looked through the parallel doorways with her back against the metal. She shoved her entire weight into the damn thing and yelled, "A little help!"

It was futile. She let out a grunt that produced an involuntary sob. Of all the ways to die, this was not one she favored. Isabelle couldn't swim, and they were hours from land. She stepped away from the door and the persistent water shoved it open. There was no point in trying. Gahi could see that, couldn't they?

She glared at Leo while making her way back to him. She stepped over the second doorway when the strange blond boy ran down the stairs. Galen splashed noisily toward Leo and patted him on the back with enough force to induce a resurgence of life. Leo stumbled forward and found Isabelle's gaze. Fear was written in his eyes and along the lines of his face. She almost laughed; he was a man who had heroic ideas but failed to carry them out. He was no hero at all. He was a coward.

"Was standing there part of your plan?" Galen asked, and Isabelle thought Galen ought to slap Leo upside the head for good measure. But he didn't and instead bounded toward Isabelle.

She turned back and started working on closing the door again. Galen joined her side, and they operated as a unit, using all their strength to fight against the overflowing water.

"Let's get this over with," Galen said, his face contorted in concentration and energy exertion. They closed the door with a final, excruciating shove, and Galen latched the clamp in place. It was sealed; not a drop seeped through.

Isabelle crossed her arms and shivered. Motives didn't matter now, as long as he was there to help and not to kill them. She looked Galen over, noticing the blood splattered on his face and stomach and the bruises covering his knuckles.

He'd come back. He'd been apprehensive and critical, and he'd come back. Why? Hadn't he said the lives of others didn't matter?

"We should close the rest, just in case," he said.

"Did you find one?" Isabelle asked, wishing she could repeat the word 'lifeboat.' She knew it when she heard it, but she couldn't get herself to say the word aloud—her tongue twisted. How had Micah passed the exam without knowing fluent Latarian? Without his training, she'd be clueless.

"Eli is saving one. Hopefully, he hasn't left."

Isabelle should've felt more relieved than she did.

The rest of the doors were easier to shove shut, and by the time they were done, Leo was deathly pale and leaning forward, hands on his knees and gagging. She looked away, unable to watch him puke again. He spat instead, then wiped his mouth.

"I'm sorry," he had the gall to say. "I don't know what came over me. I just couldn't move."

His hands were shaking. He rubbed at his wrists with twitching fingers. Galen shot him a pair of accusatory eyes, not a hint of empathy. "That's not something that can happen again. You'll get yourself killed."

"I know."

"The only lives the examiners care about are their own and the ones who pass. Everyone else is expendable. It's time to go."

Isabelle followed Galen upstairs, admiring his scolding. She couldn't have said it better herself. She grabbed Galen's shoulder lightly from behind. "Are you okay?"

He didn't act or look tired, but his bruises and the splattered blood were cause for concern. He acknowledged neither. "It's how you'd expect it to be up top. Whole lot of fighting and bodies. Do you fight any better than you did earlier?"

She'd forgotten he'd seen their fight against Abel. She

blushed, recounting her laughable attempt at fighting, which was a full-body tackle and a myriad of furious punches.

Her lack of response seemed to be enough for him. "Then I suggest you stay below deck. Some people have guns."

Once they reached the bedroom level, Leo deadbolted the door behind them. The room was pitch black now; the windows revealed nothing but a vast nothingness she couldn't bear to look at. Collective darkness and silence terrified her, and she hastily rushed up to the second floor. It remained empty aside from dead bodies and the cowering girl.

Isabelle was not prepared to set foot on the main deck—she never would be—and briefly entertained Galen's suggestion of staying behind. There was no telling how it looked up there, how many people were still alive.

They stopped where the snack tables used to be, cookies and chips and tiny sandwiches strewn upon the ground and crushed to smithereens. Leo was, for the first time, devoid of opinions.

Galen raised his eyebrows at them. Leo refused to make eye contact, and the pale boy's attention gravitated to her. His choice of clothing made her uncomfortable—showing skin was taboo back home—and she couldn't quite get herself to look at him, either. His dark green eyes were piercing and expectant of an answer. She wasn't ready to give one.

"Will the two of you be accompanying me?" Neither she nor Leo spoke. Her eyes drifted toward the sobbing girl in the corner. Isabelle did not want to be hesitant. She didn't want to be scared. But there were dead people at their feet and the examiners were heartless.

Micah's killer would continue to roam free if she gave up now. No one else cared about his death, not even their father. Once someone left, it was hard for the village to accept them back; Micah had been welcomed back with public whippings meant to absolve him of his sins.

She brought her attention back to Galen, courage slowly bubbling up. He tapped his foot angrily, brows raised impossibly high. Why was she so intimidated by him when he was nothing more than short-tempered? "Look, I can't keep Eli waiting. I'm not about to be stuck on this ship. Make up your minds so we can go."

"We're coming. Obviously," Isabelle hissed, tugging Leo by his arm toward the ascending stairs. Isabelle walked up the steps with a nervous smile, her decision compensating for her fear of whatever was above. She was making the right decision. Micah would see the justice he deserved. It would be okay.

She took one glance at the ground and nearly screamed. Moonlight revealed a spectacle of mangled and very dead bodies, blood soaking the wood. A brute held his armless shoulder and sobbed while others stood along the railings in anguish, wills broken by the notion of failure and inevitable death.

Galen peered over the ship's edge; Isabelle and Leo followed suit. All the lifeboats had been taken on that side. By the lack of fighting around them, she deduced they'd all been taken except one, which had been broken to bits and floated aimlessly in the waves.

Galen led them to the other side of the boat. Isabelle expected to see Eli, but the sea was black and empty. Galen hit the railing with a fist. "We took ten minutes, at most! How could everyone be gone already?"

Isabelle crossed her arms. She should've known. But they'd done the right thing. That's all that mattered. Her fingers curled into fists of their own, heat rising to her face. She would have to wait another six months to take the exam again. She had no home to go to—unless she wanted to be whipped, and she certainly did not—and no money. And Micah's murderer was out there somewhere, living their life. Did they care? Did they feel remorse?

She looked out to the sea and caught sight of a neon orange raft bobbing in the waves. Pieces of rope connected five lifeboats around it, though she couldn't tell how many people there were.

"At least the examiners made it easy to spot them," Leo said, waving his arms over his head to catch Eli's—or anyone's—attention. Isabelle joined in, assuming Eli had already rowed all that way.

"They aren't coming over," Galen said impatiently. "At this point, we should take our chances and jump in. Try to swim over."

Isabelle looked down again and shook her head, perplexed. "No. No, sir."

"We lost the first phase. We really lost. I'm a fool. The three of us are fools."

"No one forced you to help," she mumbled.

Galen scoffed and squinted at her. "I said I'm a fool, didn't I?"

"Stop arguing," Leo interjected. "We can't change our choices, and it doesn't matter. Look. They're coming back."

Isabelle watched the horizon; the orange blot had moved perhaps a yard closer. The lifeboats were still connected, and the ropes dragged them flimsily behind. She'd never seen such a strange yet funny thing.

The sudden jerks of the lifeboats sent some contestants spiraling into the water. By the time they resurfaced, the boats were gone, pulled by the propeller of the orange metal contraption speeding toward the main ship. They were left behind, forced to swim back with the hope of catching up in time. Isabelle silently prayed for them. There were tales of leviathan that lurked beneath the waves, large and long creatures with reptilian scales and webbed feet. Creatures that quenched their hunger with the flesh and bones of humans.

The water was so calm yet so dark, unique in its tangy smell and thoughtlessness. If things were normal—if 'normal' existed at all—perhaps she would learn to love the ocean. But this was not that world, and she was afraid. This would be the last time she stepped aboard a ship.

Emmarcia held up a microphone as they grew near, and it cackled to life. Her flippant voice penetrated the air. "Were you the ones to close all the hatches?"

"That's them, alright," Eli said somewhere in the darkness. "I told you they'd be coming."

Isabelle watched the examiner's stern gaze shift to Eli. There he was, sitting in a lifeboat with a cloaked person. Isabelle had been the one to suggest looking out for themselves but hadn't thought about the feeling of betrayal that came along with it.

The examiner said something Isabelle could not hear. Eli untied his lifeboat from the orange one and paddled to the edge of the large ship.

"Does this count as passing?" Galen called out.

"It does. Use one of those pulley ropes and come down."

Isabelle stared, wholly dumbfounded. Galen assessed the ropes with a gleeful, smug smile as Leo stood with his mouth slightly agape. This was the work of Gahi.

The nearest rope was held together by a few strands, and Isabelle used her knife to cut it loose. She tied the rope around the railing in a fashion akin to her teachings. Tying knots was one of her favorite pastimes, and her skill was finally proving useful. The rope was shorter now, but the drop was reasonable, and she was certain they would pass the exam.

She'd finished the task so fast and effortlessly that when she turned around, Leo and Galen were simply staring. She smiled awkwardly. "It'll do. Please. Don't let me fall."

"Don't worry," Leo said. "We're here to help."

She peered over the ship one last time and took a deep breath. She wanted to believe him, but Leo had proved inefficient under pressure. He could very well cost them all their lives.

A hoard of other contestants came to their side, gaping and jeering at the examiner and the boats attached. A potbellied man pointed an accusatory finger at the examiner. "Look how much room there still is! At least thirty more of us can pass! Why do they get a free pass?"

The microphone erupted instantly with the aggravated words of Emmarcia Parigold. "This exam is to weed out the weak from the strong; the heroes from the common folk. Trying to save a sinking ship is the most heroic thing one could've done in this phase. Now, if anyone else tries to board these crafts, make no mistake, you'll be killed on the spot."

The woman smiled sinisterly behind the microphone; her crooked nose appeared bigger in the shadows. Her warning was also a dare, Isabelle realized. Emmarcia wanted someone to cross her. She wanted to execute someone to prove a point.

Nobody budged. Eyes drifted to the three of them. Isabelle ignored their stares and climbed over the railing with a firm grasp on the rope. She pinched the rope between her feet and slowly started her descent. Her muscles quelled with tension. The drop was far, deadly, and her hands shook from the weight of her body. The process was long and painful, an immense strain rippling through her forearms and calves.

At the end of the rope, she let go, expecting a rough landing and an aching butt. Hands tried to catch her, but gravity brought Isabelle down on their stomach. She sat up to see Eli's chin as he rocked his head back and groaned. He rubbed his wrists and then grabbed her sides, slid her off him, and wheezed. "Remind me to never try that again."

Isabelle knelt and met Emmarcia's snickering gaze. "Will they be saved?"

"A clean-up crew is already on the way."

Leo plopped onto the boat next. It shook from his uneven weight and his face paled. "I don't like the sound of that."

Galen made a speedy descent and scooted to the back, picking up the free oar and twirling it horizontally. "It doesn't matter what you like; the Overseers can do anything they want to us. Besides, is there really anything we can do for those people that we haven't already done?"

He was right, of course, but the idea of a 'clean-up crew' sounded wildly disturbing. Isabelle wished she could negotiate with the examiner, but she knew her inability to speak fluent Latarian would muddle her point. Besides, the examiner would do what she wanted, regardless of what Isabelle said.

Leo remained quiet; his eyes closed as he held onto the side of the boat. She wished he would unlock his confidence, but it was lost.

"I gotta say," Eli said as he moved closer to the hooded figure. His back lightly leaned against theirs as he faced Isabelle, a sign he trusted whoever was underneath. Isabelle looked over her shoulder, realizing she treated Leo the same. She wouldn't call what she felt toward him trust, however. Unthreatened was a better word for it. He was now partaking in the emptying of his stomach over the lifeboat's edge. "I'm surprised you guys really did it."

"I'm surprised you left," Isabelle retorted.

"Was it you or you that said we should focus on our own survival first?"

"And which one of us begged to work as a team?" Leo asked.

Eli crossed his arms and smirked. "The one that was right. If we hadn't worked as a team, you'd have failed."

"We're disconnecting everyone from our craft now," Emmarcia interrupted. "It's time to embark. Please follow us to the next location."

The Exam Leader and her crew of six untied the lifeboats hastily. Once all the boats were disconnected, they pulled out oars of their own and began tossing back waves, paddling to a destination unknown. The craft was larger than the other lifeboats and heavier, but they had more paddles and more stored energy. Though the propellers were turned off, the examiners rowed at an exhilarated, inhuman rate.

Small bulbs illuminated off of the orange boat suddenly, blinding Isabelle. If they couldn't keep up and lost that light, they'd be stuck forever, or until they starved to death. Suddenly, drowning didn't seem so bad.

The hidden person—a girl—volunteered to keep rowing and Galen took the back. Isabelle couldn't gauge the strength of either of them, nor their motives, but her energy was depleted. Her legs were stiff from the freezing water, and she could feel bruises forming on her thighs and shoulder.

She, Leo, and Eli distributed their weight evenly within the boat, taking up their own seats. Things became quiet once Leo stopped puking, and it made her think about the people left behind. A clean-up crew was coming. How cruel that sounded.

She was thankful when Leo broke the silence, his words directed at Eli. "Did you fight anyone?"

"No, not really, but I dodged well. Oh," Eli added as an afterthought, "and sorry for fleeing. You guys did a good thing."

"If it worked," Galen muttered. Isabelle was growing to dislike him with every syllable that escaped his mouth. His lack of fear was admirable, but everything he said came across as cold-hearted.

"You know, for someone who was adamantly against the ship idea, and a strong enough fighter to advance without us, why'd you go back to get Is and Leo?" Eli asked.

Galen shrugged nonchalantly. "Leo's the only one around here that looks to be my age, and… well… I guess I just liked how confident he was that we should save the ship. Even with everyone and the odds against him, he still believed he could do it."

"Huh," Eli said, stroking his chin. "We're one and the same. I guess confidence really is the key."

"I understand why you ran," Leo chimed in, clenching his stomach as he leaned closer to the lifeboat's edge. He gestured toward their other rower. "New friend?"

He leaned over the boat and upheaved before an answer could be spoken. Isabelle reached over, running her fingers along his back in light circles. How could the boy who attracted others based on his confidence be so utterly weak and uncharismatic at the same time?

"Yes, but her identity must remain a secret for now." Eli lowered his voice. "It appears she has a situation like ours on her hands."

"Ah, a dick-like situation," Isabelle said, the words flowing before she could stop them. She didn't swear often, nor did she like the way they sounded, but it seemed like the most appropriate term. And, of course, Micah went out of his way to teach her such profanities in Latarian. The anonymous girl snorted and released a sharp laugh before recoiling into her tough and quiet shell. Isabelle liked her already.

She appraised the crew she somehow gained over the course of the day. How had she stumbled upon such a strange group of companions? And they were good ones, too, even if Leo was proving to be a disappointment.

They kept pace with the examiners, surrounded by the other lifeboats. Some were falling behind, while others had three or four rowers and maintained a solid pace. How were Galen and the hooded girl strong enough to keep up?

Time began to bleed together. Leo read off his wristwatch every fifteen minutes until his stomach settled and he drifted to sleep. Isabelle loved the notion of sleep, but every time she closed her eyes, she saw dead bodies covered in blood. With every blink, the images got more grotesque; a body cut to bits, innards strewn on the walls and railings.

She stayed awake and kept her eyes on the orange lifeboat with her knees tucked into her chest. It took maybe two hours for her to ask, "Do you want to switch?"

The hooded girl answered with wispy comfort. "I'll be fine."

"I could do this in my sleep," Galen called back, his voice hardly a call at all.

Isabelle yawned. Sleep. She wanted it so badly and it was just within her reach, but no. Another blink and her eyes were stretched wide open. She pulled her knees even closer, hiding her face between her legs.

"If the three of you want to sleep," the girl added, "that's fine. We'll wake you up if we need you."

"A-are you sure?" Isabelle asked. "What if we get attacked? What if one of you gets tired?"

Her body stiffened at the idea of the leviathan attacking and crushing them whole. She needed to stop thinking.

"My family has us train extensively," the girl assured. "My upper arm strength is killer. Quite literally."

"And if we're attacked?"

"I've got it covered."

Isabelle wasn't sure what that implied; if this girl had killed anyone before or if she was putting up a front. It didn't matter, because at that moment, her eyes drooped, and her vision began fading out. She imagined horses jumping over white picket fences, counting each one as it disappeared.

"Your family trains you, too?" Galen asked. "Get along with yours?"

"Not even on a good day. You?"

Isabelle listened half-heartedly as her head lolled to the side. The sudden movement startled her, and she jolted upright. She glanced behind at Leo, who leaned over a wooden seat with his face snuggled against a folded arm. Eli softly snored in front of her, scrunched between two seats and lying on the floor. It would have been peaceful, if not for the murderers and impending doom that surrounded them.

"We'll see," said Galen. Isabelle wished to inquire further, but her tired body begged to curl up on the floor. Before she knew it, she drifted to sleep with the sway of the sea.

PHASE
2

CHAPTER 12
ELI

ONE MOMENT, HE was enjoying a nice dinner with his family. The dinner table was long, with shiny glass dishes lining the edges. The center was stocked with steaming ham and mashed potatoes. His identical twin brothers, Felix and Iris, sat across from him. Beside him was his younger sister, Alyssa, and his parents were at each end.

They all had food on their plates except for him. His father's voice faded in and out. Eli caught glimpses of what he was saying—something about the cruise line and who would inherit it. Felix was technically the eldest, born two minutes before Iris, and was therefore supposed to gain control of the family fortune.

His father stopped jabbering and turned to Eli with sunken black eyes and a crooked smile. He outstretched his palm to his youngest son, revealing the keys. *The* keys. To everything. To anything. It was metaphorical, of course; there were no keys to something so complicated. Eli swallowed, his heart racing around an endless track. He reached out. He had to. He didn't want to, but he had to. Anything to make his father happy.

And in the next moment, his shoulder was shoved, and his eyes snapped open. He involuntarily sat up, his forehead connecting with Othelia's. Eli's head fell back, hitting the wood it'd once been resting on. He rubbed his temples as a rush of pain erupted throughout his head.

When he opened his eyes again, it was incredibly hard to adjust to the darkness surrounding them. How long had he been asleep? His head was groggy and throbbing. An overdrawn yawn escaped him as he squinted, trying to make out which vague silhouette belonged to whom. Leo was beside him, stretching lazily and releasing a sleepy sigh.

"About time," Othelia said, now standing and looking down at him with a look of irritation, her palm over her forehead.

Standing? She was standing on the boat?

Instinct took over—the rules of small seacrafts were very clear. Eli reached for her other hand and pulled her down. A gasp escaped her lips and when she was crouched to his level, her brilliant blue eyes were filled with radiating annoyance.

"What are you doing?" she asked, jerking her forearm out of his grip.

"You mean what are *you* doing? You can't stand on a boat like that. It'll flip."

"We're on land." She swung her leg up and over the lifeboat. "We have been for a few minutes now."

Eli reached over the lifeboat with haste and the expectancy of water. Instead, his fingers were met with many tiny, slimy rocks. The pebbles made a barely audible crunch as he dug deeper until he eventually hit wet yet solid dirt.

"You two were impossible to wake up," Galen said, looking between Leo and Eli before his gaze rested squarely on Eli. "And she slapped you, twice."

He smiled. "Well, then I hope that headbutt hurt."

Eli couldn't see her from this far, but he suspected an eye-roll came his way.

"The examiners are over there." Isabelle gestured away from them. All he could see was the beam of a flashlight pointing at the Exam Leader's—what was her name, again? Marcia?—heels. "We wait. For stragglers."

"How'd we keep up?" Eli asked. "Did I sleep through my turn to row?"

Isabelle shook her head. "Those two. *Chalkluntso.*"

He raised a brow. "Come again?"

"Witchcraft," she repeated in Latarian. He couldn't place the language she spoke, racking his brain for any hints in what she said. There were twenty languages across the world that were established, and he knew three of them fluently—the two universal languages and Ishlish.

To his credit, he tried his best to familiarize himself with the others; he could struggle through six semi-well. At the very least, he could say 'hello' and 'goodbye' in each. Closing oneself off to trade because of a language barrier was of no interest to him.

"Where are you from?" chimed Leo. "If you don't mind me asking."

She stared at her feet. "I mind."

"That sounded like Urkinian to me," Othelia said, her confidence brimming. "Or am I wrong?"

Isabelle's head shot up, but she quickly corrected herself and walked in the direction of the Exam Leader without a word.

"How'd you know?" Eli asked, eager to understand how the princess' mind worked. She was the inheritor of the throne, and Ishla traded low quill sums for freshwater from Eli's country. Striking an early bond with her could be his key to success. Once he became a member of the NGRC, perhaps he could convince her to see his ways, convince her that her father was a money-grubbing con. A favorable outcome was unlikely, he knew. She was bred from the same cloth and undoubtedly groomed to become Queen, fed the same rancid philosophies that her father held.

She responded with a shrug and an off-putting tone. "I've been blessed by the stars. I suppose that's how I know."

Othelia sped ahead as they neared the examiners. Ah, yes. He'd revealed a little too soon that he knew her language, and subsequently, who she was. Eli couldn't help it; he'd understood her Ishlish proclamation perfectly, and he *had* to respond with their royal greeting.

He'd been filled with giddy excitement ever since he guessed Ishla during the pre-exam. Eli knew it was unlikely to run into her, but he couldn't resist entertaining the possibility and looked around for her every chance he got. And then somewhere the stars aligned, and it happened.

So far, she wasn't like he expected, namely because she'd saved him a number of times. If he knew the rich, and he knew them well, she was a snob in disguise and one who didn't care for other people. He'd thought she would want endless attention, too, but then she asked to stay anonymous. Of course, Eli also noticed Abel Casterral and Samuel Sandoval loitering about, which meant little Miss Othelia was hiding from them. But why?

They stood around with a clump of participants, quiet and attentive. The breeze was sharp here, and the relentless wind made his face flush and numb. A tall building stood a few yards from the beach, exterior lights hanging above the long and wide windows. The rooms beyond were dark and ominous.

The Exam Leader swept her flashlight over the crowd of onlookers; her lips curved into a frown. "Hm, that's all of you?" She released a sigh. "Well, no matter. Some years are less gifted than others. Please, follow us."

And thus began their ascension up a small but rocky hill. The climb became an increasing hassle; his palms began to bleed from tiny, shallow cuts. He reached the top and wiped his hands against his pants, panting and wincing at the searing burn the scratches made. His palms were covered in mud and blood, the idea of infection making him gag.

Beyond the hill was flat land with thick strands of grass stretching past his knees. The building loomed ahead with dark red double doors. Alarms went off in his head. The examiner clicked off the flashlight. He panicked, adrenaline triggering his fight or—let's face it—flight.

In the darkness, something gleamed in his peripherals. He searched and—there—he saw a piece of yellow reflective tape on a contestant's shoulder. It occasionally got caught in the moonlight before disappearing again. He took a deep breath, trying to get his nerves under control. The process was slow and agonizing. After being attacked back on the boat, he couldn't completely shake the terror that hung over him. Potential death was everywhere, and he was not adequately prepared.

He needed to engage in conversation before his thoughts drove him insane. Eli came up beside Othelia and did just that. "So, you didn't get any sleep?"

"No," she said with a suspicious eye. If there'd been trust between them, it'd been broken the moment he spoke Ishlish. A fixable error, he hoped. "But it's alright. I feel fine."

"You should've woken someone up. One of us could've helped." He was surprised she offered to row in the first place.

"A lady can make her own decisions," she said sharply. "I'm fine."

"Right, sorry." Eli focused on his scraped hands, running a

finger over each cut delicately. His hands were colder than the air around them and they worked to soothe the aching.

His fingers were trembling. He hadn't realized they were shaking until then. Come to think of it, he was still damp all over, and his shoes sloshed with every step. He'd forgotten about getting tossed into the ocean. And it'd happened because of Othelia, too. Perhaps he should've felt mad.

Instead, he said, "I didn't mean it like that, uh, I just meant. You know. You can ask me for help if you need it."

His inability to talk sent a bright blush to his cheeks. Thankfully, it was hidden by the darkened sky, though it was embarrassing, nonetheless. He could speak in front of a thousand strangers during his graduation, but talking to one princess and he was stuttering like a fool? Felix and Iris would laugh if they saw him now.

"Thanks," she said. "You can help by not drawing attention to me."

Eli looked around, trying to spot the other contestants. He could hear scattered chatter throughout the area, black blobs against more blackness. It was kind of scary, hearing the grass rustle but being unable to see who or what caused it. He had to remind himself that he had a group of people he believed in and if they were to be attacked, he was safely surrounded.

From what he could tell, no one was in their vicinity. "I think you're fine out here. No one seems to be paying us any mind."

She inhaled slowly. "That's something you simply don't know. Anybody could be listening."

"Fair." He admired her apprehension. "But what would be the benefit of listening in if we talked about non-secret things, like say, what's your favorite thing to do?"

He could've sworn he felt a long and hard glare from her.

"I'm glad you asked. My most favorable of hobbies is walking in silence."

With that, Eli took the hint and kept his mouth shut, absorbing the silence. The quiet was truly torturous. He reached for his flip phone to check the time and pulled away with dismay. It'd been swept away at sea when he'd fallen off the lifeboat. Classic.

A wave of panic washed over him, and he checked his front pockets. His shoulders relaxed when his fingers brushed against the cool metal of his flask. His super-secret flask with just enough taq for six swigs. He took one now, discreetly tipping back his head. Eli didn't feel much by it—his tolerance was becoming uncomfortably high—but every inch of him yearned for a drink. He needed to feel the burn of his throat as it went down.

It was pathetic, he knew. "Leo, the time?"

"One in the morning."

Galen whistled for the second time that night but offered no words in return.

"Stars, do you think we'll get a chance to sleep?" Othelia asked, a twinge of fatigue bleeding through. Would phase two start right away? He didn't know if he could handle two or three sleepless days. He was the type who needed all nine hours of rest to be fully energized for any given day. But Galen and Othelia were in more worrisome shape than Eli. They must've exhausted themselves from the rowing and the fighting. Surely, they wouldn't survive.

The red doors were bigger up close. Much, much bigger, and above them hung a string of bright blue letters that read 'Broadcastia.'

He couldn't resist pointing to the name and whispering to the others, "This is a TV/radio show studio. They're most popular for game shows if I do recall, and I do."

"Do you think that means…" Leo began.

Eli grinned. "One can hope."

Where was Broadcastia located again? Off the shores of… the country of… it was no use. He couldn't recall.

They filed in, one after the other. The lights had been flicked on by Marcia—no, that name didn't sound right—the Exam Leader, revealing a suspiciously normal lobby and a single hallway lined with doors. The floor was decorated with black-and-white tiles. Many of them were engraved with words. Names, he noticed. Names with birthdates and deathdates. Some had quotes. He shuddered. It was too morbid for him.

Eli shifted his gaze to take in his surroundings, examining the vacant receptionist desk, atop which were fresh purple flowers sprinkled with white spots. Leo came up beside him and stroked his chin. "Wow, I've never seen a pentail up close."

Eli's eyebrows shot up. "Know a lot about flowers?"

Leo nodded. "I farm flowers back home. Grew a liking for them. Pentails have unique petals that look lik—"

"Let me guess—tails?"

Leo nodded. "And they're supposed to smell like oak."

"So, you like flowers and you farm. Are you from Edna?"

Leo hesitated to answer, his inability to trust anyone seeping from his pores. Eli resisted rolling his eyes. "Well, at least your attire and farmer's tan make sense now."

Eli moved closer to the flowers, ready to take a whiff when the Exam Leader stood on top of the front desk and tapped a tiny bell. The packed room became hushed, and all eyes gravitated toward her.

"Right," she said, pulling out a black top hat from behind the desk. "You'll be working in groups of two. You must pick your partner. Then one of you will come up here and draw a number. That will determine what room you'll compete in."

Rationally speaking, he should've reached for Leo or

Isabelle. After all, they'd solved the pre-exam together. And yet, he found himself turning his head toward Othelia. "Would y—"

Othelia was no longer by his side. Instead, she was next to Isabelle, their arms interlocked. Warmth spread to his face, and he turned to Leo, confident he would say yes. But Galen seized the moment and grabbed Leo's arm gently and looked Eli directly in the eyes with a cocky smile. "He's mine."

Eli sighed, supposing this was karma the stars placed on him for not electing to save the ship. What was he supposed to do now? He didn't want to work with anyone else. And what if he was wrong, and the phase was really a one-on-one fight? Eli didn't bring a weapon, thinking he'd be able to use his wits to get out of situations. He was screwed. Overconfident and talentless.

His self-talk was unacceptable. A politician should never fear the inevitable. They should embrace it and adapt.

Eli waved his hands above his head. He was already squished against the desk at arm's length from the Exam Leader. People were crowding her, fighting to pick a room number first. Her eyes skimmed over the herd but didn't acknowledge him. Instead, in absolute suddenness, she cut her free hand through the air and pulled the top hat away from their hungry hands. "Enough!"

The contestants stopped, but it was too late. She pointed a bony finger at the three people closest to her. "The three of you are out. Leave. You'd make the Expedition Overseer title look foolish."

They gaped at her. The Exam Leader shooed them away with a flick of the wrist, disdain in her sneering lip.

"Excuse me," said one, "but I'm not goin'ta leave until I get a real explanation! I've done nothing wrong!"

Two of the male examiners shoved through the crowd,

their brawny bodies bigger and taller than anyone there, and stopped at the three men she'd pointed at. The examiners grabbed them by the wrists. Although they struggled and hissed incoherent swears, they were unsuccessful in breaking free and were tossed out into the night.

The Exam Leader's gaze shifted to Eli as the crowd of people remained settled in their spots. Well, stars, this wasn't good. Her eyes were piercing into his soul. She kept the hat raised out of the participants' reach, who had all become tame and respectful. "And what did you want? Or were your motives the same as theirs?"

Eli stared up at her in stunned silence. He didn't like this feeling, the clenching of his stomach as his nerves soured. Sweat slid down his temples as he became increasingly aware of how hot the room was. How did he expect to get anything done if he kept listening to his nerves? This was foolish. He'd had no problem approaching Leo after witnessing such bravery. He usually had no problem with approaching people, so why should this time be any different? Eli relaxed his shoulders.

"Oh, pardon me, no," he said, oozing charm with a courteous smile. "It appears I don't have a partner. Would it be possible to do the next phase alone?"

She shook her head while lowering the hat once more. "Wait until everyone else has chosen rooms, then. If there's an odd number of you, you can certainly work alone. Though, I wouldn't say that's the ideal choice."

"I'll be your partner," a voice said behind him. Eli turned to find a silver-haired man in a silver suit approaching from the crowd. He looked to be of Eli's age, his smile and demeanor dashing.

Eli felt his nerves calm. He hadn't noticed anyone resembling his age before, and the guy looked kind enough.

The man stretched out his hand. "Raphael."

"Eli," he took Raphael's hand. "Thank you for saving me there."

Raphael smiled. "Why, of course. Anything for a man of great taste."

Eli peered down at his suit. He'd worn the one his father suggested, handsewn by a famous designer. He'd attracted quite a fellow. Eli wasn't one to keep up with the fashion world, but he could guess Raphael's attire was made from a similar source.

"So do you, my friend. Where are you traveling from?"

"An island. It's been newly populated—Abberstein. And yourself?"

Eli's eyes widened. "You're an heir of Harrington, then? I wasn't aware the Kingship approved the 7th family. And I'm a citizen of New Guayi. Moved there when my father bought out BrillCruise."

Raphael smiled again, something gleaming in his pale green eyes. "The Kingship is announcing it today. I'm surprised you know of Abberstein."

Eli nodded with a smile and opened his mouth to speak before getting cut off by the examiner.

Their attention moved to her as the room grew quiet. "You will now pick your rooms for the next phase."

People began forming a line quietly in front of the examiner, picking numbers out of a hat one by one. Eli lingered by the hallway while Raphael stood in line. He'd been partnered with—no, chosen by—a royal. He was in an unnerving situation. There wasn't enough information about the Harrington family to gauge if they were worth winning over or not. He'd have to stay on his toes.

"Good luck," Leo said as he and the other three passed.

"If this has anything to do with fighting, you'll need it,"

Othelia said with a sly smirk, walking away before he could retort.

He prayed to the stars that the next phase wasn't fighting. His entire career counted on passing this exam, and he didn't want to wait another six months to try again. His family didn't care if he won or not—they thought it was a pointless endeavor. In fact, his father begged him not to go. Eli was meant to help with the family business and eventually make his own.

Becoming an O-MC—the title of a Master Class Overseer —wasn't needed to become an entrepreneur, especially with a family who could fit any bill. There were Average Classes he could take instead, but Eli couldn't settle for average.

Most people cared more about the money they received from passing the International Exam than the EO-MC-T that came with it—a bar code tattooed to the left wrist if you passed the exam and became an Expedition Overseer. It would be shining gold if he passed, dull green if he'd taken an Average Class exam. This perk wasn't advertised to the public, for reasons unknown, but Eli had connections, and those connections led to finding out why such a thing was to exist. But none of that was important right now.

"Five," Raphael said as he approached, holding the paper up between two fingers. His smooth voice bounced off the walls as the lobby thinned out.

"I bet five will be my new lucky number," Eli said.

Their dress shoes clanked against the concrete floor as they made their way down the hall to room five. He ran his fingers along the mouthpiece of his flask, desperate for another swig. Resistance was key.

A silver plaque beside a dark red door read their assigned number and underneath was the title of 'showroom.' There were no indications of life on the other side of that closed door, and he decided it was best not to hesitate. Get it over with. He turned the knob and walked in.

Words bounced off the walls and remained so as they entered, yet he'd heard nothing until then. Strange. The room had four raised floors, each with a row of chairs. The chairs were separated into six pairs per floor, and there was one pair left open. First row, third in from the right. There were the exact number of seats necessary for the contestants. No more, no less.

A thin, muscular woman with two black pigtails stood at the head of the room behind a podium. The podium went up to her stomach, and she bore a name tag on the left side of her shirt. When he squinted, he could barely read the name, 'Liviola.' She smiled at him, a spring in her step as she spoke. "Ah, the last group! Please, sit!"

Eli examined the other participants. There were eleven other groups, twenty-two people. He spotted Othelia and Isabelle sitting in the top right corner; Leo and Galen weren't there. Othelia didn't appear to notice him walk in, but Isabelle waved. He smiled in acknowledgment but didn't spare a wave back. After all, Othelia didn't want attention drawn to her, and he was a man of his word.

On their vacant seats were black, metallic boxes with a red button in their centers. Three was written in white on each side of both. Everyone else had a box, too, though their numbers were different. Eli picked it up and sat down; Raphael followed suit.

"This shall be fun," Raphael said, examining the box. "A multiple-choice test, perhaps?"

"Did you train at all?"

Raphael shook his head. "I thought the exam would solely be fighting. I fear I focused on the wrong thing. And you?"

Eli smiled. "A bit. We'll see how far it takes us."

"Let's begin!" Liviola said cheerfully, tossing a hand in the air dramatically. The contestants stared at her with blank expressions as they exuded exhaustion and consternation.

"I am Exam Leader 2E, Liviola Ovelent. Welcome to late-night trivia! There are fifteen questions. Each question is worth 1 point. If you get the answer wrong, it'll cost 2! The top five groups will move on to phase three! To answer, press your button. The person who reacts first goes first! Does anyone have any questions?"

She waited along with Eli. He expected someone else to ask, but when no one did, he raised his hand. She pointed to him. "Group 3?"

"After we hit the buzzer, is there a time limit for our answer?"

Liviola winked and added with a giggle, "Ah! Good one, I forgot! You get fifteen seconds to answer! Oh, and keep your buzzer numbers in my field of vision so we can keep track of your scores!"

Eli wasn't sure how his trivia skills ranked among others. He liked to know current events and some geography, but that was where his expertise ended. And boats. He knew one too many things about boats.

The wall behind Liviola lit up. He looked around, searching for the source of the projection and coming up empty-handed. Five categories appeared, each with three question marks vertically stacked underneath. From left to right, Liviola read them aloud. "Geography. Plants and Animals. World Government. First Aid. History."

Damn. No boats.

Still, the world government category would work in both his and Raphael's favor, and maybe geography and history would, too. He got this. He just had to believe. Eli took a deep breath and envisioned answering all the categories correctly. Sweat less, envision more.

"Excuse me." Raphael raised his hand, and the examiner pointed to him. "What happens if we don't pass this phase?"

She winked with a wide smile spread across her lips. "You die, of course."

Eli gulped. He supposed he should've expected such an answer, but it hadn't crossed his mind. Murdered for simply not knowing trivia? Adrenaline coursed through him—or perhaps it was fear.

"The order of choosing a category starts with group 1, and we'll go in numerical order," Liviola continued. "Oh, and last rule, I swear! If your teammate buzzes, you both can answer within those fifteen seconds! All right, sir, care to start?" She pointed to group 1.

The first man was middle-aged and wore a skin-tight tank top, bulky muscles protruding from his sleeves. Stubbles of brown hair erupted from his chin and above his upper lip, and he was tall, at least six-foot-three. His partner was the polar opposite; a young woman with a long braid, no taller than four feet, and legs too short to reach the floor from her seat.

She reminded Eli of a doll his ten-year-old sister would play with. Alyssa only had girl dollies, and she loved to make them kiss more than anything else. Eli would only play with her if she begged, and he'd set the same rule every time: romance was off-limits. He wasn't asked to play often.

The buff contestant cleared his throat. "Geography."

Underneath the category, the top question mark faded to gray, and the screen changed to reveal the first question. "We're now standing in 'Broadcastia,'" Liviola read aloud, "famous for their radio game shows. They first began on the shores of Midral, but relocated to the shores of where?"

Aw, damn. He should've known. He pressed the button,

certain he'd figure it out within the time given. But Liviola pointed to a group in the second row. No one in the room breathed. His muscles remained tense as all his focus turned to group 7. The buzzer was a pale, middle-aged man, his brown hair disheveled and full of white lint. His sleeve-less tank revealed a long and blue leviathan tattoo that stretched down his left arm. A bold choice. "The shores of Equive."

Equive. Eli felt a quell of frustration bubble inside as Liviola lifted a finger. "Correct! One point for Group 7!"

The young man high-fived his partner, a girl of similar age with long and curly red hair and a face speckled with freckles.

He brought his attention back to his incompetence. Twelve years of primary education and three years of higher learning, and he still couldn't remember half the things he was supposedly taught. Equive shone brightly in his mind's eye the second he heard it. Did they row that far? He supposed they'd also taken a ship out to sea before being forced into lifeboats, so it was possible. It was easily thirty miles, if not more. But Othelia and Galen rowed the whole way without help. Was that viable?

There was something else that was important on Equive, a landmark of some sort that separated Broadcastia and the port city of San Juale. But he couldn't seem to remember that, either. A desert, maybe? A forest? The answer sat on the tip of his tongue and that's where it was intent on staying.

His memory used to be better. His grades during primary school were stellar, and he'd landed on the honor list every year of higher education. About two percent of students got on the list, and he was one of them. But then he started drinking.

Everyone in his family drank; it was inevitable he'd run into the peer pressure. It was pesky Iris who suggested slipping a shot into his orange juice, and the next thing Eli knew, he was asking for more and more until he was puking on their kitchen floor. And now he suffered the consequences, including a fading memory and a flask in his pocket with a hand itching to reach for it.

Group 2 chose 'First aid,' of which Eli knew nothing about. Fifteen seconds ticked by, and no one buzzed in. Just like that, the point was gone forever.

"Group 3?"

Eli jumped. He hadn't realized it was his turn, and now all eyes were on him.

"Oh, uh." He turned to his partner. "World Government?"

Raphael nodded in agreement. Eli's heart thumped loudly in his ears. This was it. He had to get it right. With a shake in his voice, he said, "World Government, it is."

It felt like minutes before the question appeared, though in reality, it was mere milliseconds. "There are six members of this gro—," Liviola began before being cut off by the sound of two buzzers.

Eli slammed his thumb on the button and stood abruptly, his vision blurred from overwhelming adrenaline and confidence. He opened his mouth as Liviola pointed in Eli's direction. "K—"

"Group 12!" she interjected, her eyes looking past him. "You have buzzed first!"

Eli stilled. He looked like a fool. He sat back down and turned to the group behind him.

His eyes widened.

"The Kingship," Othelia said, keeping her head down and avoiding everyone's gaze entirely in a bold attempt to remain anonymous. He cursed to himself. How much faster had the answer occurred to her?

"Correct! One point for Group 12!"

Eli sighed, and for the next three rounds, both he and the girls didn't answer a single question. Group 7 was having the hardest time now, seeing as they'd gotten the last question wrong and now had a negative score. Group 11 quickly swept up the point, gaining themselves a spot on the board, as well as group 1. But none of them really mattered because they weren't him or his partner. He needed to act, and fast.

It was easier to think than to do. At the seventh question, the third and final round of geography, Eli's ears perked up, and he found that familiar adrenaline coursing through him once again. "A country known for its expansive, lush fields. The only things native here are cows and farmers."

Eli pressed the buzzer halfway through the question and then again when she was finished reading it off. He prayed to the stars above and to the constellations. If there was any time to prove a higher power, it would be now.

And then her finger was pointing at him. And the words, "Group 3," were called from her lips. He forgot how to speak, his jaw locked as everything around him disappeared and his mind focused on Liviola's pointed finger.

"Edna." The air he'd stored in his lungs came out in a powerful burst. Time seemed to stand still as it ticked away.

"Correct! One point for group 3!"

His shoulders relaxed, and he slumped back in his seat. Finally, he'd been able to give an answer. Eli had Leo to thank for that question.

"I certainly picked a suitable partner," Raphael said. "I need to get my head in the game. Especially with that little princess over there."

Eli gaped at him, unsure of what to say. There were two routes he could go, and he decided on the boldest. He regained composure and said, "Ah, you noticed that, too. Abel Casterral and Samuel Sandoval are here as well."

Raphael nodded. "They're nothing. I wouldn't think she is, either, but I was told only Samuel would be participating."

"Is there a reason as to why all the Royal families aren't competing?"

Raphael smiled. "Of course. But I wouldn't know of it or tell you if I did."

"Fair enough," Eli said, setting his mind back on the game. By question thirteen, six groups were tied with one point each, and group 1 had four points. Eli hadn't answered the second world government question, and his partner hadn't answered anything. He was essentially taking this phase alone.

And then there were two questions left, one in First Aid, and the other in Government. The order of choosing a category had looped back down to group 2, who decided on First Aid. "A type of gauze that can help heal broken bones."

He didn't know the answer to that one, either. Eli missed being smart. He missed knowing things and telling people the things he knew. If there was anything to come of this exam, whether he passed or not, he hoped he could walk away with some form of new knowledge.

"Medibreak," someone called out. Eli repeated the word in his head. He'd remember something, at least.

"Final question," Liviola said, immediately reading it off. "Assigned the task of keeping tabs on all other foreign governments, this branch of security is considered quite controversial."

Eli pressed the buzzer without a second thought. The answer flashed through his mind so clearly that he was brimming with confidence.

"Group 10?"

His heart sank. Once again, someone had reacted faster.

The woman took a moment to answer as she contemplated the right thing to say. Her words were separated by drawn-out pauses in a thick Baltarish accent. "The... Continental... Security... Commerce?"

Eli's heart skipped a beat, and he held his breath.

"No, I'm sorry! That's incorrect! Would your partner like to guess?" Their partner, another woman who looked to be sixty with wrinkles and a low hunch, shook her head shamefully. "You now have negative two points." Liviola feigned sadness before turning to Eli. "Group 3? You buzzed second. What is your answer?"

He smiled, blown away by the work of the stars, and said, "Continental Security Commission."

Liviola didn't react at first, allowing suspense to overtake the crowd. His shoulders tensed despite knowing he was right. And then she became fully animated, her smile bigger than before. "Congratulations! Groups 1 and 3 have passed!"

He jumped in the air, slinging a fist into the sky; he wouldn't die today. Eli didn't care how he looked to the others, not now, not when he passed another phase of the exam. All on his own, too. "Yes!"

The rest of the room remained quiet. He whipped around and realized he was the only one celebrating. Not even the other winners were adamant. He blushed and came to his senses. Looking around the room, he was careful to catch the eyes of anyone looking back at him. "I've lost my manners. Forgive me."

Eli sat and looked at Raphael, the man composed with arms crossed over his chest. "A bit overzealous today, are we?"

"A bit," Eli replied abashedly.

Liviola continued, "If I say your number, you have automatically failed and must exit the room."

"Like we'd freely walk to our deaths!" someone yelled from behind. Contestants began standing with vigorous protests and shaking fists. The pale man from group 7 waltzed up to Liviola, a fist reared back to strike. Liviola moved at a quickness unseen by the human eye; her body disappeared from Eli's vision before reappearing behind the man. She wrapped her hands around the back of his head and snapped his neck in one fluid motion. His body fell to the floor in a heap.

The exam room door burst open, and six muscular men and women entered and ushered the failing contestants out. The final woman grabbed the dead body off the floor. Eli gulped, the sight of death replaying in his mind. He would yell if he could get himself to so much as open his mouth. The sound of his neck snapping rang in Eli's ears, muffling the screams that erupted from others.

Liviola turned to them with a smirk. "Please, do not cause a ruckus if you fail. The results will be the same no matter how hard you struggle."

By the time the room was cleared, eight of the original twelve remained, six awaiting their potential demise.

"Those who have yet to pass, all with 1 point, are two, five, six, nine, eleven, and twelve. Those who have already passed must stay until the final round is complete." She paused, building the tension in the room until it was thick and stuffy. "Now it's time for our lightning round! There will be three questions."

A final round. He gulped. Only three groups could move forward, or none at all. He didn't dare look back at Othelia and Isabelle, fearful that his gaze alone would throw them off. Eli glanced at his partner, whose eyes were now closed, his head leaning back against the chair. He was either disappointed in his performance, tired, or bored.

"You no longer need to press the buzzer! Instead, the first person to shout the answer will get their team a point. If you or your partner answer wrong, you'll be eliminated immediately. If you answer a question right, both you *and* your partner will move forward.

"Question 1: *Bestine* is a bright orange fish, known for the toxin it produces, which can stun its prey. This type of fish is most common in which part of the sea?"

"Dead Sea," someone from group 6 called. They were right —of course they were—and they passed.

"Question 2: Forty years ago, Brent Barbo invented what?"

"The electric chair," a shout came. It was followed by, 'incorrect!' and the group members saw themselves out.

"The electric *car*," another yelled, and they were right. Eli's heart dropped. All he could do was listen.

"Question 3: What village is considered barbaric for being the only one to still implement whips?"

"Reinta."

Eli spun around in his seat, a common theme within the last hour, and Isabelle was standing with her eyes locked on Liviola. They burned with fury, a passion behind her actions he hadn't seen before. "And we're people, you know. Different does not mean 'barbaric.'"

Raphael's attention had been seemingly grabbed by Isabelle, his eyebrows shooting up as he looked at her. Eli's attention had long since drifted to Othelia. Her face was peeking out from under her hood, her soft chin pointed up at Isabelle as she watched the display of defiance. Her blue eyes were the most striking, a lightness akin to ice.

Eli swung his attention back to Liviola. Now was not the time to stare in awe at someone both more beautiful and more powerful than he. That, and he couldn't help his seeping hatred for her father. It bled into how he looked at her, and he was disgusted at the idea of thinking of her as anything other than a novice.

The smile dropped from Liviola's face for a brief blink and then returned in full. "Correct! You're the final group to pass! Groups 11, 5, and 2, I'm sorry, but you're out. Please leave the trivia room."

There were protests—death awaited them, after all—but Eli chose not to listen. It was best to avoid the reminders that they could die for failing a phase. Eli took this opportunity to hop up the stairs and stand beside Isabelle, Raphael trailing behind. Defying his own thoughts, he looked at Othelia instantly. As he approached, her left leg was leaning against the chair in front of her, the other planted on the ground.

To Isabelle, he said, "Thank the stars. I was nervous you wouldn't make it."

Isabelle huffed and crossed her arms. "The disrespect. They really said 'barbaric?'"

"Tya-kyt," Raphael said, and Isabelle's attention snapped to him, a dumbfounded look overtaking her features.

"You know my language?"

Raphael smiled. "I do. It's quite beautiful. My mother is from Reinta."

"What did he say?" Othelia asked, trying to repeat the Urkinian word and failing. "I don't know that one."

She didn't seem to recognize Raphael. Was she pretending not to know him?

"Tya-kyt. Idiots," Isabelle responded with a smile.

Othelia nodded toward Liviola, who returned to the front of the room. "Tell her. You can't expect things to get done if you don't do them."

There was a moment of hesitation, but then Isabelle gave a sharp nod. She exchanged pleasantries with Raphael before confronting Liviola. When she was gone, Eli sat beside Othelia and propped a foot on a chair right alongside her. He could feel Raphael watching and listening, and Eli expected him to. They were both mesmerized by the addition of the princess to the exam.

"You know, you stole a point from me." He looked ahead

but couldn't resist taking a spare sideways glance. She was smirking but had an eyebrow raised in confusion.

"Rightfully took it, actually. Stealing would imply I didn't play by the rules."

"Hey," he said with a playful smile. "You're the one who said it, not me."

CHAPTER 13
LEO

THE FIRST POINT Leo earned was in the plants and animals' category. A light blue flower that grew in the snow and shriveled up in rain. "Amalyse."

"Correct," said the host, Dominic. He was stout and of medium height, his skin the color of charcoal. He wore a peculiar hat that Leo had never seen before, flat with a small bill protruding out the front. It was bright red, while the man's loose pants and shirt were creamy white. He sat attentively in the front, an arm lazily resting on the podium beside him. "One point for group 6!"

Galen gave Leo a low-five and whispered, "Nice! I got the next one."

The next four questions were all answered correctly by Abel and his blond partner, whom Leo hadn't noticed until entering the room. He wasn't sure how he'd missed the new man, but now the blond was engrained in Leo's mind as a potentially lethal opponent. Both he and Abel were dressed formally and carried themselves as if they were of high importance. His light blond hair and bright blue eyes heavily contrasted with his dark, tawny skin. And, on top of working with Abel, he'd already answered two questions.

Almost everyone in their room had gotten one question right. The groups who failed to do so were overzealous and cocky, guessing without thinking of the repercussions. The bucktoothed, short man two seats down had quite the trigger finger and dragged his team's points down to negative five.

"Sorry," Dominic said, his voice nasally and low with just enough energy to sound like he cared. "You guys might as well be out, so I'm going to ask you both to head back to the lobby. You've failed the exam."

Seeing people get kicked out increased the pressure. Leo's body was unequivocally paralyzed. All he wanted was to see and talk to his parents—wanted to know what they thought of his decisions, and if he was making the right ones. On the lifeboat, Leo had dreamed of milking cows with his mother, of all things, and he could hear her raised and reprimanding voice from that dream now. *"Don't you ever risk your life like that again. If you do, I'll disown you."*

His stomach gurgled then, memories of her endless pies filling his thoughts. Hot cinnamon apple and banana cream, burning his palette but tasting too good to stop eating. Just yesterday, he couldn't think of pie without getting nauseous. Now it was all he wanted.

He needed to stop thinking and focus on the exam. There were only two more questions.

"Our second-to-last is in the combat category," Dominic exclaimed. "This type of move involves the act of erasing your presence and is often referred to as 'stalking.'"

Leo hadn't noticed Galen's reaction, hadn't seen how quickly he pressed the red button underneath his thumb. But Dominic pointed to them, and Galen answered with a smirk, "Tip-toeing."

Leo raised his eyebrows as Dominic exclaimed, "Correct! Another point for group 6!"

"That's not fair! I buzzed first, sir," a girl with curly red hair yelled. Her hand was waving in the air sporadically, her freckled face upset and determined to voice it. She pointed to Galen with an unexplainable hostility. "I knew that answer!"

Her partner grabbed her by the wrist lightly, his moon-shaped eyes filled with terror and his thick brows drawn together. He wore a tight red jumpsuit that emphasized his stomach rolls and large appendages. "The point ain't worth it, Mari. They ain't worth the hassle."

She turned to him. "You don't speak for the examiner. And don't give away my identity, *Kiel*. Why do you sabotage us every time, huh? It's like you want us to fail."

He removed his grasp from her and looked away with an angered flush. "That's enough, Ma—team member. I try just as hard as anyone else that participates."

She either didn't catch his words or blatantly ignored them. "There's no point in calling me a team member now, jackass. You've already said my name."

Dominic sighed and motioned with an extended, flat palm for her to sit down. She did so with an exaggerated huff as Dominic said, "You are correct in that no one speaks for me but me, and I've already spoken, have I not? The two newbies get the point."

Mari gave Leo and Galen a pointed glare. Leo looked away; he hated the thought of having enemies. Instead, he focused on Galen, who smugly peered back at her. Galen was strange, but Leo liked how fascinating that made him. "You know a lot about combat?"

"I know a fair bit. It runs in the family." Galen's smooth voice brought Leo back to the present, where they existed with two points and a golden ticket into the next phase.

"Combat runs in the family?"

"Something like that."

Leo smiled. "Is that why you're taking the exam? Your family?"

"More or less."

"Me, too. Minus the combat."

"You don't fight?"

"Not at all."

Galen's mouth hung open. "I should've known when you froze back there. How do you expect to pass the exam?"

Leo shrugged off his embarrassment. "Wits? Luck? I came with a knife. That's worth somethin', right? And, say, shouldn't exams omit fighting to the death?"

Galen laughed at that, and Leo felt a rush of red erupt to his cheeks. "Not this kind of exam. Wow, are you only here for the money? There's more to it, you know. Tiers to become powerful, depending on the type of power you want. An EO is tier one."

"I've never heard of tiers. What's the point?"

"What's the point of anything? To have power. Overseers exist beyond the World Government. They obtain *real* power. Real control. EOs exist to conquer and discover new lands. That's their point. And sometimes you need to kill to conquer."

"Whose land are we conquering?"

Galen shook his head. "So, why are you taking the exam? If you don't want the title, what do you want?"

"To clear a debt."

"Oh."

"Oh?"

"I just thought there'd be a more exciting reason than that."

"Sorry to bore." The conversation ended there, and

Dominic read off the last question. Although neither of them knew the answer, they passed with two points along with three other groups.

Dominic looked around the room sheepishly. "It looks like we went over the five-group quota. Oh, well. Congratulations! You've moved on to phase three! But first, you get some time to rest! Gentlemen, come with me! Ladies, Exam Leader 2C will arrive shortly to escort you to your rooms."

Someone with a sharp jawline and long black hair raised their hand. Dominic did not wait for the question to be posed and answered. "If you identify as other, someone will come for you shortly as well and you'll have your own, separate room. Please make sure you are verified as 'other' on your identification card."

"And if I don't have that?"

"You must be verified as 'other' to stay in that room."

"But—"

"Those are the rules. No exceptions. Please, take it up with Emmarcia if you have a complaint. Gentlemen, come with me." Dominic did not address the concern any further and hobbled toward the door. Leo and Galen followed him through the hallway and into the lobby. It was spacious now, no longer uncomfortably sweaty, and they could break away from the other victors.

Dominic stopped them there. "We'll need to wait until all the games are done—we're waiting for one more room."

Some victors were already waiting in the lobby, but it was far less packed than it had been earlier in the night. He checked his wristwatch. 3:30 in the morning. How had time moved so quickly? It didn't matter, because Dominic said they could rest. Sleep. He could only dream of sleep.

Leo looked around the lobby for Eli, but he wasn't there. Disappointment penetrated his thoughts, and his shoulders went slack. He stood on the tip of his toes to see over contestants' heads—there were twenty or so—but he was far too short. Leo sucked in a breath and tried to look on the bright side. He'd passed phase two, and so had Galen. Maybe the girls made it. He'd have to wait until morning to find out.

"How are you feeling?" Leo asked. They stood by the receptionist's desk, next to the pentails. He simply loved their smell. "You must be tired."

Galen leaned his elbows against the countertop, facing the contestants. "As you would expect. I should be ready to go after a few hours of rest."

"Your arms aren't sore? You rowed for two hours straight. And those bruises…"

"It was four hours, actually. Four hours straight. And I could do it for two more before actually getting tired."

"Does that run in the family, too?" Leo joked.

Galen chuckled. "Now you're getting it."

His face grew serious, and he looked around to see if anyone was eavesdropping. Leo looked along with him, finding Abel and his companions conversing in the corner. "But listen," Galen whispered. "That girl who was rowing with me? She was pushing faster. I hate to admit it, but she's way stronger than me. And she didn't look too tired, either."

"What are you suggesting?"

"What if she's like him, like that man over there? What if she's abnormal, too?"

That wasn't an idea that occurred to Leo. In fact, he'd forgotten about what Abel had done, how he'd pushed Isabelle through the air with some invisible force. "I'm not sure. We'll have to find a way to ask her."

How, though, he didn't know. Usually, he would pry for anyone's name and life story, but the mysterious girl threw him off, and he couldn't explain why. Surprisingly, he was largely disinterested in her, and it felt mutual.

"If she and Abel can do the same thing, that means others can, too. How do you think it works? Mag, you think?"

Leo shook his head. "That's impossible. The notion of humans using mag has been debunked time and time again. Mag is simply a natural nutrient for plants and animals, an additive to their health, but nothing more than that. Our bodies don't absorb it; mag doesn't affect us."

Galen bit at the edge of his thumbnail. "I don't know a lot about mag. One of my sisters was an MO/MC—a master class magical items collector—a few years back, but I never asked her about it. I should have."

"Sisters? How many do you have?"

"Four. Three older, one younger. And a younger brother, too."

Leo's brows shot up. He envisioned the amount of noise that must've gone into the daily life of six siblings, the contrast of their youth. Leo and his sister barely talked anymore, and she hardly came home. She probably wouldn't find out Leo had left until a few weeks after he got back.

"That's a lot," Leo opted to say, unenthused to share his lackluster experiences with a single sibling. "Almost too much, I'd say."

"Almost."

"The final group is finished and on their way to the rooms. Follow me, lads," Dominic said with a sweeping motion of his hand to follow. They were led down the same hallway as before, then down two long corridors before reaching large brass double doors. Inside the large room were cots. They were evenly spaced along the walls, lined with windows out of reach and overhead lights centered on the ceiling. Two giant ceiling fans whizzed round and round. It didn't take too long for him to get dizzy from staring at them.

"We've made the official count," Dominic announced. "There are fifty of you left. Thirteen women, thirty-one men, and six others. You may pick your beds."

Leo and Galen chose two cots under a barred window; the Kiel guy was beside Leo, and on Galen's side was a tall and muscular middle-aged man in a skin-tight tank top Leo hadn't noticed before. The tiny mattresses came with a thin blue blanket and an unfluffed pillow. He grimaced as he tested the pillow with his hand. It completely deflated, his palm connecting with the mattress on the other side. He was beginning to suspect the examiners didn't want them to sleep.

He spotted Abel and his group on the other side. They were sitting on their cots and chatting. The blond was showing off a golden sword. Light from the overhead bulbs reflected off of the smooth and shiny metal. The men were too enthralled in their own words to notice Leo watching them.

Beside him, Galen scanned the room silently. He was oddly quiet and soft-spoken, yet he wasn't afraid to confront ideas and other people. He clearly wasn't harmless; the blood of others on his face and the bruises on his knuckles were proof of that, but he didn't look to be manipulating Leo, either. And Galen had come back to help them, while Leo stood there, frozen. Isabelle had yelled at him, her words muffled behind a wall of fear, a type of fear he could not explain. It overwhelmed every sense, and suddenly he'd found himself unable to move.

Leo spotted Emmarcia standing in the doorway, seemingly undetected by others. Her eyes found him, and she smiled before she turned and left, disappearing along with any indication of when the next phase would begin. What if sleep was a ruse and the third phase began in a matter of minutes?

The creaking of a door grabbed his attention. His head

snapped to the right, where he noticed a rounded green door. 'Bathroom' was scrolled down the center in five different languages. He caught sight of the door in mid-swing, and Eli sprouted from the other side. Leo waved the man over with an exhale of relief.

Eli caught his eye and approached. He'd taken his suit coat off and it dangled around his forearm. His tie dangled around his neck loosely; the white shirt underneath was long-sleeved and tight, tucked into his formal trousers and held together by a thick black belt. As he got closer, Leo noticed Eli's shoes and socks were in hand. His bare feet slapped against the concrete floor.

His hair was now composed of loose clumps entangled in a web atop his head. Most curious were the red and bruising rims around his neck, but Leo thought it best not to ask about them. As Eli approached, a silver-haired man passed him on his way to the bathroom and tapped Eli across the chest with a smile. "See you in the next phase."

Eli nodded back cordially and said with a matching smile, "Assuming no one kills us in our sleep."

The silver-haired man laughed. "Not on my watch. I'll make sure of it."

Leo watched curiously but stopped himself from inquiring further. Eli was quick at making friends, it seemed. Perhaps too quick. The silver-haired man, as Leo recalled, had been the one who'd frightened Magenta Marigold before Leo had boarded the ship.

"You guys made it!" Eli said as he stood at the end of their cots, looking down with hands on his hips and a silly grin. "Thank the stars; I thought you'd end up dead! What'd you end up scoring?"

"Dead?" Galen asked.

Eli's lips parted in surprise. "Your examiner didn't tell you? The penalty for losing was death."

Leo's heart nearly stopped as he remembered the group that'd been kicked out. They didn't know they were going to die and had left willingly. The Examiners were ruthless; he was a fool to think otherwise.

"We scored two points," Leo said, trying his best to get his potential fate off of his mind. "One each. You?"

"Two points, all me." Eli pointed at himself. "Isabelle and Madame Mystery had to compete in the lightning round, but they passed too."

"Who was that guy?" Galen asked, undeterred as Leo had been. Great minds think alike, Leo thought, as he watched Eli's reaction carefully. Was their group being played by him?

But if there was any hesitation in Eli, he didn't show it. "Raphael, my partner in the last phase. You know, the phase you all ditched me in."

"I guess we were making up for how you handled the first phase," Leo retorted.

They ended up discussing the entire match, rehashing everything they could remember. Eli sat at the end of Leo's cot as the night wore on, their voices gradually becoming hushed as more people went to sleep.

"You had world government?" Galen asked. "That would've been a nightmare."

"Uh, how? Politics is the single most interesting thing on this planet, and you cannot convince me otherwise," Eli rebutted. "And it's always helpful to know the political layout of any country you step foot on."

Galen snorted. "Someone that invested in politics must be involved in them themselves."

Eli cocked his head with a look of scrutiny but didn't give any indication of the validity of Galen's assumption. Leo wasn't going to ask—it wasn't his place to—but curiosity itched at the back of his brain and the question was blurted before he could process his actions. "Where?"

"Come again?"

Leo took a deep breath, feeling his chest rise and fall ever so slowly. "Where would you, you know, do... your political... things?"

Leo winced at his own question. He didn't know or care to learn the political structures of other countries, but he knew Edna's well enough; they were under the rule of the Farmers Directive Board, which mostly collected taxes and piled on the debt of farmers. Citizens, as far as he knew, had every right imaginable, barring crimes, of course, and they had the lowest levels of crime, because no one bothered to visit, and they were all too busy tending to their own farms.

"I think he means what type of position would you have? If you were a politician?" Galen added with a sigh. He didn't appear to care for Eli, or his answers, all too much.

"I want to join the NGRC," Eli whispered. "That's the New Guayi Republic Committee. Twelve members who serve 5 years each. The voting is staggered to every other year for new candidates. That's where I'm from, New Guayi. They have complete control over the country. I want to be a part of it."

To say Leo was surprised would be an understatement. He wanted to be a politician for the ability to control? That didn't sound like Eli. But as Leo thought, and he thought hard, he realized Eli had been the one to confront him first. And he'd been the one to befriend, or at the very least, recruit, the mysterious girl and that silver-haired man he'd partnered with.

He was confident and unafraid to do what he thought was good for himself. Suspicion grew in Leo's gut. Maybe he was right all along, and Eli was using him.

Leo asked the very sudden question of, "Why?"

Eli cracked a smile and leaned in. Galen and Leo drifted closer to him with eager ears. "I want to destroy the rich by infiltrating their decision-making. Did you know that 80% of the population is in poverty? How is that possible? How did it get that way?"

Leo knew only from the vague teachings his mother had given him. Hearing the country's name brought back images of the historical text he'd been forced to read. He sifted through the information, picturing the pages and words with perfect clarity; a mental image of page 25 revealed a gigantic wall around a lush kingdom, where the rich lived. Outside the wall were shacks made of wood that lined the muddy streets. They used buckets instead of toilets, which would have to be tossed in gutters. Rats, cats, and dogs alike scurried down the street and fed freely, and it wasn't uncommon for epidemics to overtake the towns.

"I've watched people die," Eli continued, his voice strained, "at the hands of greed. It's disgusting."

His disgust, however, quickly dissipated as he smiled, tapping Galen on the shoulder. "What about you?"

Galen provided his own smirk, but it looked more nervous than cocky. "That's classified."

Eli wrinkled his nose. "I told you my secret. Why not return the favor?"

"No one forced you to."

"You both know why I'm here, too," Leo added quickly. "My family is in debt."

Galen raised a brow. "Are you trying to convince me?"

He nodded. "You're next."

Galen's shoulders tensed, perhaps unexpecting of Leo's forwardness. Leo didn't mean to pry—well, actually; he did. He just felt bad about it.

Galen turned his gaze away, staring straight ahead. They sat in silence for a few seconds, Leo and Eli clinging to their hope of knowing.

The boy closed his eyes and released an agonizingly long breath. "It's a family tradition. For us, when you turn eighteen, you pass the exam."

"And if you don't?" Eli asked.

There was a longer pause as Galen seemed to contemplate his next words. He was just as cautious as any other man in the room. Leo watched him attentively; Galen's eyes lowered, and he fiddled with the loose skin on his index finger. Finally, Galen said, "When you turn eighteen, you pass. That's just how it is."

"That's a... unique family tradition," Leo said.

"Wait, I know you," someone interrupted from behind. They all turned to find Kiel pointing at Galen. His eyes were still round and terrified, but for different reasons now. "I mean, not *you*, but I know your kind."

"His kind?" Eli asked.

Galen frowned and tilted his head. "It's not nice to eavesdrop, you know."

Kiel turned to Leo. "I'd be careful of him. There are families that send their children at eighteen. A bunch of families, not just his. I wouldn't trust him if I were you."

Leo stared at Kiel for a short while, taking in the absurd omen at face value, and said sternly, "Thank you for the concern, but he's been transparent in his needs for passing the exam, and so far, he's been nothing but help."

"For now," Kiel replied.

A female examiner with two black ponytails walked in before the conversation could continue. She clapped her hands and shouted, "It's time to rest! Please, no talking from this point on. If you wish to use the bathroom, it's that door on the far right. You'll have seven hours to sleep. If you kill anyone during this time, you'll be eliminated from this and all future exams! Thank you!"

She clapped three times, and the lights dimmed until the room was pitch black. Leo could feel shuffling at the end of his cot and a body plopped down beside him. An elbow jabbed at his side. Frustrated, he sat up and turned to face the intruder.

"Excuse me?"

"Sorry," Eli whispered. "Hope you don't mind. It's too dark to find an open bed."

"Fine, but keep your elbows on that side, please." Leo rolled over as Eli struggled to get under the covers.

"As long as I get some of this pillow action," Eli whispered. Someone in the room shushed them and they fell silent. It was admittedly hard for Leo to fall asleep at first; he was surrounded by strangers, defenseless, and open to being murdered. Would any of them dare break the rules and kill someone as they slept? Hopefully, no one was that brash. But in this darkness, it would certainly be possible to get away with it.

Eli began snoring beside him, his knee digging into the back of Leo's leg. Leo closed his eyes and envisioned lying in a green pasture, surrounded by flowers, with the sweet and sour scent of nitren in the air. He took a deep breath, releasing his fears as he gently fell asleep under the hot, sunny sky.

INTERMISSION

CHAPTER 14
OTHELIA

ISABELLE SHOVED HER awake. She sat up with a start, peering around at the rest of the ladies. There was a line of women standing outside the bathroom, and Liviola was standing in front of the hallway door. The examiner was dressed in tight black shorts and a shirt, far different from her colorful blouse and white leggings the day prior.

The room they sat in was smaller than she'd care for, each cot scrunched close together. If she hadn't been so tired, she may have complained or slept in the hallway. But she had been exhausted, and she'd fallen asleep the second her head hit the pillow. Her wooly carcass kept her uncomfortably hot and sweaty throughout the night, but she was too paranoid to take it off. She'd even slept with the hood covering her face.

"We can shower," Isabelle said, struggling through the Latarian words. Othelia had translated the phase two questions for Isabelle, her Urkinian good enough to be understood by the native speaker. "They're providing towels, soaps. Breakfast, too."

"I slept through all that?" Othelia asked, rubbing her head. After the energy she exerted the other night, she'd acquired a migraine. A common side effect of using maoho for too long. At first, she rowed without using her power, but her arms grew embarrassingly tired after the first two hours. She didn't want to admit defeat, not when Galen was still rowing with his raw strength. It was unnerving to think someone was stronger than her. He was certainly on her radar. And one day they would have to fight.

Isabelle nodded. "Slept through most of the showers. Three minutes each. You're last."

"How's the water?"

"Amazing," Isabelle sighed with a blissful smile, then added in Urkinian, "Absolutely amazing. In Reinta, we bathe in a river. The same river we drink and fish from."

Othelia crinkled her nose in disgust. "Is that sanitary?"

"Probably not, but there are no other options."

Othelia hadn't thought about bathing in other countries—she'd assumed everyone had a bathing station inside their homes. Each child in the Sandoval house had a private bathroom connected to their bedroom. There was no tub; instead, the ground gradually descended into a drain and a large showerhead hung above. The water was hot and fresh but used sparingly, as most of the island's freshwater was imported from other countries. Five minutes a week were allotted to showering, and to Isabelle that itself was considered a luxury.

"How'd your talk with Liviola go?" Othelia asked, her head continuing to pound. Her arms ached. There was still so much more to be done, but she was overexerting herself. She dreaded not knowing how many phases there were and when this madness would end. She hadn't expected the exam to go like this, not at all. What a mess she'd brought upon herself.

"She said she understood," Isabelle said with a satisfied twinkle in her eyes. "And apologized."

Isabelle's passion for her country was something Othelia could only dream of achieving. She couldn't remember the last time she cared about her country's well-being or worldly reputation.

"Good. Good way to take initiative. I'll be back in three." Othelia stood and stretched, then made her way to the now lineless and vacant bathroom. The last of the towels were folded beside a square mirror, specks of dried paste and dust hiding her full reflection. A pink sink sat under the mirror, filled with soapy and dirtied water. The shower was similar to what she grew up with; a gradual incline toward the drain.

Othelia looked over herself briefly; her hair was both puffy and stringy, a dastardly combination, her sac was covered in blood, and bruises had formed around her ribs.

The shower was short and sweet. She scrubbed her flesh with soap and lathered her hair. It was the fastest operation of her life, and she realized afterward that she hadn't had an entire thought throughout the process.

At three minutes, the water stopped automatically, and the silence was deafening. She stood under the showerhead, her arms shaking with every ache. She rubbed at the knots in her shoulders in a failing attempt to soothe them. The relief her fingers gave was temporary, and the minute she reached for the towel, a shooting pain erupted in her head. It was enough to send her doubling over, rubbing frantically at her temples to rid herself of the invisible evil.

When it reduced to a dull thud, she dried off and checked her pants pockets. The flower heads and blade were secure, and she ran the bloody blade under the sink water before it, too, shut off automatically. She reluctantly tossed her clothes and wretched sac back on. The hot water had made the room sticky, and sweat was already pooling around her armpits.

As the number of participants dwindled and her brother remained, she was becoming increasingly nervous about their inevitable encounter. Perhaps one more phase, maybe two? And how many phases would there be in total? She wished the schedule was stated somewhere, but that would defeat the purpose, wouldn't it? Whatever twisted and unusual purpose there was.

Their breakfast spread was in the same lobby as before. She looked over the options greedily. There were only four items to choose from: various berries, scrambled eggs, crisped bacon, and tiny sandwiches. Othelia picked a sandwich up and examined it, realizing with overwhelming delight that they were filled with honey. She guzzled one down, then two, then three.

"Ahem." She looked up. Liviola stood on the other side of the table, her hand pointing at a sign beside the sandwiches. Othelia's gaze drifted to the black letters that read 'Three per person' in about ten different languages.

Othelia furrowed her brows and thought about arguing. But who was she to complain? They were supplying free food. She resisted the urge and gave the examiner a short, "Sorry."

Liviola smiled wickedly and pointed to the ground. "A hundred push-ups. Now, please."

Othelia gulped, her eyes switching from the dark brown muck that covered the floor and the examiner's smug and amused face. She realized then that the examiner liked this— liked to watch people struggle and suffer and maybe even die. Othelia wasn't about to touch the dirtied ground, not after having just showered, so she opened her mouth to protest this time.

"Oh, sandwiches," Isabelle cooed as she came up beside

Othelia and inspected the breaded goods. She picked one up and brought it to her nose. One sniff sent her tossing the sandwich back onto the platter with a look of disgust. Isabelle looked between Othelia and Liviola with disdain and a crinkled nose.

And then, Othelia had a thought. She smirked and gave Liviola a quick sideways glance. Smug as ever, Liviola was. Othelia resisted the urge to lick her lips. There was nothing more filling than seeing someone's expectations shrivel up.

"They don't smell good?"

Isabelle shook her head. "Honey is meant for *teantes*."

"So, you aren't going to eat them?" Isabelle shook her head again and Othelia hammered in her point. "Is it okay if I have the three that were for you, then?"

"It makes no difference to me," Isabelle said.

With that, Othelia gave Liviola a wonderful display of sneering lips and narrow eyes, a look she'd toss in Samuel's direction any day, maybe even later. Isabelle looked hopelessly confused, her hazelnut eyes the size of questioning saucers. She must've missed the entire interaction, Othelia realized, but it mattered not. She smiled and grabbed a bowl, tossing in handfuls of nuzzleberries and strawberries. Isabelle followed suit.

Liviola released a disappointed sigh. "This group is no fun."

Othelia didn't bother with a farewell and looked around the room as the examiner walked away. She had no clue where the men were, but now was as good a time as any to look for them. There was only one reason as to why she stuck with Isabelle and the others: they'd been right about the boats. They'd figured out the docks were a decoy, and they'd all made it through the phases on their own merits.

"Suppose you know where the others are?" she asked

Isabelle, who nodded and gestured with her chin to follow. Othelia did so with her head down, watching her own shuffling feet as they peeked through the sac. There was a great deal of risk in raising her head when Abel and Samuel were wandering about. The lobby was packed well enough, but now there was elbow room and with that, more gaps to see through.

She started noticing other contestants' shoes as well. Dark purple, rubber-based flats attached to petite feet. Bulky calves tapering off into stuffed sneakers. Clothing and footwear could show a lot about someone; it was true back in Ishla and it was true now. Isabelle, for example, wore all black from head to toe, and a hood despite not wearing it. Unafraid, yet cautious. But if not wearing the hood made her unafraid, did that make Othelia a coward?

Her thoughts were interrupted when she bumped into Isabelle's back. They managed to stay upright and, for a second, Othelia thought they'd recovered quite well. But her bump was enough to send Isabelle's berries helplessly flying onto the floor, a massacre occurring as clunky heels transformed the berries into bright pink mush.

Othelia looked up, ready to apologize profusely. Her words were derailed at the sight of their three male companions. They were stuffed shoulder-to-shoulder in the farthest corner of the room, damp from their showers and holding bowls in their hands.

"I'll get you some more," Leo said, jumping into action.

And he was gone before Isabelle could protest. Isabelle didn't appear upset that her berries were pummeled to pieces, but Othelia still apologized with a bow, and all was well between them.

"So, did you sleep well?" Eli asked. His damp hair clung to the nape of his neck, and it'd been parted; the left strands were tucked behind his ear while the right strands hung in front of his eye.

She squinted at him. People with light skin didn't live on Ishla. The climate was too hot; they burned too easily. Yet he knew Ishlish. He knew Ishlish, which meant he undoubtedly knew who she was. What motivated him to learn Ishlish?

Eli offered a close-lipped smile in return for her obvious skepticism. "Unless Samuel and Abel are hiding in that wall behind me, you're free to look up and enjoy the scenery instead of looking at the ground the whole time. The scenery being me, of course."

"Funny," she said dryly.

"Hey, I was just stating a fact." He wanted something—it was clear by the way he dressed and the way he spoke. He wanted something, and he was trying to be charming to get it. She'd met plenty of princes who acted as such; acted as if being nice warranted her cooperation or sex. She figured Eli was no different.

"What do you think'll be next?" Leo asked as he came up beside Othelia and handed Isabelle a fresh bowl. She couldn't imagine what the exam had in store; she was under the impression no one really knew at this point.

"There's a lot of speculation about the phases on the net," Eli said. "Some people have charted what happens each exam to see if there's any correlation or repeats."

"And?" Othelia asked.

His gaze shifted to her, his hazel eyes piercing her own. She could hardly stop herself from asking why he knew Ishlish. "There are similarities and themes, but never the same type of phase twice. Otherwise, the exam would be too easy. Out of 358 exams, the most common phase has been a one-on-one fight. It's been recorded to have appeared in 60."

"How many phases were in the previous exam?" Galen asked.

"Six. I can't remember what all of them were, but I know they had to cook a squid at some point."

"I hope there's cooking," Galen said. "You name it, I can cook it."

"He's mine," Eli declared, grabbing Galen's shoulder. He looked into the eyes of the other three individually. "If there's a cooking phase, I'm his partner."

"Deal," Othelia said. She was hoping she and Isabelle would stick together throughout, though she wouldn't have minded working with Galen. But Leo and Eli? Leo, she found no particular interest in. He didn't seem to have any outstanding qualities so far, and her apprehension toward Eli spoke for itself.

"I can make vegetable casserole," Leo added, as though he could read her mind. "That's about it, though. And some desserts…"

"More than anything I could make," Eli said. "That's what parents are for."

"Why can't you cook?" Isabelle asked with a confused furrow of the brow. "What kind of man can't cook?"

Conversations blurred together then; Isabelle and Eli argued on the definition of manhood. Galen and Leo talked of recipes and meals they enjoyed. She heard their voices, but their sentences meshed into one. Eli's previous words had ignited a deep pit of utter darkness in her, one that made her eyes well with tears.

She looked down at her shoes, blinking them away. This bout of sadness made no sense; meals were supposed to be made by servants. But that wasn't true for most people—most people got home-cooked meals and family dinners. And she'd never have the chance to cook or eat with her family again. The

Queen had died giving birth to the final Sandoval son, Eb, eight years ago. Only Samuel and Othelia were old enough to truly mourn her, and they'd not once spoken of her death to their father or each other.

"Is something wrong?" Eli asked. Her head shot up to meet his worried gaze. All their eyes were on her. Even worse, she could feel a tear rolling down her cheek. She took in a shaky breath.

"No," she said, wiping away the tear. "I just reminded myself of something."

"May I have your attention, please," Liviola's voice boomed from behind them. Othelia turned and found the woman standing on top of the banquet table. Her hands were cupped around her mouth to make herself louder. The heels of her black laced boots extended five inches in the air, carefully positioned around the items on the table.

The chatter died down almost instantly. Liviola gave a nod of satisfaction. "You'll all be given a map to your next destination and a compass. You have four hours to get there. That is all I can say. The time will begin once everything is handed out and we open those doors. Hear that? We, not you. If you attempt to leave before we open them, you're disqualified. Got that?"

No one was sure what to yell back. Leo gave a meek, "Yeah," and blushed when none of the others did the same.

The maps and compasses were slowly doled out. Othelia had never used a compass before, nor did she know anything about tracking terrain. It wasn't part of the training within their stone walls. With luck, that meant Samuel and Abel would struggle as well. She could only hope this group could pull her through.

The slice of paper they'd received was hardly a map. Instead, it was a crudely drawn shape of what she presumed to be the continent they were on and a tiny star in the center. The four cardinal directions were on each side of the land mass, with the north facing the star. There was a dot by the shoreline with the word 'you.' That was it. No names of towns, no indication of what the land was like. What types of animals lived out here? Were there countries to cross? Cities? Were the people friendly? There was no scale, no way of knowing how far they'd have to travel.

The muscles in her arms continued to ache relentlessly, a reminder of all the energy she'd exerted. If they had to climb mountains or cliffs, she'd be done for. But if they walked, ran even, she could handle it in short bursts.

Othelia snapped her fingers, bringing the group's attention back to her. "When was the last time any of you drank water?"

"Come to think of it," Leo said, stroking his chin, "it's probably been at least two days."

"That's—okay, wow. That's item number one. Item number two is to figure out how to read this thing," Othelia said.

Emmarcia opened the doors and people walked out with polite fear; no one shoved or rushed. Some started jogging after crossing the threshold. Their group stayed behind, however, and followed a sign down the hallway to the first door on the left. It read 'water station' in Latarian on a silver plaque beside the door. On the other side were a small room and a short man attending a metallic table, atop which were yellow cups filled with water. A thick plastic hose was connected to the wall behind him, trailing up onto the table with a stopper at the base.

Six other contestants loitered about, sipping water casually and glancing around the room silently. There was a single girl, a tall redhead, who chatted loudly to her companion, a doughy man in an unflattering red jumpsuit. Othelia tried to blot out the girl's abhorrently obstructive voice and got to drinking. She recognized three other contestants from her trivia room; the man and woman from group 1 sat against the wall, and Eli's partner, Raphael, sipped idly by himself with a hand in his pocket.

"Hey, partner," Eli said cheerfully as he approached the silver-haired man. Raphael nodded to him and walked over. Isabelle's interest seemed to be piqued immediately as she said something in Urkinian, to which Raphael responded in kind. Othelia tuned out their conversation and watched as Galen gulped down a cup of water, his focus resting solely on hydration. She grabbed two cups and chugged them to keep pace. All the while, she could vaguely hear Leo asking the name of the man handing out water.

Once she finished her fifth cup, she was ramped up and ready to go, shaking out her hands and jumping on the balls of her feet. Galen began working on stretches and she pantomimed his every move, touching her toes and performing perfect lunges. She wanted to know his secret. Did he use maoho, too, and hide it better than her? Or was his strength pure?

"I thought that was you." She jumped at the sudden presence behind her and whirled around. Hanako H. Byrde stood before her, a sly smile spread across his lips. He took the time to look over the people she surrounded herself with, one by one, before falling back onto her. By then, his smile had faded.

"Congratulations," she said sardonically, looking down at her outlandish attire pointedly. "Come to dole out more meaningless threats?"

"Threats? I've not once threatened you. Unless you think truths are threats. Your head has been hurting, yes?" His voice was smooth and calculated, and it made her skin crawl.

Othelia gulped and took an instinctual step back. "Who are you?"

Hanako sighed. "Look. I'm not supposed to tell you. Your father specifically told me not to tell you, or even speak to you, for that matter. But I find myself to be a nice guy. I may not come across as such within these circumstances, but I'm a nice guy. I'm a believer in justice and being fair."

She took out her knife in one swift motion. As she reared it back and lowered herself to strike, he unsheathed his sword; the blade sat on the tip of her nose, a prickle of blood forming. She took another step back. "He sent you here to kill me?"

"I don't fancy fighting until the job is done. Do you think he'd be so cruel as to kill you unjustly?"

She wasn't sure.

Isabelle came up behind Hanako and lunged forward with her dagger aimed at his stomach. He whirled around, his sword hovering inches away from her neck. She stopped and stumbled forward; her footing was a clumsy, stumbling mess. She nearly fell into the blade, Raphael catching her arm before impact. Galen took a step forward and prepared his fists.

Othelia threw out her arms and yelled, "Stop!"

Galen's sharp gaze spoke for itself. His brows were furrowed, and he was bouncing on the balls of his feet with a faint smile. Someone was excited to fight.

Othelia shook her head. "Not now."

The four of them already knew too much. The possibility that Eli recognized her was bad enough. She chuckled nervously and nodded for Hanako to follow her into the empty hallway. Before leading him to the lobby, she pointed at the others. Leo stopped mid-sentence and looked at her with wide, curious eyes. "No eavesdropping."

She closed the door and went out to the lobby. She spoke

in harsh whispers as she walked up to him, "Father couldn't have known I was coming! He never told me of the exam."

"The King had his suspicions. I was hired as a precaution. I have to say, I'm quite surprised he raised such a... rambunctious young woman."

She pointed to the doors behind him. "Leave before I kill you."

"Your hostility is charming, princess, but you need not worry. I'm only instructed to take you back home if you pass the exam."

She cocked her head and almost released another nervous laugh, but she controlled herself. She must've looked crazy with her display of emotions; her eyebrows wriggled, and her mouth was contorted into a half-smile, half-frown. "Only if I pass?"

He laughed and reached into her hood to ruffle her hair. She winced and jumped back, keeping a hand outstretched between them. She'd blast him into oblivion if that's what it took. To think her father knew her so well. To think he would use that to his advantage.

How embarrassing. She hadn't considered such a possibility. Worst of all, she was scared, her adrenaline replaced by sheer panic. She disobeyed again. The final straw, she imagined. Would she be brought back and locked away forever? Or would there be more beatings and more training? Would she be allowed to reign over the kingdom instead of her brother?

No, probably not. She'd broken the rules and tricked Alexander. Even if she passed the exam, she'd never get a chance at the throne. This was not good. Not good at all. Hanako was clearly stronger than her. There was no way out.

She got ready to attack him with her power. Her plan was to toss him into a wall and leave him unconscious and tied up, so he was forced to fail. Hanako narrowed his eyes. He knew what she was gearing up to do, and that frightened her most of all.

"Your father didn't hire me to fight you. He hired me to take you home. Do you think he would choose someone he didn't find capable of the job?"

"And if I don't pass? What then?"

"You'd know if you hadn't interrupted me, but I'll let that go. I'm a nice guy. I try to be, anyway. And I do believe you deserve to know. Fairness is key, so I'll say it as plainly as I can— If you do not pass the exam, your father has instructed me to bring you before the Continental Security Commission. Your father has signed a statement that says you've committed treason and you'll be put in prison. No hard feelings from me or anything, I'm just the hired help."

"I haven't committed treason," she said. "I've never spoken ill of Father to anyone; I think the way he looks after our country is noble and just."

"He has told me you're quite the conceited liar, so please spare me. I'd best be going now. There is much more of this exam to get through. I'll take care of you later."

"What if I gave you the money I win?" she bargained. "All of it, whatever the amount."

He shook his head, eyes full of pity. He was maybe twenty years older than her, wrinkles forming under his eyes. "Silly little thing, you are. Loyalty cannot be bought, not in my line of business. Only earned. To accept such an offer would be tasteless."

She hated the way he looked at her; his bemusement whittled her down to nothing. Hanako H. Byrde didn't give her an outright nasty glare, but she could see the distaste in the way his brows came together, and the way his forehead creased.

He whirled around and left, as simple as that. The door he gracefully glided through clicked shut behind him. She rubbed at her wrists with a shiver and focused on her breathing. She wanted to feel hate toward him and her father, but all that lingered was a sense of dread. No matter what she chose to do, she was condemned to be locked up.

The emptiness of the room was daunting. Her deep breaths permeated the stillness of the lobby, and it sent her hurrying back to the water room. She felt crazy, her head filled with a painstaking ache and her body feeling sluggish despite the sleep. And now this? Some father he was. Tears pricked at the corner of her eyes, but she pulled herself together.

CHAPTER 15

ISABELLE

HER INTEREST IN the mysterious girl's endeavors was cut short by the man standing before her. Isabelle had yet to meet another who grew up in Reinta—and he spoke Urkinian so fluently! His piercing green eyes as he sized her up made her body tremble with excitement.

"I must confess," Raphael said in Urkinian. "I am a prince."

Her eyes widened. "Why would you tell me? Surely that's something you'd keep hidden."

He shrugged. "You don't seem like the type to care. I wanted to see how you'd react."

"I don't suppose you want to know my past now as well."

"Only if you fare to give one."

"Perhaps another time. Say, why is a prince taking the exam?"

He chuckled, his eyes full of delight. "That's not how this works. I cannot divulge *all* my secrets. Could I see that dagger of yours, by chance?"

Her eyebrows shot up. She'd hardly used her dagger thus far; an ample weapon squandered. It was nothing special in a traditional sense; it was merely something her brother bestowed upon her before he left Reinta for good. How she longed to hunt with him again, to hear his voice. There was nothing that could compare to how he treated her, the kindness to teach and listen. Only Gahi was there to listen to her now.

"My dagger? What need would you have for it?"

"Gahi has led me to you. I can sense there is something of note regarding your weapon. I can explain more once I take a look at it. But if you'd prefer to keep it at your side, I understand. I am nothing but a stranger to you."

His ominous words struck a cord within her. He could very well be a threat oozing in charm, but he was right. Her weapon was important, at least to her. Isabelle handed over her dagger, surprised at how willing she was to give it to him. Perhaps it was due to how open he'd been regarding his identity, paired with his ability to speak Urkinian. If what he said was true, and his mother was from Reinta, there was a chance her family knew of his. But Reinta was a small village, and she had never heard of a man named Raphael.

He appraised the weapon and raised a brow with a faint smile before handing it back. "This is quite something, I will say. Whoever gave it to you meant well."

"How do you know?"

He winked. "You do not sense it? You will learn in time."

"That isn't much of an explanation." She sheathed her weapon, feeling the weight of it in her hand as if she would never have the chance to hold it again.

"There are certain things I cannot discuss, I'll admit. But this may be a more powerful dagger than you know. And I'm deeply sorry for whoever owned it prior—they met a terrible demise."

The wind was knocked out of her by the sheer force of his words. They'd received a letter that Micah had died, but she had a sliver of hope that he was out there somewhere, traveling free from the constraints of communication. She put the dagger back in its sheath.

Isabelle held back tears as she said, "My brother. My brother gave me this."

"Ah," he said, a look of genuine concern crossing his features. "I didn't know. I can only sense their wishes and their deaths. I'm sorry."

She shook her head. "I suppose that uncovers my desire to pass the exam—I want to find whoever killed him."

Raphael considered this. "And here I was, just wanting to get away. I'm not sure if I can help you in any way—my connections are limited—but I shall let you know. My mother has long since passed, but anyone from Reinta is family to me. What was that saying, again? 'Family is an extension of all those who are well and lost?'"

His recitation of one of the few Reinta mottos further cemented her trust in him. There was no doubt in her mind that he was who he said he was. Even if his previous words raised suspicion, he was someone she had faith in.

"Y-you don't have to," Isabelle pressed. "You barely know me."

"I don't need to know you to see the strength and determination you carry. We are bred from the same cloth; we are family. Let us see how this exam pans out. I bet there are far more connections as an Expedition Overseer, many more if you're in the Master Class. I hope to see you on the other side."

"Travel with us," Isabelle blurted, her face growing hot.

There was something about him, the way his smooth voice carried each syllable.

"I'm afraid I wish to take the exam alone as much as I can. Thank you for your consideration. I'll remember y—"

The door burst open, cutting Raphael off. Isabelle had been hooked onto every word—she, too, would remember him —but her attention was brought to the frazzled girl entering the room.

"I must be going now. Safe travels," Raphael said with a smile. He placed his hands lightly on hers and said, "May Gahi watch over you."

He left the room, passing their hooded comrade with a knowing nod. The girl ignored him and started to speak, but Isabelle wasn't listening. She hadn't noticed Raphael until he'd approached the night prior, and she couldn't help but wonder how he passed the first phase alone. His suit was unscathed, and he didn't appear to have any weapons. And he was a prince. She didn't know what to do with this information, didn't know how to digest such a peculiar thing. She supposed it didn't matter, that the exam was more important than whatever her thoughts were leading to now.

Isabelle slowly brought her attention back to her group, wondering if she'd ever meet him again.

PHASE 3

CHAPTER 16

OTHELIA

HER BREATH HITCHED as she entered the room and panic consumed her thoughts once more. She urged herself to act calm. The water room was much livelier than the lobby—until Othelia walked in. Isabelle and Raphael were in the midst of a conversation and turned to her almost immediately as she crossed the threshold.

"We should get going," she said, heading over to the water station to drink more in order to soothe her nerves.

"What was that? Did you know him?" asked Eli.

Othelia shook her head. "No, but there's no need for you to concern yourselves with him. I'll have to deal with it when the time comes."

Leo was chatting with the man behind the booth still, his attention never stopping for her. Galen finished another cup along with her and asked, "So, they aren't hired to kill you? Or us?"

"No, and, as I've said, it's not something any of you need to worry about."

"We can help you," Eli said. "We could try, at least. Tell you what, if that man comes around again, I'll punch him until he's unconscious and have him thrown in jail. That's what I'll do. He's got no business threatening us."

"He's threatening me," Othelia said. "It's my business and I'm not saying it again. Besides, you wouldn't be able to knock him out. You wouldn't even land a punch."

Galen snorted, and she turned to him. He was on another cup of water, speeding through the pre-prepared glasses like they were shots of taq. "How many have you had?"

Galen held up six fingers before gulping down his seventh. She proceeded to drink four more—she couldn't be beaten, after all—and lined them up beside his empty cups. Aside from their group, everyone gradually cleared out of the room. Galen leaned against the booth with his arms crossed and his eyes on the door leading out. The loud redhead and her companion stared back at Galen briefly and whispered to each other before leaving. He waved at them with a smile.

"You know them?" Othelia asked.

He shook his head. "Not one bit, but it looks like they've taken an interest in me. We've got to start being more careful."

"Indeed," Othelia said as she walked toward the door and spun around to grab the others' attention. "We have less than four hours now. Let's get going."

As they exited the building, she drifted to the back of their pack as her entire attention landed on the compass. She understood it well enough; one side of the needle pointed north, the other south. They were going south and when she turned to face north, the Broadcastia main entrance was looming over her.

It was mid-morning, and the air was a dash warmer than it'd been inside. The sun shone bright but didn't burn, and the ground was damp and muddied, exposing a path of layered footprints leading around the Broadcastia. The building was surrounded by tall and thick grass on all sides, but there were a few inches of empty space for them to walk through.

They followed the path of footprints, which cut off at the grass behind the radio station. The grass stretched high above their heads and was densely packed with thick strands. There were fragments of human trails; scrapes in the grass blades, a few bent or trampled, but none had seemed to be cut down, only crumpled under the weight of bodies. Footprints extended along the backside of the Broadcastia. Isabelle walked to the other end and peered around the corner to get a view of the other side.

As she walked back, she reported, "No trails."

Galen stepped forward and held out a palm. "Knife, anyone?"

Isabelle and Othelia both grabbed for their knives, but Isabelle had fewer layers to burrow through and got to hers faster. Galen took it with a smile and slashed at the blades of grass. Some scratches appeared, but Isabelle's dagger didn't suffice. Galen tried Othelia's knife next, but it was to no avail. The grass was uncuttable.

"Impossible," Leo said grimly. He had the voice of someone who'd already given up.

Othelia stepped forward and cautiously tested a blade between her fingertips. It was covered in fuzz, reminding her of a fruit that grew in the palace courtyard, pyaloes. It was blissful. "This is the softest thing I've ever touched."

Eli came up beside her and tried to do the same, but he winced as he bent his fingers. Her eyes widened as she looked at his scraped hands. "What—"

"Messed them up during all that rock-climbing last night. Hurts like you wouldn't believe. Shower helped it some," he said, his hazel eyes tired but kind. She gave him a sympathetic smile and mouthed the word 'sorry.' He turned a faint red— apparently, doughy eyes and sympathy were all it took—and said to the group, "W-what do you guys think? I've never heard of grass that can't be cut before."

"Because it's impossible," Leo repeated, rubbing his thumb along a deformed strand. He tried tugging at it, digging both feet into the ground and using his full strength to pull it out. It wouldn't budge.

Eli waved away Leo's answer. "Yes, yes, we know what you think already. Anyone else? I'm thinking it's genetically engineered grass. Grass built by humankind to be indestructible."

"What could soft, indestructible grass be used for?" Isabelle asked.

He held up the map and compass and gestured around them in large sweeping motions. "Phase three of the exam, perhaps?"

"Maybe it's natural," Isabelle suggested. "Could animals live inside, survive with no sun?"

"Or mutated bugs," Othelia said with a shiver. Eli and Leo jumped back from the grass in unified horror as the possibility struck.

"...or it's mag," Galen said. Othelia turned to him; he was staring back critically, almost accusatory.

"Plants, humans, and animals can't be magical," Eli said. "Only items."

"Bugs?" Othelia asked.

"I would hope not."

"But what's an item? Couldn't a piece of grass be one?" Isabelle asked. The same question had crossed Othelia's mind, seeing as the talithes were considered magical items despite their flower-like appearance.

"An item is anything inanimate or dead. So, I guess,

technically bugs or grass could have mag," Eli confirmed. "As long as they're not living. And these don't look very dead to me."

"Do you have all the answers?" Othelia asked with crossed arms.

He smiled in return. It fit perfectly on his face, and dimples formed beside thick lips and radiant white teeth. "Only the important ones."

She brought the map closer to her face, blocking out Eli before her thoughts lingered on him any longer. She'd be damned if only a few witty remarks won her over.

The tiny star in the center of the continent taunted her. The lack of a sizable scale to measure distance was unsettling, as was the amount of time it would take to get there. What if it took exactly four hours, and they were already too late?

"Does anyone know how to use this?" Leo asked, turning around in circles while staring down at the compass with growing agitation.

Isabelle sighed. "Follow me."

"You're sure?"

"Yes." She ran her finger along the map, from where they were to the star. "Northeast. The red will want to point north."

Othelia relaxed. Isabelle further proved her initial theory that this group was worth sticking with. They were going to pass the exam if they worked together, or in this case, followed Isabelle.

"We should hold on to each other's shoulders while we're in there," Galen said, nodding toward the nightmarishly tall threads that stood before them, "and we need to be ready for anything."

Whatever was in there, they could beat it. She told herself she was unstoppable. She told herself the only person who could ever beat her in a fight was Alexander. Keep that confidence up, she reminded herself.

They lined up and Isabelle pushed her way through, Othelia clutching her shoulders as darkness shrouded her vision. The soft, plump blades tickled her below the knees. When she looked up, the sun was nearly gone. Rays peeked through in spurts, and occasionally the grass would open up into pockets big enough for one person to fit and see at a time. In these pockets, the sun was harsh, and the dirt was crusted over.

Behind her was Eli, then Leo, then Galen. All she could hear was the breathing of the others and their footsteps on the sinking ground. At first, she thought the soil was wet from rainfall or too little exposure to the sun. It was when they stopped for Eli to pee that she realized the ground was actually sinking. After thirty seconds, the bottoms of her flats were absorbed.

She gripped Isabelle's shoulder and tried pulling a leg out. The mud, if it could be classified as such, stretched thin as she pulled her foot up further. She grunted, trying to shake the substance off. It clung mercilessly and began slowly retracting back into the ground. She used her hands next, using her long nails to pry the sludge off. Her operation was successful, the stringy mud snapping off one shoe. But now there was another predicament because it stuck to her hands instead. The ground was holding her hostage.

Something within the mud, or perhaps the mud itself, gave a forceful tug and pulled her down to her knees and hands. Horrified, she tried pulling her palms out, but her strength was incomparable to whatever lay below. Her hands and knees began to sink along with her calves. She desperately looked around for help.

Isabelle was working on her own legs, trying to free one at a time. The grass obstructed her view of the others, and her sanity was quickly waning as she realized no one was coming to her aid. There was nothing but grass on every side, the scent of sweet nectar filling her nose and overwhelming her eyes. The ocean she could handle, knowing that at some point they were bound to stumble across land. But this? It made her claustrophobic.

"A knife," Othelia yelled at Isabelle. "There's one in my pocket. Cut me out!"

Othelia attempted to pull herself out again, becoming increasingly frantic with each additional failure. Her heart was going to burst, and it wouldn't matter because she was going to be devoured by the dirt and suffocate, anyway. This made her tug harder, but the harder she tried, the harder it fought back.

"Wait," Isabelle called back, pulling out her weapon and stabbing the ground beside her sunken foot. A shrill shriek erupted in response and Othelia almost screamed in return. The event unfolding was beyond abnormal. She could handle magical items and mutant animals. Fantastical powers, sure, why not? But mutant dirt? If she wasn't experiencing it firsthand, she would call the notion of animalistic mud utterly ridiculous.

Isabelle got to sawing the area around her foot and worked the knife underneath. Othelia watched in pain-stricken anticipation, her wrists and feet submerged. She felt like a helpless idiot, and bet she looked like one, too.

Othelia reminded herself that it was best not to wallow in situations that couldn't be helped, so she looked back at Isabelle in the feeble hope that she'd made progress. Thankfully, Isabelle managed to break one leg free and began working on her second foot when they heard another yell. It was close, presumably a man.

"Guys!" Othelia yelled, her voice rich with worry. She couldn't see any of them. "Guys?"

"Coming!" one yelled. Leo, she thought. He sounded close, perhaps behind her. No, in front of? Next to? She couldn't be sure. A few seconds passed until the same person shouted again, "Wait, can you say something again?"

And Othelia did, her uselessness permeating her mind. She could feel tears filling her eyes, yet further proof of her incompetence and inability to control her emotions. There had to be something she could do herself. She didn't need anyone's help, she thought, if she could just come up with a plan.

One thing came to mind, a last resort. She gulped, closed her eyes, and envisioned her power coursing to her fingertips. When she was ready, she released her maoho with the hope of forming a nice-sized hole.

Instead, a sharp twinge of pure agony radiated throughout her hands. She screamed. Alexander had dealt plenty of painful punishments in the past, but it was nothing compared to the sheer burning of her flesh. It seared, blisters forming and bursting within the same second. She panted involuntarily, saliva dripping from her mouth as her screams hitched into a sob. The world around her began to blur as nausea and dizziness took hold.

Rustling erupted from the tangles around her, and she froze. Be rational, she reasoned with herself. It was probably one of the guys. But she couldn't get herself to think, not really, and her fear remained. She screamed, a sob escaping through it all. How could she be so weak?

And then Galen was in front of her, his pants caked in mud. A small, retractable knife was in one hand. He tucked the knife in his pocket and came up behind her, looped his arms under her armpits, and pulled her up with so much force that she thought her arms would be ripped from their sockets.

Galen grunted in her ear but did not speak, focused on the grueling task at hand.

Othelia's hands rose from the mud, her flesh spongy and destroyed. The pain morphed into numbness in half her fingers and both her wrists. Galen let go and hopped around to keep his feet from sticking. Leo appeared next, his forehead and cheeks damp, his chest heaving.

"I lost my map," he said. Othelia hadn't thought about those things, and both the compass and map had been consumed, but it was the last thing on her mind. For the first time in her life, she felt a pang of longing for the palace. For home. For things to go back to how they were despite the beatings and walls and lack of freedom.

Galen pulled out his pocketknife and sawed his way through the strands connected to her feet and arms. He worked fast and with a steady hand, his mouth shut in concentration. Leo started to help, pulling at her feet until she could stand and walk. At last, they had freed her, and they all joined together in a dance of hops to avoid the same situation from occurring. Isabelle, too, had successfully broken free. She'd done it herself, and Othelia had needed not one, but two people.

Her hands were covered in a grotesque array of mud, blood, and blisters. Her fingertips were peeling and oozing, and both the front and back of her hands were rubbed raw. Bright red and wrinkled. She couldn't twitch a finger without a tremendous sting rippling through her hand. Where had that glorious numbness gone?

Othelia cursed at herself, knowing fully well that this was her own fault. She had attempted to throw her maoho into the mud, a rather stupid thing to do, she realized. The mud was thick and solid, acting as a barrier. Her hands burned because the power had nowhere to go.

She assessed the rest of their situation, arms dangling

limply at her sides while the four of them continued their hopping jig. Galen tossed his pocketknife to Leo, who caught it flimsily and stashed it in his backpack. Isabelle still had her map, and Leo still had his compass. Everyone else had lost theirs in the scuffle. Well, everyone except—

"Where's Eli?" Othelia asked, using her forearms to wipe away the tears streaming down her face. They acted as added humiliation, and she opted to keep her head low, hoping no one could see.

"Here," he said from behind. She whipped around, finding a perfectly unmuddied suit and body. He rubbed the back of his head as a flush of red entered his cheeks. She'd never met someone who blushed so often. "Sorry, I got a bit lost trying to find you guys. And sorry for making us stop, as well. Guess this is kind of my fault."

Othelia shook her head. "None of us could've seen this coming, so it's no one's fault. Let's just get moving."

"How'd you remain unharmed?" Galen asked Eli, skepticism written on his face.

Eli shrugged. "I'm not sure. I was standing in a sunny spot outside of the grass, over there." He pointed through the towering grass. "The ground was dried."

"Those must be safe spots," Galen pondered. "Did you know?"

"Of course not. I just stopped where I was standing to, you know, go."

Othelia couldn't gauge if he was lying or not—she couldn't gauge if any of them were—and she didn't care. At least the others wouldn't have left her for dead.

The ground seemed to latch on if they stood still. Jogging was voted too dangerous given the density of the grass, so they maintained a quick pace as they trudged on. Othelia couldn't grab hold of Isabelle's shoulder, so she trailed along at the back of the group, behind Galen. She struggled to keep sight of him; grass would replace Galen's presence as though he was never there, and claustrophobia was igniting fear.

Her wooly garment lacked pockets, so her ruined hands were left on full display. They ached with each brush of grass. She desperately wished gauze would magically appear, or a doctor, or pain medication. Anything. But wishes didn't come true, did they?

She thought of the mud interacting with her open wounds, how the sores could easily become infected if she wasn't careful. If she didn't have her hands, what was she good for? What were her skills? She couldn't even make a fist.

They stumbled upon a circular clearing within the grass, large enough for them to stand shoulder-to-shoulder. The mud was crusted over, the sun beaming above. They stopped and stood and didn't sink. She smiled, thanking the stars. Galen had been right. For now, they would be fine. Assuming nothing else lurked in the grassy trenches.

"Whoa," Eli said as he came up beside her. "What happened there?"

She hesitated to answer. Othelia was fairly certain that average people didn't know of royal powers; the Kingship probably had a reason to keep it a secret. Should she divulge that information? Certainly not—that could be exactly what Eli wanted—but what would be a good explanation?

Othelia rolled her shoulders and tried to maintain an air of stoic collection. "I'm not sure. My hands sunk pretty far into the ground, and it seared my skin."

"It screamed," Isabelle added. "The ground *screamed*."

"It was sticky and stringy, like that cheese," Galen said. "Devorage, I think."

"I can't say I've ever heard of carnivorous dirt before." Leo kicked at the ground, and flecks of dried dirt flew a few inches into the air. "I'm going to have nightmares for weeks."

"You know your hands are bleeding," Eli interjected, bringing the conversation back to Othelia. *I didn't lose my sight, you buffoon,* she thought in a bout of anger, *just my hands.*

None of them were medical experts, and she didn't particularly trust them to try. There was nothing she could do but feed the ground with her blood as it dripped along. "It'll be fine. Don't worry about it."

He ignored her request and started fumbling with his tie. "Here, can I use this to wrap one or both, if possible? Just to stop the bleeding and, you know, infections and stuff. That's a thing, right?"

"They'll probably get infected if we don't clean them," Galen said, edging closer and bending to inspect her hands at eye level. He peered up at her curiously. "Those look painful. Can you feel your fingers?"

She nodded and choked back a sob as he gently grabbed one. "They hurt."

"I have some water," Leo said while taking off his backpack and uncovering a half-filled plastic bottle, "and an extra shirt we could use to wrap them."

Eli took the bottle from Leo and splashed some water on his tie. He gestured toward her hands. "May I?"

She raised them meekly. "If you feel that strongly about it, go ahead."

And he did, without hesitation. She withheld a scream as Eli dabbed his damp tie on her wounds. She wondered if she would contract an infection and if it would kill her. There were worse ways to go, she supposed, but it didn't sound all too pleasant.

The mud washed off easily, turning viscous and dark

brown until peeling away. Othelia watched Galen rip Leo's extra shirt into strands; the activity would've kept her mind off what was happening, if not for the unbearable pain.

Once her hands were rubbed raw and semi-clean, Galen handed the cloth scraps to Eli, who individually wrapped each finger and her palms. He tied it snuggly at her wrists. The tightened fabric felt strange at first, chafing against the burns and creating a dull ache. But then the ache subsided, and her stiff hands felt almost comfortable, wrapped around a cozy fleece blanket.

"Thanks," she said, looking down at her hands. It was the work of someone clueless, the fabric too loose around the palms and too tight around the fingers. It was nothing like the pristine work of a palace nurse. Still, she was impressed with his effort, and her hands felt better than before, perhaps due to the riddance of the wretched mud. She smirked and said jokingly, "You could be a doctor."

He let out a short laugh. "Oh, stars no. I'm not one for gore. Your hands are about as much as I can take. Politics is all I know."

She wrinkled her nose, his pronouncement startling, though it shouldn't have been so. If anyone were to know Ishlish, it would be a politician. However, he hardly seemed the type; he didn't have the ruthlessness of a politician—the cunning ability to do whatever it took to sway other people. Nothing about him stood out against a crowd, not even his 6-foot height, and his eyes were too kind. That, and he had some rather negative ideas about the rich, whom he'd have to encounter regularly. At least now it made sense why he knew their royal greeting.

"Are you going to tell me what you want?" she asked suddenly.

His eyebrows raised, and he stood quietly, staring back at

her with wide, confused eyes. He smiled nervously and sputtered, "A-am I that obvious?"

"I'm not asking again."

"We're running out of time," he said, and a blush was already rising to his cheeks. "To finish this phase, I mean. Leo, the time?"

"One in the afternoon. H-Hey, do you guys think any others ran into that?"

"What, you mean were they swallowed into the ground? Probably, but I didn't see anyone," Galen answered. Leo gulped. The idea they'd walked over someone who'd been buried, or eaten, alive was far too much for him, Othelia supposed. She was too shocked by her own encounter with the mud to mull over the details any further.

"We have two hours left," Eli continued quickly. "But I'll tell you later, I promise. It's a long story. I have no intention of hurting you or anything, but it's a story best for another time."

Isabelle placed her hand on Othelia's shoulder and looked at Eli in defiance. "If you try, you're out."

Eli backed away and opened his mouth to speak, eyes still wide and surprised, but it was Galen who said, "He's right. Now's not the time. We should go."

Othelia let the conversation drop, knowing they were running out of time to find the fourth phase. Her suspicions had been correct, and that was a problem. She was stuck worrying about Hanako, her brother, and Abel, and now with the possibility of Eli trying to harm her or use her.

Well, whatever he had planned, she'd be ready.

CHAPTER 17

ELI

THE WORLD OPENED up around them, revealing a gigantic field that spanned what seemed like miles, tiny mounds erupting throughout flat plains. The grass was far shorter, up to their ankles, and the dirt looked and acted normal. Sparse, leafless trees populated the field, a few bushes at their sides.

He stopped and wiped away beads of sweat forming on his forehead; the others were spread out beside him. Eli hadn't anticipated what had occurred in the grass, and he felt unequivocally terrible for being the sole cause of Othelia's damaged hands. He'd made a mistake, holding in his bladder and waiting until they were in harm's way to relieve himself.

"So, we made it out," he said to himself. "But made it where?"

"I hope the ground doesn't sink," Leo mumbled beside him. "I'm tired of this exam. Tired of all of this."

Eli raised a brow. "But not too tired to complain, it seems. Have no fear, young Leo, we're almost done. We're at three of five."

"Or six."

"Or six. But hey, halfway there is better than dead."

Eli watched the princess as she and Isabelle whispered to each other. He wished he could say and do the right things, wished he could gain Othelia's trust. But he knew he was coming across as menacing to her, and he didn't know how to change.

"What is that?" Isabelle asked, pointing to the north. Further beyond was a gray and dense cloudy wall blocking their path. Yet another obstacle. He had to agree with Leo; he was tired of taking this exam. "Looks like... rain, maybe?"

"More like fog," Leo said, using a hand to shield his eyes from the sun. "We get that sometimes back home. It's harmless, just makes it harder to see."

Eli pondered for a moment, racking his memory for the common landmarks in Equive. And then the answer hit, and he snapped his fingers with a triumphant smile. There was nothing better than being right. "It's mist. I remember, now. A mist desert."

"Desert and mist? Don't those two things contradict each other?" Galen asked.

"That's a common misconception. A desert is a barren land where nothing can grow due to either the lack of precipitation or too much."

"Let's go," Othelia said. "We're running out of time."

As much as he detested the controlling nature of the rich, he had to admire Othelia's ability to take charge, especially after having her hands fried by living muck.

"Yes, ma'am," he said with a salute. To his surprise, he was greeted with a small smirk from the princess. Perhaps he was slowly growing on her.

They walked on—the field was long and devoid of any distractions. Although they should've run, everyone appeared sluggish and worn. They were losing stamina and confidence, two things that they desperately needed to keep themselves going. The exam was only meant to get harder as the phases continued, and now was no time to lose their stride.

"Say," Eli said, attempting to break the deafening silence and lift spirits, "I think you've all been doing wonderful so far. We make a great team."

"All we've done is obtain a lifeboat and win trivia games," Galen said plainly. "Is that impressive to you?"

Eli should've expected such a reaction, but it was no matter because he had the perfect response. He always had the perfect response. "I believe you pummeled quite a few people on the boat, Galen. And trivia is no laughing matter. Not many can—"

An arrow cut through the air, the sharp blade grazing Eli's cheek as it whizzed past and slid into the tree behind him. He stood, stunned. The others paused in their tracks as the world slowed to a halt. Leo's wide eyes bounced between Eli and the direction in which the arrow appeared. Galen smiled, his eyes focused on something, or someone, far in the distance. Isabelle shrieked while Othelia unsheathed her dagger.

Blood trickled down his cheek from the gash of the arrowhead, the stickiness, and sharp pain pushing him into motion. He pointed toward a tree a few yards away. "Shooter," he yelled. "In the tree!"

Eli ducked at the sight of another object flying through the sky. The second arrow landed in the grass beside his feet. He yelped, jumping away from the protruding object. "Why is he shooting *at me*?"

Leo dashed behind the nearest tree, shoving his body against it with his eyes clamped shut. Eli was compelled to do the same, but something within him told him to stay out in the open. Stay alert but out.

"I got him," Galen said. "He's sitting in the tree branches."

"I'll distract him," Eli proclaimed. "He seems to be drawn to killing me first."

"You'll die if you do that. Take up Leo's position and hide behind a tree. Galen and I will take care of this," Othelia said.

Galen sprinted toward the assailant's hide-out, an arrow whizzing past him as he ducked and dodged it. Othelia and Isabelle followed suit, though he wasn't sure what Isabelle was going to contribute. He'd seen how she fought; she didn't know how to. Eli glanced over to Leo, sighed, and followed the others. Sure, he didn't bring a weapon. Sure, he was useless in a fight. But he wasn't going to sit back and watch his companions defend him without helping them in some way.

The field was open, making it easy for the shooter to target them. Eli opted to run in a zigzag, hoping he wasn't the first to be shot at as they ran. He passed two, three bodies on the way over; they weren't the first to be attacked. Hopefully, they would be the last. Blood was dripping down his chin now, cooling his cheek as the wind smacked into his face. It was too windy for the arrows to be precise, he realized.

Galen was the first to arrive at the tree, the bowman visible now. It was a big, muscular man in a jumpsuit that perfectly matched the dark brown of the trees, a scar along his cheek. Eli watched as the man loaded his bow and pointed an arrow at Othelia as she neared. She didn't appear to notice—her eyes were on Galen as he prepared to climb the tree.

"Othelia!" Eli yelled, ramming into her side as the arrow was shot. They fell to the ground a few feet away from where the arrow struck and rolled; Othelia hovered over him with her arms pinning him down. She was panting, the run and her injuries likely catching up to her.

"You idiot," she hissed. "You just revealed my name."

"Correction. I just *saved* you. Now, please get off me before we're killed."

She huffed and stood, brushing herself off. Eli stood frantically and watched as Galen jumped up and grabbed the nearest tree limb behind the bowman, keeping himself hidden from the man's view.

Isabelle used herself as a distraction, waving the bowman down. "Hey! What business do you have with us? We've done you no harm!"

The bowman didn't answer, and instead loaded yet another arrow and aimed at Isabelle. Eli held his breath; he wasn't close enough to save her. She was going to die.

And then the man's grip loosened on the bow as his arms fell to his sides. His head lolled, and his face grew slack as he fell from the tree. His body thumped to the ground; a sharp and sudden snap sounded as his head smacked into the dirt. Eli jumped back instantly, his heart squeezing as he realized what the noise was. The man's neck had snapped, killing him within a second. The man's eyes hung open, staring ahead at nothing and everything all at once. That sound would haunt Eli for the rest of his life.

Eli peered up to find Galen in the tree, balancing himself on the branch the bowman had been on. Galen stared down at the dead man with a frown. "Huh," he said. "I thought that was going to be harder."

Isabelle, Eli, and Othelia huddled around the dead man while Galen checked the perimeter for any more unsuspected hunters. His jumpsuit slowly changed from the brown of the tree limbs to pitch black.

"This man," Othelia said. "He's a contestant. I stood beside him on the boat."

"He must've been waiting around to kill contestants. What a brilliant plan that turned out to be," Eli said.

"I thought he was going to be more powerful than that," Othelia stated with a shrug. "Oh, well."

"He did almost kill you. And me," Eli responded, touching his cheek. His hand came back with fresh blood, and he wondered if the cut would leave a scar later.

Galen came up beside Leo, his search around the perimeter complete; a grimace was still painted on his face. His eagerness to fight and kill wasn't something Eli was too fond of, but Galen made a fit partner, and Isabelle would probably be dead now, if not for him.

"Well," Eli said, clapping his hands. "Should we go back for our little friend back there? See how he's holding up?"

Isabelle sighed. "Coward, he is."

"Perhaps. But then again, those who grow up on sheltered farms don't often encounter such awful things."

"Oh, and you do, Mr. Politician?" Othelia asked sarcastically. He couldn't tell if she liked him or despised him. Maybe it was a bit of both.

Her question struck a chord in him. The things that occurred in New Guayi were that of nightmares. People starving, finding nothing but cats, dogs, and the like to eat. The poor were drowning, and people who lived on the right side of the wall were thriving. He may have been born lucky, but the vast majority were trapped in endless torment.

"More than you'll ever know."

CHAPTER 18
ISABELLE

THERE WAS AN air of unease from them all, particularly Othelia, who'd grown incredibly quiet and stared ahead with trepidation etched in her features. Eli had blurted her name and outed her apparent secret. Although Othelia's name struck no semblance of importance to Isabelle, the young woman appeared to be hiding something. Whatever it was, Othelia had been nothing but helpful and kind thus far, and Isabelle found no reason to distrust her.

After being attacked, the walk to the looming, dark clouds was uneventful and hushed. Leo was clearly embarrassed by his further display of cowardice, as he should've been, and the others seemed exhausted from their encounter with the bowman.

When they finally reached the edge of the cloud, they stopped and stared at it in silence. White and gray clouds danced together, hitting an invisible wall and curling inward on themselves. It was so unnatural that she almost denied its existence. This was a dream. There could be no other explanation for all that was occurring. Back home, the soil was normal, and the weather was always warm but never too hot or cold. Fog could certainly form and roll off mountains, but it looked nothing like this.

Was it safe to walk through? Was it even safe to touch? There was no way around, at least none within her eyesight, and there were no other competitors around. They must've gone through this fog, or whatever word Eli had used to describe it. Still, she was afraid of touching it on the off chance that it, too, was alive. If the ground tried to eat them, what was stopping the air from doing so? There was also the chance of participants lurking within, waiting to slim down the competition—if any were still alive.

Eli moved forward, taking the chance no one else dared to. He stuck his hand out, thrusting it into the fog as Isabelle yelled, "Wait!"

Her warning came too late. Eli's entire forearm was submerged in the gloom. From where they stood, she could see a few feet inside the fog before the land gradually faded away. Nothing was growing from within, aside from a few tall and leafless trees. Their branches spiraled from their trunks in an ominous and bleak way and the bark was midnight black.

Eli's arm was still intact on the other side. The swirls of gray contorted around his flesh harmlessly, so Eli became more daring and stuck his whole body through. He spun around to look at them from the other side. He appeared duller, the colors of his clothes washed out. More curiously, however, was the way his hair became damp as dew droplets clung. His white shirt quickly adhered to his body and became transparent, his nipples peeking through the fabric.

He looked down at himself and then held out the palm of his hand, squinting with amusement. "I knew it, didn't I? A Mist Desert."

Isabelle shook her head incredulously, but no one else seemed particularly fazed by what he was saying. "Danger," she asked, "in there?"

Eli stepped back onto their side, his body soaked to the bone, and shrugged. "Now that, I'm not sure. I definitely should know, but I have no clue at all. I wouldn't be surprised if something was lurking in there."

Isabelle shuddered and prayed to Gahi that leviathan hadn't found this place and mutated into a horrid hybrid. There was no proof the creatures and stories within the Holy Book were real, but every Reintian believed in them. How could she not? Especially now.

She swallowed her fears and nodded. She clamped her eyes shut and crossed the barrier, instantly feeling the strange sensation of water hanging in the air and lightly poking at her skin. It felt like a bunch of tiny pinpricks on her face and hands, not quite painful but very apparent and uncomfortable.

Isabelle raised her hood, covering her face to the best of her ability, and tried to look deeper into the haze. There was sparse plant life, black shrubs clinging to cracks in the ground. Sunlight poured in through circular beams, shining down onto select trees and allowing them to grow pink flowers.

The compass needle spun sporadically, and condensation pooled under the glass. How was this possible? Their planet's magnetic pull never wavered; the only disruptable force she knew of were metallic objects and large rocks. But the cause hardly mattered, because now the compass was ruined along with the map, ink bleeding off the page and staining her fingers.

"That's not good," Othelia said, her voice beside Isabelle's ear. Isabelle jumped, having not realized how close she'd gotten. "What's the point of giving us a compass if it won't work halfway through?"

"We have an hour left," Leo said wearily, kicking the

ground thoughtlessly. She watched him kick up the dirt. It fell back to the ground with a soft crunch. His incessant whining was getting on her nerves. "I have the map in my head, not like it's much to remember," he added. "Or helpful."

A crunching noise from what was supposed to be dirt? She knelt and scooped up what she thought might be sand. The tiny grains were around the size of salt, but they weren't sand. Isabelle squinted at the circular, microscopic rocks piled atop each other and shifting in her hand.

She dug a hole with the point of her shoe; the pebbles slid over each other and slunk back to their original positions once her shoe was removed. There was no reachable bottom, and the needle continued to spin no matter how far she held it down the hole.

"Look for things," Isabelle said suddenly, desperately searching for the right words. She opted to pantomime what she meant. She pointed to herself and feigned being dead, then pointed to the sole of her shoe, then a tree. Bodies, footprints, landmarks. "Anything."

One of the crucial steps of hunting, she came to learn, was finding the inconsistencies or minor details that could lead to the animal you sought. Were there hoof prints? A nest that indicated a family of birds nearby? A hole in the trunk of a tree?

The others fanned out, keeping within eye distance of each other, but she stayed in her current position. She had a plan. A flimsy plan, but it was better than nothing. She surveyed the trees, trying to find any patterns in the way they were lined up. There were none, the dead and living minding their own business with no meaning, no reason.

"There's a body," Othelia called. There was a pause and then, "Make that five."

Isabelle could make out Othelia's silhouette from where

she stood, so she dug another hole with her shoe to serve as a checkpoint and walked over. Two of the five bodies had been gutted, innards sprawled out as a buffet for the two-legged, feathered creatures sitting on their stomachs. The dark brown birds pecked at pink flesh. Isabelle's eyes met their blank gazes, and she gagged, covering her mouth and looking away reflexively. She crouched low beside a tree and upheaved. Eli and Galen came up to observe the bodies.

"That's wicked," Galen exclaimed with intrigue. She looked at him from the corner of her eye, his lips creased with excitement.

"Wickedly gross," Eli said, turning the other way and gagging.

"It's just some dead bodies." Such a strange boy, Galen was. Isabelle didn't think too fondly of his nonchalant tone toward the dead as she hurled a second time. Only bile came out now. "You wanna come see this, Leo? The human body is endlessly fascinating."

"I'd rather not," Leo responded from somewhere distant. She couldn't place where he was.

"Can we focus?" Isabelle asked, wiping her chin. Her breath tasted horrible, and her face was hot from the dispatching of her breakfast.

Othelia put her hands on her hips and aimlessly looked around. "What do they expect us to do? Get through here by luck?"

Her agitation was both clear and warranted. Panic seeped into Isabelle's thoughts. There wasn't much time left. She looked up at the dead trees with wonder and confusion. She hated it here. It was meek and depressing, and the dampness seeping through her clothes made her shiver even in the humid climate. She didn't like the cold or the rain, and this was a morbid concoction of both.

Gahi created a world with no meaning or reason, no discernable end or motive. A world where creatures could make their own decisions and decide their own versions of right and wrong. She should've suspected that these types of phenomena could exist, that this desert was more natural than unnatural. Nothing had a reason. It just was.

"The compass doesn't work in the sunny areas, either," Leo reported from afar.

"Of course not," Isabelle said. Then, to Othelia, she said in Urkinian, "The sun doesn't affect the magnetic pull of our planet."

Othelia repeated Isabelle's sentence to Leo. Although Isabelle didn't think her words were harsh, his mouth clamped shut, and he turned away. She'd made a mistake, but now was not the time to correct it. There were no footsteps engrained in the rocks, and no other bodies, dead or alive.

So, she stuck with her original plan; the one she had no faith in. Isabelle gestured for them to follow her, and she searched for the hole she'd made. It took some seconds to find, and she stopped walking when she did.

"If we go," she held up the compass and pointed to the NE, then pointed directly in front of her, "we'd get there, right?"

The group was slow to react, sharing glances with each other. Finally, Galen said, "Sure, yeah. Theoretically. But how can we know if we're walking in a straight line?"

"I imagine mist like this is fairly easy to get lost in," Eli said, "because it's so dense. Not even a flashlight could point us in the right direction."

She looked at him while stroking her chin. "Good point. Othelia, can I use Urkinian? I have a plan."

Othelia nodded. "I'll try my best to translate."

Isabelle paused, mulling over her idea before she said it

aloud. After all, if it sounded dumb in her head, it certainly wouldn't translate well into words.

"Well...?" Othelia prodded.

"Well," she began, "we can't just walk in a straight line, considering all the trees in the way. But what if we started by spacing each other out—in a straight line? Then, the person in the back could run up to the front and we could make sure they're perfectly in front of everyone else. If something is blocking our way, we can use that as a marker for keeping our path straight."

After the translation, Galen asked skeptically, "And you think that would work?"

"What else?" She turned to Eli. "How big is desert?"

"Unfortunately, I don't know," he said sadly. "A mile minimum?"

"Is it possible for our destination to be inside the mist?" Othelia asked.

"Unlikely, I'd say. Building infrastructures would be a nightmare in here."

"I think we should try it," Leo chimed in. "What else could we do?"

Isabelle nodded and cleared her throat. "Is everyone on board?"

"I don't think so," Galen said with an overdrawn and conflicted sigh. "It's just too... convoluted? And it would take up too much time if it's a mile or more. Here, let me try something."

Before anyone could protest, he dashed toward the closest tree. She watched in awe as he jumped with his arms extended and grabbed a thick, suspended branch. He clung to it with an iron grip before pulling himself over the top. He hopped from one to the next until he reached the highest accessible point.

She understood what he was doing, and she cursed herself for not coming up with it first.

Galen remained up there and out of view for a minute or two before appearing again. He sprung from the lowest branch and tucked himself into a ball while hitting the ground. He rolled twice and popped up on his feet effortlessly.

Isabelle stared and stewed in mild resentment. She could not do such things, nor could she come up with a better plan, or be perfectly fine with seeing the dead. How did she expect to serve justice for her brother when she couldn't look at a dead body, much less kill someone herself? She was a failure of a leader and practically spineless. At least she could save a boat.

As Galen approached, Eli pointed at him and looked at the others in astonishment. "Did he just do that? Did you just do that?"

"Yeah. If you roll as you hit the ground, it'll minimize the impact of your drop," Galen replied, his voice silvery yet quiet. "The desert ends. It's actually not too far, I don't think. There are fields on the other side, and what looks to be a village."

"Did you see any people? People we could recognize?" Leo asked.

Galen shook his head. "Too far for me to see faces, but I saw some people. We should head in that general direction. I can climb a tree every once in a while."

Isabelle debated whether to refute his idea. She wanted to be right, to be chosen, and not proven wrong so easily. By Galen, of all people. But he had a point, didn't he? She thought her idea was bad, yet she'd said it with such confidence. She had embarrassed herself.

Galen walked away, his swagger burning a hole in her. He hadn't asked if they agreed or not, and he didn't seem to care. Did he care for anyone other than himself? He may have helped Othelia out of the mud and come back to unsink the ship, but what if it was all for show? Or did he somehow find it within himself to care for the people he partnered with?

Othelia was the first to follow, then the boys one after another. Reluctantly, Isabelle swallowed her pride and took up the rear. The checkpoint she'd made was nothing more than a tiny, useless hole now. She wanted to crawl into a hole now more than ever.

"We should run to preserve our time," Leo suggested, and they did.

Isabelle's wet clothes rubbed her skin raw, causing a ferocious itch on her already aching thighs. With every step, her knees begged to buckle. She used every fiber of her being to ignore it.

They ran together, a group of synchronized steps until Eli began trailing behind. Leo fell back to keep him company; Othelia and Galen took up the front. Isabelle was in the center of their two groups, watching the mist as it swirled around Othelia and Galen's bodies. She wanted her physical strength to be better; she wanted to be like them, but there was only so much she could do.

A low branch obstructed her path, and she ducked. As she straightened up, she skidded to a halt and held her breath. Her eyes widened, terror-stricken, but a scream dared not escape. In front of her stood a seven-foot-tall, bug-like creature. Its segmented tail was long and narrow, curling over the base of its long body. It had eight legs and pedipalps with pincers and it stared at her with four black and vacant eyes.

She took a slight step back carefully, the pebbles underneath crinkling as her foot slid across them. At that moment, the creature lunged forward with a pointed tail, a stinger at the end dripping with venom.

Isabelle took a quick step to the left and backed away, her back hitting a tree. The stinger dug into the spot she'd just been standing in, the creature shrieking as it realized it'd missed. It scuttled backward, pebbles sprouting from the ground as it removed its stinger. She screamed and ran in the opposite direction, realizing with dismay she'd picked the direction of Eli and Leo, the two weakest of the five. She was leading them to their deaths.

She looked over her shoulder; the creature was feet away and running at an immense speed. Her breath hitched; she was a goner. Isabelle braced herself for impact, her head turned away. She didn't need to see the creature as it killed her.

Impact never came. An incoherent yell sounded from behind her. She turned; the creature had been tossed in the air and onto its back, legs kicking frantically to flip over. Leo—Leo?—was standing there, foot outstretched, a knife in hand. Had he kicked it?

He stood frozen, always frozen, staring at the creature and then at her with wide eyes. At least he'd acted this time around.

"Run, you idiots!" Eli yelled as he passed Isabelle and Leo. "Oh, stars, *run!*"

She bolted, the creature still struggling as she passed; the legs crackled as it squirmed. Angry squeals sounded, igniting further fear and speed into their steps; Eli somehow outran them, panting profusely and wheezing.

Isabelle looked back, hoping to see the creature stuck or gone. But nothing was going the way she thought, and she watched as the thing flipped itself upright. It charged toward them with the tail curled over its body. Isabelle yelped in surprise, her legs propelling her through the desert like a bullet. Adrenaline took over, and her mind went blank.

Something struck her ankles from below, and she stumbled forward, her breath hitching as the wind pulled off her hood and sent her body toppling to the ground.

But instead of hitting the ground, someone pulled her

upright by the back of her shirt. She gagged; her windpipes were squeezed by the tight fabric. She found her footing and continued running, gasping and holding her red-rimmed neck. Othelia appeared beside her with a grimace. "That was a close one."

Othelia's right hand was twitching; a sore had opened and was bleeding through the fabric, turning it a light pink as the mist droplets connected. Othelia let out a throaty grunt and said no more, speeding past Isabelle. They were running from a creature that was smaller than them, yet Isabelle couldn't imagine trying to kill it. She didn't want to get anywhere near it. With any luck, they would reach the end of the desert, and it would sta—

A sharp sting shot through her ankle. She cried out, pulling her foot away as she twisted around. The creature gripped her flesh with a pincher and held her, sawing into her skin with its sharp edges. She screamed in agony, pulling out her dagger and holding it over her head. Its stinger drew back.

Leo appeared behind the creature and slashed at the segmented tail with his much smaller pocketknife. The creature let go of her as Leo's knife made contact. It shrieked again, this time as it writhed in pain. It staggered back and turned to Leo, lowering itself and readying to pounce.

Isabelle hesitated—the smallest error could get her killed—before rushing forward and driving her knife into the center of its body. She pierced the exoskeleton, black blood oozing from the wound. She breathed in deeply and twisted the knife. Her hands were shaking, but she stabbed once more, this time at the base of its neck. The screeches slowly waned until the desert grew silent.

"Th-thanks," she said, favoring her foot. She gulped down the searing pain radiating from her ankle. Isabelle looked down at it; fresh blood drizzled to her muddied shoes and the pebbles beneath her feet.

Leo nudged the creature with his foot to ensure it was dead. Its legs curled in on themselves, shriveling like a raisin in the scorching sun. He looked up at her with eyes dark and lost, but he softly smiled and said, "That was pretty cool. Can you walk?"

Isabelle bit her lip, trying to ignore the pain but failing miserably. Even after her harsh words, he was still nice to her. It was bothersome. She wanted to yell at him, tell him to be angry. Tears pricked her eyes. Her ankle ached, her thighs were raw, and her mind was spinning. She shook her head and gasped out, "Yes. Uh, yes. I am fine."

Her wound throbbed and the only consolation was the mist, which cooled the inflamed skin and washed away the blood. The last thing she wanted was for someone to offer help, much less him. Accepting help was admitting weakness. She should've known Leo would offer, anyway. "I could carry you."

"No, thanks," she said, wobbling forward. As she put pressure on her ankle, she clamped her jaw shut to suppress a yell. As she did so, she bit down on her tongue. A jolt of pulsating pain forced her mouth open, and she yelled despite her efforts. Leo grabbed her hand to help her balance. Defeated, she said, "Fine."

He scooped her up in his muscular arms and kept her close to his chest. Then he ran. He wasn't like Galen and Othelia; she weighed him down and he gasped for breath. And it was her fault. She was putting them both in danger.

Isabelle was seething inside. After all, she'd failed the exam, hadn't she? She couldn't do anything that required anything strenuous or physical, and Leo wouldn't be able to help forever. They had to watch out for themselves as she had suggested. A quell of sadness crept up her throat. Her village would celebrate her return, rejoicing in her safe travels before doling out a punishment for leaving. Her father would look at her with shame and pity and wonder how he could lose both his children to the outside world. He'd tell her she'd been corrupted, that she should've stayed gone.

"You are a failure to the family name, Micah. A disgrace."

She shuddered and tried to focus on Leo's heavy breathing and the pain in her ankle. She'd rather feel pain than think about her father and the village. Isabelle missed him deeply, but she knew what the consequences of leaving town would be and that losing him could be one.

Galen climbed another tree and reported they were close. A loud and prolonged squawk erupted from above and they took to running again. Her heart threatened to break out of her chest, her mind becoming a frenzy of fearful thoughts. She peered over Leo's shoulder as she bounced in his arms, searching for the beast. An off-white bird with long, curved wings came soaring down. Its beak was long and bared with ferocious, jagged teeth. Its talons were outstretched and ready to burrow into Leo's shoulder. No one saw it but her.

She thought perhaps life would flash before her eyes, but all she saw was the bird and its pointed talons as it approached. Leo couldn't possibly run any faster with her in his arms. They were doomed.

Just as the bird came within inches of grabbing Leo, Isabelle found it in herself to shout, "B-behind!"

Something connected with the bird and sent it reeling backward. Well, it must've been something, but she hadn't seen anything. An invisible beam tossed the squawking beast backward, and it tumbled helplessly in the air. Leo ran past Othelia, who'd stopped, her hands pointed to the sky. Isabelle understood. She understood, and it terrified her. The one person she connected with the most was a witch.

Othelia yelled and fell to a knee. The cloth wrapped around her hands was dripping with blood. Isabelle watched from over Leo's shoulder, watched as Othelia grunted and turned. Her face was contorted in pain, but she ran with a final gasping cry. Her attack proved successful; the oversized bird struggled to keep a consistent path as it disappeared into the mist.

"How'd you do that?" Isabelle asked when Othelia caught up with them.

Othelia offered a sly smile and winked. "*Chalkluntso*, was it? Witchcraft?"

Her smile dropped, and she let out a faint sob as she looked down at her ruined hands. "I don't think I can use them for a while. Or my power. It's not... it's not working correctly." Her lip quivered, and Isabelle had the sneaking suspicion Othelia was crying, though the mist made it impossible to tell. "I-I can't believe I made a mistake like that."

Isabelle gulped, frightened by yet another element of life unexplained by the Holy Book of Gahi. The Holy Book had one mention of an unsavory mag user, a person named Abedas. They were in their late twenties with a male stature, though they identified with no sex or gender. Abedas brought joy to the children of the town with goofy antics and magic tricks. They'd heal people that were sick. But they could also contort nature. Suck the oxygen out of a room. Bring the dead back to life. Which, in retrospect, was a very unkind thing to do. The story was supposed to be a lesson—that nature was best to be left undisturbed.

But if there was such a way for humans and mag to interact, and Othelia could wield it, then the Holy Book was wrong. Othelia wasn't evil at all. She'd saved them from an oversized bird, rowed them to safety without a complaint, and told Isabelle to stand up for herself and Reinta.

The Holy Book was never wrong.

"Don't worry," Isabelle said to her encouragingly. "We'll have someone look at your hands when we finish the exam."

Othelia nodded but covered her face with her hood and doubled over, throwing up honey sandwiches in prolonged and ghastly hurls. It subsided every few minutes, and Othelia would keep running until she'd pause and puke again. After their fifth stop, she leaned against a tree, her tawny skin flushed.

"What's the matter?" Isabelle asked.

Othelia kept her eyes closed and exhaled slowly before trying to stand and run again. "I've got some head pain, is all."

The rest of the run went somewhat smoothly and silently, despite an occasional stop. Isabelle mulled over the prospect of asking Othelia to help her find Micah's murderer. Someone with such fantastical strength and power would be of good use, provided Othelia wasn't an evil witch.

The mist weighed Isabelle's shoulders down, continuous movement the only thing that had kept her body warm, and now her lips were turning blue, the cool droplets slowing down her circulation. She thought she might freeze to death before they arrived at their next destination.

And then, the mist dissipated, the sun as radiant as ever over a flat, brown plain. She smiled and basked in the light, allowing her body to absorb the heat. She was damp; her hair was parted in strings and clung to the back of her neck. She pulled off her hood and tilted her head back. Leo struggled to maintain his hold on her, but she didn't care. The warmth was perfect, and she was in paradise.

Paradise was short-lived as the searing pain of her ankle reared its ugly head. She fended off a sob as a throbbing sensation coursed through her foot and leg.

"There's that town I was talking about," Galen said,

pointing to a supposed 'town' half a mile away, made up of a single street with two-story houses on each side.

She prayed as Leo held her and the others walked, everyone tired and weak. They took but fifteen steps when she saw a lump of clothes sitting in the grass. Flies buzzed excitedly as they hovered over the bundle. A putrid smell rose to her nose, one unlike anything she'd ever encountered. The smell of rotten meat sitting out in the sun. She covered her face with her shirt to act as a barrier, but the smell wafted through that, too.

As they passed, she gagged, realizing it was a person. Their face was pummeled to a pulp and unrecognizable, but she knew them by their attire; the woman from group 1 of the trivia phase. But where was her partner? Isabelle could've sworn she saw them together in the water room.

"This exam," Isabelle said, "is too much."

Leo nodded. "The dead are going to outweigh the living." He grunted as he shifted her weight in his arms. "I won't be able to carry you and fight when we get to the town."

"Yes, yes. Put me,"—she gestured toward the ground—"when we are there."

"You should keep your dagger on hand, too. This looks like a life-death phase."

A path of dirt formed a few more paces east, leading them to a giant sign. It stood in the center of the path, made up of wooden posts. A red 'X' was printed on the left, and words were scrawled in scrunched and small letters to the right. It was a language she did not recognize. Leo leaned so close to the sign that Isabelle's shoulder rubbed against it roughly.

"I've never seen this before," Leo mumbled.

Othelia came up to the sign, and Eli followed immediately after. She read the words aloud in Latarian. "'There are ten items scattered throughout the village. They are being guarded by criminals. Successfully obtain one item and keep hold of it for 24 hours. You may not leave town once you pass this sign. Only—'"

"'—death will come!'" Eli finished with an overzealous twinkle in his eyes. He planted his hands on his hips in satisfaction and then furrowed his brows after a moment of thought. "So, we either try to go back, get stranded and die, or try to take the exam and most likely die?"

"I wonder how many people tried to leave because they don't know Ishlish," Othelia muttered. She turned to Isabelle and repeated what the board said in broken Urkinian. Isabelle shivered when she was done.

Death relentlessly loomed over them. She'd prayed and prayed that the next phase would involve something else entirely. A puzzle of sorts, much like the trivia of the second phase. Isabelle wouldn't be able to fight or defend herself with full strength now, and that wasn't good paired with her lack of training. But if she turned back, she'd be failing her brother. She'd go home, if she ever found home, and be treated as what she was. A disgrace.

Galen bounced on the balls of his feet, stretching his arms over his head. Othelia began doing the same, copying him move for move. They flexed their muscles and bent to touch their toes. But it was Galen who said, "Finally. We're going to have a little fun."

PHASE 4

CHAPTER 19
ELI

H E WOULDN'T EXACTLY label a man of staggering height with a spiked club aimed at his head 'fun.'

The man swung with a grunt; his thick fingers wrapped around the base of the bat tightly. Eli ducked before stepping around him, using his terror to fuel his speed. He didn't bother trying to fight, instead dashing behind the fifth house on the left in hopes of not being followed.

The dirt path had taken them directly to the so-called town, gradually widening until it became a road dividing the houses. It was a town with no stores or doctors or schools. Just sixteen houses, eight on each side. Most had porches, like the one Eli ducked behind, but their conditions were varying. While some had splintering paint or completely barren wood chips, others seemed to sparkle in dazzling bright oranges and blues under the morning sun. The house he chose was a light, dusty violet.

The rest of the group had split off; Leo with Isabelle, Galen by himself, and Eli—bless the stars—with Othelia. The downside unfortunately being that Othelia couldn't fight much anymore, and Eli never could to begin with.

Speaking of, she was hot on his trail, leaving the club-wielding man in the dust. When Eli peeked around the corner, the man had disappeared completely, presumably bored with their lack of cooperation. Six or seven of the dead littered the road. Mouths open, eyes gazing aimlessly. His hands trembled at the sight. Why hadn't he brought a weapon? He knew the kinds of challenges the examiners came up with, yet he couldn't bring himself to pack so much as a knife. He was silly enough to bring a flask, but not a weapon.

And the town was quiet. Too quiet. People were either hiding or battling inside. Or dead, like those poor fools he passed.

"Damn it," Othelia said through gritted teeth. "My hands are fried!"

Eli sympathized; he'd never felt pain beyond a toe-stubbing and his recently sliced-up palms and cheek. Her injuries brought about fear in him; he thought her hands may never work right again, and that her pain would stay forever. He kept his worries to himself. There was no point in voicing his thoughts when she undoubtedly felt the same.

Behind the violet house was a white picketed patio raised by three steps and a sliding glass door, which was ajar and shattered on one side. Inside sat a white cat, three or four feet in height. It released a low meow as it stared at him, its fur matted with blood on both its mouth and paws. He had never seen such an animal. Beautiful, if not for all the blood.

"Think all the items have been nabbed already?" Eli whispered as they ducked behind the next house over. It was a bright shade of red, the shade of red that deterred someone from entering.

She nodded, avoiding his gaze. Revealing his knowledge of

Ishlish had been his second biggest mistake, the first being his refusal to bring a weapon. "We must be careful. Can you fight?"

"I can talk," he said. "I'm good at stalling or convincing them not to fight."

"That's high praise. Do you think you're capable of that?"

"I'm hurt," he said dryly. "...If I can't, we can run. Or I can punch, you can kick. It'd be a real team effort."

"Have you ever punched someone before?" She crossed her arms, winced, and looked him over with blatant skepticism. He shook his head and received a scoff in return. "Then you should bank on your words."

He peeked over the red patio pickets—which would reach to his stomach if he were standing—and tried looking inside via a single glass door. He could see the edge of a fireplace, ablaze and crackling, the rest blocked by a couch filled with three people facing the fire. None of them moved. He watched for a dash longer, wondering what type of 'items' they were looking for. They could be anything, and anyone could have one.

The eeriness of the unmoving figures made him shudder, and he nodded for her to follow him to the next house, the second to last. This one was white and set up with a patio as well, though without pickets surrounding it. There were sliding glass doors, but they were shut, and black curtains were drawn.

There was a tree too, one of the few normal-sized trees in the area, and Eli paused under it. The sun was high and hot, and the shade felt like protection, a way to hide. He looked up at the yellow apples growing within the leaves and watched as one fell to the ground with a soft thud. It was the absence of people that scared him the most. The silence of a town that should've been thriving with action. His shoulders ached from the weight they carried.

Eli observed Othelia, who was boldly inspecting the inside of the seventh house with her face pressed against the glass door. He opened his mouth to protest when something silver reflected from above. The branches rustled as a shape fell toward him.

There was no time to move out of the way, his reflexes dampened by confusion. He was pinned to the ground by two powerful legs on his thighs and fingers curled around both his wrists, holding his hands above his head. A woman with knotted brown hair and scratched-up, pale skin stared down at him, amused.

Eli writhed around like a hooked worm, but her grip was strong. He resorted to head-butting her, a knee-jerk reaction, and her grip loosened enough for one of his hands to break free. She pulled out a long boning knife and aimed the blade at his chest. He yelped as he reached up and grabbed her wrist, the blade inches from his chest. His hands were trembling from the weight he was pushing against. The fight she was putting up was good—too good. Eli grunted and did what he could. But she was stronger.

His grip began to falter. The blade slowly descended upon his chest, inch by inch, until the tip of the blade pricked his skin, and a small bead of blood stained his shirt. The woman sneered, and Eli's grunting turned into frightened yelling. She released her grip on his other arm and prepared to shove the knife into his flesh. Eli reached for her neck a moment before she drove it down, and the knife flew up and away.

Both his hands were preoccupied around her neck as he wrung it, pressing his thumbs into her windpipe with desperation he didn't know he had. She did the same; her face turned red and her grip weakened around his neck.

And then the pressure lifted from his legs, the hands disappearing from his skin. He gasped, rubbing at his neck while sitting up and looking for who freed him. It was Othelia, who was now rearing her foot back and aiming it at the woman's face. He thought he saw a tooth go flying as her kick connected. Something inside the woman cracked, and Eli looked away. Othelia kept kicking, a rampage of force.

"You think that's good enough?" he asked.

Othelia faltered, her foot inches from the woman's chest. The lady had stopped moaning and moving, a limp arm covering her eyes. Othelia rested her foot on the ground with a meek nod; she didn't look too thrilled to be paired with him. He knew she'd prefer Isabelle or Galen, and he didn't blame her. He wasn't exactly useful.

Eli released a pained grunt as he leaned on his forearms and stared down at the dab of blood pooling in the center of his shirt. Though the cut wasn't deep, it stung when the fabric rubbed against it. This wasn't how he thought things would go; he may have just witnessed the princess kill someone. His eyes were glued to the unmoving body, even as Othelia helped him stand. She checked the body for any items and came up empty-handed. The *body*, he thought with horror.

"Y-you—"

"It had to be done."

There, standing over a dead person so tall and calm, she looked like who she was, a rich noblewoman with no regard for the lives of others. She was just like the rest of them. But he'd rather work with Othelia and pass the exam than stick to his conscience and lose. At least he had a conscience.

"Yeah, but—"

She cut him off again, voice raised. "You want to pass, don't you?"

Her eyes grew wide with instant regret, her words loud enough for others to be drawn to.

"We need to go," Eli whispered.

Othelia nodded. "But hey," she whispered with a soft smile, one that would usually calm his nerves. "You used your hands, and I used my feet. That team effort is worth something."

In another scenario, he would've jokingly responded about other things they could partake in as a team, but he couldn't find the words when he'd just witnessed her murder someone.

Before taking the lead, Othelia grabbed the blade out of the woman's hand and tossed it to him. Eli jumped out of the way and the knife tumbled to the ground. He rushed to pick it up, face growing hot with embarrassment. "Sor—"

Othelia was long gone, already entering the backyard of the last house on the left. Eli ran to catch up to her. His steps were louder than hers—his big feet rustling the small spurts of grass and crunching the fallen leaves. She ran silently, a phantom. Was that part of her power? What an absurd thought to have—'power' like hers shouldn't exist. Could she use it anywhere or with only her hands? How did she call to it? What *was* it? And if Abel and Samuel could wield this power, then could the other royal families use it, too?

His pondering was cut short by the appearance of the last house. None of the others looked appealing to enter, but somehow this one was the creepiest, painted completely black yet sparkling when hit by the sun. There were no windows, and the door was boarded up.

Othelia didn't waste time and kicked feverishly at the lowest board. Each time, the wood splintered but didn't break. Eli offered his knife, but she shook her head. "That'll take too long."

She threw her body into the door. He winced at each thud and whispered, "Would be quieter, though."

She ignored him and continued slamming herself against it. Eli weighed the knife in his palm. He should've been happy to have found something to defend himself with, but it gave him no comfort. The handle was engraved with the initials, A.M. Did they belong to that woman, he wondered, or had she stolen the knife from someone else?

The door broke open and Othelia clumsily fell inside. Eli's head snapped up in time to see Othelia catch herself with her hands. She sucked in a deep, pained breath and groaned. She was suffering, and he couldn't help her. Perhaps he should've become a doctor, someone who could find the answers to her injuries. Instead, he was an expert on boats. Useless, indeed.

Eli peeked inside, his eyes slowly adjusting to the dim lights. The room they'd stumbled into had a kitchen to the right and three people tied to wooden chairs to the left. Their eyes were covered, and their incessant screams and cries were heavily muffled by thick, silver tape. A shadow moved from the open kitchen and disappeared behind the wall before Eli could get a good glimpse of who, or what, it was. All he knew was that he didn't want to move.

Othelia let out another groan as she stood and took off toward the kitchen. He both admired and feared her lack of forethought. Were her burnt hands a product of this same nature?

Unable to compel himself to follow, he started taking off the contestants' blindfolds and tape. His heart nearly dropped at the sight of Abel and Samuel. The third man he didn't know. His hair was dusty blonde and his skin rosy, eyes hooded and narrow. They were the color of the ocean, and the ocean was overflowing as the man wept before Eli. Four of his nails had been peeled from his fingers.

What was Eli supposed to do with them? If he untied them, he'd be attacked, but he couldn't leave them defenseless, either. Eli clasped his hands together behind his back as his gaze shifted between each of them. "Do any of you have an item?"

"Does it look like we'd have one?" Samuel snapped. His cheek had a cut smeared with mud, and the corner of his lower lip was turning a dark purple.

"I'm going to search you," Eli said, reaching into Abel's pockets and shoes. Abel didn't seem to recognize him—which was quite all right. "All of you."

Most contestants didn't bring more than a weapon or two, so he looked for anything out of the ordinary, anything at all.

No luck. They were dry.

Eli sighed and put his hands on his hips. Right back to square one. What was he going to do with them?

"Uh," Abel said, wobbling in his chair. His eyelids were sunken in dejection, and he sounded just the same. "Can you let us go, please? We'll go peacefully."

Eli stroked his chin. "Why would I believe the sons of kings?"

They were interrupted by Othelia, her back thrown against the kitchen wall. She landed on her feet and kicked her shadowed opponent in the groin not once, not twice, but three times. Eli watched in amazement. His family didn't bother with teaching fighting techniques, nor did he believe violence was the answer. But he had to give her credit for her resilience and skill. She was good at what she did.

The man fell, moaning as he slapped against the tiled flooring hidden behind a counter. Othelia reached for him but stopped halfway and sheepishly looked at Eli. Her hood had fallen back during the scuffle, and he found himself wholly captivated by her beauty. He wanted to speak, but his thoughts became jumbled and words refused to flow. How annoying.

"Can you help me?" she asked. He nodded and headed over, trying to use his tall frame to block Samuel's sight of her.

"Othelia? What are you doing here?"

Her smile faltered as her gaze shifted to her brother. "I should be asking you the same thing. But we're busy right now."

Eli arrived at her side and peered down at the unconscious man. One of the criminal guards, he suspected. The man had multiple tattoos and lip piercings, and he sported an ankle bracelet.

Othelia pointed to a golden bracelet wrapped around the man's wrist and Eli's mouth dropped open in delighted shock. Eli slid off the bracelet with careful and eager fingers. He dangled it between himself and Othelia. She didn't need help to fight; she needed help with grabbing the item. At least he was useful for something.

He expected her to take it, but she shook her head and walked toward the door. As she stepped over the broken-down boards, she said, "Leave them."

Incredulous, he shoved the bracelet into his pocket and glanced over at the tied-up fellows. The criminal was unconscious, his chest rising and falling softly. He'd awaken again, and when he did, there was no telling what he would do.

Samuel wriggled around and fought with his bindings, sparing angry glances toward Eli—perhaps presuming Eli would blindly listen to Othelia and leave them. Abel, on the other hand, hung his head with his mouth sealed shut. He'd already given up. Eli did a quick sweep of the house for Abel's two cronies. Empty. By Abel's dejection and their absences, Eli surmised they were dead.

"Please let us go, please," the third man begged, tears streaming down his cheeks. "I won't hurt you, please. I just want to go home."

That was the deal breaker. Eli couldn't leave them for dead, even if they would've done the same to him. It wasn't right. And for Othelia to turn her back on a sibling? Well, he didn't think that was right, either, no matter how wretched Samuel probably was.

"Oh Stars, you better not betray me. Here." Eli sawed at the ropes that bound the men, thankful for A.M.'s knife. It was his only advantage if they were to attack him.

He released the crying man first, who stood and hugged Eli, whispering words of gratitude. He ran out then, gone and away. Next was Abel, who rubbed at his wrists and refused to look at Eli. That was fine; Eli didn't need appreciation.

Samuel was last, for obvious reasons, but he, too, remained docile. He stood with a nonchalant stretch, burying his fury well while standing at eyes-length from Eli. His breath was hot against Eli's face.

Eli backed away with the knife between them. Samuel was too calm for his liking. "Well, you're welcome, but I best be going now. Don't follow us."

He turned and stepped over the broken door, soon to be free from that dingy house.

"You're friends with her?"

Eli stopped and turned back around with an eyebrow raised curiously. "We're acquaintances. Partners in crime."

"You aren't of the royal families," Samuel said, his voice thick with intrigue. His eyes scanned Eli from head to toe with a grimace. Eli had the suspicion he was caught in the middle of something he most definitely wanted to be in. Anything regarding the Sandoval line was crucial.

"Astute observation."

"How do you know each other? Are you of Ishla?"

Eli wiggled a finger and offered a dry smirk. "Sorry, but I

don't answer to you. Why don't you ask her? She's your sister, after all."

Samuel tsked. "Can you let Othelia know something?" He didn't wait for an answer. "Her recklessness is what caused this. She needs to go home."

Eli tried his best to hide his surprise and nodded. He had no intention of spreading the word, but naturally, he said what would get him in the least amount of trouble. "I'll pass on the message."

"I don't know what she's done to earn your respect, but you aren't important to her. You'll be left the minute she doesn't need you anymore."

Eli let out a short laugh and walked out while muttering to himself, "She'd have ditched me after the first phase."

Othelia was waiting around the corner, sitting with her back pressed against the black exterior of the house, and arms wrapped around her tucked knees. She looked vulnerable, almost sad with her eyes transfixed on the horizon beyond. The sky was bright blue with not a cloud in sight. Birds were in the distance, flying high and free.

"What took you so long?" she asked. "Fraternizing with the enemy?"

"Do I seem the type?"

A small smile rose on her lips. "Anyone interested in politics seems the type."

"And that excludes you?"

"What do you want?" she demanded, her eyes switching to his, burrowing into his soul. "What was your purpose for approaching me on the ship?"

"I told you then; I know a lot about boats, and I wanted to help. I haven't lied to you."

"Tell me, or I'll tie you up with them."

He sighed. Eli didn't want to tell her about his plans, not

yet. He wanted to smooth out her edges and build trust until he could tear down the love she felt for her father. But trust was a dream of the past at this point. "Are you familiar with New Guayi?"

Her mouth hung open and then she said, "Of course. They have the largest natural water supply in the world."

"Do you know how much money your father pays for two tanks full?" She shook her head, and he continued, "100 quill, what could easily be 800 or more, I'd bargain. You really don't know?"

"You're using me to get to my father? Is that it?"

He hesitated. "New Guayi is going into steep debt because of him. He takes without giving. I was hoping to befriend you and help you see my side—that King Sandoval is a growing tyrant. What's he planning to do when he finally bleeds us dry? Take it all for himself?"

Eli looked out into the ever-expanding and lonesome fields, waiting for an answer. He was at the edge of his seat, eager for her input but scared of what she might say. He could feel her eyes boring into him. Every muscle in his neck wanted to turn to her, to watch her. It was insufferable—his attraction.

Finally, he felt her eyes leave him and she stared into the distance as well. "I'm afraid I didn't know about any of that. Father has been excluding me from the political realm for quite a while now. More so than I thought. I'm sorry, but I'm of no use to you. I'm of no use to anyone."

Eli twisted his head toward her sharply. She'd been excluded from everything? And for how long? What had she done that was so horrible?

He pulled the bracelet out from his pocket and put it on her knee. "Of no use? I seem to recall you kicking the asses of several people in the last two days. You even saved me moments ago. Seems to me you have plenty of use, just maybe not in the way you first thought."

She frowned. "Well, I'm assuming my wonderful brother spoke to you, and if he did, then you already know I'm telling the truth and don't have business with him, either."

"That's a bold assumption," he shot back lightly.

Othelia stood, the bracelet sliding off her knee, and tilted her head to indicate she was leaving. She jogged toward the opposite side of town. He followed with a moment's hesitation, bending to pick up the item and looking back to make sure Samuel and Abel weren't following.

Eli and Othelia spent a second in the open and then found refuge behind the parallel house. This one was bright orange, perhaps the brightest of them all. They paused under a closed window with the blinds raised.

"I think you should know by now that I'm no fool," she whispered. "I don't particularly care what Sam has to say about me, but there's no point in you lying. I thought you wanted to befriend me?"

Her forwardness was enduring, but her lack of urgency was not. He nodded, out of breath and panting from their short run. She was right; he should've known by now. Her intelligence just added to her beauty.

He needed to stop lusting over her. Othelia killed someone right before his eyes, and she didn't care about the politics of her own country, much less anyone else's. She could evoke change if she wanted to, but she didn't want to. But he needed to remind himself that she seemed upset by being left out of her family affairs. Maybe he could convince her to care.

"Okay, okay. Yes. He said, 'this' was all your fault, whatever that means." Eli peeked through the window; the room was lit by the sun pouring in from the other wide windows. There was someone sitting at a dining table, staring back with open eyes, a scar over the left. He didn't move, and he didn't blink.

Eli wasn't stepping foot in there. Nope. Nuh-uh. He nodded for Othelia to follow him to the next house. She looped her arm around his, pulled him back, and pointed. "We do this one. I can feel it."

"You know what I feel? Creeped out."

"Exactly. That guy in there? He's one of Abel's friends. Obrien, I think. He was the strongest of the three of them."

"And now he's dead. And that doesn't worry you?"

Othelia didn't respond, instead jabbing her elbow into the window. It shattered with a deafening crunch. *Apparently not,* he thought.

"It was to my understanding that we didn't want attention," Eli said, looking around frantically and fearing the worst.

"We want to get this over with."

"Without drawing attention. You're going to get us killed!"

"We'll be fine." Othelia barreled in, tossing her body through the cracked opening and rolling in a way reminiscent of Galen. Eli picked shards of glass out of his way before he swung a leg over the sill.

The dead twin had a mouth twisted in pain, his head slumped forward with discomforting, empty eyes, and a meat knife was lodged in the back of his skull. Eli gagged, reeling backward until his back hit the refrigerator. He closed his eyes and tried to steady his breathing, but the smell of blood in the uncirculated air made him gag harder.

Othelia disappeared into the house, either unaffected by the smell or good at ignoring it. There was a single hallway leading to five rooms. Sweat protruded from his shaky palms as she scurried down the hallway, and he wiped at his brow. Two doors were open, one with audible shuffling from Othelia, and the other staring back at him with apparent vacancy.

Eli chose the farthest room to search—the door shut. Stars, he hoped no one was on the other side. The sweat drenching his body was heavier now, slick along his back and armpits. How could Othelia so easily search the rooms? How could she so easily kill another person?

He couldn't wait any longer and opened the door. As he took a step over the threshold, something sprouted from the other side and connected with his forehead. He flew back and landed with a loud thud, his head ricocheting off the wood-paneled floors. Black spots clouded his vision and disoriented his senses. Nausea consumed him. He flopped onto his side with a groan, unable to stand or see or think or control the drool spooling from his lips.

A hand wrapped around his ankle and yanked him in.

CHAPTER 20

GALEN

GALEN HADN'T ANTICIPATED splitting off from the others. At the very least, not from Leo. But when he first saw the vacancy of the town, there was no question in his mind. They'd have to work quickly and quietly, and that sort of plan couldn't include four other people. Besides, he wasn't there for other contestants—he wasn't even there for himself.

A man swinging around a club came charging at Eli as they all took off in separate directions. While Eli and the mag girl ducked behind a house to the left, Galen took off down the center of town, inspecting the front of each house he passed. He jumped over a dead body, a man with a crooked nose whom Galen could almost recognize, someone he'd seen on the boat with the male mag user.

Some doors were beaten in, others tightly clasped closed. He'd just have to pick one and go. His legs sent him veering toward the sixth house on the right. Galen skipped the four steps leading up to the front porch and landed on his toes without making a sound. The walls were made of dark red wood, and the front door was a thick block of metal. The roof was concaved as if the infrastructure was about to collapse in on itself.

Galen pressed himself against the wall between the front door and window before testing the doorknob. It wouldn't budge. He prepared to peek into the open window, but the sound of movement inside gave him pause. The movement of the knob must've tipped them off.

He got halfway down the stairs when the door opened. Galen glanced behind his shoulder to see a giant man with an ugly mug and tattoos of once vibrant dragons lining both of his meaty arms. The head of each dragon ended at his elbows, staring back at Galen with wide eyes and slithering tongues. Galen recognized the man immediately.

Nicknamed 'the Axe,' Herbert Cummings had a 500,000Q bounty on his head, namely for breaking into people's homes and murdering them as they slept with, as the nickname suggested, an axe. His interrogation later revealed that killing in the dark gave him extra 'pleasure.'

Now, Cummings did not have an axe. He ran toward Galen with a formed fist instead, technique nonexistent but eyes full of fire. Galen watched the man swing, figuring out the trajectory of his punch as it came.

Galen smirked. Cummings' side was wide open, and Galen kicked him there, hoping to hit a rib. Galen was shorter and smaller, and his kick didn't move or injure the man. As his foot connected, Cummings grabbed hold of his calf and twisted it harshly. Galen huffed, muffling a scream with a clenched jaw.

His other leg fell out from under him, and his body twirled in the air. There was no time to think; gravity pulled at his upper body, his face plummeting to the ground while his foot was still clenched in a calloused hand.

Galen saved himself with an outstretched arm, stopping his

momentum and pushing himself into the air and back the way he came. His free foot soared higher than the one caught in Cummings' grip and landed squarely in the delinquent's face. He was thrust backward, losing hold of Galen's leg. Galen's shoulder slammed against the ground with a thick thud. Air was squeezed out of him. He wheezed; the dirt and houses and sky meshed together in a blurry mess.

But there was no time to hesitate. He pulled himself upright and stood with a grunt. Cummings was standing and steady, staring back at Galen with a hard, unreadable expression. Galen expected to be attacked and braced himself, rolling his shoulders and cracking his neck. He tested his leg, the muscles of his calf sending sharp pain to his foot. He winced but kept his eyes on his opponent.

Cummings maintained his sharp gaze as his lips transformed into a haughty smile. He waved Galen forward. "Come in."

He turned his back to Galen and made his way up the patio stairs. The steps creaked under his weight. Galen watched the man go, his mind reeling. It should've been a simple decision; he should've attacked Cummings right then and there. The first rule of The Bounty was to incapacitate the hunted. Keep 'em alive for the money, but make sure they can't get away once you've got 'em. Galen had considered bringing a pair of handcuffs to the exam but ultimately decided to do without. His sisters hadn't needed them.

And, given Galen's thinner physique, there was no way he could beat the burly man one-on-one. The key to dealing with faults was recognizing and working with them. So he followed, curious where this hospitality would lead. There was always the possibility that this was a trap, of course, but Galen was fast. If he was outnumbered, he knew the exit points, and he would use them. No point fighting a losing battle when the penalty was death.

Galen watched the back of Cummings' head; the man's hair was buzzed down to nearly nothing. Black and white swirled tattoos ran from his scalp down to his neck, freshly inked and bright red around the edges. The tips of the swirls were swollen and lumpy—infected, no doubt. Good. Karma came in many forms. But how was a prisoner to get a tattoo while locked away?

The inside was well-lit and sparse of furniture. A row of tall lamps lined the farthest wall, the lightbulbs exposed but turned off—the only light came in from the windows behind them. A table sat in the center, empty, aside from a can of beans with a fork protruding from the top. Beside the table sat two black bags with pink plus signs on their sides.

Cummings sat on one side and crossed his legs. There were no chairs, and his knees were squished against the table legs, but he paid no mind and ate his beans idly, speaking not a word. It was an insult, and Galen was greatly insulted.

"Is this a joke?" he asked, searching the wooden kitchen cupboards and under the sink. Everything was empty. He turned a faucet handle, opened a fridge, and tried the stove. None of them worked. Would they create a fake town strictly for the exam, or had they turned off the electricity to make the game fairer?

Galen released a deep sigh and tore through the rest of the home angrily, looking for anything he could get his hands on. All six bedrooms held unmade beds, and he flipped the mattresses over hopefully, expectedly, but there was nothing. The bathroom only had a bar of soap and wiping paper, and the toilet didn't flush. A waste of his time.

He huffed and went back to the sitting room, where Cummings was shoveling the last of his beans into his mouth.

He looked at Galen from across the table, arms crossed over his chest. Galen mimicked him and tilted his chin up—he felt taller that way—and narrowed his eyes.

Cummings ran a hand over his stubby hair. "You're about an hour too late. Though there's no way to tell time here, so who can be sure?"

Galen stood a good few feet away from him, keeping all his senses in play. Unless he missed something, which he found very unlikely, then the house was truly empty. That posed the question of *how* the item was taken and Cummings' life was spared. But neither of those things really mattered. He was asking all the wrong questions, and that included the one he asked aloud, "Why aren't you trying to kill me?"

"I had a job, and I failed, as you can see. I have no reason to kill you."

"So? You're a murderer. Wouldn't you want to fight me? Doesn't your kind like to murder?" Galen's blood boiled as the man's expression didn't change, a look of unrelenting boredom etched in place.

Galen had never fought an actual criminal—that was for the big leagues—but he had an extensive amount of training. An occasional sibling dispute would be solved with a fight too, of which his current standing was 8-10. His odds of beating this man were low, but Galen still wanted to fight. It was the best way to let his frustrations loose. And, more importantly, it would be fun.

"My kind? That's interesting of you to say. Some may be so vile as to not have their own standards, but I certainly do. Defending a house ain't one. I break into them. At night. As you can see, it's broad daylight. And all they supplied me with was food. Not a single weapon. Where's the fun in that?"

"What about those?" Galen asked, pointing at the black bags with pink pluses.

The criminal shook his head at Galen's relentless effort. "There's nothing of use to you in there, either. This is the medical house, apparently. They didn't bother telling me that until I got here, though. I don't know nothin' about that stuff."

"Medical house? For who?" Galen asked, unzipping both bags. They were filled with neatly packaged medical supplies of varying degrees. Needles, gauze, wipes, burn treatment.

"Competitors can get patched up here if they come in. For criminals who get injured, too. The examiners aren't complete barbarians."

Galen nodded along; that wasn't the answer he was expecting. He pulled out a packet of needles. "You could've used these to fight."

Cummings scoffed. "Didn't I say I have standards?"

"Can I take some?"

"Not a chance."

Galen glanced up at Cummings, ready to protest, and froze as a sudden jolt of anxiety coursed through him. Cummings bore a sly smile, his first notion of interest in Galen since he sat down. He oozed murderous intent, his eyes blank. Primed for a fight. Should he badger Cummings some more? No, there was ultimately no point. Although, it would be fun. He was being forced to take the exam, sure, but he still wanted to get in on the action. Aside from the first phase, the whole thing was proving to be a slog.

Galen left the bags on the floor open and headed toward the door. "I'll be back later to hide here. I have partners that could benefit from the gauze in there. Don't let anyone else use it. In fact, don't let anyone else inside."

"And why would I do that for you?"

Galen paused. "Why not? Unless you've already made a deal with someone else?"

Cummings clasped his hands together and placed them on the table, his smile receding. "I recognize an Aguelon when I see one. Tell me, do they breed you all the same? As shallow, money-hungry fuc—"

"You killed innocent families while they slept."

"Your mother tossed me in prison. You know what a life sentence in prison is like?"

"You deserve several lifetimes."

"Perhaps I've been prone to following through with some bad... urges. But you and your family aren't much better."

"What's that supposed to mean?" Galen didn't like being recognized; it took away what little power he had. And much to his dismay, he was offended. His mother and elder sisters were some of the best bounty hunters of the decade. Perhaps they enjoyed earning money, but that wasn't comparable to murder.

Cummings didn't answer, his gaze somewhere off in the distance. Galen was quickly losing interest in him, mostly because he found murderers without a cause boring. They simply liked to kill. What kind of motive was that?

Galen didn't particularly like killing. After all, everyone had someone who would miss them. He'd only meant to stun the bowman, and causing the man's death was unnerving to Galen. He'd have left this gross man and house and never come back if he hadn't remembered Isabelle's ankle and the mag users' hands. If either of them lived, anyway.

"Keep it empty until I get back, and I'll see to it your sentence is reduced," Galen offered. It wasn't something he'd follow through with; he was an Aguelon, after all. Justice had ruled Cummings a lifelong sentence, and that's what he would serve.

Cummings scoffed. "Go ahead, prove me wrong. If you can. Your kind isn't interested in forgiveness."

Galen gritted his teeth and turned his back on the man. His fingers were itching to form fists, but he held back and stormed out the door. The street was eerily quiet, the blistering sun beating down and creating waves of radiating heat around him. He could already feel sweat staining his maroon crop top, the long sleeves dangling over his hands.

He wanted to find the others; the exam wouldn't have been as interesting without them. But no, he should focus on his own success. There was too much on the line. Trying to find these 'items' was strictly based on luck and close-range fights. He wasn't too good with luck, and he wasn't relying on it now. He'd search every house if he had to.

He took note of the house's address—5010—and then ran off to a purple house three down. The outside was rimmed with white, the paint brighter than any of the others. Around the house he went, finding a back door lying in the grass a few feet away. Galen held his breath as he grew closer to the opening.

"I don't want to do that," someone whispered from the other side. Galen paused and tried to make out the rest of the conversation, but it was muffled. How many voices were there? At least one female and one male, maybe two. Were they close to the door or deeper inside? He couldn't tell, so he depended on his best guess.

Galen hopped over the threshold of the doorway, steps inaudible, and took in his surroundings. As predicted, there were three of them to the left, on the other side of a bulky couch. Two men and a woman. Their hushed whispers were magnified; they were arguing, he realized, undisturbed by his presence. Good. He had time to think of a plan. He quickly sorted each room into categories. To the right were the kitchen, a bathroom, and a table. To the left were the living room and stairs. There was a short hallway with three open doors.

Based on their lack of alertness, he pinned them as novices and prepared himself to attack. There were no weapons out in the open, which was promising, but he kept his guard up as he jumped over the couch and locked eyes on his first target. A boy, no older than Galen, with a doughy frame and high-pitched voice. His red tracksuit stuck out against the brown walls and looked vaguely familiar, though Galen couldn't quite place from where.

Galen came up from behind and hit the pressure points behind his neck and along his spine. A gasp escaped the boy's lips, and he fell to the ground in a heap. As he fell, Galen was onto the next person. The second boy and redheaded girl stopped talking in surprise and turned to him, but their reactions were slow. Galen jabbed his elbow into the second boy's nose and kicked the girl in the stomach.

Amid everything, he remembered the name of the tracksuit kid, Kiel, from the trivia phase. The one who'd warned Galen's partners of his family. The girl was from trivia, too, Mary. No, it was something weird, like Mari.

She stumbled backward, and her flailing arms revealed a crowbar. Mari caught herself and stepped forward, aiming the crowbar at his arm. Galen backpedaled with his hand out in defense. The solid metal slammed against his fingers; the pain reverberated through his hand and up his arm. He yelled despite his efforts to suppress it and ducked as the crowbar came swinging at his nose.

He remained crouched and grabbed her weapon from underneath before forcefully pulling it down. She had an iron grip on the damn thing, so he stepped on her toes, then looped his foot around her ankle and kicked it out from under her. The crowbar twisted out of her hand as she fell backward. She landed on her butt and looked up at him with furrowed brows, rubbing at her wrist.

Galen held the crowbar between them. The other boy gave up easily, holding his gushing nose while cowering behind Mari. Kiel would be unconscious for the rest of the day, maybe even the next.

But Mari wasn't done yet. She sprung up and lunged forward, catching him off guard. Galen stepped back and held the crowbar like a bat. He wound his arms back, ready to swing. Her resilience was admirable, but he didn't find her a challenge.

She backed away from each swing—on the defense as he kept control. Exhilarating adrenaline coursed through him, and an involuntary smile overtook his lips. She gave up, unable to land a hit or gain any semblance of power. Mari stood beside her partner. Their mouths shut, and hands relaxed at their sides.

"Any of you got one?"

They shook their heads. The boy looked notably terrified, blue eyes dewy with tears. His hair was electric blue and piercings ran along his earlobes and fingers, but his tough exterior meant nothing here. It was strange, having someone cower before him. Galen had to admit, there was a certain entertainment there, a certain excitement. That was a horrible thing to think, he knew, but it popped into his mind, nonetheless. Some urges couldn't be controlled.

Mari was putting a damper on his enjoyment, her accusatory eyes pinned on him, lips curled in disgust. When he looked her way, however, her eyes darted away. They were both avoiding his gaze, he realized with amusement.

"Give me one of your items and I won't kill you." He wouldn't kill them, not unless he had to. He was leaning more toward doing to them what he'd done to Kiel. But trying to do that to two people in such close proximity would be hard. He didn't know their capabilities. Hopefully, they'd cooperate, so he didn't have to worry about it.

"We don't have any," the girl shot back, stomping her foot. Her bluntness was bothersome; he almost believed it. But no, she was scared beneath those hazel eyes. Terrified, even. The same look his youngest sister, Tatiana, had when his mother made the announcement for him to take the exam. She'd hugged him and cried.

"Overturn your pockets and roll up your sleeves, please."

"Fuck you."

"Very well." Galen took a bold step toward her with the crowbar raised.

The boy thrust his body in front of Mari as a means of protection. It was comical, the way he tossed around his arms and puffed out his chest. "There's no point in lyin', Marianne."

Her eyes widened. "Why would you say my *full* name in front of him?! Are you stupid? I ought to smack some sense into you, you wretched simpleton."

"Hey," Galen said roughly, waving his hand. "Item first. Bicker later, 'kay?"

The boy shook his head silently as he reached into his pocket and produced a pair of opal earrings. The stone was transparent, crystalline white. Galen contained his giddiness with a gulp.

"I-I stole them off another guy," the boy blabbered. "Say, m-maybe if I kept one and gave you the other, we'd both pass?"

Galen shook his head. "I can't take any chances. I'm sure you understand."

The boy stared at him for an uncomfortable amount of time. Galen extended his hand out. "Well? Hand them over."

The earrings were given with a whimper. Galen felt bad, to an extent, but the weak were meant to be picked off in a game like this. He shoved the earrings into his pocket and tossed the crowbar at their feet. "Thank you for your service."

Galen headed for the back door, a grin still on his face. He'd secured a nice pair of earrings *and* he would pass this phase of the exam. One step closer to going home.

He was stepping over the threshold of the doorway when the back of his head was struck. He fell to the ground, nose connecting with the wooden panels at an awkward angle. A sharp crack splintered through the air as one of his lenses shattered. A shard of glass snapped inward, penetrating the center of his eye. Galen didn't feel any of this, however; the single blow had rendered him unconscious before his cheek hit the ground.

CHAPTER 21

LEO

HE RAN WITH Isabelle in his arms, hunched low. He watched the others break off and quickly followed suit, running to the far right before he saw which houses they'd ducked behind. The man with a club was particularly terrifying, his grimace permanent and angry.

Leo carried her to the side of the first house, leaning against the wall to catch his breath. Unless there were any straggling contestants that came down the dirt path, they were safe. For now. Isabelle was getting too heavy for him; he was strong, but tired, the physical endurance of the last few days catching up to him. Of all things, he thought his strength would be an advantage, but he was naïve. Naïve and weak.

She hit him on the shoulder. "I said to... to..." She gestured toward the ground.

"Oh. Right." He helped her stand and lean against the wall beside him. She favored her right foot but didn't remark on how it felt. Her shoulders sagged as she let out a deep exhale. Leo wanted to comfort her, but there wasn't much he could say.

This would prove to be the hardest challenge yet, especially since neither of them were fighters. He recalled how she attacked Abel on the boat, shoving her entire body into him and throwing both of them to the ground. Not an attack he'd call 'good.'

Leo glanced around, not another member of their group in sight. He took in the quiet nature around them. A door opened across the way and Leo caught a glimpse of the club user going in. Everyone else had disappeared. Why hadn't he kept track of Galen? Not only would his combat skills be cool to see in action, but they'd find the items in a matter of minutes. No, no, now was not the time to fantasize about what could've been; what was the best scenario *now*?

He turned back to Isabelle. "We'll have to hit one of these houses. You still have your dagger?"

She nodded meekly and shrugged. "We're out, Leo. I'm not trained to do this."

"So? Were you trained to stop a boat from sinking? Were you trained to—"

She muttered something in her native tongue before saying through gritted teeth, "It's a losing battle."

Quitting wasn't an option, not by a long shot, but what could he say to convince her?

'If we don't pass, they'll probably kill us?'

'Remember when they said a clean-up crew was coming for the contestants in the first phase? You want that to be us, too?'

Leo slunk to the ground with defeat and Isabelle followed, keeping her good leg outstretched and the injured one crossed over it. They'd never bandaged her gash up, but by now the bleeding had stopped and the exposed tissue was sticky with clear ooze and dirt. It would most likely get infected if she didn't receive help.

Isabelle was examining her wound with tired, low-lidded

eyes, rubbing gently around it. She sniffled, and he knew she was crying.

There was no tried-and-true method for handling a crying girl. It made him nervous when anyone cried, and he could feel that rise of unease now. He attempted to gulp it down, but her look of despair persisted along with his discomfort. When his sister was sad, he'd usually give her time alone and avoid talking to her at all costs.

He needed to think of something to say. Her sadness was lingering in the air. He ran his fingers through his hair. "Why'd you want to take the exam? You came from, uh, Reinta, was it?"

A tear fell from her long lashes as she nodded. She leaned back and closed her eyes. "My brother. My brother, um, told me."

"Did he pass?"

"Yes." His chest tightened. There was more underneath her words, something he could detect but couldn't quite see. "Papa disapproved. When Micah came home, he was"—she drew a smile with her finger—"but not as, um, humble. He made bad friends after he left."

"I-I see. So, you're looking for him?"

"Someone killed him."

"Oh... I'm sorry. You don't have to, you know, talk about it, if you don't want to."

"It's okay. Two months later, we got a letter." She drew a rope in the air and grabbed her throat. Hanging. What kind of crowd had her brother fallen into?

"Do you know who did it?"

"No."

"But passing the exam could help?" Leo mulled through all the benefits he remembered hearing on the radio. Nothing about finding murderers rang a bell, though he supposed the winners became part of a network, part of the Overseers, with connections to the underbelly of society.

"I thought so, but, but—"

"Enough with that." Leo stood and reached out to help her up. "We haven't lost yet and we ain't going to. You deserve to know who killed him."

Isabelle rested her weight against him, using his shoulder as a crutch. He blushed as he realized their closeness, something he'd never experienced beyond hugging a family member. It wasn't something he was particularly fond of.

"You're that sure?" she asked, testing the pressure she could exert on her foot. He knew she probably didn't believe in him, not after his display in the first phase and with the bowman. But he couldn't give up on his optimism, fake or not, for the sake of their survival.

"Why not? Just because our odds are slim doesn't mean they ain't there," he spoke with a forced smile, a ruse devised to convince them both. "So, which house should we pick? Did you see where any of the others went?"

"Not sure."

Leo nodded and checked the street. Six bodies scattered the ground. Had they always been there? He didn't hear any signs of a struggle. No shouts, no guns. But there they were, still and rotting, eyes vacant and mouths agape. He listened for an enemy, but all he could hear was his own ragged breathing and the rustling of nearby leaves.

He jumped when Isabelle asked, "You have that knife?"

Leo forced his gaze away from the fallen contestants and looked at her with confusion. And then he felt the straps of his bag digging into his shoulders and remembered that it was secured against his back. He shrugged the pack off and shuffled through his things. The water bottle he brought was empty from trying to clean off Othelia's wounds, and his spare shirt had gone to the same cause. He removed his crumpled 10Q and tossed it to the side, finding the pocketknife resting at the very bottom with his pencils. His notebook called out to him, begging for a sketch of the ocean, the fields, the mist desert. Anything to avoid the grueling process of confronting his own nerves.

Leo pulled out the pocketknife and snapped open the blade. "Small, ain't it? It'd be good against one person, but no more than that."

Isabelle pulled out her dagger from the sheath against her tight black leggings and twirled it between each finger daringly. She stopped once the handle reached her thumb, and she extended it out to him. "Use mine, since you're more... able than me."

Leo waved it away. "I'd be no good with that. In all honesty, I'd probably accidentally stab myself. You should use it."

She released a final, trembling breath. "The pain... I can manage. For a little while. Enough to try."

He slapped her on the back. "That's the spirit!"

Isabelle stumbled forward and grimaced as she pulled on his shirt for sudden support. He reached out to help her further, embarrassed by his lack of coordination and apparent awkwardness. "I-I'm sorry."

"It's okay," she said, scrambling to adjust her foot while cleverly avoiding his wide hazel eyes. "If I can't handle this, I'm as weak as someone banished to the Unholy Land."

The latter half of her words were a mix of her native tongue and Latarian, but he could make out the semblance of the words 'weak' and 'Unholy Land.' Leo was unfamiliar with said land, though he could guess it was related to her religion.

"When'd all this defeatist talk start?" he asked before taking another gander at the dirt path separating the houses. The body count remained the same and his shoulders remained stiff. How many others were out there, waiting, watching?

He looked back at Isabelle, who pointed at the gash on her leg with a sour expression. "Can't fight. But I'll try. You ready?"

Leo attempted to boost his morale, playing scenarios in his head where he defeated the first two people they came across and successfully stole their items. It was wishful thinking, he knew, but there was no other way Leo could convince himself to move otherwise.

"Yeah, I guess so. Which house first?"

Isabelle peeked around the corner with him this time, the coast clear.

"This one?" she asked, jabbing her thumb toward the one they hid behind.

Leo nodded, having no preference of his own, and took the lead. He took mindful steps up the three stairs leading to the patio. A swinging bench hung from the left side, suspended by two tough and shiny chains. The body of a man was sprawled over the seat with wide eyes and a gutted stomach. He gulped.

The house itself looked old compared to many of the others, with torn and poorly touched-up yellow paint. The final stair creaked as he placed his weight on it and he froze, eyes glued to his mistake. Every fiber in his being told him to turn and run, yet he stayed in place. If he backed down, so would she.

Keep going, he insisted, and somehow one leg moved, then the other. He swiveled his heavy head around to check on Isabelle. She was trembling, but she nodded for him to continue, and he did.

Purple curtains cascaded over the front windows, blocking any semblance of movement from inside. There was a peephole drilled in the center of the door and he kept his eyes locked on it as he made his way forward. Was someone staring back? Was there a gun on the other side, ready to blow his head off?

He shoved his shoulder into the door while turning the knob with the brief hope that it'd open; it didn't. Leo used the back of his foot to kick the handle, slamming onto it until the pain forced him to stop. His efforts were a semi-success, the knob busted enough to be wriggled free. His foot hurt tremendously, and he realized with horror that he could've tried using his pocketknife instead. Though how, he wasn't sure.

Isabelle shambled up from behind him and assisted with tearing at the knob until the lock gave. She stumbled as the door swung open, but he grabbed her by the wrist and pulled her upright. She nodded in thanks and pushed her way inside.

Leo hesitated to follow, his attention drawn to his throbbing ankle, which was already turning a nasty shade of black and blue. The throbbing was sharp and distinct, radiating up to his knee. He grumbled incoherencies associated with anger and fixed his sight on the ground, his jaw clenched in pain.

"Coming?" Isabelle called. Her voice was filled with distress. Leo's heart plummeted, but he gulped back his fear and tried to use his foot. He grabbed the doorframe as he stepped over the threshold to steady himself, the bruises creating an insufferable, invisible stabbing. He had to push through; there were more important things at hand.

Isabelle was stopped a few feet ahead. He looked over her shoulder to see a silhouette blocking the hallway. The house was far too dark to see their face; the brass sun behind Leo shone on their feet, revealing brown sandals with thick chains clamped around their ankles. Shattered chain links trailed behind them. They must've been a criminal. Where was everyone else?

The silhouette was nearly half his size, their hair sticking in odd positions on every radius of their skull. Their muscular arms were thick, and Leo had the sudden realization that he very well may freeze up again. His heart ricocheted from his chest, but his feet wouldn't budge. The pocketknife was in his hand, shaking profusely; Isabelle had already noticed his apprehension and took to testing her foot until it settled on the ground.

Leo looked around the room with haste, finding a pile of bodies to his right, presumably long since dead. So, that's where everyone was.

He kept his face slack despite his screaming thoughts, breakfast crawling back up his throat. He swallowed, but it didn't help. Leo was going to puke—there was no question— and all the while, the silhouette stood perfectly still. Watching. Waiting.

The figure shot forward at the same time Leo doubled over, contents spilling from his lips. His ears remained focused on the flies that swarmed the pile. He was aware something was happening, something bad, but he couldn't break his concentration away from the buzzing, and he couldn't stop his gut from emptying. The smell of death was an intoxicating thing.

Leo was thrown against the wall by a wild beast; they pinned him with their forearm against his neck and jabbed a short blade into his side. His body throbbed from the instant pain as a gasp escaped him. He was losing oxygen, and all Leo could come to think of was the damn farm and the brightness of the fields and how vast it felt. Leo couldn't find it in himself to fight; he'd been drained long ago. He was a coward, wasn't he?

He remembered his pocketknife and his fingers twitched to life. Leo gagged and tried to swallow, only to come up short on air. His throat was being crushed. Leo desperately drove the pocketknife into his attacker's shoulder. It connected, but the blade was dull and worn; it couldn't penetrate their arm any more than a few inches. Leo pulled it out and tried again, this time the blade snapping off from the handle. His weapon was useless. He was useless.

Leo dropped the bladeless handle and took to scratching at the sharpened and brightly painted nails of his captor; their feminine face and bulky physique blurred as he gasped for air. His head was swimming. Pockets of moments spilled into his mind. Baking cornbread with his mother. Being taught how to use sign language by his sister. He missed his sister. How many days later would she discover he was dead?

"I-Isab—" he choked out. His limited thoughts began to wane, and his fingers were growing numb and loose, his motor functions failing him. He tried to say Isabelle's name again, but words were lost to him.

And then his body crumpled to the floor, smacking against the wooden planks with a harsh thud. Leo coughed, gasping incessantly. His lungs burned, and his entire body shuddered with every deep and raspy cough. The blade his captor had driven into his side stuck there, blood pooling from within.

He couldn't register what had just occurred, not at first. He could vaguely hear a scuffle, shoes chafing the floor, and a throaty grunt. Leo's body was in a heap, tossed lazily onto the floor as though he was nothing but trash.

He finally managed to look up and observe their struggle; Isabelle had latched onto the back of the attacker and held their neck in the crux of her elbow. Her legs were wrapped around their midsection and her second hand gripped onto her dagger, which was now lodged in their neck. They gasped for breath and jerked their body back and forth, clawing at their own neck while spasming uncontrollably. Isabelle yelped and hopped off them with the dagger still wedged in place.

Leo attempted to scramble to his feet, holding his side with the knife still lodged in place. He used the wall behind him as leverage. He didn't dare look at the wound, terrified of fainting from shock. Leo approached Isabelle slowly, but she backed away from him with wide eyes. She shook her head, daring him to leave her alone for good. Leo kept making the same mistakes, didn't he? He could see the betrayal behind her eyes and knew the answer.

"See?" he said meekly, words haphazardly trailing out. "You could do it. You aren't weak."

"Thank Gahi for that," she said with a pointed chin and narrow eyes. Just like that, her animosity resurfaced. The person she'd stabbed writhed on the ground until they gave out a long-winded wheeze and their eyes stared blankly at the ceiling.

She overturned the criminal's pockets. "Are you okay?"

"I—I don't know," he said, falling to a knee. She looked over and her eyes widened.

"Holy Gahi—You've been stabbed!" She rushed over and inspected his wound; her anger toward him appeared to have temporarily dissipated.

"Yeah," he said, the pain nearly unbearable. "You didn't notice? Should we—should we take it out?"

"No, no. You'll bleed to death."

"It doesn't feel very deep," he said. "But it—it hurts like crazy."

She assisted him to the vacant couch and laid him down. "I'll look for the, um, 'item.' You lay. Don't move. Stay awake."

She dashed through the house in a quick shuffle, looking around desperately for, well, something. He didn't like to wait, nor did he like to be so utterly useless. Leo grabbed the edge of the couch and pulled himself upright. He groaned at the pain, pulling himself off the couch and holding the area around the knife with his hand.

Leo made his way to the L-shaped kitchen; smack in the center was a tall, blackened marble island. He looked at the countertop incredulously. It was much too modern for an otherwise rundown home. His hand brushed against the length of the countertop as he hobbled around it.

His fingertips grazed a small chain. It was pure black, blending into the surrounding darkness. He pinched it between two fingers and brought it closer to the busted open door. The silver chain became thicker until it reached a small, golden gauntlet at the end. What a strange item, he thought, but it was an item. He was sure of it. "I-I think I found it!"

Isabelle hustled over to him and leaned against the marble countertop to steady herself. "I told you to lay."

Leo ignored her and held the chain between them before lowering the necklace into her cupped hand. She examined it with a scowl of scrutiny. "How can we be sure?"

He shrugged, making his way around the island and tossing open cupboards one at a time. "Did you find anything in those other rooms?"

"No," she said from behind. "But this could be a... a fake."

All the cupboard doors were slung open, revealing vast emptiness. Leo patted down the shelves, finding nothing, not even dust. "It could be, but I doubt it. No one knows of the exam phases until they happen, right? How could they bring a decoy?"

"I don't know the mind of a *criequez*."

"Well, regardless of if it's the real deal or not—which I definitely think it is, by the way—you can have it. Since you did the fighting."

Her eyebrows shot up with surprise. He thought she might

deny him and give the item back, but she nodded and shoved the necklace into her pocket instead. "We should go."

Isabelle walked over to the dead criminal and took the dagger from their neck with her eyes clenched closed. She wiped the blood on their clothes. Leo watched, amazed, and admittedly resentful, of Isabelle's ability to take control of their situation.

They left the body behind as they hobbled back into the scathing sun. Leo shielded his eyes, noticing a foot before it disappeared behind the furthest house. The movement was so quick that he questioned if it'd been real or not.

Leo struggled down the creaking steps onto the warm soil, his side burning. The stab wound hadn't appeared to do any lasting damage; he could move freely, his only hindrance the jarring pain. But, he reminded himself, he could die if it wasn't properly managed.

His watch still worked and indicated that it was noon. They still had twenty-four hours. There was no telling what could occur within those hours, no telling if the wound would become worse and destroy his insides until he dropped dead.

Now was not the time to worry. Now was the time to find an item. This entire exam would be pointless if he didn't pass.

A bright purple house caught his eyes and, like a bug drawn to light, he walked to it. He headed to the back of the house, hopeful of finding a back door. He was relieved to find that not only was there a door but it'd been smashed through.

He expected to find an empty house or one filled with the dead, ransacked and deserted. Instead, there was a boy lying face down on the ground. Their glasses were split in two and their light blond hair was sticky with fresh blood. It took Leo all of thirty seconds to figure out that it was Galen, and he fell to his knees.

Leo rolled him over, and his jaw dropped. Galen's face was

covered in streams of blood. Shards of glass pricked at his closed eye; one was large enough to stick out from his skin. Blood oozed from the damage. He must've fallen harder on one side because the other lens was cracked down the center but otherwise intact. He held himself together enough to not puke. Leo may not have known Galen for long, but seeing him in such a state was gut-wrenching. He wanted Galen to pass the exam, too, whether it be for his family or for himself.

He put his ear up to Galen's nose, which whistled softly with every shallow breath he took. He was alive. Leo wanted to relax, but of course, he couldn't. Galen's eye was punctured, he was unconscious, and no one was coming to help.

Isabelle appeared behind him. "Looked around. There's nothing." She paused, realizing whom Leo was kneeling beside. "Oh, my—he okay?"

Leo looked down at their comrade. "I wouldn't say that, but he's breathing. Looks like he was hit pretty hard."

"Nothing we can do... we can't leave him, can we?" Isabelle asked, squatting down to examine his face. "Gahi. Will he be able to see?"

"Of course we can't leave him. You have your item, so you should stay, and I'll go looking for mine," Leo said.

"But your woun—"

"Lie low," Leo said. He didn't wait for an answer and jogged through the short hallway of the house. As expected, there was a bed in one room, a white sheet covering the mattress. He worked the fabric off and bundled it into a ball while running hastily back, tossing the material to Isabelle. He winced with every step.

"I'm sorry for asking you to do this," he said, "but can you try to bandage him up, too? If you think the glass should stay in until he gets proper treatment, then that's fine. But, please, at least the back of his head, alright?"

Isabelle nodded dutifully. "I'll try. Good luck, Leo. I'll pray for you."

He smiled awkwardly. "Thanks, Is. I won't disappoint you this time."

Leo gave her a final nod and left. If he made any of the same mistakes again, Isabelle wouldn't be around to save him. He gulped—his hands juddered, and his back was tense and hunched from the pain of his stab wound.

He'd intended to move one house over and break in through the back once again. That was, until he saw a familiar wool-covered figure, her hood down. Even from where he stood, a good two houses away, he could see her furrowed brow and curled fists. And she was talking to someone. Eli was nowhere in sight. His mind raced. Had she left him? Killed him? Who was she talking to?

Their voices were just loud enough for his ears to pick up an occasional coherent word. Leo ducked behind the nearest corner, watching the altercation and determining if, and when, he should make his presence known.

CHAPTER 22
ELI

HIS ARMS TRAILED along helplessly behind him as he was dragged into the room; his knuckles scraping against the wood. He could vaguely feel the handle of his knife loose in his grip. The door slammed shut above his head and the faint click of a lock snapped in place. A boot sprung from nowhere, kicking the knife out of his hand and across the floor. Eli groaned and looked around; his vision was hazy after his head had bounced on the wooden floor.

As his sight slowly reemerged, he could identify two others in the room—a man and a woman. The woman was tall and muscular, her crop top exposing thick, outlined abs. Her arms were comically large compared to the rest of her, and she had a shotgun caressed in her hands. The man was at least a decade younger than her, his chin and upper lip covered in light scruff.

Wait, Eli realized, it was the man from group 1, wasn't it? He could tell by his tall stature and sullen, focused eyes. But the woman, she wasn't his partner. Who was she? Could he talk his way out of this by simply recognizing the man?

They both stared down at him as though he were a science project, curious and ravenous for more experimentation. He tried to look around for his lost weapon, head pounding and heavy. So heavy that it took extra effort, all his effort, to swivel it sideways. There, in the corner of the room, the knife stared at him. It was too far, and his body was a stone.

Othelia banged against the door, but it wouldn't budge. How she could break through a boarded-up door and not this one, he didn't know, and it didn't matter. He was stuck. This was, perhaps, the worst possible situation to be in.

Eli tried to lift himself up, arms shaking under his weight. He could feel the man and woman watch as he struggled, but Eli kept his eyes on the knife as if it were going to sprout legs and disappear if he looked away. He kneeled on a wobbly leg, and he thought, well, stars, maybe he'd make it.

His efforts were cut short when the butt of a gun connected with his nose, his back slamming back onto the floor. A sharp crack of bone was met with a jolt of coursing pain. Sticky and warm blood was already spooling down to his chin. Eli flailed without thought, tossing around his fists haphazardly. His head, his nose, his body throbbed as he let out sobs of agony. He was going to die, and with a destroyed face, no less.

Eli attempted to pick himself off the floor once again, but it was no use as the woman trained the nuzzle of the gun inches from his face. He slapped at the gun desperately, waiting for her to pull the trigger. His throat was hoarse from his screams and swirls of color danced in the overwhelming darkness behind his eyelids as he clamped them shut.

A hand wrapped around his left wrist and pinned it down. He reached for the arm as his eyes sprang open. A knife came crashing down, stabbing the center of Eli's left hand. He screamed as the knife was pulled out. Blood gushed from his palm. The man stared down at him with an amused smile, his face hovering over Eli's.

Eli didn't dare look at his hand, he couldn't, and in a rash frenzy of fear, he head-butted the man. The man backed away with an angered yell, holding his head in his hand as he stood. Eli sat up and used his legs to scoot away from them, waving his hands in defense.

Blood trickled down his palm, a hole in the center. Eli was sure, at that moment, that he was going to wet himself. "Woah, can't we j-just talk this out? Y-you're from group 1, right? You did well. You did the best, actually. Surely, we can reach a conclusion other than violence?"

They wouldn't accept his offer—no way—but he had to buy himself a sliver of seconds. His eyes flashed to the woman's face, and his stomach swirled at her eager smile. Not his stomach, his bladder. Warmth spread down his pants, but he didn't look. He was too terrified to be embarrassed. The man glared down at him, knife dangling at his side as he looked at Eli with a mix of pity and surprise.

"We don't do negotiations," said the woman, her eyes narrow as she raised the gun. At that moment, Eli didn't think. He jumped up and pushed the barrel away from himself while punching her across the cheek with his good hand. Her head ricocheted to the side, and the trigger went off with an overwhelming boom. A high-pitched whine shot through Eli's ears, and he stumbled, dizziness taking control.

He frantically checked over his body and the door, fearful either he or Othelia were shot. His gaze met a bloody pulp on the ground. He screamed. Suddenly, his dizziness was gone, replaced with aching anxiety and terror. The tall man was nothing now, his face long gone, and his brain splattered everywhere. On the ground, the walls, and the ceiling. His head was split down the center, legs still twitching and fingers spasming around his knife.

Eli hadn't just screamed; he was still screaming. His hand ached from the punch and bruises were forming on his knuckles. The woman stared down at the mess she'd created while cradling her reddened cheek. It wasn't much of a hit, but she was surprised and fixated, mouth open and eyes glued. Her gun was at her side, pointing at the ground.

There was only one thing he could do with her diverted attention. Eli clamped his mouth shut, retrieved the knife from the man's warm and bloody hand, and thrust it at her neck.

A soft gasp escaped her as the blade met flesh, and the gun fell from her grasp. She'd been calm and non-threatening when he'd attacked, but now her eyes were filled with sorrowful rage as she jerked away from him, grabbing at the knife and pulling it out. Blood spurted out and drenched her hand, quickly draining down her elbow and dripping to the ground. She released a gurgled cry while she clutched at the gushing wound.

He needed to assure his safety; he needed to kill her. She was deranged and vengeful, and he didn't doubt her ability to attack him before she died of blood loss. He knew what killing her meant—that he was a hypocrite. He was just like the rest of them. But it had to be done. He didn't want to die.

Eli reached for the gun. It was surprisingly easy to cock and pull the trigger despite its weight and his damaged hand. The kickback sent him flying off his feet, and the bullet diverted off course. The woman's screams ripped through the air. A horrified cry escaped his trembling lips as he realized what he'd done.

Her arm was disconnected, suspended above the ground by stringy bits of muscle, bones shattered. He cocked the gun again, maintaining his position on the floor, and fired. It clicked. Stars. That wasn't good at all. Tears began streaming down his face; his time was up.

The woman didn't approach him, however. Instead, she stared at him wordlessly and shambled to the bed. She laid back on the pillowless mattress, the room oddly quiet while she bled out. Eli worked quickly, nervous the woman would get up and attack. He pushed down his wooziness and checked the man's pockets. The woman started moaning; a horrible guttural incantation of sorrow.

He gulped and pulled out a long necklace with a small ruby eliase dangling in the center. Were all the items jewelry? Assuming this was one. He glanced back up at her; the bed was covered in blood and her skin was growing pale. Her lips were parted as more inhuman moans erupted. He would remember this for the rest of his life.

Eli fumbled with the lock and pulled open the door. Othelia was on the other side, her eyebrows drawn in worry. He held up the necklace with a weak smile. "Ta-dah."

Her eyes panned to the mush on the ground, then to the moaning woman behind him, followed by his wetted pants. And, finally, she looked into his eyes. Hers were glassy, but she did not cry. "Did you—"

"It had to be done, right?" He laughed bitterly. "Let's go. I can't stay here."

They left through the back door, both items stashed in Eli's pocket. He slunk down the steps of the vacant porch and wedged himself between the corner of the stairs and the house wall. Othelia sat beside him.

The gunshot and the woman's blasted arm replayed in his mind like a sick joke, followed by the man's headless body. He sobbed, covering his mouth with his good hand and training his eyes on the blurry horizon.

No, that wasn't good enough. He reached for his pocket

and pulled out his flask. He sucked down two gulps before Othelia started batting at him with her elbow. Eli was taller, and his long arm dangled the flask out of her reach. She didn't appear to care and continued to bat at his extended arm. Taq splashed from the top. His throat still burned from his first round, and all he wanted was more. Just one more sip. Just enough to make things a little better.

He yelled in frustration and brought the flask down to his side in defeat.

"Shhh," Othelia whispered forcefully. "We still need to survive for 24 hours. You can't give up our location now."

Eli wasn't listening; the image of the woman's stringy arm brought the flask to his lips. It was empty. He tossed it to the ground with an angry grunt. "Why would you do that?"

"Because resorting to alcohol is for quitters and you aren't a quitter, are you?"

"I may as well—"

"No, you aren't. That's the right answer. No."

"I'm not a quitter, just a guy who wet himself in fear!" He sniffled, and his bottom lip quivered. He knew he looked weak, but there was no escaping what he'd done. There never would be.

Eli looked at the sky with eyebrows drawn together. "Stars, what have I done?"

The stars didn't answer, and Othelia didn't, either. Her silence only made him feel worse. Because he was weak, wasn't he? Everyone else around him were fighters or murderers and they did it well. How could he stand up against the Sandoval monarchy or be a politician when he wasn't as ruthless as them? And, between all his doubts, the thought that rang the loudest was, *I wish I was drunk right now.*

"You were defending yourself, Eli. That doesn't make you a bad person."

He looked at her, eyes puffy and red. "But what makes my life more important than theirs? What gives me the right to defend myself?"

"I was on the other side of that door. I heard you trying to talk them out of killing you. You're as important as anyone else. Being human is about surviving another day. That's the only criteria we have. So, you saved yourself, and maybe that's selfish, but that's better than being dead."

"I guess," he said, tears streaming down his face once more.

Othelia sighed and stared at her hands. "I'm sorry. Did that make sense? I don't really know how to—how to comfort people well. But, you know, if you regret killing them, then that's something, right? You can't be bad if you regret it."

Eli leaned his head against the wall and closed his eyes, smiling lightly. "You're a good person, you know."

Othelia snorted and shook her head. "I guess."

She said nothing more and wrapped an arm around him, pulling him closer. Eli desperately wished she would keep talking. About anything. These thoughts mixed with the killing he'd done only made his guilt grow stronger. She'd show her true side eventually, the side she inherited from her father. Then Eli would grow to hate her once more and wish to never hear that silky, soothing voice again.

His thoughts became faint, and his head lolled to the side, resting on her shoulder. He opened his eyes, squinting, but struggled to keep them open. What was happening? Was this what shock felt like? His body was exhausted and paralyzed, begging him to close his eyes again and sleep for an eternity. He could vaguely feel Othelia's ginger fingers hold up his bloodied, slashed hand. As his vision faded, he could see the concern that lined her face while she ripped away the bottom of his shirt.

"This hurts, you know," she said, nodding toward her hands. "You're lucky I've decided I like you."

"Can..." he murmured. His lips had grown heavy. He wished he could find the energy, any energy at all, to flirt with her. But her words were a comforting blanket, whisking him to sleep.

"What?" she asked softly.

"Don't tell them I wet myself," he stumbled out, eyelids falling closed. "Please."

He had secured a spot during this phase of the exam. But, as his thoughts drifted away, he couldn't help but think about what Othelia had said. Eli had done what the selfish did. What the rich did—he killed someone so he could succeed. He was becoming like her; he was becoming like them.

CHAPTER 23
OTHELIA

ONCE SHE WAS done wrapping up Eli's hand, she realized he was unconscious. Blood had dried around his mouth and chin, his nose bent in an odd way; an injury she did not have the skills to attend to. He looked broken and sad, even in his sleep.

She carried his limp body to the nearest tree and propped him against the trunk. She examined the tree branches to make sure no one was lingering above. The house they hid behind was windowless—a hopeful sign that no one was watching.

Othelia sighed. The air was hot and sticky, her body a sweaty mess. She supposed the wool cloak she wore no longer mattered, considering she'd finally come face-to-face with Samuel, and she peeled it off. The air immediately became cooler, her greasy hair settling on the nape of her neck. Othelia wondered what she truly looked like with her burnt hands and bruised legs. She tossed the coat to the side and sat beside Eli.

The silence was oddly peaceful, and Othelia leaned against the tree with her eyes closed. She took in the quiet; the sweet-smelling air reminded her of flowers and summer and home.

She heard their footsteps before they turned the corner.

Othelia popped open an eye, curious to see her newest competitors. Despite all that had happened in the previous phase, she enjoyed the exam far more than she thought she would—namely, the fighting. She was a natural, and the thought of fighting produced a rush of adrenaline throughout her body. She could ignore her headaches and nausea if it meant a good altercation.

Her heart sank when she realized it was Samuel and Abel. She scowled before they caught sight of her. She knew how they were; they would try to fight her. She wanted to fight, sure, but not with her brother or pesky, weak Abel. Not now, anyway.

Samuel was the first to notice her, pointing with a grimace. Abel's eyes followed his finger; they landed on her with an expressionless gaze. She waved and settled on a cocky half-smile. Eli mumbled incoherently beside her, and Othelia looked away from her brother without a second thought, checking to see if her companion was waking up. To her dismay, his eyes remained closed as his head moved and his chin sat on his chest. His black hair was draped over his eyes as he slept soundly.

"Othelia," Samuel said with a smug, upturned nose and arms crossed over his chest. "Given up, have we?"

"Someone let you out of your binds?" she asked, her eyes daggers. "I'm surprised someone would pity you so. I can't say I'm surprised that you got yourselves tied up in the first place, though."

His eyes shifted toward Eli. "It was your friend who untied us, actually."

Othelia knew he wanted a reaction, so she kept a straight face, maintained eye contact, and made a mental note to chastise Eli later. "I figured as much. You guys talk, too? What'd you talk about, hmm?"

His eyebrows shot up. "He didn't tell you? Your taste in men is uncanny."

They glared at each other in mutual silence. Finally, she let out a sigh. "I'm not interested in your judgment, Sam. Neither of us has an item, so can you spare me, please? Just this once?"

"You're lying," Samuel said. She held his gaze yet again, this time rising to her feet. He smiled, seeing through her ruse completely.

"So, what? You want to fight? Is that it? Both of you?" Her gaze shifted to Abel, who shrunk away from her icy stare. He looked, to put it lightly, horrible. His hair was a knotted mess, and his eyes were distant, brought back only in moments of fear. She'd known Abel her entire life. She'd seen the way he held himself—tall and dutiful, with a dash of raging arrogance. But, here and now, he was sluggish and slouching. His movements were irregular and unnerving. He meant no harm to anyone.

Abel shook his head and stepped around her, holding up his hands in defense as her eyes followed him. He slid against the tree trunk, taking the spot where she'd been. She didn't like how close he was to Eli; if Abel hurt, or even touched Eli, there would be no telling what she'd do to him.

Not a word escaped Abel's lips. Othelia pointed toward him with her thumb. "What's his issue?"

"Not everyone's as lucky as your friend over there," he said. Ah. No wonder he was so dejected. Obrien and Marcious were dead.

"How'd you escape from Alexander?" Samuel continued. "I figured he'd be doing everything in his power to stop you."

She shrugged. "People can be swayed. In the end, I

convinced him to come with me and try the exam out. I told him I was choosing the middle boat and—"

"And since he had to choose first, you lied and left him behind. Wow," Samuel said, shaking his head in disbelief. "And that dumb bastard really fell for it."

"Clever," Abel added with mild amusement. Othelia twirled around to face him. He was staring up at her with those meek, cloudy eyes. She'd never seen the face of someone who'd given up before, but this had to be it. He was still handsome underneath his worn-down demeanor, she noted, and his new quiet nature was far better than his usual haughty attitude and condescending tone. Usually, she hated the guy, but now she only felt sorry for him.

"I'm sorry about your friends," Othelia said in earnest. "May they rest deeply and soundly and be one with the stars."

He responded with a sullen nod. She turned her attention back to her brother, her hands dangling limply at her sides.

"I'm going to ask one last time, Sam," she said, wishing she could dole out a threat. If only her hands worked properly. "What do you want?"

"I think you should give me your item. I know you have one."

"I believe that's considered cheating," Othelia said, finding his notion utterly preposterous.

"Let's fight for it, then. I'll make it fair for you. No weapons or maoho. I'm assuming your power is waning like mine. Do you have headaches, too?"

She scoffed, not daring to confirm his assertions. "Fair for *me*? No wonder you don't have an item yet; it's because you're an idiot."

Abel barked a single laugh. She wished it'd been Eli instead; he would've laughed and added another quip alongside her.

He curled his fists. "Abel, countdown from three!"

The prince did as he was told. As he hit the final number, Samuel lunged forward. Othelia dodged and curled her fingers into a fist before shoving them into his diaphragm. She screamed at the rippling pain. He stumbled backward and let out a throaty cough before regaining his footing and striking again. He launched several punches at her in quick blows, each one harder and harder to dodge until one connected with her shoulder and sent her spiraling backward.

Othelia landed on her open palm and a knee, gritting her teeth. A blister burst, and she screamed again. She kept low to the ground and spun with an extended leg, kicking under his feet. He fell onto his back and pedaled his feet wildly in the air to keep her at bay. She jumped up and released a kick at his side. Samuel reached out to stop her, but his reaction was a second too late and her foot successfully connected.

She stared down at him, stealing his look of conceit and claiming it as her own. Othelia could barely contain herself as she asked, "Why did Father send you?"

He coughed, and she kicked his face. His head snapped to the side and blood erupted from his nose. He stared up at her with a scrunched face, tears pricking his eyes. She'd only ever seen him cry a handful of times, namely when they were younger. She tried to think of the most recent account; it'd probably been over four years ago.

His mouth was drawn, his lips quivering. She watched as he sat up and wiped his nose. She could feel Abel's eyes on her, as well as an extra pair. Eli was still sound asleep. Someone else was watching.

"I need to pass," Samuel said, his voice breaking. She brought half of her attention back to him. The other half was solely invested in those watching. How many people were out there? As much as she hated to admit it, her hands ached. If she kept using them, she feared the pain would last forever, and they'd become unusable. "I'm sorry Father sent me instead, I really am. But this is a matter beyond you. Please, Othelia. I'm asking as your brother. *Please.* I have to pass. I have to."

He wept, his eyes shifting to the ground. The only indicator of his genuine sorrow was the tears that hit the grass between his crossed legs. Othelia couldn't tell whether his groveling was sincere. She highly doubted it, and his pathetic display sent a curl to her lips. She understood to an extent. Their family resorted to beatings both as a way of punishment and a way of becoming stronger. Yet somehow, he still loved their father. He still wanted to prove his worth.

But she had no sympathy for her brother.

Othelia drew back her foot and reared it toward his face, expecting to both break his nose and knock him out. Samuel blubbered and waved his hands frantically. "You're no better than them!"

She faltered, her foot inches away from his chin. It hovered there as he looked up at her, a look of both hatred and confusion in his eyes. But the fear was the best part.

"You think you are. But look at you." Samuel looked her over with pure disgust. "You aren't."

Othelia set her foot down slowly. Her hands were shaking, and her breathing was ragged. She took in the mess that sat before her. His bleeding nose once looked like a surefire victory, but as she watched it drip from his chin, it only looked sad. No, it was horrible. Monstrous, even. Was this what Alexander saw every time he beat her?

There was no telling what their father would have done to Samuel if he failed the exam. If Father discovered she'd won and Samuel hadn't, it'd be over for him. Why else would the King send Hanako after her?

Hanako, who she hadn't seen yet. Was he the one

watching? Would Samuel be tossed in prison if he failed? Othelia thought she'd fare well behind bars, albeit extremely bored, but she didn't foresee her brother making it a day, much less a lifetime, in a cell.

She tsked and walked over to Eli, reaching into his pocket and producing the diamond-studded eliase necklace they'd retrieved. She held it over Samuel's head.

Ah, damn, was she really doing this? And for what? So she could feel better about herself? Or was there a possibility she loved him? Looking down at his sniffling face, she couldn't possibly describe how she felt toward him, but it didn't feel like love.

He remained where he sat, overcome with grief and tears. "Thank you, Othelia."

"On one condition."

"Of course."

"You give me the prize money and tell me anything you find out about magical items."

He raised his brows and stroked his chin. "Yes, I suppose I can do that. You're looking for a magical item?"

She gave him a small smile and tossed the necklace at his feet. "Don't say I never did anything for you."

She sat against the tree on the other side of Eli. She was acutely aware of her shoulder pressed against his. But whatever thoughts that may have arisen were foregone by the pairs of eyes on them. Two, three at most. Did any of them have an item?

She wished Eli would wake up. She didn't want to leave his side, but she wanted to pass. Badly. *Not bad enough*, she thought dryly.

"I'd leave if I were you," she instructed Abel and Samuel loudly, hoping the bystanders would hear as well. "Some people are watching us and I don't feel like fighting as if I'm on your side."

As if on cue, footsteps sounded from a few feet away. She recognized Leo as soon as he appeared. His shirt was still unbuttoned, and his hair was a knot of curls. His neck was red, and there was a knife bulging out of his side.

"Where are the others?" she asked, realizing Isabelle and Galen weren't trailing behind him. "And how are you walking around with that thing sticking out of you?"

Leo hobbled over, grasping his side with bloodied fingers. He watched her brother and Abel with questioning and nervous eyes. "I'm not sure, but I'm managing. It's not too deep, I don't think. Isabelle and I found Galen; she stayed back with him. He's not in good condition. Knocked out. How's he?" Leo nodded toward Eli.

Othelia sucked in. "He fainted, but he's okay. Someone stabbed through his hand, though."

"Yikes. A lot of stabbing going on today."

"You got an item yet?"

He shook his head. "Did I just see you give yours away?"

"Evidently. That's my brother."

He raised his brows and gave Samuel a sheepish smile and wave. "I thought you guys looked similar. I'm Leo and you... are..."

She should've expected as much. He really had to introduce himself to everyone. Hadn't he seen her kicking Samuel around?

Samuel squinted against the sun. "You don't recognize us?"

Leo tilted his head. "Should I? I mean, we were in the same trivia room, but I don't think they said your name."

"Ignore him," Othelia said. "His inflated ego has brainwashed him into thinking he's somehow important. We should drop Eli off with Isabelle and get our items. Do Is and Galen still need one?"

"Galen does, I believe. But he's probably not waking up anytime soon," Leo admitted. "I was thinking I'd look for myself first and find one for Galen if I have time. It's the least I could do."

She nodded. "True. He did climb trees for us."

Leo smiled. "And rowed with you, which I never did say thank you for, by the way. So, thank you. And thanks for being on board with helping Galen, too."

She wanted to help Galen solely in return for his essential aid throughout their partnership. Maybe that meant he was a friend. She couldn't really tell, nor did she care much, and Othelia focused her attention on searching for other onlookers. She could've sworn she felt another pair of eyes, but there was no one else in sight. They'd have to be careful.

Othelia crouched between Eli's outstretched legs to become eye level with him, contemplating the best way to pick him up.

She used the back of her wrist to raise his head, careful not to move her fingers. "Eli," she cooed. He did not stir, so she tried again a little louder, "Eli!"

"I'll try to help with carrying him," Leo said, groaning from his wound as he slowly bent down. He slung Eli's arm over his shoulder and crinkled his nose. "He smells like a tavern."

"I noticed that, too. Smells like taq," Abel said.

"He didn't have much," Othelia assured.

"Having any is too much," Leo said with a shake of his head. He gestured toward Abel and Samuel. "You guys are welcome to come with. Provided, of course, you don't try to steal or kill us."

Samuel shook his head, but Abel gave a sharp nod. "Yeah, okay. Don't worry. I'm done with this exam."

Othelia gawked at him. "But surely you'll have the same punishment as Sam or I. I thought the King of Xivis was a less forgiving man."

Abel let out a deep and tired sigh. "I know I should care, but I don't. Not anymore."

"What about you, Othelia? Will you be coming home after this?" Samuel asked.

She laughed. "Oh, goodness no. Not in a million years."

"Father will put a bounty on your head, you know. Why'd you even come? You would've been chosen if you'd just stayed in line like the rest of us. You missed your chance to, and yet you're here, trying anyway?"

Othelia rolled her eyes. "You should be careful how you talk to me. I can easily take that necklace right back, Sam. Don't think I won't." He clamped his mouth shut. Satisfied, she turned to Abel. "Like he said, you're welcome to come with. Just don't try anything stupid."

Abel nodded in understanding and followed along as Leo led the way; Samuel reluctantly trailed behind. Othelia walked beside her companions, resting Eli's other arm around her neck.

"Am I supposed to know who you two are?" Leo asked her with a grunt. Eli was heavier than she thought he'd be. "Did I hear you mention a king?"

She thought over her options, taking in Leo and wondering if she could trust him. Regardless of whether she could or not, Leo would be easily beatable if he ever betrayed her. He wasn't a threat in any way, shape, or form. "We're children of the Ishla king. I'm the oldest, then Sam. We have two other siblings, too, though they're years too young to participate. Abel here is the son of Elderage Casterral, King of Xivis. It's another island."

He nodded along, absorbing this new information. There was no telling how he would react. "Why would the children of kings be taking the exam?"

Othelia was surprised by how quickly he made the same queries she had. She was thankful for it. "Right. I've more or less been exiled from the family, so I don't know why, and sweet Sam won't say anything."

"You're here to find out why?"

"Partially. Maybe. I'm curious, I'll give you that. But I find myself caring less and less each hour. It's not like their scheme will work; whatever my father tasked Sam with is something he can't do. He couldn't even get an item without begging me for one."

"I can hear you," Samuel said from behind, his voice gruff and angry.

"Good," Othelia replied. "You need a wake-up call."

"So, what's the main reason?" Leo pushed.

She sighed, debating whether to speak of her intentions in front of her brother and Abel. She had no plans of running into them again, so what was the harm? "There's a magical item I was recently drawn to, something that I want to find out about."

"That's... peculiar... but neat."

Othelia chuckled and looked at him with bemusement. "I just told you I was drawn to a magical item, and that's your response... you're a strange one, Leo."

"Thanks?"

She stared ahead, counting the bodies that littered the ground as they walked. "How many people do you think are left?"

Leo gawked at her and shrugged. "I-I wouldn't guess too many. There are a lot of bodies. Twenty, at most?"

The estimate sounded small, but the village was desolate.

There were only eight items, so it made sense many would perish while fighting. Samuel, Eli, and Isabelle had three. Somewhere out there, in this silence, were at least five others currently holding their own. The more she thought, the angrier she got. Was it weak to give up her item? Would she be stronger if she'd kept it for herself?

Leo guided them through a broken-down doorway, the inside of the house filled with solid darkness. There were four bodies piled on the floor and no sign of life. Nerves crept along her spine, but she kept her emotions in check as she inspected the rooms; the four boys remained in the living room.

"Are you sure this is the right house?" she asked as she walked back to them. "They aren't here."

"What do you mean?"

"I mean, they aren't here," she repeated with a twinge of frustration. "What're we supposed to do about Eli? I'm sure as stars not keeping him with these two."

"I'm sure Isabelle left a message behind somewhere," Leo said, scanning the floor for anything. "She still has her knife. See if she carved anything."

Othelia followed his demands. He was a good leader, she mused, and made snap decisions. He may not have been a fighter, but he would probably serve useful on a hunt for magical items. Her thoughts were confirmed when he pointed to the floorboards by the kitchen island. She stood beside him and read what she saw aloud. "5010. What is that?"

"A time?" Samuel offered.

She scoffed and gave him a taunting glare. "Can you follow Abel's example and shut up, please?"

He did, crossing his arms in an act of defiance.

Othelia looked at Leo, who was staring at the adjacent wall as he pondered. He snapped with his free hand. "An address?"

They locked eyes, and she smiled with a nod. He could

make snap decisions and produce adequate theories. For the first time since they met, she took some interest in Leo Montero, if only just some. "We'll try it."

And that's when the commotion outside began.

CHAPTER 24
ISABELLE

GALEN WOKE UP a few minutes after Leo left. Isabelle had moved him to the bed inside and was tending to his damaged face, clearing off the blood and glass the best she could. His undamaged eye flung open and an animalistic, pained howl erupted while he clamped it shut again. She jumped from his suddenness and a yelp escaped, though her tiny noise was masked by Galen's cries.

There was nothing there that could help him. The bedsheet stopped the bleeding from his head, but his eye was irreparable. He writhed on the bed, his body curling in on itself as tears pooled at the corner of his eye. His face contorted in pain; he clasped his hands around his damaged eye and winced before yelling again.

Her hand hovered over his shoulder. There was no definitive way to console someone, especially someone in immense pain. Micah had received whippings when he returned home. She had nightmares of his screams when he was bound like a pig around a spike. She'd take a washcloth and daintily dab at the open wounds while humming a childhood song, one her grandmother would hum while tucking them into bed. Eventually, Micah would join in softly, then in full force.

But that wasn't an option now, was it?

"Galen? Galen? Listen. Okay? Calm down. Breathe. In and out, okay?" She motioned with her hands for him to follow along with her. Her body was vibrating. The pain in her foot had subsided, but her nerves were setting in.

Galen looked at her with a squinted eye and his mouth sputtered open as though he'd just risen from a long swim underwater. He was trying to hold it together, but something inside him switched and he howled again before sobbing softly with his good eye smashed against the mattress. He let his mouth hang open, drool spooling out. "Galen? Can you hear me?"

"My eye's fucked, not my hearing," he said, his voice strong for once. His tone was cross, and she pictured him as a dog, snapping its jaws at her. She suppressed the urge to snap back. Galen was just in pain, she reminded herself. She shouldn't take his words personally. He didn't know what he was saying.

He groaned. Through gasps of trembling breaths, he asked, "What happened?"

She sat on the edge of the bed beside his feet. "Leo and I found you. You were hurt."

"Do I have the earrings?"

She shook her head before realizing he couldn't see her. "I don't think so. I'm sorry. Leo doesn't have one, either."

"Where is he?"

"Looking."

"So, I'm stuck with you?"

Isabelle folded her arms. "You'd have bled without me."

"Would you have helped me if Leo hadn't asked?"

"Would you have helped me?"

"No," he said plainly before writhing again. Good, she thought, regretting it immediately. One wasn't to wish bad luck on anyone, no matter how wretched.

She gritted her teeth, imagining a perfect world where Galen was unconscious, and she could wait out the rest of the exam in peace.

Her hand gravitated toward the necklace Leo had found, and she rubbed her thumb over the smooth underside of the gauntlet. Isabelle's scowl turned slack, her mind back on track. "Thank you for your honesty. I cannot do more. You'll have to see a doctor."

Isabelle expected another outburst of unkind words or grunts of pain, but he noiselessly faced the ceiling and released soft sniffles. "I was so close."

"It's okay," she said. Admittedly, she didn't believe her own words. She knew he didn't, either. It was not okay at all. His eye was ruined. "Do you know who..."

She did not know the Latarian pronunciation of the word 'attacked,' but Galen appeared to understand what she was getting at. "There were two of 'em left... but I try to envision them and all I see are unidentifiable blobs. The details are fuzzy... I took those earrings from 'em, I know that much. I know that much..."

Galen drifted into sleep for a minute, a very long minute where Isabelle watched him with wide eyes, fearing he was dying. She went up to his face to check if he was breathing when his eye snapped back open. He got to crying and yelling again; it was agonizing on the ears.

Galen continued angrily, "I must've thought they were weak if I let my guard down like that. Damn!"

He tossed his fist onto the bed; it hit with a dull *thud*. She didn't enjoy feeling bad for him, but she did all the same. Was this how Leo felt when she cried? Pity? All she wanted to do was hug Galen and heal his eye like Gahi's apprentice. She silently prayed for this impossible feat.

"There's a bag of medical supplies in house 5010," he said. "I remember that. We should go there. I—ah!"

He stopped talking and cried some more. Blood had seeped through his bandages and transferred onto the mattress, staining it dark red. His left eyelid was sealed shut by the glass. His voice was small and soft. "Please."

She let out a deep breath. She could carry Galen to the house he spoke of, but there were too many variables to consider. They'd need to leave Leo a message and run outside with full hands and no means of protection. Galen didn't mention a medic along with the supplies, which meant there probably wasn't much that could be done.

The word 'no' was pressed hard against her lips. As she continued to look at him, she couldn't bring herself to say it. *Damn me to the Unholy Land*, she thought.

"Okay." But she had to do something first. She rushed out of the room, already unsheathing her blade. Isabelle looked around the back room where they'd first entered, examining the floorboards. She opted to carve the numbers right next to the door, but the boards were thick and sleek, impenetrable.

Isabelle's heart sped as she gulped. From here, she could hear Galen's whimpers, sounds that made her nerves rise. The kitchen appeared to have different flooring, and similar wooden panels, but rotting at the edges of the kitchen island. She made quick work of her carving, dragging the knife hard into the ground, splintering the area around the numbers.

Satisfied with her hasty work, she ran back to Galen and scooped him up as Leo had her. He was lighter than she expected. Galen curled himself into her arms, legs draped over her forearm and his head against her chest.

Isabelle stumbled toward the front door and awkwardly

tried to use her preoccupied hand to open it. She stood there for what seemed like forever, fiddling with the knob while balancing Galen's body, which was slowly slumping closer and closer to the ground. Finally, she heard a soft click and shoved her way out. The sun was overwhelming to her pupils, and she was temporarily blinded. Galen groaned in her arms. She gulped, frantically searching with squinted, watery eyes. From here, it was impossible to see the addresses of the houses across the road.

"Color?" she asked, which garnered another moan in return. It was weaker this time, distant, and she feared he was falling unconscious in her arms, overtaken by his wounds. She shook him lightly. His mouth parted in a sharp yelp, his eyelids convulsing. "Stay awake. Which one? Tell me."

"Other side..." He let out between segments of groans. "Middle."

"Got it." She hobbled down the front steps; the back of her foot slid against the final stair, and she stumbled forward. Her weight became uneven, and she nearly lost Galen in her tumbling act. She cursed her bought of clumsiness.

"Careful," Galen snapped.

"I could drop you right here," she muttered in Urkinian. She had to control herself; it only made sense he'd snap at her, especially when she made such mistakes.

She dashed to the other side of the 'road' and searched for the addresses. It was still difficult to read some of them; the thin black numbers blended in heavily with the dark-coated houses. Galen groaned in her arms as she maneuvered around a dead body. Her eyes were trained on what was ahead instead of the dead.

Isabelle was proving unsuccessful in her attempt to not think about what she'd done. Flashes of her dagger plunging into the person's neck made her tremble, and the idea of her

Savior looking down at her with disdain rocked her to the core. It'd been hard to push the blade into the thick muscles of their flesh. That was perhaps the worst of it—how much weight she had to put behind her blow. Yet the blade slid out easily, leaving behind a trail of splattered blood on the floor and her shoes.

Isabelle hadn't meant to kill them; she only reacted in self-defense. She hadn't meant to. But she'd aimed for the neck, the one place a stab wound would kill anyone. If Isabelle hadn't wanted to take their life, she could've aimed anywhere else. Anywhere. They'd gurgled on their own blood, choking and gasping while staring at her with dead-set eyes. Isabelle shook her head and a tear fell. It wasn't on purpose. It wasn't.

Her attention snapped back to reality. There, that was the house. She could see the first two numbers if she squinted hard enough, and as she shuffled closer, the last two numbers matched up. It was the only house painted red, and she wondered with a quell of anger why Galen didn't just tell her the color.

"You there!" someone shouted from behind. Isabelle stopped at the bottom of the porch stairs. They sounded familiar, but she couldn't place who they were. Isabelle looked up the steps to the door. Beads of sweat rolled down her jawline and onto Galen's exposed midriff. They'd been so close. "I said, you! Over there! Stop at once!"

Her eyes were bulging from their sockets as she tried to figure out who it was. Faces of contestants flashed in her memory, but she came up empty-handed. She breathed out of her mouth, her heart racing, and Galen groaning. She turned around.

It was the man with long black hair and a black-trimmed white coat. He was but five paces away, staring back at her with a postured demeanor. She couldn't remember his name, but he'd been the one to threaten Othelia's life. He didn't look like a murderer. A guard, perhaps, or someone royal, but not a murderer. But then again, she didn't look like one, either.

"Are you here to kill me?" Isabelle asked. She was surprised by her forwardness. Her voice trembled, but she stood tall and glowered at him.

"It's not within my interests to kill you, miss," he said, but his hand was on the hilt of his sword. Galen was silent in her arms. She didn't want to place him on the ground for fear that any more drastic movements would damage his eye further. She didn't want to be responsible for that, too. "But I do have a question."

"Tell him no," Galen grumbled.

"Is Othelia in there?" He looked at her brazenly, a look she equated to Abel, though this man seemed less cruel and judgmental, and more so dutiful.

"Why?"

He sighed and pulled out his sword, slashing it thrice before bringing it to his side. "I know you're with her. I can very well guess she's in that house."

She turned to the dark red house slowly; its gloomy and towering frame made her shutter. Isabelle kept her back to him. The thought of a sword at his side only made her want to scurry away faster. "I don't know where she is."

Victory was at her fingertips, but there were still endless hours to go. Hours of wondering if a lunatic like him would come knocking on her door. She walked toward the house, hoping to reach the inside before he got the chance to strike.

"Hey!" he yelled, voice filled with anger and astonishment.

"I wouldn't go near her if I were you," a new voice called. Isabelle stopped and turned around again; her eyes widened in surprise. It was Raphael, his suit and hair as silver as ever. He stood behind the sworded man and looked into Isabelle's eyes with a smile. In Urkinian, he said, "I was hoping to find you out here."

"And who might you be?" the sworded man asked, turning his back on Isabelle.

Raphael chuckled. "I'm surprised you do not know me. I thought your people knew everything, *Hanako.*"

Hanako gripped his sword tightly and held the blade in front of him. "Your magnation is strong. I wasn't aware there were others tied with Othelia or the Royal Families. But if you wish to battle in this girl's place, I suppose I have no choice."

"Othelia? Oh, bother, no. I have no immediate interest in the princess, or you, but anyone who is a threat to Isabelle is a threat to me," Raphael said. He reached into his suit jacket and pulled out a much smaller sword, one she couldn't imagine would fare well against this Hanako man.

Raphael looked at Isabelle again, his eyes a beautiful blue she wished she could swim in. She would've cursed herself to the Unholy Land for such a thought, but she doubted they would ever meet again. Even without knowing the two men, she could tell he was the lesser in this match.

In Urkinian, Raphael said with a smile, "Go. I'll meet you inside."

She nodded and yelled, "May Gahi bring good fortune to you."

She turned back to the house then, allowing fate to take control. The prospect of losing her only known ally with the ability to find out more regarding her brother's murder was fearsome, but she wasn't one to fight in a losing battle. Not with Galen in her arms and a swollen ankle to weigh her down.

Isabelle hobbled up to the porch and attempted to open the door. It was locked. She knocked twice, hoping that whoever was on the other side wasn't gearing up to end her life.

Was this the right house? Was Galen deceiving her and leading her to her death?

No one answered. She knocked again. Nothing.

She turned around briefly to view the fight unfolding behind her. Raphael jumped to the right, dodging Hanako's sword by mere inches. The fabric of his silver suit was stained with blood at the cuff, a gash running through it. Their swords clanked together as Raphael lunged forward and Hanako blocked the attack; their swift motions were hard to catch with the human eye.

Movement from the left caught her attention; a woman was shambling over from a house across the way, a foot dragging behind her. She held a large stick in one hand, leaning against it to stand upright, and a hatchet dripping with blood in the other. The woman ignored the two men fighting, her eyes locked on Isabelle—no—on the boy Isabelle was holding.

Isabelle pounded on the metal door frantically while sparing glances over her shoulder. The woman passed the two men as she made her way across the dirt road. Isabelle was sure at that moment she would be hacked to pieces. She may have deserved such a gruesome departure; it was befitting of someone who stabbed another human in the neck.

"Open up!" she yelled.

"It's me, the Aguelon," Galen yelled in a half-shout. He appeared to be putting all his effort into his plea. "Please let us in!"

She hadn't expected his plea to work, but a heavy bolt was lifted, and the door swung open. A large man stood on the other side, bending to see her under the doorframe. He looked her over with disdain, but he nodded and moved to the side. She barged through and placed Galen on the ground in a scrambled attempt to close the front door.

"She's coming!" Isabelle shouted, hoping her warning was

enough to convince the burly man to either close the door or scare off the woman.

"I can see that," he responded. The man left the door wide open as he stared at the approaching woman, his arms crossed and a broad smile on his face.

She pulled out her blade as she approached the man, suddenly fearing she would have to fight both him and the deranged woman outside. His eyes bulged with wild excitement as he saw her knife and reached out his hand. "Toss me that."

"Not a chance. Lock the door!"

"She'll just cut through the metal door or the wooden walls surrounding us. It's best to kill her. Here, let me do it. Give me your knife."

His eagerness was enough for her to reach a conclusion. "She'll wear herself out."

"By then you won't have a door to hide behind, now, will you?"

Isabelle scowled in response. There was no one she didn't like back home, but she was finding plenty during this exam. He made a good point, too, but she was not surrendering her weapon to anyone, much less a killer who got a thrill out of it.

She ran up to the door and examined her opponent one last time, ignoring the man completely. The woman's eyes were wild and angry. Her hair was an array of untamed red curls, and freckles covered every corner of her face. Her upper lip was split down the middle, and blood trickled from her temple and extended down to her jawline.

"What're ya doing there, lady?" the woman yelled from the steps. "I thought that blond boy was dead, but you're over here carrying him 'round like he's still breathing. He still breathing? I knew I shoulda hit him harder."

Isabelle slammed the door shut and locked it. She wasn't

looking to murder again or watch another person die. The burly man looked at her with disappointment, and Isabelle gave him a glare in return. "You want to kill her? Go out there and do it yourself."

He shrugged and walked over to the only table in the room. He sat, a fresh can of beans opened in front of him; two empty cans were pushed off to the side. He pulled the fork out and waved it at her jokingly. "When she breaks through, I will."

She sheathed her knife and knelt over Galen, determining how to pick him up and sling him onto a spare bed, assuming there were any beds in the house. He appeared unconscious, but as she knelt over him, he asked, "Did it work? Did my name work?"

"Yes. What did you call yourself? 'The A-guelon?'"

"Ah-gwe-lon," he croaked. "It's my last name."

"People know you by your last name?"

"Only the unlucky ones with a high enough bounty on their heads."

Isabelle sucked in a breath. So, she was sharing a space with a criminal. What luck she had.

She struggled to scoop Galen up, grunting as she put all her weight into her legs. Galen was perhaps the strangest of their group—she would never understand him—but he was a life. She carried him down a narrow hallway and into the second room, a stray couch with a black box and screen facing it. She'd never seen such a thing before, and it hadn't been in any of the other houses prior. Was there a theme to this town? Was it a town at all?

Isabelle made her way back to the main room; the blade of the hatchet chomped against the wooden wall beside the door, and she jumped at the sight of the blade sticking through. Her heart sank. Nothing could ever be easy, could it?

Grunts sounded from the other side as the woman

struggled to dislodge the blade. It took more than a few tugs before she successfully ripped it away, taking a chunk of splintering wood with it. A medium-sized hole was formed in its place. There was no telling how much time they had left before she hacked the wall away.

"You stupid, dumb bitch," the woman howled in a shrill, high-pitched voice. "I'll finish the job, you hear me? That boy threatened my life; he's a menace! A menace!"

Isabelle turned to the man, who shook his head sullenly and said, "Sounds like she's got the right to be angry."

She gestured to the door with a tsk of exasperation. "Not to kill him."

He laughed. "Where are you from, girl? That's what the International Exam is. An excuse to murder."

"And you thought I'd give my knife?" she asked, repulsed. He must've been delusional. "You are *desheez*." She made a face resembling disgust. "Why are you here?"

He stretched his arms and looked at her, his washed-out brown eyes turning softer, the adrenaline he once felt evaporating the longer they spoke. "I was merely sent by the examiners. I don't need an excuse to kill people. 'The Axe' is my street name, though I can tell that it means nothing to you."

His boisterous tone sent her seething inside, the way he sneered as he admitted to the enjoyment of murder. And then she remembered Galen's words back when they read the phase four instructions. He'd been excited to fight. To kill. How many had Galen killed before he became the victim? Was this woman's anger warranted? Had Galen killed one, two, all of her friends before she got the jump on him?

She clenched her jaw. "No wonder you get along."

The Axe let out a hearty bark, a type of laugh only a truly moronic and murderous person would have. She clenched the handle of her dagger with a clammy palm as another deafening crunch of the hatchet filled the room. A glint of the metal protruded within, taunting her. "I am nothing like that boy and his family. Now, are you going to give me the knife or are you going to keep watching 'til she breaks through?"

A bright, blinding light shot in through the windows, cutting off whatever response she may have had. The house lit up as though a million bulbs had been turned on at once. She and the man turned away; the hacking temporarily paused.

"Gahi! What—"

"Hey," a voice called from the hallway. "Are you still here?"

She pulled out her dagger instantly, her racing heart and blotted vision sending her into a panic. Just like that, the blinding light was gone, replaced with the woman continuing her hasty work. Whatever caused the blinding light didn't matter, because, at that moment, her safety had diminished with the addition of an unknown threat.

The voice had come from the hallway. She pressed herself against the wall beside the corridor, peeking her head around the corner. Her shoulders dropped at the sight of Raphael leaning against the hallway wall, holding a bloodied arm as he shambled toward her, a grunt escaping his lips with every step.

The backdoor from which he presumably came through was at the end of the corridor, now closed and hopefully locked. Had it been unlocked this entire time?

"What was that?" she asked in Urkinian. "And who was that man?"

"A Swordsman. My father has told me about them. People who are hired to take on jobs for those in prominent positions. It was part of my studies when Father became King." He groaned as he stopped in front of her, continuing to use the wall as support. "I'm sorry I haven't tried to stop that woman; I fear I've made an error. Didn't fight to my full capacity. A mistake, as it would seem."

She noticed red peeking out from under his suit jacket. She pulled back the flap gingerly, revealing fresh blood seeping from his side and staining the fabric. Her eyes widened.

"Did you kill him?" she whispered.

Raphael shook his head. "No, I couldn't. I'm not"—he released a shuddering breath—"trained well, yet, in that regard. My father wishes for me to become head of our international relations, not of killing."

"What did he mean by that word—mag-nat-ion?" She tried her best to pronounce the word Hanako had used, wincing at how it sounded rolling off her tongue. "Did it have something to do with that light?"

He smiled. "You're sharp. You will learn in time. Perhaps once the exam is over, I can explain it to you. My magnation is strong. My mag, not so much."

Raphael looked over at the criminal eating his beans, his eyes panning over to the bright pink bags with red pluses on them. "Those are medical bags. Here, could you help me? I can't lose much more blood."

Isabelle rushed over to the bags as Raphael slid against the wall beside them and sat with his legs sprawled out before him. Her face grew hot as she cursed herself for not noticing the bags sooner—or knowing what they were.

"Can you help him?" Isabelle asked 'The Axe.' He had to have the medical bags for a reason, after all.

He shook his head with a bemused smirk. "Why would an admitted criminal know how to help people?"

She shrugged. "People have layers?"

Isabelle began going through the bags, desperate to find anything of use. The only knowledge she had of cleaning wounds came from the aftermath of whip lashes she and her brother got. Even then, all they used was fresh water and woven cloth to do so. The equipment in this bag was advanced, white cloth spun tightly together, packaged applicants and creams she couldn't read the labels of.

The Axe sat at the small table and watched her. He lazily spun his spoon around in his empty can, producing a metal-on-metal clanking. His smile and titillated expression were gone, replaced with that of a curious child. "You know the back door was locked, and I didn't hear any windows shattering. Care to explain?"

Raphael shook his head. "If you were meant to know, you'd know."

Isabelle continued to rummage through the medical bags, needing not an explanation for how Raphael had entered the house. He had protected her, named her an ally, and he needed her full attention on bandaging his wounds.

Raphael listed off the names of the supplies she needed and helped her read the instructions in Urkinian. Her mind was reeling, hands shaking. She was terrified. Terrified of the house being broken into and murdered. Terrified of the man who wanted to kill sitting a foot away. Terrified of Raphael bleeding to death beside her.

As she prepared cream for his cut, another hack sounded from the wall. The hatchet stayed lodged in the wood as an incoherent yell protruded from the woman's lips. She let out a bloodcurdling scream, and her body hit the metal door with a thud.

CHAPTER 25
LEO

ELI'S LIMP WEIGHT was proving to be a challenge. Although farm work provided him with some extra physical strength, having the entirety of a six-foot man pressed against his side, and a knife in the other, was quite debilitating. Even with Samuel's help—hardly—on the other side.

Othelia led them toward the commotion across the street while Abel trailed behind them. He wasn't sure what to expect, but it certainly was not the rancid smell of cooking bodies that overcame his senses as they made their way around a house to the dirt road.

Leo gagged and peered away. He couldn't imagine how embarrassed he'd be if he puked again. His heaving was dry and, although he was light-headed and nauseous, he would not throw up here. It smelled worse than navy-spotted cow dung, worse than rotten meat in the fridge. Worse than a man who lived without bathing and rolled around in his own urine.

"Guy." Samuel's voice somehow found its way into Leo's ear. Leo's face turned ashen at the sight of a screaming woman swinging a hatchet into a wall. The knife in his side was causing aching pain, radiating throughout his entire body. Color drained from his face and his eyes rolled back in their sockets.

He took a step forward as his body swayed, and that seemed to rouse his mind just enough to hear Samuel say, "Don't pass out. We can't afford another one of us down. Especially since Abel is dead weight."

"Saying that isn't right, Sam. You saw what happened to Obrien and Marcious. It isn't right, saying what you just said." Abel spoke with a dejected voice filled with trepidation, reminiscent of Galen's. Leo thought of Galen's bruised and broken face and wooziness threatened to overtake him all over again.

"It's a fact of the matter," Samuel snapped.

Leo liked to consider himself a patient person, but Samuel was testing him. Every squawk from Samuel's lips was grating in his ears. Being referred to as 'guy' made Leo realize he may dislike him. A lot. There was good in everyone, he tried to remind himself to dampen his growing annoyance. There was good in everyone, and he was given the ungrateful job of finding it.

"You think that's it?" Othelia asked, pointing toward a small, red home with a concave roof and circular windows as opposed to the rectangular fashion of the others. The home with a woman swinging a hatchet at the wall. Her curly red hair bounced with every tug as she attempted to dislodge the blade.

"You or me?" Leo gestured between Othelia and himself, hoping Othelia would take the reins. After nearly getting killed, and a knife protruding from his side, he'd had enough. He didn't have an item, but he didn't want to fight someone. Especially when he'd lost his only weapon.

But Othelia glanced from the woman to Leo with a nervous twinkle in her eyes, something he thought she was immune to. Was it possible? Was she, the apparent Princess Othelia... scared? "My hands, uh, I don't think I can. All I can do is kick, and that hatchet looks too sharp to be kicking at."

His shoulders sagged, and Eli's head tilted from the sudden shift. Leo surveyed their pathetic crew. They were all tired and sported various injuries, many of which included drying blood. They all stank, a product of the decaying bodies surrounding them mixed with their heavy sweat. No one else was stepping up to the plate. This was a bona fide disaster.

"Knife?" Leo asked, a sigh escaping before he could help it. Othelia nodded and pointed to the sheathed blade at her side. He grabbed it and weighed it in his hands, tossing it between his palms.

"Hurry," Othelia urged, relieving him of Eli's weight.

"There you are," a voice said as their group began making their way across the dirt road. Leo jumped; the tall, long-haired man appeared without notice.

Othelia scoffed. "I thought I was safe until the exam was over."

"Plans haven't changed," Hanako H. Byrde said smoothly. "I'm merely here to observe, your highness."

"Who's this guy?" Samuel asked, gesturing with great annoyance.

Hanako's eyes flickered to Othelia's brother, and he smiled. "The other sibling? How rich, the scene I've stumbled upon. Brother and sister working hand-in-hand instead of fighting each other. Your father will be quite intrigued to hear that."

The hatchet woman struck against the house again with feverish grunts, ignoring Hanako and the group's presence altogether.

"Abel, take his arm," Othelia said, peeling Eli off her neck. Abel reacted hesitantly, eyes bouncing between her and Hanako and the crazed woman.

Leo was left out of the altercation completely, and that was quite fine. He was too busy trying to amp himself up to fight the hatchet-user. Leo had to step up to the plate. He had to. But it was happening again, dammit. Leo was stuck, shaking in his sneakers and watching helplessly as this woman hacked away at the house. If Isabelle and Galen were in there, the woman was going to do the same to them when she got inside.

He heard Othelia say, "You're not taking me home and I'm not rotting in jail. We take care of this here and now."

Leo could listen no more; his mind was set. Somehow, he got his legs to move, and he was propelled forward. He reached the porch steps as the woman freed the hatchet from the wall and reared it back. His mind was reeling, tunnel vision taking hold. He'd hoped instinct would take over, if such a thing were to exist, but he couldn't stop thinking about the blade in his hand and what he would have to do.

He gulped and felt his momentum slow as he climbed the steps. His chest was tightening. He clenched his jaw to stop his groans from the knife in his side. It was happening again, wasn't it? He was always going to be a coward. He would be responsible for Isabelle's and Galen's deaths.

His foot hit the porch, and his knuckles whitened around the knife. He didn't know what else to do except raise the blade in the air, but it felt wrong as he did, too heavy. He opted to use his foot at the last second and kicked her in the side. She shrieked as she stumbled to the left. He kicked her again, this time in the back, slamming her into the front door. The hatchet fell with a thick thump. As the handle struck the porch floor, she whirled around. He took an involuntary step back in sheer fear, his gaze looking from her to the hatchet as the blade hit the ground.

The woman lunged for the hatchet, curly hair covering her face. Her fingertips were stained with blood and had just barely brushed the hatchet handle when he raised his foot again. His toes connected with her chin; her head flew back, and he saw something white—a tooth?—fly out of her mouth. What was he doing? What kind of fight was this? He was emulating what he'd seen Othelia do to Samuel, the only reference to fighting he really had. Like using the knife, it didn't feel right either.

Leo stopped, hands trembling, and breathing rigid. His kick wasn't powerful enough to do much damage, though her angry cry suggested otherwise. What caught his eyes were the earrings clipped into her lobes—thin golden frills attached to crystalline opals. The woman rubbed her chin, but only for a stunned, gasping second. Then her gaze landed back on the hatchet, and she was diving for it again.

"Step on her hand!" Samuel advised from the cushy sidelines, but Leo didn't react fast enough. She grabbed hold of the weapon and started swinging frantically, aiming at no one and nothing.

She yelled incomprehensibly, "They're dead... yes... I'm going to... he'll be mine... soon... and that bitch... that dumb bitch... soon... yes..."

Leo backed off, nearly slipping down the porch stairs and back onto the dirt road. The woman's smile was crooked and toothy. As he looked at her, he realized she was around his age. Around his age and from... from somewhere. From the exam... trivia, he remembered with horror. It's the same girl?

"Mari, was it?"

She stopped swinging. One of her eyes peeked out of her entangled hair, wide with surprise. It lasted for but a second, and then her brow furrowed and her lips curled in disgust. "You! You know them! You're his friend!"

"Who—?" But any attempt at communication was futile.

"Responsible," she yelled. "You're all responsible! They'd be alive, if he hadn't... yes, if he hadn't!"

Mari turned herself back around and got back to chopping. There was nearly a hole big enough to shove through now. Leo's mouth hung open. Her actions were unusual compared to how she acted during the trivia phase. He'd marked her as someone independent and headstrong, but her current state was anything but, and he had a sneaking suspicion Galen was the culprit of whatever she was enraged about.

"Isabelle, you in there?" Leo called, to which he got an almost immediate, "Yeah!"

"Can you come and help?" He was desperate for someone, anyone. There was silence on the other end. He was alone. Was this her way of punishment? Her way of forcing him to commit to something? Commit to murder?

He glanced over at Othelia briefly. A sword was at her throat, resting underneath her chin, and her face was a bloodied mess. Leo let out a final, intoxicating breath and came back up the steps.

He didn't hesitate this time, nor did he try to think as he sliced at Mari's shoulders from behind. Mari turned around furiously and swung at his head. He ducked and sliced at her stomach. It slid easily through her shirt and flesh, drawing a slash of blood over her navel.

The movement sent another piercing stab from the knife jutting out of his side, and he yelled. She swung at his neck next, and he jumped backward. His back connected with the wooden post of the porch. Leo ducked, squatting as low as he could with hands covering the back of his neck. The blade bore into the wood above him and was easily dislodged. He yelled again, tears spilling from his eyes. He didn't know how much longer he could fight with his wound.

Leo scrambled away from her on his hands and knees, pushing himself to the side as she swung again. Mari had no aim; she just wanted to chop him to bits, and that was enough.

He stood and lunged at her as she was dislodging the hatchet from the porch floor. The point of Othelia's blade was directed at her stomach, his wrist at an awkward angle.

"That's not how you hold it!" Othelia yelled.

"Why don't you come over here and do it, then!" he snapped back, his terror turning to anger. This was mad. He signed up for the exam even after everything his mother told him. This was nothing but desperate people pitted against each other in hopes of riches and respect.

The blade missed, and he retreated. Mari came for him again, this time holding the hatchet above her head. Leo dodged to the left and pointed the sharpest edge of the knife outward. He sent the tip into her back, and she screamed. He winced, nearly screaming himself, but he didn't see blood seeping through her clothes. It didn't feel real, what he did, what he was doing. It didn't feel real, and it didn't feel right.

He pulled the dagger out, and blood dripped from the blade. When he saw the back of her white cotton shirt, it was stained, too. She dropped the hatchet and charged forward with a fist. He hadn't expected such an attack, and her fingers connected with his jaw. The knife in him shifted as he tried to regain his footing, and his screams were muffled by his inability to fully open his mouth from her punch.

Mari punched him twice in quick succession and then stopped, her knuckles bruised and broken. The knife fell from his hand and, instead of keeping it for herself, Mari kicked it over the porch edge.

His face was growing hot with pain and his lip was bleeding and inflated. He wiped at it, but the spot was numb, a metallic taste in his mouth. Leo grabbed for the handle of the hatchet, and she followed suit. They pulled on it with both their hands, a strange tug of war occurring in an otherwise quiet town.

Leo desperately pulled it with all his strength, and it ripped out of her calloused, brittle fingers. He stood with a speed he didn't know he had and hovered the hatchet over his head. His feet were planted, his heart thumping so fast he thought it may burst. Mari stared at him in confusion for a moment, her weapon gone. He gulped and said, "Don't make me do this."

She stood slowly, staggering while she touched her back. When she brought her hand to her face, there was blood. She stared at it with mouth agape in stupefaction. Then her brows furrowed, and she clenched her bloodied hand into a fist. She took one step forward, rearing up to hit him.

He brought the blade down. It connected with the center of her head, cracking through her skull. Her body spasmed, her lips sputtering and eyes convulsing. Leo backed away. He held his breath, his own eyes bulging in terror. She fell to the ground and continued to writhe like a fish out of water. His skin turned ashen, and dizziness took hold. Leo reached for the patio pillar and used it to steady himself as he saw double.

Her spasms turned into twitches until she finally took her last breath. Her eyes stared vacantly into the vastness of nothing, and he remembered with a rising dread that he knew her name. She had a name, friends, family. She had a life, and he took it from her. And for what, he asked himself, for money?

He attempted to stand upright, but his side forced him to remain hunched over. Every muscle in his body was screaming, and the world was becoming dimmer. He knew he had to lie down, his chest heaving as air filled his lungs in short bursts. Panic escalated quickly, but not because of his physical state.

Leo stared ahead at the front of another house, this one light blue. It reminded him of the sky, so he looked up at it. It was serene and bright. A beautiful, cloudless day. He told himself to imagine clouds drifting along without a care. Think of the nitren, their sweet yet sour smell, their light maroon petals shedding off and traveling in the wind. He ran a hand through his hair. When he pulled his hand back, he realized it, too, was covered in her blood. His hands were trembling. Had they been this whole time? He felt he should puke. If there was any time to puke, now would be it. But nothing came up.

"Leo!" Isabelle's voice brought his attention back, reality morphing into view. Mari's body, the handle sticking upright, the blade still lodged in her skull, her boisterous curls now soaked and flat.

The door was open now. Isabelle stood in the doorway, a man sitting at a table behind her. She wasn't using anything to prop herself up, her busted ankle resting perfectly fine on the floor. She could walk just fine. Sadness and shock boiled over into anger.

"Why didn't you help me?" He turned to Samuel and Abel. "Why didn't any of you bother to help?"

No one responded. Isabelle shrunk away, cowering in the darkness of the house inside. She'd been right there, right on the other side of the door, listening. Listening to the entire confrontation while not doing anything to help him.

"I was... I was helping someone," she whispered, but Leo didn't care.

"You're all cowards," he choked out. His words sounded muffled from his puffy lower lip. He felt his cheeks. They were wet, pools of tears gathering at his fingertips. When had he started crying? "All of you."

Leo bent down and gingerly unhooked the earrings from Mari. He sniffled and stifled sobs as he did so, his face bright red with fury. When he had both, he entered the dingy home and brushed past Isabelle.

"Leo, I'm s—"

"Spare me." His voice was smooth and icy. "You were

behind that door this whole time and you did nothing. No apologies. Where's Galen?"

Her mouth sputtered, opening and closing with no words. He tsked in frustration and didn't wait for an answer. Instead, he tore through the small corridor and searched for Galen. Of the three closed doors within the hallway, Galen was behind the first. He was lying on a couch face-up, his chest rising and falling peacefully.

Had they fled here because Galen had woken up and told Isabelle to? Was Galen really the reason Mari was so upset? Had he injured or killed her friends? Leo shook his head before his thoughts got too far. He couldn't place the blame on anyone. No, he couldn't blame anyone but himself.

CHAPTER 26

OTHELIA

AS LEO WAS struggling to prepare for his fight with the hatchet-wielder, Othelia had other business to take care of.

"You're not taking me home and I'm not rotting in jail. We take care of this here and now," she said. Hanako H. Byrde was watching her with amusement, a twinkle in his eyes that she didn't like all too well.

"I was informed by the King that you two aren't very close," he said, nodding toward Samuel.

"We aren't."

"And yet you're working together?"

"He's still my brother. I may not like him, but he doesn't deserve to fail. Speaking of,"—she paused for dramatic effect—"I'm not passing. So, how should we settle this? Will you try to kill me?"

He shook his head and walked toward her. She stood her ground and kept her head held high. Fearlessness was the only form of power she had over him. She wouldn't be able to kick him like she could with Samuel. She couldn't use her power or her hands. Othelia had heard of prison and the things that happened once tossed in, and it wasn't a place she was heading. She supposed the only thing she could do was die with dignity.

"I've already told you what happens if you don't pass, your highness. The King and I have been friends for years. I wouldn't slaughter his daughter. Not unless he asked me to."

"I may as well be dead if you send me home. I'd rather be dead. There's nothing there for me. Why are you all so keen on keeping me locked away?"

Hanako ran a gloved hand through his hair and sighed. "I'm not too fond of repeating myself. I've told you the conditions I've been given and there is nothing more to it. It's nothing personal. I told you that, too. It's not personal for your father, either. The Kingship is meant to have its secrets and a little trollop like you running around with an open mouth is not within their interests."

"That's deranged."

"That's the sacrifice of being blessed. The stars have blessed your family, of all the people on this planet. To spread the word of your power would be detrimental to the Kings. There are no hard feelings here. Don't you get that? You're given love. Love and money and power and anything you could ever want. Surely you can't expect everything without a price."

Othelia clenched her fists and winced, her burnt hands a joke on top of it all. She had no plan, no idea of what to do. There was nothing she *could* do, not physically, at least.

She crossed her arms, sandwiching her wrists between her ribs and arms to avoid rubbing the burns against her clothes. He looked at her with confusion, then laughed. "I see. You're hurt. Well, those will get all nice and healed up in the prison infirmary. There are still twenty hours left of this phase, yet you've given up?"

Othelia scoffed. "I haven't—"

He didn't give her time to finish; his sword was sheathed, and he thrust a fist into her cheekbone. Her head snapped to the side and her body followed, legs twisting over each other as she unwrapped her hands to catch her fall. She braced for impact, but he moved faster than she fell; he grabbed her arm with an ironclad grip and hoisted her upright. Othelia saw a glimpse of his bemused expression before he punched her in the other cheek.

His moves were a step beyond quick, a superhuman speed that launched her head from one side to the other. There was nothing she could do to stop it. Her brain rattled against her skull and a dizzying array of black dots sprouted in her vision. She stumbled backward, an eye swollen and her nose busted. At some point, she must've bitten her tongue, because the metallic taste of blood was in every crevice of her mouth.

She looked at him through hazy vision, wanting nothing more than to lie down and sleep. She glanced over at Eli, who was still unconscious, and felt a pang of jealousy.

When she turned back to Hanako H. Byrde, his sword was thrust underneath her chin. She stopped moving and gulped. The blade nicked her, and dabs of blood sprouted as a sharp pain warmed her neck. Othelia tried to take a step back, but their movements were synchronized, and the blade remained under her chin. She pointed her palms at him and tried to channel her power, but it only made her head hurt. She let out a soft cry, and the blade slid along her flesh, begging to break through.

This was it. She'd never find out about the talithes or know why her father sent Samuel here. She'd never see the ocean again or venture into the outside world. Othelia had finally met people outside of the palace, most of whom she actually liked, and she'd never speak to any of them again because she'd be gone and lost to the stars in the night sky.

And, by stars, it sent tears to her eyes. The physical pain was numbing, but the idea of dying sobered her up enough to look up at him with radiating annoyance.

He tapped the sword against the bottom of her chin and said, "Now, now. Don't look at me with such disgust when we both know *you* are the problem here. I made my presence known because you deserve to know I'm watching you. I'll be watching until this exam ends, and then I will take you with me to one place or the other. If you fail after this phase, I'll fail as well, and take you to prison."

The commotion on the porch got caught in her peripherals, and she temporarily ignored the blade resting underneath her chin to watch. She didn't know Leo well, but she knew enough. No doubt he would be struggling. He'd never used her type of blade before, either—it was specially made by the royal blacksmith, designed long and curved inward. The blade was so strong it could cut through a person's midsection in a single swipe given the right momentum. The outer curved edge was also sharp, and it was used best for cutting necks.

Leo, in all his blazing glory, was charging at the woman with the tip of the blade pointed at her stomach. Her heart nearly jumped from her chest as she yelled, "That's not how you hold it!"

The flat edge of Hanako's sword bounced against her chin and the point cut into her neck. The cuts were sharp and forceful, but not enough to pierce further than the skin. She kept her eyes on Leo, ignoring the pain. She'd felt far worse.

Leo dodged the woman and shouted, "Why don't you come over here and do it, then!"

Her eyes flickered to Hanako. She took another daring step back, only for the same synchronized dance to occur. "Who are you?"

"I've already told you my na—"

"What business?" she demanded. "Occupation. Job. Work. Who *are* you?"

His eyes narrowed, and he stared back in silent contemplation. His mouth was a tight line, but she could see something there, perhaps intrigue. Perhaps he was even amused —did she remind him of her father? "I am one of the Five Swordsmen."

"The who?"

"Has your father not taught you of such matters? Surely that would be in the curriculum. Or perhaps you were as bad a student as you are a fighter?"

"First, he does not teach me; our tutors do. Second, we're taught everything but the history of other countries and other political systems. I can't say I remember hearing anything of the sort," she said, conveniently leaving out the fact that she was a rather horrible student. They were given tests after each lesson, and she notoriously got the worst grades out of the three eldest siblings.

He shook his head. "Of course, I can't believe you in the slightest, but I'll ask the King about the validity of that statement once this is over. If what you are saying is true—"

"It is."

"—then I'll tell you now, for the sake of it. Becoming a swordsman is an overly complicated process, but I'll boil it down to simple terms for you. A man, and only a man, is chosen to inherit the title by whoever is a current member."

"That sounds simple enough."

A flash of anger appeared on his face, and she thought he might just stab her to death. But he didn't and put his sword away. "I can assure you it is not! There are many people on this planet, many, but how many can be the best of the best? Only five! Now enough with this squabbling; it will reach no other conclusion than more bruises on your part, I can assure you of that. It looks like your friend is done fighting. Come."

Hanako brushed past her and made his way to the house Leo had just defended. She stared at the open fields behind the houses; a new world she'd never be able to discover. Even after the sinking mud and mutant mist creatures, she still wanted to see more. Hanako said she had everything—love, power, and money. Yet she wanted more. Would more be enough? Or would nothing ever be?

She scoffed to herself and brought her attention back to her brother and Abel. They stared at her with wide eyes but didn't speak a word. She waved Samuel away from Eli and carried him up the steps with the help of Abel. The pain was unbearable, but she didn't care. Love, she thought with bitter resentment. She didn't have that. And if keeping her trapped was her father's notion of love, she didn't want it. What would her mother think of all this? Or would she have consented to the hiring of Hanako?

They struggled to get Eli inside and onto a bed in another room. Isabelle was on the floor tending to Raphael and a man sat at a table watching them with curious eyes. Galen was nowhere in sight.

Hanako and Samuel remained in the main room, and a small weight lifted off her shoulders as she and Abel laid Eli down. She stood next to Abel at the end of the bed; they both quietly watched the unconscious Eli. Eli's head tilted to the side, and her heart rate accelerated, hoping he would awaken, only for his eyes to remain shut. His mouth parted as his chest continued to rise and fall, a soft snore escaping.

Othelia broke the silence. "Your father didn't send anyone to take you home?"

Abel looked at her pitifully. She reached up and touched her swollen eye, remembering what she looked like and all the damage that had been done. Irreversible damage, just like her hands. Just like her gauzed-up forearms.

"I can't say he did, no. Not to my knowledge, anyway." Abel chuckled softly and looked back at Eli. "But who knows what goes on in his mind? He very well might have." Abel sucked in a deep breath. "You've met quite a few people. Did you know them prior?"

She shook her head.

"Huh, you look at him like you've known each other a long time," he said and, upon noticing she was awkwardly avoiding his gaze, he chuckled. His voice was hollow, but his smirk was genuine, she thought. But who was she to know? They were not friends.

"He's just a nice person," she said. "They all are. I don't want them to get hurt or die…"

She trailed off, realizing his very own friends were dead. "We could, uh, we could have a ceremony for them. Your friends, I mean."

Othelia turned to leave the room, fearful of his response and the way he may look at her. They were both going to fail the exam. They pitied each other, and she couldn't bear looking at someone like that any longer. As she walked out, he followed and said, "I'd like that."

Hanako was at the end of the hallway, leaning against the wall. His eyes were closed, and his face was soft. He appeared serene and paid no mind to either of them as they entered the room.

Speaking of someone she may have pitied, Leo walked up to her. "Galen. Have you seen Galen yet?"

She stopped and shook her head slowly. Isabelle came up beside Leo and he inched away from her in disgust. Othelia eyed him up with scrutiny. She'd been too absorbed in her interaction with Hanako to see how Leo's fight ended; she only saw the woman lying dead on the porch. The way he looked at Isabelle reminded Othelia of how her brother looked at servants. Disdain and disrespect. It was not a look she was privy to.

"His eye is bad," Isabelle said, then in Urkinian, "There's glass stuck in it, and the back of his head was bashed in."

Othelia translated for the others, and they all opted to pile into the room where Galen lay on the couch; everyone except Samuel, Hanako, and the weird man sitting at the table. Galen was stretched out, one hand dangling over the armrest and his head tilted to the sky. It was ghastly, looking at him, and she could feel tears prick her eyes. She wondered how she looked, too, and if anything would ever heal.

Leo tossed the medical bags at the base of the couch and started rifling through.

"Can you do anything for him?" Othelia asked. Leo shook his head and punched the bag with a grunt. Raphael leaned against the doorway, his demeanor hunched and tired. He, too, shook his head. "Okay," she continued. "Abel, then? What about you?"

He nodded and stepped up to the medical bag. His fingers were determined, each more calculated as his eyes searched for the things needed to patch up Galen's eye. He tilted Galen's head and examined the eye from all angles.

"Ouch, that's bad," he murmured to himself.

"Can you help him?" Leo asked.

He sighed. "Well, I can get the glass out, that's for sure. But he won't be able to see from that eye ever again if I do. Things just aren't that advanced yet. And it'll probably hurt for a long time, maybe even forever. I can probably fix it up, though. Sow it closed. I'll do my best."

Abel got to work, slipping on a pair of plastic gloves. He set a metal contraption atop the bag. He then began peeling off the rims of Galen's glasses carefully, and that's when Othelia had to look away. Her stomach clenched at the prospect of seeing a mushy eyeball. An eyeball of someone she knew.

"How do you know how to do all this?" Leo asked.

Othelia peeked over her shoulder to see what Abel was doing now, curiosity beating the gory, gross nature of it all. Abel pulled out a thin thread and a pair of tweezers. Then a thick, medium-length needle. "I'm a first-year surgeon. Graduated top 5% in the class. From the Elderage Université. Quite prestigious, if I do say so myself. Can you help me for a second? Flip him on his side."

"Wow," Othelia remarked. "I didn't know you had it in you. To graduate top of your class, I mean. Or graduate at all."

Abel chuckled lightly. "I'll take that as a compliment."

Leo did as told, gingerly turning his friend over before several coughs escaped him. He pulled his hand back and she saw fresh blood that had spilled from his mouth.

"Hey," Abel said sternly, "You need to lay down, too. You're ripping up your organs keeping that knife in your side. I'll fix you up next. Just... stop moving."

Abel got to work on Galen, gingerly peeling away shards of glass before preparing a needle and thread. Galen's eyebrows twitched, and that's when Othelia had to leave the room. She didn't want to see him in pain. Stars, such a horrible thing shouldn't be allowed to happen. Glasses should be indestructible.

Isabelle and Raphael followed Othelia out, and they huddled together in the corner farthest from everyone else.

"I messed up," Isabelle said with a quiver in her voice, communicating in her native language. When Othelia looked at her, Isabelle seemed about ready to burst into tears. "Did you hear Leo yell at me? I just stood there and listened to him fight someone, and then I watched as he killed them. I—oh!"

As Isabelle was about ready to let the tears flow, she burst into hiccups instead. She covered her mouth with wide eyes and tears fell, and she hiccupped again.

"You aren't entitled to save others when your life is on the line. That's all there is to it," Othelia assured.

"You were helping me," Raphael added. "I could've bled out if not for you."

Isabelle shook her head. "There are forces beyond our control, but in this case, I could've done something."

"Do you think you could've beat that girl if you'd intervened?"

"I could try."

"That wasn't the question," Othelia said. Isabelle released a string of hiccups and laughed for reasons Othelia couldn't figure out.

"No! No! There, okay? No. I would've been hacked to pieces," Isabelle said, snorting through the hiccups. But there was no mistaking the sorrow that ran thick beneath it all.

Leo marched over to them with a mop of disheveled, curly hair and bloodied hands. His eyes settled on Othelia.

"Are you still gonna try looking for an item?"

Othelia looked up at him with a curious cock of the head. He maintained eye contact, not once glancing at Isabelle. She squinted. "No, it's not within my interests anymore."

He nodded solemnly. "What should we do about Galen? He still needs one."

Othelia sighed. "That's not within them either."

"Bu—"

"Look. My hands are fried, she's done fighting, my brothers' a dick and, if I had to take a guess, you aren't about to kill anyone else either. So, where does that leave us?"

He closed his mouth. She could tell he wanted to say something snappy back, or perhaps prove her wrong and find another item for Galen. He frowned, and said, "You agreed with me, though. You said we should help him. We wouldn't have found this phase without him."

"I know what I said," she barked. "And I'm not repeating myself. It's too risky. If Galen has any sense, he'll understand when he wakes up."

Leo clamped his mouth shut and stared at her a second longer. His eyes flickered to Isabelle before he turned and sat against the wall on the opposite side. Hanako was watching her with fascination.

Her brother paid no mind to their conversation and sat across from the buff man. Both their arms were crossed, and they were staring at each other silently with their chests puffed out. He was going to pass the exam and be loved by their nation; she'd be going to prison for treason. All they could do now was wait for the phase to end, listening to a chorus of hungry stomachs and lamenting over what their futures held.

PART THREE

The Aftermath

CHAPTER 27
GALEN

HE FADED IN and out throughout the majority of the final phase, each time overridden with pain. When he fully gained consciousness, he found himself in a hospital bed. An IV was attached to his arm, the soft beating of his heart playing a melodic tune in the foreground.

The left side of his face throbbed and there was a dull pulsating somewhere in the center of where his eye should've been. The skin from his eyebrow down to the cheekbone was numb. He ran his fingers along the soft bandages that covered his eye and played with the edges cautiously.

"You're awake?" a voice said from his left side. He cursed his dashed peripheral vision, instead seeing a black dot of nothing on his left. Forever? Galen didn't want to ask, nor could he get himself to. He racked his brain for any memory of how the exam ended, but he couldn't come up with an explanation. He kept playing with the gauze covering his eye, wondering where the nearest mirror was. What did his eye look like underneath?

Galen had to turn his torso until Leo came into view. Leo sat on a short, black chair with one leg crossed over the other. His blue flannel and jeans were replaced by a loose white shirt and flowy black pants. His hair was notably damp, his natural curls deflated. He leaned forward with a small smile, but his brown eyes spoke otherwise. They were glassy, full of sadness. The glint of excitement and determination was gone. "Thank goodness. How do you feel?"

"What happened? D-Did I pass?"

His memory came back as he asked, and he knew the answer by the time Leo's smile disappeared, and he responded with a heavy, "No."

Galen looked down at his lap and nodded, his throat becoming dry. "Did you?"

Leo took a moment to respond, the silence overwhelming. The hospital room was big, with long windows and a skyscraper view. The sky's darkened clouds were beginning to part, and the sun was slowly edging out and illuminating the landscape. Droplets of rain clung to the glass. The glass. His glasses. Oh.

"I did. So did Isabelle and Eli. I'm sorry."

He looked at his hands. His family couldn't see him like this. No one could see him defeated. Of all people, *he* didn't pass? He'd had the earrings in his grasp, but he'd neglected to neutralize the enemy. Never take your eyes off them unless they're dead. Did his mother know yet? Surely, she wouldn't know until he came home. How would she react?

A bout of shame washed over him. He'd failed. Even after his victories against his eldest sister during training, she had passed her exam, and he had failed. He gritted his teeth. This was supposed to be easy. Another day of fighting and winning, just like any other task he was assigned.

"How many others?" he asked.

"Eight."

"And that was it? That was the last phase?"

"I'm sorry," Leo said again. Galen wanted to be mad at Leo, furious even, but the feelings wouldn't come. The worn, bloodshot edges of Leo's eyes were enough to discard any harboring animosity Galen might've had. He wanted to view Leo as a friend and to do so meant trusting him and his word. As hard as it was.

"Thank you for keeping me alive," he said. "Don't feel bad. It's my fault. You don't owe me anything."

The last thing he wanted was for Leo to blame himself. It was truly Galen's fault. He'd broken a cardinal rule of bounty hunting, and these were the consequences he had to face. Still, he wished there was someone else to blame. Perhaps his family? They basically sent their children on a death mission. One they were all able to pass except him.

"You didn't deserve this," Leo said softly.

"And yet it happened. Please, let's not talk about it. How long was I asleep? What happened to the others?" He wanted to thank Isabelle for carrying him and protecting him as well. It'd be a shame if she'd left without saying goodbye. His eyebrows—though it was more like one—shot up in surprise at his own thoughts. Was she a friend, too? Though he vaguely recalled being rude to her, he found he could truly trust her, a trait few people had.

"They're around, probably in the dining hall. You were unconscious for about a day and a half. We were all discharged this morning. You should see the first floor; they have shops with decent clothing and anything you could think of buying." Leo snapped. "Oh, are you hungry at all? I could buy you a donut or two. They're delicious. I mean, absolutely phenomenal."

"Everyone waited for me?" Galen couldn't hide his

astonishment. He hadn't really expected that, mostly because they barely knew each other. His family encouraged having friends, as long as they were strong and intelligent, but he was never good at talking to people. He much preferred sticking to the sidelines—listening in on the finer details of conversations, and noticing the differences in mannerisms. He still found himself lonely despite this, never having someone to report those details to.

Leo gave another semi-genuine smile. But Galen could see that far-off look, the one someone had when they couldn't reconcile with what they'd done or seen. Galen wanted to help but knew he couldn't, not really. That didn't mean he couldn't try. Simply being there for Leo would be enough. Anything to get him back to his old self.

"Of course. We're a team after all," Leo said.

Galen sensed a hint of malice in his voice, or perhaps mockery. It wasn't directed at Galen, but he couldn't decipher what the cause was. Was there a traitor among them? Or had something else happened? He had too many questions, unable to choose one to start with.

"Oh, and we got you a present!" Leo said, transforming into a shell of a giddy schoolboy. He bent over and picked up a brown paper bag by its thin straps. Galen reached for it with his left hand but missed, inches off from the straps. He tried again, missing by nearly a few centimeters. Again, Galen couldn't find anger in himself, only sadness and longing for his mistakes to be undone. But praying was hopeless. There was nothing to pray to.

"Here," Leo said gingerly, grabbing Galen's outstretched hand and guiding it to the bag. He thanked Leo sheepishly, red hues rising on his ashen cheeks. He reached inside and pulled out a rectangular box containing a phone. One of the fancy, new types, with a sleek touch screen. He had no words. Leo reacted as though he could read Galen's mind and spoke for him. "Isabelle, Eli, and I all got 100Q of our million to buy new clothes and such; we all chipped in on a group call plan, the cheapest there was. And don't worry about paying us. It's the least we could do."

Galen opened his mouth to say thank you again, but a nurse came bustling in. Her eyebrows shot up at the sight of his liveliness. She stopped in her tracks and covered her mouth with pink, polished fingernails. "My goodness, you're awake! You"—she wagged a playful finger at Leo—"were supposed to let me know if he woke up!"

Leo chuckled, maintaining his friendly demeanor and scratching the back of his head nonchalantly. "Sorry, Caroline, I got caught up in the moment! Have no fear; he's alive and well."

"I'm required to check in every ten minutes, Leo; it's been nearly an hour and a half! I even left the premises; I could get fired if I don't know the exact times. All because you assured me it'd be fine."

Galen's eyebrow shot up. They talked to each other as if they were friends. Were they? Or could Leo reel everyone in with his freckled nose and honest smile? Galen stared at Leo as they continued their banter. "I think your real downfall is security cameras. It's been ten minutes, at most. Provided no one was keeping a keen eye on you, your job is secured."

The nurse stared at Leo with her hands on her hips and rested a pointed glare back at him. Leo held her gaze and mesmerized Galen in the process. Galen was so enthralled by their strange conversation that he hadn't heard the knock at the door. It wasn't until the person cleared their throat that his gaze shot to them.

He plopped his new phone in the bag from which he'd drawn it, and gulped, his hands shaking with stunned horror. One eye was wide, the other in constant pain. The lack of his left field of vision made him woozy, bringing about a sense of vertigo even as he sat perfectly still.

"Oh yes, I was going to say. A woman claiming to be his—your—mother is here," the nurse said with a flash of red across her smooth face. Galen couldn't bring himself to smile at the sight of his mother. Instead, he felt like he was on that boat again, his heart sinking to the bottom of the sea. She was no shorter than six feet tall and her abdomen and arms were brawny. They stuck out strongly against the light purple dress she wore.

"Hello, my son. All is not well, I see." Francesca Aguelon approached her son's side but did not hug him. He squinted at the far clock, but his vision blurred the farther he tried to see. Galen was the only one of his siblings who needed glasses, and now he was the only one missing an eye.

He wanted to cry and curse his wretched luck, but not in front of her, not when he'd already caused so much damage. He focused on her features, taking in the scent of perfume she always drenched herself in, fitted to smell like that of a daphne flower. Their smell reminded him of ambrosia, a type of fruit salad fused with marshmallows. His mouth salivated at the thought of food and images of bacon swarmed his head.

Galen missed cooking for his siblings and the hectic mornings that came with it; making one egg after the other and frying heaps of bacon that were devoured within seconds. The children didn't care how hot the bacon was; their fingertips long since numbed to withstand excessive heat.

Leo sat awkwardly at Galen's side with his eyes locked on Francesca. It was common for people to look at his mother with confusion and disgust—her looks weren't traditionally feminine, and she wasn't afraid to speak her mind or dress how she pleased. She was in her late fifties, married to a man in his thirties, but her face was almost perfectly smooth and young-looking, aside from a dash of creases here and there along her forehead. Her lips were thin and a natural, vibrant red.

Leo's foot tapped anxiously against the tiled floor as Francesca walked over to Galen's bedside. She stopped in front of where Leo sat. Leo suddenly stood, the chair legs softly squeaking as he pushed it back. He peeked around Francesca's bulky shoulders, his face riddled with nothing but concern. "Do you want me to stay?"

Yes. But it was his mother who would make the decision. He didn't know if he should rejoice at seeing her again or fear her, and her expression gave no indications. Her hair was in a tight bun, as it always was. Gray strands were visible only when hit directly by light, and they gleamed now against her blonde hair as she turned to Leo.

"Are you a friend of Galen's?" Although he could only see her side profile, he knew her smile was radiant, pearly white veneers seamlessly posing as real teeth. Her voice was butter melting in a pan, a smooth crackle of excitement and intrigue layered underneath.

"Yes, ma'am," Leo sputtered. "I 'suppose so."

His gaze flickered to Galen, pleading for an answer. Galen couldn't bring himself to speak, paralyzed with fear of whatever his mother would say. Leo gave her a wavering half-smile, his confidence slowly reemerging. He extended a hand, and she shook it. "Leo."

"Splendid! I've never met one of Galen's friends before! I'm glad one exists," she said, resting her other hand on Galen's left shoulder. He felt the momentary, tight squeeze she gave, but he couldn't see her do it. He craned his head a strenuous amount and his face grew hot with embarrassment and frustration. Did she already know how to take advantage of his weak spot? A stupid question; of course she did. She was the queenpin of the family, the most ruthless and cunning of the bunch. She handed out smiles to people like party favors, then killed them at the party.

Despite how scared he was, he tried to remind himself of all the good she'd done for him. She'd taught him all the rules of bounty hunting—how to aim a gun, how to successfully fight and slit a throat. Most of all, she gave praise. Constant and almost overbearing praise doled out as back-handed compliments. Praise that made him stronger and fight harder.

"Please, be a doll and wait out in the hallway. I don't intend to stay long." Her voice was smooth and sweet.

"I'd like to hear Galen's decision, if that's all right with you."

Galen looked at them with his mouth hanging open. They both stared back at him, waiting. His mother was patient, her eyebrows up in surprise at Leo's rather condescending tone. He was more combative than before. What happened while Galen was unconscious?

"I'm, uh, pretty hungry," Galen said sheepishly, wishing he could find the courage to tell Leo to stay.

Leo gave a tight nod and salute. "Say no more. Donuts are on the way." He turned to Francesca. "It was nice meeting you."

Galen watched as he and the nurse left, the beeping of his heart monitor ricocheting off the charts. His mother pulled up the chair Leo had once resided on and sat beside him. Her face turned to stone. "He's a nice boy. Feisty, but nice. How did the exam go?"

"How'd you know where to find me?"

"I have connections with an examiner. She informed me late last night that the exam had ended, and you were here. Now, tell me," she pressed.

Galen could tell she already knew the answer. There was something in the far depths of her eyes that quelled with sadness. Unless some other tragedy occurred, it was because she knew he'd failed. Knowing this and having to explain what had happened, what he'd seen and done, was torturous.

He told her everything quickly and monotonously. Galen had dreamt of what his arrival home would be like, the excitement of showing his family the EO-MC tattoo. They'd celebrate, and he'd bake them all their favorite sweets. He could picture it now. Tiny chocolate cakes for Litheial, the youngest of his siblings. Lemon bars topped with coconut shavings for Daphne. The twins, Scarlett and Henrietta, would share vanilla pudding and, for Eric, an apple pie.

When he mentioned saving the sinking boat with Leo and Isabelle, his mother's eyebrows shot up for the second time. It wasn't within his family's nature to think of the whole over the objective, and he couldn't tell if she was proud of this decision or disgusted.

She never interrupted him throughout his explanation, offering nothing more to convey her feelings than her eyebrows. He coughed as he reached the end of his tale, his mouth a dry desert. "I grabbed the earrings, and he begged me to let him keep one. I said no and turned around. My back was to them, and th-they hit me on the head, I guess.

"I woke up with crushed glass in my eye from my lenses, but that's all I really remember. I-I—" He began to cry, his left eye stinging and throbbing in a vicious cycle. He wanted to reach up and hold it. No, damnit, he just wanted it back. His jaw clenched, and he diverted his good eye to the wall in front of him. "I lost."

She was silent, soaking in his confession and fresh tears. Crying was yet another way he deviated from his family. He cried at everything. When he was sixteen, the twins found a dying bird. It laid on the grass, squawking with a twitching leg. He'd caught one look at it and broke down. Scarlett and Henrietta poked at it with a stick and laughed.

"It sounds like you made a wonderful group of friends," she said with an encouraging smile and nod of her head. He didn't know if he could consider the others as such, as they'd only known each other for three days. But he enjoyed their company, so that was worth something.

He nodded back, unable to return her smile. His voice trembled only at the beginning of his sentence, becoming hardened as he went on. "What's going to happen? No one's ever lost before."

Francesca's shoulders tensed, and her gaze shifted to her lap as she twiddled her thumbs over her interlaced fingers. He watched them along with her, taking in more dreadful silence. Why didn't she want to speak?

He tried again. "The exam occurs biannually, right? I could take the one in January. The clues were beyond easy this year, so I'm sure I could ace it properly next time."

She let out a shuddering breath, a single tear shedding down her porcelain cheek. She dashed it away gingerly with a single brush of a finger. He'd never seen his mother cry before.

"I'm sorry, Galen. For never telling you, or any of the young ones. But I'll tell you now because you're one of them."

"One of who?"

"Your other siblings. There were a few others before you and your elder sisters."

He didn't try hiding his utter shock. Other siblings? He tried to rack his memory of growing up around anyone else, tried to pick apart old faces, voices, body types. His search came up blank. "Wh-what do you mean? What happened to them?"

She closed her eyes and pressed her lips together, providing him with more silence and questions. Did he even want to know? Or did he already know, deep down, what she was going to say?

Finally, just as he opened his mouth to say something more, she spoke. "They, as you probably suspect, didn't pass the exam, either. The line of Aguelons are soldiers of peace, capturing criminals deemed the worst of the worst. Someone who cannot obtain an EO-MC-T isn't strong enough for our type of work. "

They. Them. Who? Who had they been before and who had they become after such a wretched thing?

"How many?"

"Seven."

"*Seven?* Why don't any of us remember?" Surely there weren't children long before Daphne was born, so long ago that none of the family could've known them. Daphne was the eldest at 28. She wasn't home as often anymore, but he'd gotten a letter from her two weeks prior to the exam. She would be in town to celebrate with him afterward and hinted at a fair amount of partying to be had.

His mother sucked in a rigid breath, as though this was the hardest thing for her to say. "We've had all your memories blocked. Yes, you have met them. Played, trained, dined. You've even shared a room with one, a boy. We lost him three years ago."

"Lost him?" he asked quietly before he became fully unhinged, shouting as he spoke. "You didn't *lose* him! You gave him up! And you're giving me up? We're your *children*."

She remained calm, but her lips were pursed together, and tears were at the corners of her eyes. "There's a lot we've hidden from you, things that would explain away what you're asking. I'm sorry, truly, but I cannot tell you said things. It is not within my power, within my right. There are greater works at play than you will ever know."

He was both dumbfounded and angry. The bluntness of her abandonment and now knowing things he used to know but had forgotten. Been forced to forget. It was too much; it was too cruel. "You're not sorry about what you've done. You're sorry you had to tell me."

He searched her expression for any sense of regret, of someone who truly missed her children. On the surface, she was full of sadness and deep sighs, but if she had regrets, she wouldn't be letting him go too.

She retreated into her silent shell, sucking him along with her and forcing him to think. His stomach flipped and nausea swept over him, the dull ache in his eye growing stronger. He winced.

"Will they forget me too?" He loved his sisters. He got along best with Daphne, as she was the most genuine, he thought, of the bunch. Galen still appreciated the others, despite the antics the twins got into. They were his best, and only, friends growing up. Without them, who was he? Where did he have to go? This wasn't real. It couldn't be.

Galen felt all the things he wanted to say. She was horrible. The worst. Despicable. He hated her with all his heart. Sweat protruded from his forehead despite the cool air from the vents above, and his chest was suddenly tight. Everything he did wrong replayed in his mind. It was all his fault. He would have his eye and pass the exam if he'd just kept the crowbar in his hand. If he'd just knocked them all out. If he hadn't turned his back.

Francesca smoothed out her dress with beefy fingers. She did not waiver when she spoke; every word was read off a script, every tear a crafted fable. One she knew he'd want to believe. She shook her head. "Litheial and Eric will no longer remember. If they pass the exam, they'll get to have their memories restored, if they'd like."

His mouth was agape, unable to comprehend her confession. No, he understood perfectly, but he didn't want to. "You... you mean Scar and Henri, and Daph, they all—"

"They were asked to keep it a secret from the three of you."

And they listened. All the nights they played cards together. All the nights they dined and trained together. It was all hidden. A farce. He gritted his teeth, but he couldn't bring himself to be angry anymore. His head and eye were pounding, and he sank into his pillow. The ceiling stared back at him blankly. "You're all liars."

"It's for your own good. If you can't handle the International Exam, you can't handle being a bounty hunter. You'd die if we let you stay. There are tiers to power, Galen. There are tiers and you failed the very first one."

"There are other ways to handle this." His whirlwind of emotions left him feeling numb. He liked the plainness of the ceiling; how much purpose it served and how unobjectively unproblematic it was. Just a ceiling. No thoughts, no wicked deeds, no motives. Just a blank slate serving a purpose.

"We're practically rich," he continued. "You could help me build a restaurant, a reputation as a Premiere Chef. What about the other kids you tossed? What were they good at? Do you even know? What about me, mom? Do you know a single thing about me? Do you know anything about any of your children at all?"

His voice broke. He couldn't look at her. Did she look at him and see an utter failure?

"Our family's reputation has no room for artists or chefs or anything else aside from what it already has. I'm happy you've made friends. I'm proud of you for that, but this is how things are run in this family, and we do not break from tradition. This is an unfortunate outcome for all of us."

"You, but—" He wanted to fight back, but what was there to say? 'Don't abandon me, mother, I need you? I need my family?' She wouldn't listen. If she did, she'd call him weak for being so dependent.

She stood and looked down at him with tear-filled eyes.

"You have no right to cry," he said, his fingers curling into the sheets. He gripped them tightly. "You have a choice here. You don't have the right to cry when this is your choice."

There was a pause in time, one where their eyes were locked. A moment of understanding that what was done could never be undone. She had no right.

"Take care, Galen. You'll be sent away if you try to come home. Have no fear of your belongings; they've already been rid of. The best you can do is learn from your mistakes and grow."

Francesca walked toward the door, stopped in the open frame, and looked back at him for the last time. He didn't know what to expect, but whatever it was, he didn't want to hear it. Ever. He wanted her out of his sight, gone forever.

He didn't want her to leave.

"Do you want to remember them?" she asked.

What kind of question was that? "Of course."

Her lips were tight, eyes wide and unreadable. Her demeanor had changed, her back notably straighter and her head cocked notably farther. She nodded. "I thought so. If you pass the next exam, I'll take the block out of your memory, but you won't be allowed back into the family. Though, if you meet the right people, I'm sure someone else could do it for you. The choice is yours. Farewell and good rest, Galen."

Francesca Aguelon slinked out of the room without

another word. As she passed through the doorway, he swore he could see a faint smile play across her lips. It only confused him further, and he took to staring at the ceiling again. Tears slipped down his temple and dampened his hair. Sobs lodged in his throat as his chest tightened into a knot; he covered his mouth to stifle the mournful symphony unleashing from within. He didn't want her, or anyone, to hear his cries.

The room became astonishingly lonesome when he realized he had no one, and he didn't even like himself. The people he met throughout the exam were great, but they all had lives outside of this. They all had places to be and things to do. He tried to drum up some positive thoughts to ease his mind. Whenever he got to crying, his mother would tell him to man up. It was Galen's father who told him to make a list of five good things in his life. He pondered but thought of only one: *At least I didn't lose* both *eyes.*

The clicking of the clock kept Galen within the realms of reality and made the room feel like a prison. Only it wasn't a prison, and the door was wide open. He very well could've left right then. But he kept on staring, alone with his thoughts and the clock and the beeping of his heart monitor.

He laughed in spite of himself. Galen was left with no money, no family, and no sign of goals or aspirations. Should he try the exam again and look for his abandoned siblings? He didn't know what he'd do or say after finding them. What would they be like? What mistakes had they made during the exam?

He thought of Daphne with her long black hair and freckled nose. Two of her front teeth were crooked, but she never hesitated to smile when she saw him. If he got in touch with her, maybe she'd let him in on the secret. But it was a lost cause because he didn't know her phone number or her address and he was essentially banished, wasn't he?

His left eye throbbed incessantly while the other released an endless stream of sorrow. Various thoughts swirled rapidly through his mind. He imagined himself screaming at the top of his enraged lungs, breaking everything in the room and shattering all the windows.

Just as his breaking point hit, there was a knock on the door. He opened his eye, realizing only then that he'd closed it. Leo held up a brown paper bag by the handles, oil staining the bottom. Galen's panic steadily evaporated as Leo strode over and plopped on the bed beside Galen's thighs. His dark brown eyes shone in the radiant sunlight peeking in from the windows as he pulled out a vanilla donut with chocolate frosting. Galen grabbed the greasy, circular snack and eyed it with regard.

Donuts weren't completely foreign to him; however, his family hardly ate unhealthy foods. Vegetables, meat, fish, fruit. No dairy or sugary items. They were only allowed to drink water. On special occasions, they could have sweets or drink tea. He gulped, his appetite promptly lost at the idea of celebration, and he set it in his palm. Another perk of being left behind, he thought bitterly. No more rules.

"What's wrong?" Leo asked, his donut half gone already. He looked around the room before resting his gaze back on Galen. "What'd she say?"

Galen wanted to tell him. More than anything in the world. He shook his head with a sullen half-smile. His vision became cloudy again as a tear dropped. He was pathetic and weak. It disgusted him. "Let's not discuss it right now. I'll tell you later. But for now... for now, I just want to talk. About anything. Anything else."

Leo stared at him for a long enough time to warrant discomfort, but something about his presence calmed Galen.

"Okay," Leo contended, his smile and charm returning. "I won't ask anymore. On one condition."

"Name it."

Leo pointed to the donut in Galen's hand, the glaze slowly melting in his palm. "You have to eat that. The whole thing. And you have to like it."

Galen smirked. "Deal."

CHAPTER 28

OTHELIA

"**H**OW LONG ARE you going to keep looking at yourself?" she asked Eli in Ishlish, curious to see how fluent he was in the language. While Leo was upstairs with Galen, the rest of the crew waited in the hospital cafeteria. AmberWright was one of the largest world-renowned hospitals, composed of twenty stories. It was located in Equive's port city, San Juale. The first floor was solely dedicated to shops and restaurants. The options were endless—vintage books, paintings, clothes, liqueur, souvenirs of the Mist Desert and Broadcastia.

Eli held up his freshly wrapped hand and pointed at it with the other. "I can look at my battle scar for as long as I please."

The cafeteria itself spanned the majority of the first floor, filled with round tables and wire chairs. To their left, the cafeteria opened up to a buffet. To the right, there were four shops, including one that sold souvenirs exclusively to Overseers.

They'd chosen a table in the center of the otherwise

sparsely populated cafeteria. Most of their interactions were limited in the morning, as they'd been busy with doctors, showering, and washing their clothes; all of which were provided by the hospital. Though free showers were offered to anyone, free washing and drying of clothes were only provided to Overseers. Thankfully, Isabelle had easily snuck Othelia's clothes in with hers.

Samuel appeared bored; his dark blue eyes were trained on nothing in particular while he leaned on the backrest. He'd been the quietest of them all, sticking around purely because there was still a meeting for those who passed. He also owed her money and any information on magical items, of course.

Abel kept his mouth shut, too, as he sat across from Othelia and studied the metallic tabletop. His motives were unclear.

Isabelle was focused on setting up the phone they'd just bought. She faced away from the table, hunched over the small device and muttering to herself. Othelia had already mastered adding other phone numbers and how to call; the only two features a phone had besides telling the time, which automatically updated. Othelia was amazed at the idea of hearing someone's voice on the other end regardless of how far they were from each other. She'd never seen or heard of such things. Signing up for a 'group call plan' was Eli's idea, unsurprisingly.

"How are we supposed to keep in contact without phones?" Eli had argued.

"You already have one," Leo reminded him. "Why get another?"

"Had, my friend. I *had* a phone. Unfortunately, I lost it somewhere between fighting for my life and getting stabbed in the hand."

Now, Eli pulled out his undamaged hand with giddy glee and held it beside his face. A gold barcode had been stitched above his wrist during his time with the doctors. A 'tattoo,' he had called it. "This is a dream. It has to be. I mean, look at me. I'm an Expedition Overseer now."

Othelia grabbed his arm and pulled him closer with her slick, black-gloved fingers, examining the barcode as if she could decipher what it meant. Her doctor had looked over her hands with a twinkle of both pity and disgust in his eyes. Usually, he informed her, buying leather gloves from the hospital was expensive due to limited supply. But the doctor had shaken his head, handed them over, and said, "It's the least I can do." They were never going to fully recover.

"Stop rubbing it in my face," she said, letting go of his arm. As she did so, the sleeve of her shirt rode up against the table, exposing a few inches of her bare forearm.

She blushed—the doctors had taken her gauze off and forgotten to replace it—and hastily covered her arm. She looked around the table, hoping no one had seen the three thick scars that ran around her upper wrist. Much to her dismay, all eyes were on her except Isabelle's, who was far too invested in her new phone.

"What happened there?" Eli asked. She shot him a glare, but he only smiled with sincere curiosity.

"It's impolite to ask girls about their bodies," she retorted, blushing profusely. She hated her scars more than anything else. They were a reminder of the control her father had. The control he still had.

Samuel still divulged nothing regarding what the Kings had in store, nor did she think he knew anything. But she was itching for answers. And Hanako. She hadn't seen him, but she knew he was around. Watching. Listening. Waiting.

"He's right to ask, though," Samuel said. It was the first

time she'd heard him talk in over two hours. "Alexander did that to you?"

Their eyes locked. She'd pushed Alexander out of her mind entirely, too focused on the exam to be bothered with him. And he was probably dead or beaten. No thanks to her.

"He did. Why? Hasn't Penelope done the same to you?" Samuel's guard looked much like her own, tall with short black hair, muscular but still thin. Othelia couldn't remember the girl's age, but she was probably in her mid-to-late twenties.

Samuel shook his head. "She doesn't give punishment, not like that."

"What kind, then? Pray tell, brother."

He eyed her up suspiciously. "You won't tell anyone in our family?"

"Take a guess."

"Do you really think you can hide from Father?" he inquired, dodging her question. "From that man he sent for you? Even if you somehow slipped out of his fingers, and I know you'll try greatly, Father will just keep sending more. I bet Alexander is on his way now if he hasn't been killed for losing you."

"I'll be long gone before they find me," she said. "I plan to leave later today. Besides, even if he captured me, I wouldn't tell him a thing. I swear, Sam, your secrets are safe with me. Or, us, I guess." She gestured to the rest of the table. "Shouldn't you be more worried about Abel speaking of whatever you're hiding, too?"

"I already know," Abel sounded with a heavy sigh. She tsked; she was out of the loop on everything.

Samuel sucked in the air and released it slowly. "We're dating, Penelope and I. Have been for a while."

"How long is 'a while?'"

"Five years, six months, and three days." He shrugged nonchalantly. "I keep track."

"Impossible. That means you started dating when you were, what, 12? 13?" Her mouth fell open when he averted his eyes. She scoffed. "How old was she?"

"19."

"Disgusting."

"We were and are in love. Age doesn't matter."

"She's hired to beat the shit out of you. Surely she did before you dated." He nodded. She leaned back in her chair, distancing herself from him. "How could you be in love with someone who did that to you?"

"Wait—your father hires people to *beat* you?" Eli asked, his eyes widening. They both ignored him; Othelia was far too invested in her brother's tale than in explaining her upbringing.

Samuel shrugged. "Is there ever an answer to love? Spare me your judgment, sister. I know you've been fiddling around with the servants, of all people. If you were smart, you would've done the same. I'm only beaten upon request now."

Othelia had plenty of time to unpack what he'd said, but it would be pointless. There were too many other things that exceeded the level of importance of his off-putting love life. She curled her lip and sneered at him with crossed arms. "I'd rather be scarred than give myself a way to someone who's hired to hit me."

"To each their own. If you tell Father, I'll see to it you're tortured slower than you've ever been, and he makes way for your cold and merciless death."

"If I told Father, he'd be making way for *your* cold and merciless death," she said, adding with a smirk, "Speaking of Father, why'd he send you to take the exam?"

Samuel stood abruptly. "I'm finished with this

conversation. If the examiners are looking for me, I'll be at the taffee bar."

He sauntered away with balled fists. She watched him go until he was out of sight and then drew her attention back to her companions. Taffee, from what she knew of it, was a plant-based drug that could be vaporized and smoked. It could also be condensed and chewed. She'd never tried it herself, though it wasn't uncommon to see guards around the palace chomping on it.

"He smokes? Since when?"

Abel nodded. "Been chewing for almost a year now. I know you don't like each other much, but I'm surprised you've never noticed."

She wasn't. Most days, she didn't talk or pay mind to Sam unless they were training. Even then, their conversations boiled down to grunting and taunting. He was younger than her and therefore lesser, so she needn't bother with his interests and love life. It also didn't help that he was a colossal dick.

"What was that? Fiddling with the servants?" Eli asked, breaking his way into the conversation. "Care to put me on payroll and add me to the list?"

Her mouth parted to provide a witty quip, but she saw Leo and Galen stride into the cafeteria from her peripherals. Leo waved as they approached, and Eli stood with wide waves of his own; Othelia joined in with a single wave and a smile.

Galen still wore the hospital gown. It hung to his feet and exposed his arms, which were untouched aside from a long, purple bruise on the right. The area around his good eye was black, though he seemed able to open it fully. The bandaging covering the other was thick with white padding.

Eli gave Galen a strong pat on the back, followed by a side hug. Othelia couldn't help but laugh at how awkward Galen looked scrunched against Eli's towering shape. Galen's pale blond hair stuck out in every direction over the gauze wrapped around his head, and Eli had Galen's arms pinned at his sides.

"Alright, I think you've squeezed him enough," she said, coming to his rescue. "He just woke up!"

"Fine," Eli said before promptly planting a kiss on Galen's cheek and letting him go.

Isabelle glanced up from the light of her phone and smiled. "You're okay!"

After Leo had butchered that woman, he and Isabelle hadn't spoken, much less looked at each other, and it appeared as though their feelings hadn't changed.

Galen tried to smile, but the pain was written plain on his grimace. "Okay as I can be."

"You're discharged?" Eli asked with a hopeful glint in his voice. "Leo, here, didn't let the EO meeting start until you woke up. Simply refused to go. You should've seen the examiners faces. They were *pissed*."

"That's an understatement," Isabelle said.

"They want me to stay for a few more hours, just to make sure the surgery was done right and everything's in order. Abel —" Galen paused. She could tell he was mulling over whatever he planned to say.

Abel stopped midway through raising a spoon full of soup to his mouth and glanced around the table until he realized it was Galen who spoke. "N-no need to thank me. If anything, it was good practice. Please, don't worry about it."

"Come," Isabelle said, patting the chair next to her. "Sit next to me."

He did, turning his head at exaggerated angles to fully grasp his surroundings.

"Oh, and Isabelle," Galen added, "Thank you for carrying me during the final exam. I owe you one. I'm sorry for how I spoke to you. It wasn't right."

A flash of apprehension and guilt spread across her features, and she looked out at those who walked along the strip of shops. "No thanks, please. I-I didn't look for an item for you after, after I—"

"Don't worry about it. My mistakes are not yours."

Othelia was stunned; she imagined they all were. Galen's wisdom far exceeded any of theirs, when he'd shown no signs of such during the exam. She thought he was merely a trained fighter and tree climber.

Isabelle had expressed great distress regarding Galen the night before. They'd slept on an open cot on one of the upper floors, designed for people who were homeless on a first-come, first-serve basis. There were around fifty beds with tiny pillows that lined both walls, charging ports for electronics beside every sixth bed. Othelia had felt bad for taking up two cots, so they slept in one together. "I told him I would find him an item. I lied. Oh, great Gahi, please show me mercy during my trials."

Othelia's eyebrows crinkled in confusion. "You need to go to trial to get into the Holy Land? Isn't he omnipotent? Shouldn't he just know if you're good or bad?"

"Gahi knows no gender. Omnipotent beings are just that, separate from our labels entirely; calling Gahi a 'he' is both inaccurate and insulting. And yes, there is a trial, so you can understand your placement and come to terms."

"But what's the point of understanding your placement if you're stuck there for all eternity, anyway?"

Isabelle shook her head with a sigh. "You don't understand. And now my trial will include lying, lusting and—"

Othelia had tapped Isabelle on the forehead with her nose; her hands still hurt a fair amount. "Stop worrying so much. Just let it happen."

"Let what happen?"

"Life, you imbecile. All you can do is apologize to Galen

and repent or whatever, and if your wonderful savior still banishes you, then *they* don't sound like a very good being to worship."

"Ahem," someone said from behind, interrupting her thoughts of the night before and bringing the group's attention toward the source of the noise. Othelia's heart sank at the sight of Liviola, who wore a tight maroon one-piece, extending from her neck to ankles.

"I've just received word that the boy has awoken?" Her eyes scanned them and landed on Galen. "You?"

Galen nodded with a light tinge of red blossoming on his cheeks. He looked as though he may cry; his exposed eyebrow was furrowed, and his eye was glossy. She supposed she should be sad, too, but she couldn't bring herself to care, not really. She had her magical flowers, and now she'd have the money and knowledge to find out about it. The only downside was the impending life of imprisonment she had coming to her.

"Right, well. I've been sent to gather those who passed. I count three of you... where is the fourth?"

"Taffee bar," Abel said.

The examiner curled her lip but waved them along. As Isabelle stood to follow, she leaned against the table and whispered to Othelia, "I'll let you know what we find out."

"Hey," Eli leaned in next, a hand on his hip. "That's my line!"

Othelia snorted. She had to admit; she didn't mind having someone so obviously infatuated with her. Did she find him attractive, or was he just the first person to show an interest in her outside the palace?

She cocked her head up, looking at Eli's side profile. Strands of his black bangs were hanging over his eye and he pushed them aside. His white shirt had been too bloodied to salvage, so he exchanged his suit for gray sweatpants and a white, short-sleeved top. A sliver of his stomach peeked out. He noticed her staring and did what she liked best—a corner of his mouth curved up into a soft smile.

"I'll be the first to tell you everything. I can't give you any of the prize money, though, so sorry in advance. I need that for my upcoming campaign," Eli said smoothly. "But I can give you other things instead."

He winked, and she rolled her eyes. "How romantic."

He, Isabelle, and Leo walked off and away, bound to discover adventures she'd never come to know. Eli looped his arm around Leo's neck and, although she couldn't see his face, she knew he was talking by his hand gestures. Leo laughed as they rounded the corner and out of sight. She wished she heard what Eli had said.

"Where are you going," Abel spoke suddenly, "after this?"

She debated on what to say. In all fairness, she had no way of really knowing what Hanako planned to do with her. Perhaps prison really meant death, and he was just lying as a cruel joke.

"Yeah, what happens now that you didn't pass? I'm surprised, t-that you didn't. No offense..."

"Oh, I certainly would've won, and should've. Just to be clear." She crossed her arms and smirked triumphantly. "I gave my item to my brother for reasons I don't even know. All I want is the money and answers. I don't really care to become an 'Expedition Overseer' beyond that."

"So, what're you going to do with that money?" Abel pried.

Othelia shrugged. "Buy a ship, perhaps. Sail. Hunt down magical items. I think that'd be fun. They're just something I need to know about, you know?"

Galen and Abel stared back at her with blank expressions, their wavelength completely different from hers. She raised an eyebrow and pointed to Galen. "What about you? What are you going to do?"

He continued to stare back, his eye becoming teary. Oh no. She was going to make him cry.

"I don't know," he confessed, his voice faint. "My mother came to visit a few minutes ago. She, uh..." He looked between her and Abel and the table before settling on the shops adjacent to him. "She said I've been exiled. I'm no longer her son. I'm a failure."

"Hey," Othelia said, feeling a flash of anger course through her. "If your family can cast you out so quickly, then they aren't your family. Trust me, I would know."

He shook his head, but she could see a faint smile creep over his lips. "It's more... it's more complicated than that and" —he let out a shaky breath—"she said there were... others. Others before me. They blocked my memory somehow. I have other siblings, ones that I used to know."

Othelia and Abel exchanged the briefest of glances, coming to the same conclusion at the same time. They were taught very little about using their power aside from manifesting it into their fists. However, they were also taught that it could be used in other ways, depending on the individual's body. Ways the kings kept hidden until it was near time to inherit the throne. Their looks said the same thing; *What if?*

No, that was impossible. No one was more powerful than those within the Kingship. The only reason the six kings didn't rule the world was because they wanted world peace and to bathe in quill rather than blood.

If Galen had seen their exchange, he didn't let it show. Othelia scoffed. "You're better off without them, then. Why would anyone do such a thing? To their own child?"

"My sentiments, exactly," he said. "I just have a lot of siblings, and now, well, you know."

He rested his elbows on the table and placed his chin on his hands. He stared dully ahead. She admired his strength and yet she also pitied him—he'd been forced to grow up too fast.

"Take me with you," Abel interjected, his arms folded on the table. His voice was solid and low, his eyebrows drawn in seriousness and golden-brown eyes filled with fear. Fear of what waited for him if he went home empty-handed. The same look her brother gave when she kicked him into oblivion. "And Galen, you could come, too."

She stroked her chin. "And why should I do that? In fact, I can't think of a single reason I should say yes."

Othelia expected him to fight back—tell her he's been nothing but kind. The words of a prince who longed to save his own skin. But he nodded sullenly and said, with a voice that reeked of regret, "I know. Remember when our families had dinner together a few months ago?"

She pretended to contemplate, but there was hardly a week that went by that she didn't remember. She snapped her fingers. "Oh, you mean when we were each given our own pies, and you shoved my face into mine?"

"That's the one."

"You made my nose bleed all over the banana filling."

"Yes, and although it was funny back then, I regret doing it immensely."

"Is that supposed to be an apology?" Othelia couldn't believe her ears. It was so juicy, so... exhilarating to see the once boisterous boy grovel from across the table. She wanted more. She wanted to stand over him as he bowed at her feet.

If she kept thinking like this, she'd turn into her father, and she knew it. Still, the tingling in her toes and fingers, the itch for more power, was indescribable.

"It's a statement of my regret."

"And so it's been stated. The answer is still no." She

winced, not at her words, but at the sudden throbbing of her hands. The doctor informed her the blisters may fade, but the skin would always be bright red and wrinkled, and the pain would never quite go away. Another blemish; another product of a mistake she'd made.

"I'm *sorry*," Abel said. "For everything. What can I do to make you believe me? I'll do anything. I-I-I'll be your ship's surgeon. Do whatever you say."

"Huh. I'm not sure. I mean, have you ever heard of a ship surgeon before? Doctor, maybe, but surgeon?"

"I'll do it for free. Catch my own food, gather my own supplies. I'll never, ever talk to you or even look at you if you don't want me to. But please. Please. I can't go back home. Banishment would only be so lucky. My father is not like Sir Sandoval; he'll put my head on a pike in front of everyone. He'll call me a traitor to the nation."

Never mind that she was under the same stress, only without the pike. His desperation leaked off him, so much so that she could almost smell it—a dingy, musky odor.

"Okay," she bargained. "You can come as a freeloader on my ship and occasional surgeon. You'll have guaranteed safety, food, and a place to sleep. If, and only if, you tell me what the Kingship is planning. What's so important that you and I are deemed traitors?"

Abel's cheeks flushed, something Othelia had never seen before. As he flirted with princesses in the royal families, he never admitted to deviant emotions. He never looked so out of control, so hopelessly dependent.

She squirmed uncomfortably in her seat as the cogs turned in his head. If he let her in on the secret, he truly would be a traitor. But that was better than being tried as one in court, right? Better than being dead.

Finally, he let out a deep sigh. "Okay..." He took another

deep breath. "Okay, I'll tell you. But this information does *not* leave this table. None of the others can know, and you definitely cannot tell your brother."

She nodded eagerly. Galen shrugged in compliance.

"I don't know too much about it, and Samuel knows far less. But what I do know is that it isn't the Kingship; it's just our two fathers. All Father told me was that he'd gotten word of two other kings planning to overthrow the other islands. Sir Sandoval was the only other person he trusted fully to tell, and they decided that they'd have their first sons trained immediately for the upcoming uprising."

Othelia's shoulders slumped. For some reason, she'd expected something intriguing, something that couldn't be explained in a few short sentences. She didn't expect something so basic, so... boring. "An inner squabble? That's it?"

Abel shrugged. "I guess so. Father told me I had to pass, otherwise, I'd be a traitor to the cause, and thus, the island. I thought I'd pass; I thought our powers would make the exam easy."

She held up her gloved hands and wiggled her fingers, ignoring the dull pain that shot through her hands and arms. "You're not the only one." She crossed her arms, keeping her hands away from any touch, and smirked. "Anyway, your answer was satisfactory. You can come with me. Galen." She turned to him. "You are more than welcome to come too. You may not have passed, but you're strong. That much is certain."

Galen produced a wavering smile, and a tear fell from his blackened eye, then two. He wiped them away while releasing a soft sob. Othelia's mouth dropped and her eyebrows drew up in concern and confusion. "I'm sorry! What'd I say to upset you? I didn't mea—"

He shook his head quickly and let out a chuckle. "Oh, you

didn't do anything wrong." He wiped the rest of his tears away as he sniffled. "I'm just really happy."

"Well, I suppose that settles it then, Othelia." Her heart dropped as she turned around, her eyes growing wide as they landed on Hanako H. Byrde. She should've known.

CHAPTER 29
ISABELLE

THE MEETING WAS held on the fifth floor of the hospital, the business sector. Each room had transparent walls made of plastic; doors and windows included. Only the doorknobs and window frames were shiny, silver metal. Bright white lights shone above them in intervals. Isabelle peered inside each room as she was led down the wide hallway; they all had identical whiteboards and long tables with swiveling chairs. All the rooms were empty, as was the hallway.

Eli, Samuel, Leo, and Isabelle were shepherded into a room sandwiched between the rest. There were four other people sitting at the long white table; a tall woman with a bob cut and brawny muscles, a brown-haired boy with a blue leviathan tattoo, a gruff man with a bushy beard, and Raphael.

Her mouth parted at the sight of him; they hadn't spoken since the exam ended, and he'd given no indication if he'd retrieved an item or not. In fact, she'd thought he had failed but was too prideful to announce it. But there he was, in a black shirt and red pants. When she walked in, he gave her a passing glance and nod but offered no other pleasantries. He was pretending they didn't know each other. She would have to play along.

The four of them took up their seats; her beside Samuel, while Eli and Leo sat across from them. The examiner who'd run the podium in the first phase stood at the head of the table in front of a blank whiteboard, a marker in hand. She could feel the other contestants' eyes inspecting her. She was wearing what she'd come in—a freshly washed tight, black-hooded shirt and black leggings. The gruff man with a buzz cut crossed his arms and grunted, his eyes filled with pleasure as he stared at her.

A shiver crawled up her spine as his prying eyes continued to linger and she pulled her hood over her face. Isabelle slunk back in her seat, focusing on her fiddling fingers.

Galen had forgiven her; a product of pure prayer. To say she was thankful was an understatement, considering Leo's growing disinterest in her was unsettling. Especially when she saw him talk to other people. The same Leo he was to everyone —all smiles and kindness. He talked to the others as if nothing was wrong, to the nurses like they were friends; she'd overheard two of them ask for his phone number.

Sitting in that small room with the winners conjured a far too sudden flashback of the final phase, and her heart thumped wildly in her ears. There it was—a door still upright but a hole cut haphazardly beside it.

She'd heard every shriek, every yell, every sob. She crept closer and closer to the hole in the wall until she could peer through it, and that's when she saw him strike the woman in the head. Blood spurted out almost instantly, and the petrified look on Leo's face made her shrink away in fear. She'd covered her mouth with her hand and stifled a scream.

Now, Leo waved to the short examiner standing at the front with a wide, cheerful smile. "Mr. Magnum, right? How are you?"

The examiner returned the gesture with equal fervor. "Oh please, my boy, my first name is quite alright. Magenta." His bushy beard danced along with his lips as he spoke. "I'm happy to see you've made it, Leo."

Leo beamed; a radiance dampened quickly by reality. Still, it was there for the briefest of moments, and she wished there was a way to fix what she'd done, to carry that burden for him instead. "You remembered my name."

"Of course. It's to my understanding that your group stopped the ship from sinking?"

"Well," Eli said, pointing to himself. "Not all of us."

"Me and Is...abelle did. And our friend Galen, but he—"

"Got injured, yes. We've been keeping tabs on all of you to make sure no one left the premises." Magenta Magnum turned his attention to the group. He began projecting a booming voice, far louder than she'd ever thought could come from such a short man. "Congratulations on passing the exam. We're here now to go over what you've won."

Eli rubbed his hands together and whispered, "This is gonna be *so good*."

She sat on the edge of her seat in excited yet nervous anticipation. She didn't know how many prizes there were or what there was aside from money and potential connections to be had.

Mr. Magnum snapped his fingers. "You are now Expedition-specific Overseers. As you probably already know, this is one of the more sought-after Overseer titles. Your official title is an EO-MC—Expedition Overseer, Master Class. There are many things that come with such a title, including prestige, the best bounty deals, access to the full registry of magical items and expeditions, first-class treatment for various modes of transportation, and, of course, a prize of 1 million quill."

Isabelle's eyes widened; his Latarian had changed into Urkinian. But how could the others understand him if she and Raphael were the only ones who knew what he was saying? Surely, everyone else was confused and lost.

But the clapping started somewhere in the back, slowly reaching the front until Isabelle joined along. Was it possible her new tattoo was translating the words he spoke or something else entirely? No, no, that was outlandish. Witchcraft of that nature did not, and could not, exist.

Out of everything Mr. Magnum listed, the mention of bounties caught her attention. While Micah pronounced himself a hitman, he described his duties as someone hired to hunt and kill sinful men. How long had he dreamt of leaving Reinta and obtaining such a title? Did his prey get the better of him in the end?

That was where she would start; looking into all the criminals she could get her hands on—any that could be linked to what her brother used to do. It would be a challenge, one that could take years off her life. A cause she was ready to endure for a lifetime.

"There are tiers as an Expedition Overseer, or EO, for short," Mr. Magnum continued. "The higher you go, the more benefits you receive, including free entry into all public events, lodges, and hotels, along with first-class treatment anywhere you go and reserved seats in nearly all auctions."

More clapping erupted, and he waved them to stop almost immediately, ready to get things going.

"Tiers are reached through the number of jobs and exams you complete, and what areas you choose to focus on. You also receive the status that comes along with an EO-MC-T. I presume you were all given the procedure with your doctors, yes? It signifies you are one of the strongest people in the world. It is also how you can pay and access whatever you may imagine. These are all known prizes, to be expected. There *is* a final perk. But first."

As if on cue, a new woman appeared at the door; her hair was disheveled, and her thick, circular glasses were crooked. She held a bulky pile of papers as the doctor left. Mr. Magnum took the papers from her and closed the door in her face without a word. He handed the pile to Isabelle. "Take one and pass them back."

Isabelle did as she was told and scanned her copy; a small packet of three pages. The title of the document was bold and centered. 'Master Class Overseer Agreement.' The packet was written in Urkinian, and when she looked around, the other packets were in the same language as well. Witchcraft, indeed.

"What is this?" Eli asked, flipping through along with everyone else. Isabelle skipped to the third page, noticing a signature box at the bottom along with the statement; 'I hereby vow to never speak of what is said in this meeting to anyone other than a confirmed Master Class, or above, Overseer. I understand the consequences if I do not adhere to this rule.'

Isabelle looked at Eli, who was already exchanging a glance with Leo. She felt a surge of loneliness then, realizing the only person she truly bonded with was Othelia. Now she would bear these secrets alone.

"Before I go further, you all must sign this contract. If you speak of anything, *anything* to those who do not share the same status, your contract will become null, and your tattoo will fade. If anyone asks, all you can disclose is that you legally cannot say. This is sensitive information. If you were to tell the wrong person, they could use it for the wrong reasons."

"What are the right reasons?" Samuel asked. In the little time Isabelle knew him, she found him odd. Even his question struck her as such.

Mr. Magnum smiled. "I'm glad you asked. EO-MC-T's are for more than just the money. You'll all also have quotas to fill, though it isn't huge, so have no fear. We exist to uncover the unknowns of this world, as well as aid in the ridding of criminals and recovering magical items from people who may use them for harm.

"You are to attend at least four expeditions a year, which will be broadcast through phone calls. You will receive them via an automated voice message. It will highlight dates, meet-up points, and gear you may need. There are usually ten new expeditions a month, give or take."

Someone slammed their fist on the table behind her. "We didn't sign up for this! Give us the money we've earned!"

Isabelle didn't know what to think. Her brother had never mentioned such a thing to her before. Of course he hadn't. He was an Expedition Overseer. The secret died with him. But now she had it, too, all to herself. Did he know the spark he'd ignited? Did he know she would choose the same life as him?

She scanned over the document, which included a detailed list of all the consequences of exposing the EO's secrets. She saw the word treason, as well as 'tried as a criminal along with whom you spoke to.'

"By all means, you can leave now," Mr. Magnum said with a twisted, amused smile. "You won't get your money, or your prizes, though. If four expeditions are not logged for you by July 1st of the next year, your EO-MC-T will be revoked. You may only pass the exam once, so keep up on your duties."

No one moved; the tension was palpable. No one wanted to give up the title they'd worked so hard for. It didn't seem real, sitting in this room and being told these things.

Mr. Magnum smiled and started to turn, faltering when he saw Eli's hand in the hair.

Eli cleared his throat. "How do you know if we've told someone else?"

"After everyone is finished verbally signing, I'll gladly tell you."

"I'll go first then," Eli said, clearing his throat. Mr. Magnum gave him a tight nod and Eli read the statement aloud and stated his entire name. "Elijah James Kahl."

"That has a nice ring to it," Leo said.

Eli feigned surprise. "Are you flirting with me?"

"Okay, we'll go from front to back now and loop around. Would you care to start, young lady?" Mr. Magnum grabbed her attention. She nodded and haphazardly read through the statement. Reinta didn't give middle names as Eli's culture had; they were nothing more than filler between the two that mattered.

"Isabelle Chavagny." Her name appeared inside the signature box, like ink bleeding onto a page. Her eyes widened; this world was beyond comprehension.

Everyone else took their turns, even the man who protested prior. The need for money and power far outweighed the need to go on 'expeditions,' whatever that meant. There were so many more questions she had but couldn't bring herself to ask.

Mr. Magnum clapped his hands. "That's everyone! Please look at your EO-MC-T now."

She did, noticing the date she'd passed was now etched below the barcode. "Congratulations! Your informational segment is now complete!"

"As for my question?" Eli asked.

"Yes, I haven't forgotten. A higher-up has placed their mag in the ink used to create your barcodes. It's set to alert the Overseer Organization based on a list of keywords and phrases that would suggest divulging the content of this meeting to those outside the organization.

"You can't type or write these keywords, either. Trust me, we'll know. You can refute the claim, but your barcode will remain flagged and lose its color and effectiveness until the matter is reviewed. Be careful with the words you choose when around non-EOs."

"What do you mean, their mag?" Leo asked, perplexed as he leaned forward.

Mr. Magnum smiled broadly and turned his back to the table, grabbed a purple marker, and wrote the word 'Essence' on the whiteboard. It squeaked along as he pushed on the tip and her eye twitched from the grating noise it created. When he stopped, her eyes scanned over the word and she whispered it to herself, testing the syllables as they rolled off her tongue.

Mr. Magnum turned to face them once more, popping the cap onto the marker and using it as a pointer. "You get to learn about Essence!"

He snapped his fingers, and wheels clacked against the linoleum floor as a cart was rolled in. It held eight rolled-up white paper bags. A woman in tall heels and a lab coat handed them out. Isabelle took hers skeptically, examining every crevice and shaking it. Something, more like many things, rattled against each other. Micah made no mention of this.

"If you didn't know, our planet's soil has mag in it, which is a natural nutrient that plants have. We've found a way to transfer this nutrient to items. This can change their properties and allow them to do incredible feats. Scientists also know that sometimes animals can ingest a large amount of mag and become magical themselves, however, humans remain unaffected. Only within the last fifteen years have we discovered the perfect combination of natural resources the stomach can handle."

She soaked in this information with astonishment. "If we didn't know? Is this 'mag' common knowledge?"

Isabelle had never learned the term, not once, and Micah had said nothing on the matter. She clenched her jaw, suddenly scared. There was more she had to learn about being an Expedition Overseer than she thought.

"Knowledge is common depending on where you were born, miss. Some cultures deny its existence, while others worship the soil." He nodded for the cart-wheeler to speak.

She stepped up and gestured toward their bags. "Each of you has been given Essence, a drug of ten components that are 100% natural. If you so wish, you are to take two pills a month, once every 2 weeks. We recommend the 1st and 15th of every month. Instructions on how to access refills are in the bag.

"Take with a full stomach. It can be a little harsh the first time around, so expect headaches and stomachaches, but these side effects will lessen as your body becomes more accustomed to using mag. However, if you decide to stop the dosage, the same side effects will occur for a limited time."

"Thank you, doctor. Yes, now, keep in mind here, you'll feel a little head rush. It's a good feeling, let me tell you." Mr. Magnum chuckled. "But you won't know how to properly use mag unless you have the training, and you need at least two, sometimes three, pills for the effects to begin. That's why I'm recommending you make an appointment on how to use it as soon as you can. We can provide you with contacts."

"What do you mean, 'use it,'" Leo asked. He was equally skeptical as she, it seemed. She looked around at the others, gauging their reactions. Eli was fascinated, flipping the pill bottle in his hand. The bottle was pink with a white cap and a handful of pills bounced around jovially inside. Samuel's eyes were wide, his hands gripping the bottle until his knuckles turned nearly white.

"That is a good question and one for a trainer. There are five, 60-minute sessions and they are complementary, of course. You just need to sign up with your EO-MC-T."

"What is this Essence nonsense?" Samuel demanded, waving his hand in dismissal. Isabelle watched from the corner of her eye. He looked exactly like Othelia, only with a wider jaw and shorter hair. His eyes were a darker shade of blue, reminiscent of the ocean when seen in the sparkling sunlight.

He had a similar demeanor as his sister, too. Someone who thought they were above others. Isabelle liked Othelia over everyone else in their group, but she could also see the hunger for power underneath it all.

"How is that even possible?" Eli asked, running a hand through his hair.

"As I've said," Mr. Magnum explained. "You can receive extensive training and sessions on the use of Essence and what it truly entails, but not here. Do be patient."

He clapped. "That's it for today! Your 1 million quill will be added to your barcodes. Congratulations on joining Hevalth's heroes!"

The meeting ended, and as everyone slowly seeped into the hallway, Raphael caught her arm. He came up beside her with a smile as they walked down the wide hall. Her fellow 'companions,'—if she could call Eli and Leo such anymore— were already entering the elevator. She was left in the dust, forgotten about as if she were never truly there.

"He is still upset, I see," Raphael stated.

Isabelle sighed and nodded, finding no need to talk of what had occurred any longer. What was done was done. "Did you know of what we learned in there?"

Raphael nodded. "My father told me of it, though he doesn't have the tattoo. I have no clue how he knows or where he gets Essence."

Her mouth dropped. "So, that light? And how you entered the house? That was Essence?"

"Yes, I'm afraid I've been taught many tricks. I didn't want to alarm you before the exam ended. I know Reinta does not teach much on mag. Forgive me."

"It's witchcraft; impossible. Yet somehow, possible. I'm not sure what to make of it."

"You could use Essence to find your brother's murderer, no? Perhaps witchcraft isn't so bad."

"Spoken as someone who did not grow up in Reinta," she said, regretting her words almost immediately. He spoke her language, knew her culture, and was half-Reintian himself. She braced herself for a chiding, but he merely chuckled.

"You have a fighter's tongue and a savior's touch. I'll never forget that you helped me. Saved me, even."

"As I will never forget that you did the same."

He waved his hand. "Nonsense, I'd do it again in a heartbeat. You have too much to do to die during a pesky examination. Do you know what your next steps will be?"

She shrugged. "Research, I suppose. You?"

"I'll be partaking in the training; I recommend you do as well. It may be the only way to go up against whomever you are looking for. Human strength alone may not be enough, you know. You could sign up for a session with me if you'd like. Perhaps working together will help you forget about the Unholy Land."

"But... why would you want to? Why would you want to work with me, of all people? You did your part, you helped me, and I helped you. Shouldn't we part ways here and now?"

Disappointment flashed through Raphael's eyes, but he did not speak as though he was hurt. "If that's what you'd like. I, on the other hand, quite enjoy your company. We'd part after the training; I have much to do back home. But, as I've said, training together could prove to be far less lonely."

For the first time in a long time, she genuinely smiled. "It could."

CHAPTER 30

ELI

NOT ONLY DID he have to keep Essence a secret, but he'd *promised* Othelia he'd tell her everything. A blatant lie. His disgruntled thoughts persisted as he made his back to the first floor. He desperately wanted to tell her, too. The news was practically spilling from his lips already. He'd whispered to Leo in the elevator, "I can't believe this stuff exists!"

He was going to explode with giddiness. Eli could learn to do what she did; they all could. When he and Leo reached the cafeteria table, he thought Othelia would clamor for information, but she was staring out into nothing, her eyes void of anything. His excitement devolved into that of twitchy apprehension. He waved in front of her face until her attention was caught, and only then did he give a shake of the head. Might as well get the bad news over with.

"We can't tell you anything, I'm afraid."

Othelia smiled distantly, but there was nothing behind it— nothing he could see—and suddenly his mind was an abyss of wonder. Did she not hear him? He looked to Abel and Galen for answers, but they were too invested in conversation with Leo and Samuel, respectively.

"What's wrong?" Eli asked, sliding into the seat beside her.

Othelia shrugged. "Familial issues, I guess."

"Oh yeah," he said, remembering suddenly. "What happened to that man, Hanako, was it? The one that threatened you before the third phase?"

Samuel interjected by slamming his palms on the tableside. Othelia's gaze snapped to his. "It's not just us."

Her expression didn't change, and she shrugged again. "Yeah. It would seem that way, wouldn't it?"

Eli put his hands on his hips. "You know? I suppose someone who already can, uh... I don't want to say too much..."

"That's quite all right, Eli. Hanako informed me. It appears our father was drugging us. How, I'm not sure. I would guess he had servants slip it into our food, but I'll never know."

His eyebrows shot up. Eli wasn't sure why he was surprised —King Sandoval was proving to be a cruel and greedy man— but it shocked him all the same. He wished he could comment on her findings, but he hadn't the slightest inkling how much was too much to say.

Eli clapped his hands. "Well, this has been fun, but I have a campaign to start."

Leo stepped up beside him. "So eager to leave? We just passed! Shouldn't we at least celebrate?"

Othelia stood; the chair legs scraped loudly against the marble. "No, Eli's right. There's no time to waste. Is, you think you'll be able to get leads on the guy who killed your brother?"

Eli turned; he hadn't noticed Isabelle trail up behind him. In fact, he just realized she hadn't been in the elevator with them. Beside her was Raphael, and they exchanged glances before she answered. A smile spread across her lips, a blaze of determination lit underneath her feet. "I think so."

"Raphie—" Eli began.

"Raphael."

"—I'm happy you made it through! Sorry, I didn't think you wanted the others in there to know about our ties. I thought it'd be best not to draw attention to you."

Raphael nodded. "Don't worry. You were right. I was happy to see you in there as well! Men in suits always win."

"And they always stick together. That's what makes us so powerful," Eli added, slapping him on the shoulder. Raphael laughed; Isabelle watched with feigned confusion and perhaps, Eli realized, a flash of jealousy.

"Don't worry," Eli said with a wink. "I won't steal him away from you."

"Wait. Wait a second," Leo interjected. "Where is everyone going? We just got a phone plan... shouldn't we get food, at least? Or we could help Galen find some new clothes? I mean, look at what he's wearing!"

Eli laughed and wrapped an arm around Leo's shoulders, pulling him close with a strong, tight squeeze. "You're going to miss us, is that it? Don't worry, we're just one call away! What'll you be doing, Ms. Othelia? Besides calling me daily, of course."

She rolled her eyes, but something seemed to ignite within her as if a cloud had risen, and Othelia was suddenly back to her usual self. He wondered if his worry had been in his head; if she was simply tired and his brain translated that as something deeper and darker. "Abel and I are setting sail after my brother hands over what's owed to me. Would you like to be dropped off? We could certainly give everyone a... ride? Sail? It may be a while until we depart, though. I'm not sure how long it takes to get a boat and everything."

Eli's heart damn near skipped a beat. Of course, he wanted to come with. He'd been grappling with how to feel about the princess, and although he still couldn't completely rid his distaste for royalty, he liked her. It was a weird thing to admit, and he felt as though he was failing the poor in his community —after all, she was one of the enemies. But she wasn't, was she? Not anymore.

And the things she'd said to him before he passed out... The things she did... She'd been comforting. She'd helped him. She'd helped all of them. And now, at the tip of the iceberg, she wanted to sail.

Eli couldn't help but smile, his teeth shining. "You're going to sail? You like boats? What kind of boat are you looking for? Do you have a favorite type? I could totally help if you wanted. I actually have a boat guy back in New Guayi."

"You have a boat guy?"

"I do, yes. I'm sure he has connections here somewhere. We're in the Okagee district right now, in Equive's largest city, San Juale. There's quite a lot to see around here if you want to step away and get lunch somewhere," he offered. He may have been the first to suggest leaving the city, but he couldn't resist laying the offer on the table.

"You'll get lunch with her and not the rest of us?" Leo asked.

"Anyone is welcome! We'll just have separate tables."

Othelia crossed her arms and smiled. "How far is New Guayi from here?"

Eli reached into his back pocket and produced a folded-up map. Leo had coaxed a nurse into letting them use a computer. All it took was a smile and a joke. It wasn't even a good joke, from what Eli could remember. But what girl could resist the rugged charm of a farm boy?

Eli had easily found and printed a rough map of the globe,

one with the distances and measurements written at the bottom. He'd already marked Midral and San Juale, and he traced his finger along the ocean path they would have to take. The others had quieted down and brought their attention to his finger.

"It's probably a two-month sail back to our starting point. See that?" He pointed to the canal between the continents of Veloa and Phanteous, the closest waterway to Ubas from Equive.

"This right here would shorten the trip by a month, but it's narrow and there are a lot of Unknowns that live around there, people we probably don't want to run into. Not to mention the Dead Sea. Are you guys going home?" He gestured toward Leo, Raphael, and Isabelle. "We could get dropped off at Midral and go our separate ways from there?"

Isabelle was the first to respond with a vigorous shake of the head. "I'm staying here for a while, I think. I'm going to ask some of the examiner's questions before they leave. See if I can get a lead on—" She stopped short, her eyes moving from Samuel and Abel. Whatever she was about to say was lost forever. "I'm staying here. But I appreciate your kindness."

"Which means I'm staying, too, for the time being. But I'll miss you greatly, Elijah," Raphael added.

"Eli. But I'll miss you too, my finely dressed friend. What about you, Leo? You've got that debt to pay, right? And Galen. What are you going to do now? What do you think your family will do since you didn't pass?"

Sadness passed over his features; Eli knew that look well. It was a look he actively tried to avoid, namely by not thinking about what he did. He'd killed someone. But Eli would be dead if he hadn't. He repeated this justification throughout the day, but he still awoke late in the night with wide eyes and a bed drenched in sweat.

"I'm not sure what to do," Galen said, peering over the map. "I'm homeless and poor. Maybe just stay at the hospital until I can find a job or something to do?"

"You could come with me," Leo said with his usual smile and charm. Eli's eyebrows rose. He hadn't expected such an answer, and it was clear by Galen's O-shaped mouth that he hadn't the slightest inkling, either.

"Really? Are you sure? What about your parents?" Galen asked speedily, his head jerking up from the map.

Leo shrugged. "Ma and Pa wouldn't care a bit. In fact, I bet they'd be excited! My ma loves cooking, so you could help her in the kitchen. Oh, you'll have to help on the farm, though, so if that's a deal breaker—"

Galen's ears perked up, and he shook his head. "No, no, I'd love to come!"

Eli tried to imagine himself wearing jeans and a flannel, and he shuddered. Smelly animals, lifting things, excess exercise all the time and, not to mention the aforementioned informal clothes... there wasn't a single appealing thing in that sentence.

"My sister's never around, so you could sleep in her room," Leo added.

Galen's eyes—*eye*, Eli corrected—widened. "You have a sister?"

"Yeah, she's sixteen. But, like I said, she's usually living with her friend a field away. She probably doesn't even know I left."

"You measure distance in fields?" Eli asked. It sounded like a very Edna thing to do.

Leo shrugged. "Fields and mile markers off the road. So, you're sure, Galen? You'll really come?" The boy nodded, and Leo continued, "I don't think I can handle two weeks on a ship... I'll probably fly back now that I have all this money. I don't really know what I'm going to do after the debt is paid." He smiled slightly. "Eat some pie, maybe."

After everything that happened, Eli had completely forgotten about Leo's aversion to sailing. A real shame.

"Ah, that's what I was going to ask earlier," Galen said with a snap. He went back to the map, running his finger from Equive to Avala. "Wouldn't this be close to a four-day journey? How is that possible? There's no way we rowed that fast and far. Even with the few hours before the boat sank, it's simply not possible."

He was right; there was no doubt about that. But everyone stayed quiet; no one who knew could say.

"It's something you find out if you pass," Isabelle said sadly and squeezed his shoulder. "I'm sorry. I wish we could say."

"Flying may not be a bad idea, though," Eli reasoned. "It'll probably cut the trip to 5-6 days. I think they have beds and everything. Plus, I don't have the phone number of my boat guy. He deals through the black market. Cheaper that way."

"You have a black-market boat guy?" Othelia asked doubtfully. And then she reared her head back and laughed. He wanted to hear that laugh for the rest of his life. "You're a strange guy."

"You mean helpful," Eli amended, blushing profusely. "A helpful guy. How about this? I go back with Leo and Galen, and I'll talk to my guy for you."

"You want us to wait at least five days for you to call? I'll be a millionaire soon enough." She gestured toward Samuel with a confident nod of the chin.

"Yes, but money goes quick, and ships can go up to a few hundred thousand quill. The good ones, anyway. Not to mention hiring and paying a crew, maybe taking sailing lessons, food and drinks for everyone, medical supplies... Trust me, I can get a quality boat for you for 5, 10 thousand quill, easy."

"How about you call me when you've landed, and I'll let you know if I'm still interested. Sound good?"

Eli nodded, and they shook hands. "Deal."

"I should get going," Isabelle chimed in from behind. Eli and Othelia turned their attention to her at the same time; Leo kept his back facing her. Eli found his actions peculiar. He knew Isabelle had thought Leo was a coward, but after Leo had saved her from the mist creature and carried her to the fourth phase, Eli thought the squabble had been squashed. It was unsettling to think otherwise.

Abel stood and rounded the corner to stand beside Othelia, and Eli watched from his peripherals as Leo took the seat, keeping his head down.

"Call me when you've found anything out, Is. I'll be glad to help," Othelia offered.

Galen stood and smiled at her softly. "Call me, too. We'll come, right Leo?"

All eyes were on Leo as he glanced up in surprise. His hands were shaking in his lap, and he gave a wavering half-smile. "Oh, y-yeah. We'll come. Yeah, just call."

He sounded disingenuous, as though she was an afterthought. So Eli had missed something. He could tell that much, and he needed to know what it was. Eli knew he should probably ask Leo in private, but the words slipped from his lips before he could stop them. "Am I missing something here?"

Leo shrugged and glowered at Eli, which was an answer in of itself, and Isabelle shrank away.

Eli looked between them with a raised eyebrow before finally settling back on Isabelle. "Okay, then... count me in on that, too," he said. She looked up at him and smiled gratefully. "But you better come to New Guayi for my election. I need all the support I can get."

Isabelle gave him a bow and waved. "I will, just call. Safe travels."

She and Raphael turned to leave. The group silently

watched as they left, the impact of the future weighing down on their shoulders. There was so much more to do. Eli had never ventured into the political world before; he'd gone through three years of higher education to become a lawyer. He'd thought, hey, maybe he could sue King Sandoval. The King was stealing their water supply, after all. And it was certainly stealing, as he took gallons upon gallons for half of what it was worth. And what was the king going to do when he bought up all their water? What would happen to New Guayi?

But, suing a king wasn't possible, he soon found out. Evidently, kings were free to do many illegal things, so Eli would need to infiltrate the higher ranks. Tear them down from the inside, as they say. He didn't know who 'they' were, but 'they' were wise.

"So," he said as Isabelle disappeared around the corner. He turned to face the rest of them. "Is this goodbye then?"

He didn't know what he expected Othelia to say. They'd only known each other for three days, and he'd been unconscious for a good portion of it. He mourned the lack of extra time they could've had. Still, her beauty far exceeded anyone else he'd ever laid eyes on, and she was kind. He hated to admit it, but she was.

Now, he knew he wasn't the most attractive guy, especially next to Abel. Even Galen and Leo were better-looking, he thought. But, somehow, he could've sworn she seemed interested in him, too.

Othelia cocked her head. "Don't look so sad. We'll meet again."

"Yes," he said, clenching his fist dramatically. "But at what cost?"

She laughed. "Do you know the date of the election?"

"April 23rd." Eli watched as she rounded the table toward him. She stopped a foot away from him and looked up to meet his eyes. He was at least five inches taller than her, but she still looked more menacing than he ever would. She smiled as he stared into her icy blue eyes. He couldn't tell what she thought of him, not at all.

Othelia nodded. "I think I can make that work. Perhaps we could get lunch then?"

He could feel his neck and face light on fire as his heart sped up. Was this real? He stammered as he muddled his words together, "O-Of course. But, y-you know, I don't want to distract you from anything else you, um, want to do while you're away."

His eyes shifted to Abel for a second, one he hoped was brief enough for Othelia not to pay any mind to. He couldn't help the pang of jealousy he felt toward Abel. It was stupid to feel that way. Oh stars, did he know it was stupid. And it felt gross, like he was oozing toxic gunk every time he pictured them on a boat together. At sea. For months. Together. But who was he to stop her when he barely even knew her? Who was he to stop her at all?

Eli looked away from Othelia, unable to focus on anything other than her. Every part of his body was growing hot—*every part*—and he was squirming in place. How dare someone make him feel like this. Especially a princess. A princess of the king he hated the most.

Othelia laughed again and reached out a gloved hand. She placed it on his cheek and guided his face back to hers. Their eyes met and a fresh wave of heat rose to his cheeks. He was acutely aware of the others watching, but he couldn't look away. His gaze only flickered to her lips for another second, this time longer. He thought she might do it, lift herself up on her toes, and plant her lips on his.

Instead, she said, "You're cute when you're frazzled."

She backed away and bit her lip. "Don't fret about him.

Though, I leave you with the same sentiments. There's really no point in waiting around."

Eli regained some of his composure. "Not unless it involves getting a cheap boat. And calling me every day, of course."

She offered him one last smile, and he ingrained it into his memory. "Call me when you've talked to him. I'll see you around," she said, looking at Eli, Galen, and then Leo respectively. As her gaze stayed on Leo, she added, "Be kind to Isabelle. What would you have done in her position?"

She didn't give Leo a chance to answer, instead going back to Abel and Samuel's sides. Eli gulped. He didn't want to say goodbye. It would be months until they saw each other next *if* she actually pulled through and came to his election.

"Safe travels," he said. "I hope you do well. Get what you're looking for. Both of you." He nodded to Abel. Finally, Eli's eyes rested on Samuel. "And you? I hope you find peace. You are mean. You are a mean brother. I remember what you said when I freed you during the final phase. Othelia's 'recklessness' didn't cause whatever you were alluding to; it was your father. I mean, he hires people to punch and hurt you? That isn't normal."

"Of *course* you said that." Othelia snorted and glared at her brother. "My recklessness was nothing more than wanting to be different from what I am. Is that so wrong?"

"When you have duties, a family, tradition, a country to uphold, yes. Yes, it is wrong. And it makes perfect sense why I would be sent instead o—"

"Enough. No more. I don't feel like listening to you talk," Othelia said. "We really should be going. There are things to do! Good luck, guys!"

Eli couldn't help but feel sad, if only a little. He'd passed the exam. He was a millionaire now, with the only caveat of going on expeditions, of which would serve as further proof of how powerful he was to the people of New Guayi. Once the poor heard his plans for better sanitation and education, they would have no choice but to choose him. While the lower class received only one unanimous vote, the wealthy votes could be bought or earned from his expertise and familial ties to BrillCruise.

"Bye!" Eli said with a wave. "And don't forget, the election is April 23rd! I expect to see you there."

She winked. "I can't wait."

It was going to be a long ten months.

CHAPTER 31
LEO

THE TRIP HOME was not an easy one. Not because of the long journey he'd have to take to Midral and Edna, but because of what he'd done. Every time he closed his eyes, he saw the bloodied woman. A hatchet in his hand, dripping as her lifeless eyes stared back at him. Sometimes he could even feel the blow to her skull reverberate in his hands. The images themselves were sickening, bringing him to the zeppelin bathroom every half hour.

The ride itself went vastly smoother than sailing ever would have. As long as he didn't look out the window, he was fine. Occasionally, there would be a bump or two that would make him woozy, and he'd have to sit down.

Sleeping proved to be the hardest. His nightmares persisted, keeping him wide awake at night. His eyes were heavy, and his stomach constantly growled whenever he'd lay down for the night, watching the ceiling as though it had tales to offer. But when he tried to eat, two bites would fill him up, and if he took a third, he'd be in the bathroom again.

The zeppelin was long and bulky for how little room was

actually dedicated to the passengers. He and Eli were eligible for the luxury suites on the second level, but they stayed on the lower for Galen's sake. The lower level was composed of a lounging area with chairs and books, five beds, and a toiletry area. They were served lunch and dinner and the lights were merely dimmed when they slept. With a level packed of 15 people, they took turns with the beds, and Leo had slept on the floor for three of their five-day travel.

Leo didn't know how his parents would react to a new member of the family. He doubted they'd care, but once he paid off their debts, he didn't know how long his money would last to feed an extra mouth. Would he want to stay with them after the debt was paid off, anyway? He had to do expeditions now, which meant he needed to learn how to use Essence. But after everything that had happened, did he want the title of Expedition Overseer?

He had the million quill, right there on his wrist. Leo had cashed out the exact amount needed for their debt before leaving the hospital. If he cashed out the rest in Edna, he didn't need to be an Overseer. He had no need for power that entailed becoming a man who murdered more people.

As they landed, Leo looked outside, pushing his queasiness down until he couldn't bear it anymore. The clouds hung heavy overhead as if rain was begging to fall. He could feel Galen watching him quietly, before looking to the floor and holding his damaged eye. Galen had been given a new set of glasses, along with a black eyepatch that he wore underneath. His hair was thick and ruffled enough to hide the strap that wrapped around his head.

It wasn't until they landed and stepped out onto the walkways of Midral, faced with the familiar skyscrapers and apartment buildings, that Leo remembered the boat they'd left back on Ishla, the boat Eli had used to come to Midral.

Eli shrugged when Leo brought it up. "I have no need for it, though I suppose it's the best model to get where you need to go when you're in a rush. But I can afford anything I want now."

"Are you ever going to explain how we went from Ishla to Midral in a matter of hours in that thing?"

Eli winked. "As my grandmother used to say, 'secrets are your greatest weapon.'"

"So, she never told you."

"Unfortunately, she never gave specifics beyond how to use the steering panel, but I know now."

Leo raised his brows. So, it had been mag that got them there. He'd never thought about a boat being a magical item. He should've guessed. "How are you getting home, then?"

"There's a zeppelin station just outside New Guayi territory. I'll probably hang around Midral until the next zeppelin takes off to buy some gear. What about you guys?"

"We'll be taking a bus back to the farm—we should get going now, actually. The debt needs to be paid in two days. They'll be stopping by the house to collect," Leo said. The quill in his backpack weighed heavily on his shoulders in more ways than one.

Eli embraced Leo in a hug. "Good luck. It was a pleasure meeting you, even if you were judgmental at times."

Leo raised an eyebrow. "It didn't seem to stop you from drinking."

"Nothing can stop me but me, but your concern is noted," Eli said, hugging Galen next and giving him the same regards.

Eli began to walk away. Just as Leo and Galen did the same, Eli turned around with a finger raised. "Ah! I almost forgot to ask! Were you planning on paying that girl back?"

"What girl?" Leo asked incredulously.

"That lodge receptionist. You bet her fifty quill you'd pass."

He'd forgotten about her; too many other things had happened between then and now. But the more he thought about it, the more clearly he remembered. A beautiful yet critical girl with short black hair, piercing blue eyes, and a nametag that read 'Marcella.'

For once, his negative thoughts subsided, replaced with newfound adrenaline. He slapped his forehead. "Of course! How could I forget?"

He had exceeded both her expectations and his parents', which Leo supposed he should've felt better about than he did. His mother had been right all along. The people who took the exam murdered, and he was one of them. And now, if he committed to being an Expedition Overseer, he would kill more and more until he needed a pen and paper to keep a tally.

"I wish I could see her reaction; you better tell me how she takes it. I should be going," Eli interrupted his thoughts. "Othelia is waiting for my call, and I still have a few more hours to New Guayi."

Leo looked over his companion. Sadness coursed through him—a horrible concoction of loneliness and fear. Fear of change, of losing an ally he'd just met and made. He knew it was irrational; he wasn't alone at all. And, if he was so scared of change, he could simply live with his parents and Galen, maintaining a farm for the rest of his life.

But could things really go back to normal after everything he'd found out? After what he'd done?

He already knew the answer.

Even so, he couldn't help but imagine Eli coming with them. They could all converse with the receptionist together, and then work on the farm as three brothers. Granted, Eli's flirtation would probably extend to Leo's mother, and that was a soul-shattering image. Maybe it was better they split up here.

"Good luck with your campaign," Leo said, lending a hand for Eli to shake.

"I don't need luck," Eli replied with a stern look and smile, grabbing Leo's hand tightly. Then Eli was off, swerving into a nearby building and disappearing through the door. Leo stared down the street a moment longer, reality settling in. He wanted to feel calm, but his heart was a quickening drum, and his hands were shaking.

They'd been shaking profusely the last few days. It didn't just come with the nightmares, no; they trembled in broad daylight regardless of where he was or how he was feeling. He'd be hungry one minute, then overridden with anxiety the next, forced to retire to bed or a bathroom.

"Again?" Galen asked. He'd noticed the shaking the very first day on the zeppelin. They'd been given fresh fruits and canned foods to eat for their meals, but nothing that needed to be cooked with heat. Apparently, they couldn't use heat when being carried by a ball of gas. Though he wouldn't be surprised if they'd somehow manufactured a form of mag to make them fly.

Leo had been eating an apple, one that was scrumptiously sweet and juicy, and then it began. The shaking hadn't been too bad—his wrists twitched, and his fingers would occasionally strengthen their grip, but he controlled it enough to keep eating. Galen had come up behind him tentatively, observing the small, quiet struggle Leo was having. He sat beside Leo and started a random conversation, one that got his mind off the shaking and panic that rose within him.

Now, Leo sucked in a deep breath, rubbing at his fingers and wrists, and nodded. It was a crashing wave this time around. He had to clench his jaw, unable to speak for a moment.

"Think of flowers," Galen said. Leo had told him that

flowers were his go-to happy place, but lately, his thoughts entailed laying in mud instead of grass, the flowers pulling him under with sharp thorns. The sour-sweet smell of nitren was suddenly bitter.

He knew his family harvested nitren for pharmaceutical companies, but he'd never been told what the flowers were used for. Essence was made of ten natural ingredients, yet he hadn't made the connection until he read the description on the pill bottle. Something with high demand and something so supposedly powerful, yet his family got less than half of what they were owed. Knowing the truth only made it worse.

Leo shook his head, pulling himself out of his daze. "Taxi. We'll get a taxi to the lodge. A bus station is around there. That's how we'll head back."

"Should we get you water or some food first? You look... sweaty. And pale. No offense."

"I'll be fine. Let's just try to hail a taxi," he said, pushing forward. "The sooner we get back, the better."

The sidewalks were busy, a stream of people going in the opposite direction and pushing past them. He struggled to focus or walk with the rush of people around them. The streets themselves were wide with three lanes, all going one way. Leo searched for an opening between the opposing crowd. How did anyone get around in this place?

"Over here!" He heard Galen's voice from some distance away. He looked past the citizens of Midral to find Galen jumping and waving frantically for Leo's attention. Somehow, he'd slipped through the crowd, a taxi already at bay.

Leo shoved himself through the sea of people. A man and woman gave him dirty looks as he pushed between them, and he apologized sheepishly with a bow of the head. He was nauseous, his hands still shaking away. There was no escape, he realized. No matter what he did or where he was. He couldn't escape himself.

Galen stood outside the taxi he'd hailed and opened the door for Leo, who slid in and said, "Thanks."

Galen followed, slamming the door shut behind him. Leo felt a rush of terror as the door clicked closed, the edges of the car surrounding him. He reached for the window, rolled it down, and stuck his hand out. He expected the wind to flow through his fingers, to cool his body and subsequent thoughts, but the car hadn't started yet.

He hadn't heard the driver ask for their destination, the car too dingy for him to think. Leo gulped, hot and sticky sweat pouring over his brow. He could see the man's mouth move in the rear-view mirror, but he couldn't hear the words. He was at the bottom of the ocean. Vast and empty and dark. All alone.

A bump on his shoulder made him jump. His breath hitched as the world came into focus. Galen was grabbing his arm and jostling him slightly. "You sure you don't want some water first?"

"If your boy doesn't talk soon, you best leave. Ain't no pukers in my car."

Leo gulped like a fish out of water until he found the syllables to speak. "F-Fantisimo. Well, the bus station that's next to it."

The man pointed toward the back window. "If you blow, it best be outside."

Leo nodded meekly and leaned his head against the door. He gripped the seat belt to settle the shaking, but it wasn't going away. How would he be able to pick the flowers back home? Cook? Milk the cows?

Was he worrying too much? No, he thought with a shred of dread. He wasn't worried enough.

The roads were bumpy, and their driver sped with

overwhelming gusto, stopping abruptly at stop signs or when others were turning. Leo kept his eyes clamped shut, feeling death near with every jolt of the car. Galen sat in silence along with him, and the driver played a classical cello melody over the radio. He turned up the music until the vibrations rattled the speakers and billowed out the windows.

Relief washed over Leo when the taxi driver jerked to a halt and gestured toward the Fantisimo. It looked just as broken down as before, only this time it had bright yellow tape wrapped around it. There were papers stapled on the door, piled atop each other, but he couldn't read what they said from where he sat.

"Here we are," their driver said. "40Q please."

Leo leaned forward and exposed the barcode on his wrist for the taxi driver to scan. The man looked at it quizzically, his puffy eyebrows shooting up in disbelief. Leo nodded his chin toward his wrist, simply wanting the interaction to be over. The driver picked up a bulky device from the passenger's seat, which had a touchscreen that lit up with four options of scanner types.

The driver selected the second option, 'MC-T.' An amount option came up, and the driver said aloud, "Negative forty." The machine chimed, and he hovered the scanner over Leo's wrist. A gray checkmark turned green and a second later, Leo's name came onto the screen, along with the date he passed the exam.

"The voice of Leo Montero is required to confirm this transaction," the scanner said in a monotonous and choppy tone.

The driver grunted; Leo looked back with wide eyes, teetering on the edge of what he should say. "Your name, boy, say your damn name."

"Oh, um, Leo Montero."

The scanner chimed again and said, "Transaction complete."

His tension evaporated, and his shoulders deflated as the taxi driver gestured for them to get out. Leo nodded in thanks and slid out of the car. He was finally free, welcomed by a puff of breeze and more darkened skies.

"Next time, say a tip, too," the taxi driver grumbled as Galen exited and closed the door.

As the man drove away, Galen tsked and said, "Like he deserved a tip."

The calm Leo felt was quickly dispelled when his eyes landed on the yellow tape surrounding the outside of the Fantisimo. Now that the exam was over, the area was much less populated; only a few people shuffled between him and the lodge. They looked rugged and tired. Aimless. Staring dead ahead to a dreary world.

"This is it?" Galen asked as he came up beside Leo.

"Yeah..." Leo stepped up to the boarded-up doors. He looked over the sheets of paper that cluttered the main entrance. There were dozens taped on top of each other, though there were only three variations. Wanted signs.

There were different quill amounts underneath each mugshot. A man with a wide jaw and thick neck stared ahead in one, his mouth drawn in a sneer. A long scar ran from his nose to mouth and his black hair sat tall and spiked in every direction. His bounty was the largest at 50 million, followed by another man at 40 million. The second man was thinner and had wide, innocent eyes.

"Looks like someone had fun tearing things up in there," Galen said. He'd taken to the side windows, peering inside with cupped hands around his eye to exclude the sun.

Leo gestured to the flyers. "Someones."

Their names were exempt from the wanted signs, as was the

crime they were wanted for. Leo's eyes met the third culprit's picture. A girl who also sneered, a dimple forming in one of her cheeks. Her black hair was chopped short, and her bangs dangled just above her blue eyes. Her name, too, was exempt.

"It's her," he said, pointing to the paper with great fervor. His finger bounced against the flyer as he eyed the bounty on her head. 30 million quill. She'd aided in the destruction of this building? But why?

He hopped over a brown shrub and onto the grass beside Galen, copying his stance. Inside, the red velvet couches were overturned, and illegible words were spray-painted on the walls in different colors. There were dark red splotches on the carpet. Blood.

"What's so important that they'd ransack a lodge? Of all places. Surely a bus station would have more money," Leo said, exasperated.

"Maybe people are more likely to pay for a room with quill over a bus?" Galen offered.

"Let's ask." Leo tore Marcella's mugshot off the wall and led them to the bus station next door. It, too, wasn't nearly as busy as it'd been the night he'd arrived. Homeless were scattered in the waiting area, taking up two or three chairs with their sprawled-out bodies. Large ceiling fans whisked around a smell of musky mildew. To the right were large doors that opened up to where three buses were lined up, and he felt a flush of anxiety course through his body at the aspect of waiting around for the right bus to show.

There was a family of fifteen waiting for a bus, taking up the bulk of the middle sections. They talked loudly amongst themselves, laughing jovially while the kids chased each other; weaving through seats with their sticky hands outreached and touching everything.

When Leo and Galen approached the front desk, the three

workers were huddled together, talking in hushed whispers and giggling. Leo cleared his throat. The two men and woman stared him down with equal annoyance, but then the woman stepped forward with a strained smile and said, "How can I help you today, sir?"

"Uh, two tickets headed for Farm 15 in North Edna," he said. He whipped out his tattooed wrist and placed it on the counter along with the mugshot of Marcella. The woman raised a brow.

She exhaled deeply. "You know, the next bus to Edna isn't for another fifteen days. *But,* with this, sir,"—she pointed to the tattoo—"you can get a whole bus to yourself. Is that what you want?"

She made it sound like the worst possible thing he could ask for, and he faltered. He turned to Galen for a solution, who shrugged in response. "You earned all the things you can get. So why not use them?"

Leo pondered. He didn't want to inconvenience anyone, but Galen was right, wasn't he? Shouldn't Leo use his EO-MC-T for whatever he liked? He *killed* someone for it, after all. It'd be an insult to Mari if he didn't use it. "Okay, yeah. We'll take a whole bus."

The woman rolled her eyes but went through with the transaction, anyway, using the same scanner the driver had. He found it astonishing that he'd never known of such things, of so many things, and there was still so much more to learn.

But if learning came with killing, did he really want it?

He hated being presented with options. Leo desperately wished his life could be normal again. Which was ridiculous; his life would never go back to how it was, and he had more choices to make now than he ever had before.

The woman tapped on a microphone connected to a long and thick silver wire running underneath the tabletop. Her voice boomed over the intercom. "May I have your attention, please?" She looked over a piece of paper on the counter. "Route 164 will now be delayed until further notice. Thank you."

The family was no longer talking, their stunned eyes on Leo and Galen. Leo grabbed the wanted poster and peered down at it to avoid the family's gazes as he walked past. He and Galen followed the woman through a door marked 3, where a bus was parked and manned on the other side. Leo could vaguely hear the shouts of protests that followed, but he looked ahead, boarding the bus without a single glance back. He wouldn't be able to sleep at night if he thought too greatly about what he'd just done.

Galen chose not to comment, either. That was all right with Leo; he was already disgusted with himself as it was. The perks of becoming an Expedition Overseer now included ripping away transport others waited days for. But something deep inside him longed to see his parents and simply sleep in his own bed. That's all he wanted. Love and sleep.

Before they left, the woman asked if they'd like bottles of water, and they both denied the offer. Leo stopped her before she got off. "Do you know what happened at the Fantisimo?"

The woman narrowed her eyes. "If you're looking for the bounty, they're long gone by now. Them some common thieves. Part of a group that nobody can get their hands on."

Leo wished to inquire further, but she got off without another word, and they left almost immediately. Leo and Galen sat in opposite rows of each other; Galen slouched in his seat with his feet planted on the ground, whereas Leo took up his side with his legs raised over the handrails, feet dangling in the center aisle.

It was going to be a long few hours, he thought at first. But then he took out his notebook and put a pencil to paper. He tried to draw Midral from the top of the wall, then the ascending roadway. At one point, he leaned against the window and watched Galen, drawing the boy as he was then—staring out his own window with his chin resting in his palm. But the proportions of his midsection didn't come out right and Leo put his notebook away with a frustrated huff.

Leo watched the world whiz by as he thought of pie and his parents and his sister. And Galen. Leo hardly expected to make any friends, much less bring someone home with him. His parents probably wouldn't expect it, either, but hopefully, they welcomed Galen with open arms.

Hopefully, they didn't inquire about the exam.

Somewhere along the way, he thought of the monotonous nature of milking cows and drifted into a deep, uninterrupted sleep.

THERE WAS no way to let his parents know they were coming, nor that Leo and Galen were standing in the empty driveway at that very moment. The wind was much softer there, the sun brighter and the sky bluer. He took a deep breath as his eyes swept over the familiar house and farm. Everything looked exactly as it had been—the faded and chipped orange paint of the barn; their cream house with a screen door and a tattered porch. A cow mooed in the distance, and he laughed to himself. The simplicity of it all. He was home.

He went around the house, entering from the back door. The bus ride carried on throughout the night, and by the time they arrived, it was midmorning. Leo expected his father to be out in the shed chopping wood, and his mother milking.

Leo cringed expectantly, ready to hear his father's hatchet cut into a tree stump. But the air was silent, and the shed was empty. A twinge of panic seeped through his thoughts, though he couldn't pinpoint why. Sometimes his father slept in; sometimes he finished up earlier in the week and had a day off. But alarms rang in Leo's ears anyway, and he ran into the unlocked back door with trembling hands and a bursting heart.

He looked to the kitchen and stopped short when he saw his mother. She was there, perfectly fine, and cutting apples. She looked up from her work, eyes baggy and sullen. They widened in surprise, and she sat her cutting knife down. He expected a hug and endless buckets of tears, but she gave him a weary smile instead.

"You did it," she said before glancing over his shoulder. "And you brought a friend."

The rustling of papers sounded from behind him, and he whirled around. Leo's father tossed the papernews onto the couch and stood quickly, nearly running toward him. He tackled Leo in a long and strong hug. Leo wheezed. When he was released, Leo took off his backpack and tossed it on the dining table. Galen kept himself hidden around the corner of the sitting room as Leo opened the bag. Stacks of money in 100 quill intervals were nestled snugly within.

He watched his parents' reactions, respectively. His father was gawking with an open mouth and wide eyes. He laughed and patted Leo on the back as Leo pulled out another stack. "You did it! You really did it! You've freed us, my boy!"

Leo smiled, trying to appear okay. His mother was less ecstatic, her eyes on her son more so than the money. Her gaze pierced through his soul, inspecting all the things he'd had to do. Could she sense how horrible of a person he'd been? Or, perhaps, the type of person he had always been? The way she looked at him was terrifying. His mouth became dry as he shoved his shaking hands into his jeans pockets. She raised a murderer who valued money and having a home over another human life.

She remained utterly silent as his father rattled on about celebration and beer and asked, "Oh, who is this young feller?"

"G-Galen," Galen said, his voice soft and unsure.

"What happened to your eye, my boy?"

His mother's attention snapped to her husband. She waved a dishrag at him with furrowed brows and said in a stern voice, "Diego Montero! We will ask no such questions in this house! Leave him be!"

Galen's pale face reddened, and he looked to Leo for help. He would get none, however, because Leo was not there. He was too busy thinking. Thinking and thinking. By the way his mother looked at him, he knew he would never speak of what he'd done again. His actions were best to be forgotten.

Hanako H. Byrde

KING SANDOVAL WAS not going to be pleased. That much was obvious, but there was no point in avoiding the inevitable. He thought about lying at Othelia's expense, but there was no point. The King could hardly touch Hanako, anyway, no matter how powerful he claimed to be.

The palace was quaint, the guards attentive and unmoving. Hanako walked down the long, yellow-carpeted hallway. Abstract paintings lined the walls. The throne room, where the King now sat in anticipation, had two large double doors engraved with a scaled lizard. Ramna, as they were called; a native to Ishla known for its changing colors.

Hanako shoved through the doors quickly and with determination. At the end of the long carpet were three steps up to the throne. The King's son was already there, down on one knee and bowing. Hanako strode to Samuel's side and looked up at the King. His beard was long and full, white and graying against his dark skin. As he approached, he noticed Samuel's wrist overturned with the EO-MC-T facing the

King. His head remained down, his blond hair hiding his eyes.

"You arrive alone?" Nicolas Sandoval asked. His voice was soft and unsurprised. "She'll be having a jolly time behind bars, I'm sure." He chuckled. "I shouldn't have expected anything more from her. She's a subpar fighter, a deviant, and the best she can do with mag is track down magical items. *Useless* items, at that. Do you know how many are here, in this palace alone? And yet she hunts down measly, withering flowers."

"What happened with Alexander?" Samuel asked, raising his head. "If I may ask?"

Nicolas narrowed his eyes and sneered. "A fool, I hired. A fool with no spine. He's right where he needs to be, just as she is."

"What's that supposed to mean?"

"And what of the Harrington son?" King Sandoval asked, ignoring his own son altogether. "Did he pass the exam, as well?"

Hanako nodded. "It would appear so. He has yet to return home."

The King smiled. "Good. Abberstein is a splendid ally, and they are adamant that their eldest son is both strong and a considerable deceiver. He has swindled quite a number of people into believing in a cause they were once against. He will be a fine recruit for our mission. You've done great work, Hanako, as you always do."

"I didn't bring Othelia to prison," Hanako interjected.

Nicolas grasped his mighty, engraved wooden chair with meaty fingers, his eyes filled with rage. Hanako stared back at him blankly, hardly threatened by such a nasty glare. Anger was the King's default emotion, even after all these years. It was tiring for Hanako, who once drank alongside Nicolas and helped train the children when they were younger.

"Do my ears deceive me?"

"Not at all, sir. Throughout the exam, I thought she exuded fairness. She assisted her partners when they were unconscious and in no shape to pass the exam. I listened to nearly every word that was spoken between her and her allies, and she did not speak ill of you or Ishla. Her fellow allies, and she, were not 'deviants,' as you so wish to call her. She was kind. To more than just one person. And it cost her the exam."

Nicolas scoffed and stood abruptly. His bottom lip was thick and sputtering. "How could you, of all people, be tricked? Now, Alexander, Alexander I understand. He was always one to choose her lies over his duties. It was an ill fit. I know that now. But, Hanako, she is a traitor. She only knows how to disobey. I thought you were loyal. Isn't that the whole motto of your people?"

"My people?" he asked, his fingers itching to pull out his sword. How easy it would be to slide the blade into his gut. But, no, this was not a worthy or respectful time to draw his weapon.

"Was?" Samuel added, horrified. "Alexander *was*? What did you do?"

"Explain yourself, Byrde. I gave you my money and praise. Need I remind you who contacted the—"

"People go to prison for a crime. Disobedience isn't a crime, Nic. Your punishments are too harsh. If you saw what I saw, you'd understand. Your daughter may be hot-headed, but she isn't a bad person, nor did she commit treason."

"How dare you speak of my family as if you know them better than I. Othelia is nothing but trouble. I love her. Stars know I do. She is my daughter, after all. But she brings about nothing good, and you have fallen for her dastardly charm just like every other shmuck in this palace. Did you know two of my very own guards told her about the exam?"

"What did you do to *them?*" Samuel asked. He stood now, covering his tattoo with his sleeve.

"I told her about Essence, too, and a vague blanket statement regarding your plans. I told her you're meddling with things beyond your control and jurisdiction."

"You trait—"

"Relax. She has no interest in you, which only further solidified my decision. I'm a man of loyalty and *honor.* There's nothing honorable about sending an innocent girl to jail."

"Guar—!"

Hanako's sword was unleashed and at Sandoval's neck before he could finish the word. "Now, now. After all these years, you'd threaten my life? We're friends. I still respect you, even if I can't bear to agree with your actions. But, please, if you're going to threaten me, at least be prepared to lose your own life first."

"This is ridiculous! How could you possibly know of Essence as one of the Five Swordsmen? It's not within your duty to know."

Hanako sighed. "For how many years you've been around, it always surprises me how little you know. Some of us have higher authority than others, Nic, remember that. Now, as much as I'd love to stay and chat, that's all there is to be said. If you need any further help, the Five Swordsmen do not welcome you. We have our own problems to deal with, and you would be nothing more than a nuisance. I'm saying that as your friend. It'd be sad to see you flounder over something so ridiculous."

He bowed and left, not sparing the King another glance. He grimaced as he shoved the sturdy throne room doors open. It was never hard to tell someone the truth, not for Hanako. Hopefully, his words gave the King a wake-up call. If not, it mattered not. There were things and people far more powerful than a puny king, with ideas of grandeur and world domination. Such small thinking for a man with a big throne.

Hanako stepped outside and was greeted by guards blocking the horse-drawn carriage he'd arrived in, their swords drawn. They stood in a standard attack formation; a V shape of men evenly separated. There were at least ten, all with similar haircuts and yellow and white attire. Did Nicolas learn nothing at all from their nights of jousting? Hanako drew his sword and took in his enemies with bored and calculating eyes. Such small, small thinking.

IF YOU ENJOYED THIS BOOK, PLEASE
CONSIDER LEAVING A REVIEW TO SHOW
YOUR LOVE AND SUPPORT. THANK YOU
AND HAPPY READING!

TURN THE PAGE FOR A SNEAK PEEK AT
THE SECOND INSTALLMENT IN THE
FORSAKEN DESTINY TRILOGY.

THE HEROIC FALLACY

A SNEAK PEEK OF CHAPTER ONE

~

~

CHAPTER 1
OTHELIA

HEAVY RAIN POURED from the surrounding gutters, spooling onto the cobble below and flooding the uneven city streets. Water splashed over her boots and drenched her socks, instantly cooling her tawny skin as another puddle crossed her path. Shops lined each side of the street, packed together with narrow alleyways in between. Adrenaline coursed through her veins, fighting against the restraint of her growing fatigue.

She pulled her hood down further, disrupting both the rain and the sight of her face as she passed locals. Droplets dripped down her chin with each pant, her legs propelling her forward by sheer will. There was no manual that stated thievery meant a copious amount of running. Why wasn't there a manual?

Othelia squinted against the rain spilling into her light blue eyes, sure her legs would fail if she so much as moved another inch. Shouts from the men chasing her echoed off the walls as she turned down an alley, her chest heaving. The rush she felt as she turned another corner and lost sight of them sent only warmth through her bones.

Panting, she leaned against the wall and held her place, glancing down the alley corridor she'd come from. If they followed, she'd have the upper hand now, awaiting quietly for an ambush. She waited tentatively, ready for a fight and sure she would have one.

Footsteps drew closer, and she prepared her fists and steadied her breath. When she was certain they were seconds from rounding the corner, she jumped out with an arm reared back.

Othelia's body collided with another, and she stumbled backward before glancing up at the man before her. Her shoulders relaxed at the sight of not the men chasing her, but of Abel.

His brown bangs clung to his forehead as he grabbed her by the shoulders, startled by her sudden presence. His hair had grown notably longer—it was exceptionally hard to get a haircut as a fugitive—and he almost always kept it in a disheveled bun. He was thinner, too, his abs replaced with the dwindling skeleton of a man who lived off nothing more than a slim portion of rice.

Abel leaned against the building beside her, staring up at the muddied sky as it poured down on them, and let out a surprised laugh. "We lost them. We really lost them. How did we lose them?"

"Did you grab anything?" she asked, ignoring his question as she reached into her pockets. She came up empty-handed.

For a moment, he didn't answer, instead keeping his eyes on the sky above. The dark clouds rumbled with a ferocious anger she'd once felt. He shook his head. "You know, Lia, you're pretty bad at this, aren't you?"

His slender frame was hidden underneath a thick raincoat,

and he reached into the deep pockets, producing six bags of what could only hold Essence in the form of pills. Othelia's mouth salivated at the prospect of being so close to getting her mag back. "Luckily, you have me."

Othelia smiled and met his piercing golden-brown gaze. "You're a madman, you know that?"

"Only the maddest to keep you as a partner. Seriously, do you need a manual or something?"

She laughed, her worries melting away. Just five months ago, she could never have imagined partnering with Abel, the rather arrogant eldest son of the King of Xivis. He never failed to be unpleasant, and she never failed to put him in his place.

But after the International Exam, he became broken and scared, begging to join her one-woman journey around the world. She'd said yes out of pity, but now she had to hand it to him—he was more useful than she'd first thought. "I will admit, I froze when they saw us. I humbly apologize. Now, let's go before word gets out."

Abel nodded and led them through a web of alleyways. They'd spent long nights learning where the streets ended and the alleys began, memorizing the various ways back to the docks. It was best to weave between shops before inevitably crossing paths with the locals. For the past few months, they both got to know this town well, which meant they knew exactly how the locals would react to a rumored theft.

Ebbersol was small, so small that she ran into the same people on the same streets every day. She could name nearly everyone—Yanki, the paperboy; Tonay, the businesswoman; Olant, the meat shop owner. The list went on for ages, and the list meant nothing because this was the last day she would ever step foot there.

The uneven cobblestone roads carried her and Abel to the main port, where a beautiful ship awaited them. *Their* ship.

The port was lively, as it always was. With fish as their primary source of food, there was an abundance of fishermen loitering about. And, of course, it must be noon because the largest crew was just reaching the docks. The men laughed jovially as they walked in pairs of two, each carrying heavy loads of gear. There was no end to routine in Ebbersol, and today was no different.

Abel slowed to a jog as they approached the port, undoubtedly realizing how suspicious they looked. The newcomers, running down the docks wearing nothing but black, making way for their grand departure.

Othelia's heart skipped a beat as one of the younger fishermen, Edwal, turned to the sound of her splashing steps. He smiled, dimples forming on each cheek, and waved.

"Finally decided to join us?" he yelled, prompting the other men to turn and watch as she anxiously tried to weave her way around the mass before her, Abel in tow.

She laughed nervously, far more conspicuous than she'd intended. Any other day, she'd find herself mindlessly flirting with him, even if his black hair was perpetually matted against his neck, slick from grease or, in this case, rain. But this was not any other day. It was *the* day. The day she finally found the magical Essence that no one dared inform her of, baring Hanako, a man who almost tossed her into an eternal prison.

Her father, the King of Ishla, told his children they possessed something unique; magic bestowed only to descendants of royalty—maoho. *Murder.* But it was all a lie. Mag could be harnessed by anyone who knew how to find it and was limitlessly supplied to those who became Expedition Overseers.

"Ah, perhaps if it wasn't raining. My hair is soaked through," she said, instantly regretting her words. Her eyebrows drew together as she cringed. She knew how it sounded, how he would take her words as bait for a particular response, and he would bite.

The other fishermen quickly lost interest in their conversation, continuing with their path toward catching the day's feast. The captain, Rayor, paused where he stood, allowing his fellow army to pass until he and Edwal were the only two left. She could feel Abel's eyes bore into her back, watching with annoyance. They needed to go, but her ties to this town kept them rooted in place.

"Come now, Lia. Nothing could wash away such beauty," Edwal said, his voice smooth, confident.

His comment only fueled her embarrassment. Once upon a time, she would be flattered, intrigued even. But now those words sounded foolish from anyone other than, well, she couldn't think about him right now.

"Sorry, Ed, but we must get going. We can't miss the midday catch," Rayor called.

Edwal pouted playfully at her and nodded. "I see. Farewell Lia, I hope to see you again. Perhaps tonight?"

She smiled, the force behind it exemplified by the way her eyebrows twitched. "Of course. I wouldn't miss it for the world."

"Hey," a voice called from behind them. "Stop them at once!"

Edwal jumped at the sudden demand and looked somewhere beyond Othelia. She saw his lips sputter a response that she did not hear; she'd already started running. Abel's steps splattered behind her, quickly joined by a new set. Their ship, *Melancholia*, was a turn away; they just had to be faster.

Her heart leaped out of her chest as *Melancholia* came into view, and she clamored up the familiar stairs leading up to the deck. She turned around when she reached the top, finding Abel breathlessly climbing aboard. Othelia grabbed his hand, pulling him shipside with a grunt, her strength gone along with her mag.

"Cut us loose," she said, directing him to the bow, where a rope connected their ship to the port. Commoners watched from their ships, shocked at the events unfolding around them. Othelia paid the onlookers no mind, instead searching for the men following her.

They were middle-aged and largely inconsequential to the town, running a nearly condemned spice shop. While the general public didn't know of Essence, there was a network of black-market sellers in many areas of Hevalth, and Ebbersol was one of many frequented hubs.

The men had already reached the docks; one had seemingly knocked Edwal to the ground, who now sat on the brick path with confusion and hurt etched on his face. She could make out traces of blood on his fingers as he pulled his hand away from his head.

Othelia pushed away whatever guilt she may have felt and broke into action, pulling the rope that connected the steps to the dock. The steps folded in on each other, creating a board that slid into the side of the ship. As the board fully disappeared into its compartment, one of the men jumped onto the side of the ship and grabbed the edge with beefy fingers. She jumped back and reached for the dagger tucked inside her boot.

Continued in book 2, The Heroic Fallacy...
Their stories have only just begun.

ACKNOWLEDGMENTS

Wow! Publishing a book has been my dream since I was 11 years old, and it's still hard to believe that it's finally done and out for the world. Of course, I can't help but thank the people who believed in me and helped me make this a reality.

Self-publishing has been a long and winding journey, and my number one support continues to be my friends, family, and boyfriend. Thank you for listening to my endless ideas, reading my work, and giving advice on the content of the book and cover. I know I sent my fair share of cover ideas to my friends, Carissa and Kaitlyn, and my cousins, Liz and Sam. I am forever grateful for your support and suggestions.

The same sentiment goes to my boyfriend, Caleb, who was a fantastic beta reader and gave me the advice I needed to hear to make the content of the book stronger. You also dispelled my wonderful imposter syndrome and combated my anxiety with overwhelming support and positivity. I truly could not have done this without you.

With a manuscript comes an amazing cover. Thank you to Marta Obucina for her beautiful work on both of my covers. You are simply outstanding to work with and made my story a tangible piece of art.

Next, the honorary thanks to my grandma, Marcia, and my mother, Tasha. You both have always been my biggest support throughout life and always encouraged my love for writing. Even if my earlier projects were—let's face it—not the best, you both never failed to encourage me to keep going. My mom would always tell her coworkers and friends how much she loved my writing, and it gave me the confidence to keep going. You encouraged me to pursue my dreams and to never give up, whether it was with my writing, my school endeavors, or my mental health. I am forever grateful. My grandma offered excellent editing tips on anything and everything during my writing journey over the years.

Thank you to my father, Jon, for giving me endless book suggestions to read while growing up, and fueling my creativity through books and shows that gave me inspiration. I never would have read or watched Lord of the Rings or Game of Thrones without you showing them to me, and it opened the way to my interest and love for fantasy worlds. Thank you for always believing in me!

Last, but never least, thank you to all those who have read and bought this book. As a reader, I rarely ever read the acknowledgments, but if you're here, know that I could not be here without you. To have someone read this outside of my friends and family is something I will cherish forever. It is truly a magical experience to touch even one life with a book I've written, and I hope it helped you escape the world for a little while. Life is short, so I'm forever grateful that you've taken some of your time to read this book.

ABOUT THE AUTHOR

Angela Funk is an emerging author of new adult and adult fantasy. With her debut novel, Angela gives you a glimpse of what goes on in her mind. Born in Brookfield, Wisconsin, she relocated to Iowa to attend the University of Iowa for Creative Writing (and to meet her future husband, of course). Plans slowly devolved, as they do, and she graduated with a B.S. in Therapeutic Recreation, instead (it's a long story). Now, she has the title of Certified Therapeutic Recreational Specialist (CTRS) and works with adults with disabilities while trying her best to juggle the realities of the real world versus the ones she creates in her head.

instagram.com/authorangelafunk

tiktok.com/@authorangelafunk

goodreads.com/angela_funk